a m Da R

Dear Reader,

In only a few short years, the *Silhouette Summer Sizzlers* have established a tradition of scintillating, romantic reading all wrapped up in one volume that's just perfect for hot summer days at the beach, lazy afternoons in a shaded hammock, or those few minutes alone that we all manage to sneak off for now and then. This year, though, we're offering summer reading with a different twist. Turn the pages to find three stories that stand alone, and yet also fit together.

How many of us look back on the friendships we made when we were younger and wish we'd been better about following up, writing letters, making calls and keeping in touch with the people who once meant so much to us? The heroines of these three stories are no different. Once they were college roommates and as close as any three people could be. But the years—and the tears—came between them, and it's only now, as they meet again for their fifteenth college reunion, that they begin to rebuild their friendship and find something else, as well.

That "something else" is love, and there's no one who could better tell these stories of three women finally finding romance than three of your favorite romance authors: Kathleen Eagle, Marilyn Pappano and Patricia Gardner Evans. Join them now for summer in New England, where the trees are lush and green, the breezes cool and the possibilities endless. Follow three friends who take a journey of the heart and find love that will last forever. Turn the page and enter the world of *Silhouette Summer Sizzlers 1991*.

Enjoy!

Leslie Wainger
Senior Editor and Editorial Coordinator

SILHOUETTE SUMMER Sizzlers

Kathleen Eagle
Marilyn Pappano
Patricia Gardner Evans

Silhouette Books®

Published by Silhouette Books New York

America's Publisher of Contemporary Romance

SILHOUETTE BOOKS
300 EAST 42nd STREET, NEW YORK, N.Y. 10017

SILHOUETTE SUMMER SIZZLERS 1991

ISBN: 0-373-48237-X

First Silhouette Books printing June 1991

The publisher acknowledges the copyright holders
of the individual works as follows:

Sentimental Journey
Copyright © 1991 by Kathleen Eagle

Loving Abby
Copyright © 1991 by Marilyn Pappano

Over the Rainbow
Copyright © 1991 by Patricia Gardner Evans

CONTENTS

SENTIMENTAL JOURNEY

Kathleen Eagle

Summertime Reunions

Living in different places has surely been a major part of my education, but one of my life's many ironies is that, as a child, I always dreaded moving. I hated saying goodbye to friends, watching the moving van pull away with all my personal treasures and riding in a cramped car across endless miles of highway to yet another Air Force base, where I was sure I would never find friends like those I'd left behind. The worst part was leaving my "best" friend. We'd always promise to write, but I've usually been a terrible correspondent. Eventually, we'd only hear about each other through family Christmas cards, or we'd lose touch altogether. But I remember those names and faces well. It's the province of a writer to remember.

By the time I was in high school, our family had settled semipermanently in western Massachusetts, where I later attended college. To a Southern-born gypsy, New Englanders did seem a little stiff-necked at first, but I did make friends. *Best* friends. And those friendships of my youth seem no less important now simply because time and distance separate us. In fact, nowadays, I'm more apt to look up old friends when I travel than I was years ago. I find that after the initial catching up, we're back on the same wavelength because we've shared special times. Getting older just means having room in your life for more "best" friends.

I don't say goodbye anymore. I say "See you!" Maybe sooner, maybe later. Maybe in a letter or over the phone. Maybe even through a book. I've met so many people I've never actually seen, and I feel very close to others I may only see once or twice a year. For a woman who's always found it hard to make small talk, I've managed to find a lot of friends—or they've found me!

I see lots of new places on business trips these days, but vacation has more often than not been a time to go home. A time to visit family. A time for reunions with friends, for revisiting old haunts. And because one adventurous, long-ago summer landed me a husband and lifetime best friend in North Dakota, I became a transplant once again. Now there's even more family—Eagles by the dozens!—and we honor the age-old Indian tradition of coming together for summer celebrations. What could be a more welcome sight after a long Dakota winter than the faces of those we can't see as often as we'd like?

Tours and cruises are surely nice. (When will I be the lucky winner of one?) But I think summertime reunions with family and with old friends and lovers, like those in "Sentimental Journey," are part and parcel of life's happily-ever-afters.

Saturday

Velvet and oak darkened the auditorium in Fuller Hall. A faintly musty odor, borne on sodden air, permeated the room from balcony to creaky wood floor. Even on a sunny day the massive maples and sycamores, and the ivy that had covered Bartlett College's brick walls for a century, kept it cool and dark inside. But today a soft June rain fell steadily past the open windows and drew more than a few of the polite listeners to slip sweaters over their bare shoulders between rounds of decidedly feminine applause. As always, Keeley Douglas had chosen the perfect attire, this time a lemon-yellow linen dress with a matching jacket. She felt no need to add or remove clothing as she waited for her turn to speak. She hoped it would come soon, for the Arpège on her left was warring with the Nina Ricci on her right, and she felt a sneeze coming on.

It was testimony time. Keeley did indeed believe in Bartlett College's mission to educate women. Her father's money, rather than her own scholarship, had gotten her through the doors nineteen years ago, and with a little help from her friends, she'd exited four years later with a degree. Since then she'd gladly given, generously praised. She was a Bartlett Woman, and she drew quietly on the strength of the esteemed sisterhood for a good measure of the confidence most people assumed had come to her with her very first sterling-silver spoon. Testifying was part of her duty, then, but not a part she enjoyed. After fifteen years, she hadn't overcome the nagging sense that, among so many erudite women, she was an imposter.

But she would get through this with reliable style. Kip Parsons would hand her a gold filigree key, and she would accept, saying something gracious about what a pleasure it was to be a Keystone Donor for this wonderful old New England college. She would speak of traditions and excellence in education for women, and of what a privilege it was to be able to do her small part. She would announce the meeting room for the Athena Committee, the art acquisitions group, which she chaired. But all the while she would be watching the doors beneath the balcony.

Two friends. She'd seen so little of them over the years, and she remembered so much. They were the sisters she'd never had. Abby knew how to be a sister—she'd had plenty of experience—and Bess . . . well, Bess had needed some coaxing. They'd both promised to make it back this time. They'd missed the fifth. They hadn't been able to get it together for the tenth. The fifteenth was to be their reunion. For all the sophistication others had managed to breed into her, Keeley hoarded her college memories like a child with a cache of Easter candy, to be shared only with friends. *Best* friends. Women who'd passed the tests of respecting fears, understanding weaknesses, shoring up the wildest hopes and keeping the most cherished secrets.

In Keeley's life, there had been only two such women. In the postcollege years she'd spent playing all the roles expected of her, she had been forced to redefine the word *friend* just so she could tell herself she had her quota. Friends were now the women with whom she lunched, did committee work, possibly did business.

But there were few who would take a chance on teasing her about something she'd said, or being honest with her about something she'd done. There was no one who would confide in her about a family problem or a secret dream.

She was apprehensive after all this time. In fifteen years, maybe they'd changed. *Maybe?* Of course they'd changed. Keeley herself had changed. So much had happened. She had done so few of the things she'd put on her list that day before graduation when they'd challenged each other to make five predictions for the next five years. Now that those innocent times were behind them, they might have nothing in common. It might have been best to keep the memories intact, to preserve those four years in a trunk labeled The Best Time of My Life, and not let three older, wiser women tamper with something they couldn't possibly improve upon.

Keeley heard her name and moved to the podium with sleek, unaffected grace. "Thank you, Kip. Oh, it's good to be here, isn't it? This wonderful old place that never really changes for us, even though the program does surely grow and develop according to the needs of the bright young women who come here to study...."

Now there's a statement that covers all the bases. Nostalgia, elitism and progressiveness. Bess would have to give me credit for smooth, practical tactics on that one.

"We make the same commitment to Bartlett that Bartlett has made to us. A lifelong commitment to excellence in education for women. A commitment to our younger sisters and our daughters..."

*It would be nice to have a daughter, or a son. None
of us has any children. Wonder why? Abby should have
half a dozen by now.*

"... the means to build new facilities, like the labo-
ratory wing recently added to Marshall-Chaffie Hall."

*If it hadn't been for Bess, I'd never have gotten
through geology, no matter how fancy the lab was.*

"... and the money we need to beef up those schol-
arships so that the very best high-school seniors, no
matter what their financial status, will look to Bartlett
for their college education."

*Abby, that's for you. You always cared about mak-
ing good things possible for the masses. "Come the
revolution," we used to tease you, and you'd say,* "*But
there is a new world coming." And you believed it.*

"And this promises to be a very special reunion for
me. For all of us. No matter how many years have
passed, it's like coming home."

But neither face appeared at the door. Keeley ended
her talk with bloodless poise and made her way up the
aisle to the back of the auditorium. She had learned not
to permit disappointment. It was an unproductive
emotion. They had their lives; she had hers. It would be
nice if they came, but hardly necessary. She had her
commitments to the college, and she had to be here, at
least for part of the week. If she ran out of functions,
she would return to New York earlier than she'd
planned. She had Janelle Gibson's one-man show
opening at the gallery on the first of July, and there
were still promotional details to be settled.

The Hospitality Committee was serving tea and
sherry in the Susan B. Anthony Room opposite the auditorium. The soft chink of cups against saucers and the
din of polite exchanges were interrupted occasionally by

the exuberant exclamation of a name. Friends were finding one another. Keeley turned away from the big oak doors and went in search of her raincoat among the colorful array on the coatrack. She was acquainted with many of the women who were bound to be tipping glasses or cups to their lips and discussing a hundred admittedly interesting lives, but she wasn't in the mood for tea, and she had no taste for sherry.

"Lovely address, Keeley!"

Keeley smiled and turned to press cheeks with a tall brunette. "Thank you, Sarah. Wonderful to see you."

"You do that so well. I despise speaking in public."

"I've had some practice."

"I'd rather do almost anything else. Will you be staying the whole week this time?"

"I'm on the program for the symposium." She tried to recall the title they'd finally selected for her talk. "'Your Investment in Fine Art.'"

"I'll be there. It sounds lovely. My husband is coming for the dance. Then we're taking the children to Maine for a long weekend."

"The coast should be beautiful after this rain." Keeley glanced past Sarah's sleek coif and spotted her raincoat.

"Yes, let's hope it stops by then. Are you staying at the Inn?"

"Actually, I'm staying in the dorm."

"Lovely! Which one?"

Lovely, lovely, lovely. "Lawrence. The same room I had senior year."

"Oh, what fun! Do you have a roommate?"

"Yes." Fortunately. "Two, in fact. Bess Hilliard and Abby Granger."

"How lovely! I haven't seen either of them in years."

"Neither have I." She touched Sarah's arm as she edged away. "Excuse me, Sarah. I have to catch Nancy Percell before she gets away."

She didn't have to catch anybody, but she didn't want Sarah Riker Wilson to discover that Abby and Bess hadn't shown up. She wasn't sure why. It felt a little like being stood up for a date, even though dating was a piece of the past that seemed almost as remote as hair ribbons. She did say hello to Nancy, then retrieved her coat and slipped out the side door.

Out on the step, she turned up her collar and braved with bare head what was now a late-afternoon drizzle. She crossed the road and followed the paved path she'd strolled and cycled and mad-dashed over so many times, so long ago. Fifteen years seemed like a lifetime. Earlier she had run into a classmate who had a fourteen-year-old daughter. The mother of a teenager, and Keeley remembered the woman as little more than a teenager herself.

When Our Hearts Were Young and Gay, she mused. Great theme. Great title for a book. There *had* been such a time, when all things were possible and she was free to express herself as she pleased. There had been ample excitement then, the courage to take chances and the thirst for truth. There had been real friends, real promise and real love. She wanted some of that back. A bit of Abby's kindness. A touch of Bess's dedication. A small piece of her own passion, which seemed so far afield from her now. Had she known then what she knew now, she would have found some way to bottle those things. She would have recorded every late-night gab session, saved every letter, filled sketch pads with wistful, tearful, joyful moments. But the golden future had turned out to be electroplated, and now she would realistically settle for a week of remembrance, then return to her world feeling more content.

Water splattered beneath her pumps as she clipped along. She passed a puddled bed of purple and white petunias and recalled the way the early-spring rain used to bring out the earthworms. They would slither all over the sidewalk, and Bess, usually the assertive one, would pick her way along, taking care not to squash a single wriggler. Keeley paid them no heed, but she always knew she had hit one when Abby wailed, "Oh, ish, Keeley. Be sure you wipe your feet on the mat."

Keeley let herself into the spacious fourth-floor room and flipped the light on. Dreary. No luggage but her own, which she had yet to unpack. She wanted to wait for them. It was probably silly, but she'd brought the old refrigerator—the little one they'd hidden in the corner under a striped Mexican throw rug to hide it from the dorm's fire captain when she came to check how much wattage they were using. She'd even kept the red-and-orange rug.

The college provided linens, but she'd brought an extra blanket and her old red bedspread. Garish as it was, she'd saved that, too. Bess's bed was the one closest to the door. Keeley's bed, like Abby's, had its own alcove, tucked in a dormer, with access to the fire escape landing, where she had often sunbathed. She and Bess had taken a mattress out there one spring night and slept under the stars until the cold dew drove them back inside. Abby had grumbled about all the noise they'd made coming in, but they'd known it wasn't just her "maturity" that had kept her inside. It was her fear of heights.

Keeley took a pair of white slacks and a soft white top from her suitcase. No more college business this eve-

ning, she decided. No more cheerful exchanges of five
or ten or fifteen years' worth of news in twenty words
or fewer. She would shower before the rush and skip
dinner. On second thought, she would find a hamburger somewhere. A cheeseburger on white bread,
fried on a grill and dripping with cholesterol and calo-
ries.

Voices echoed in the stairwell down the hall. Keeley's heart raced as she slipped into her robe, straining
to hear, to recognize. Feminine laughter passed beneath the open transom above her door and drifted
away. She shook off...what? *Not* disappointment, but
the assumption that they were there, when, of course,
they weren't.

The bathroom was across the hall, next to the pay
phone. The first shower stall, the one she'd always pre-
ferred, still had a pelting spray. She let it massage her
shoulders and pound the base of her neck like a meat
tenderizer.

If they weren't coming, they weren't coming. No big
deal.

Keeley wrapped her thick, burnished head of hair in
a towel and padded back to the room. Her hair refused
to be sleek like the rest of her. It had its own timeless,
effortless style, made full and luxuriant just by using a
blow dryer. She used her makeup a little differently
from the way she had fifteen years ago. Concealer once
artfully used on occasion to lighten the shadows under
study-weary eyes was now a daily necessity to keep her
eyes from looking hollow. Shadows and small lines had
made themselves at home. But she needed no concealer
or shaper for her body. She had always enjoyed playing in the sun. Tennis, horseback riding, running or
hiking—those were her self-indulgences.

Her dress and jacket lay over the back of the chair, where she'd tossed and forgotten them. She made her bed, thinking that if neither friend came tonight, she would get a room at the College Inn tomorrow. For Keeley Douglas, they would make room. She wasn't going to spend the week alone in a college dorm. But for tonight, she would sleep in a place where dreams had been full of spring breaks and would-be lovers. Bright, young Adonises. Finally, for *her* chosen one, would-be had not sufficed.

And Keeley had not forgotten him.

In the many visits she'd made to the college since her graduation, she had avoided certain roads, certain old haunts, and certain real risks. But there was something about this time, something ominous about the passing of fifteen years, that led her to take the River Road to the little town of Bellefield and the place where college students, truck farmers and mill workers had mingled in search of the juiciest hamburger and the tangiest shake in the entire Commonwealth of Massachusetts: the Strawberry Shanty. This time of year, fresh strawberries from the owners' "Pick-'Em-Yourself" strawberry farm went into the milk shakes. Remembered flavors usually surpassed the real thing, but once she set out, the drive became a pilgrimage.

She passed the entrance to Peak Amusement Park and wondered whether the old carousel had been taken apart and sold to collectors. The brightly painted animals, offered individually, would have been worth a fortune.

Old Mill Road. Now there was a memory. A winding road, an old grist mill, and the comment that he hated panty hose because "they flatten the nicest curves."

Laughing, she'd held hers out the window and let the wind take them. She had been another person then.

Palmer's Miniature Golf. She'd noticed the little castle from the road, so they'd stopped and played a round. *And* played *around.* The castle was on the ninth hole, where he'd kissed her when she'd made a hole in one. Just for that, she'd made another one through the clown face and claimed a second Juicy Fruit-flavored reward.

"Pick-'Em-Yourself" covered several acres. A wealth of her favorite fruit, which, she'd discovered were replete with warm, sun-ripened juice when carried directly from plant to mouth. At the edge of the field stood the Shanty itself. The big red strawberry sign still proclaimed the house specials—burgers, fries and shakes.

The corner booth was like the first shower on the fourth floor of Lawrence Hall. Personal territory. She knew its quirks. The table would rock a little, she hoped, and there would be a cigarette burn in the red vinyl seat on *his* side. Since the Hamm's Beer sign, with the bear and the canoe, still hung on the wall next to the pool table, and since the smell of fried potatoes still edged out the aroma of pizza, there was hope that nothing else had changed. The booth was empty, and the heavy wooden table still bore his carving—*D.V.* + *K.O.,* inside a lopsided heart. Dominic Vitalli and Keeley O'Donnell. He'd done the carving on a dare. He would have done anything on a dare. Her finger lingered for a moment on the Braille-like message.

"That booth's taken."

The voice was achingly familiar, as was the line. Keeley gave herself a moment to imagine him, to paint a mental picture in preparation. She had become the epitome of poise, and she would not lose that now. She turned, smiled, and saw that he was, still, the epitome of masculine presence.

"You always told people that," she said. Remarkably, her heart was pounding so hard it made her slightly dizzy.

"It always worked." It took him a moment to offer her a handshake, and she wondered what he was thinking. He seemed less surprised than absorbed, and she shared the feeling. He looked wonderful. "Good to see you, Keeley."

His hand was warm and work-roughened, and it swallowed hers as he squeezed firmly. His nearly black hair was shorter, more controlled, than it had once been, but his dark eyes were just as bright. He still made her feel that he saw more in her face than she'd been able to find in any mirror.

She wanted to say something memorable, but she wasn't exactly brimming with clever words. Her reply was predictably pleasant but way off the mark. "You haven't changed."

"You have. You're more beautiful than you ever were." The sudden lightness she felt seemed to lend credence to his words. "And you were always beautiful."

"Maybe you have changed. You've polished up your compliments." Keeley noticed his companion. Dominic suddenly remembered her, too, and stepped aside to include an attractive, dark-eyed woman in the conversation. "We were just going to grab a burger. How about you?"

"I came up for a college reunion, and you know what those dinners are like."

"Uh-uh. No idea."

Keeley laughed. Riverdale Tech versus the hallowed halls of Bartlett again. "Well, I had a sudden craving for an old-fashioned cheeseburger."

"Join the party, then." He suddenly seemed uncomfortable to be caught in the middle as he turned to the brunette. "I'm sorry. Teri, this is Keeley O'Donnell." He winked at Keeley, signaling her stomach to turn the kind of cartwheel it hadn't done in years. "An old flame."

The woman offered a cool smile. "Teri Streeter. I'm a new flame."

"It's Keeley Douglas now."

"That's right." Dominic snapped his fingers. "You got married, didn't you? How's the ol' man? You got any—"

"Murray died two years ago, and we had no children."

"God, I'm . . . I'm sorry, Keeley. I didn't know. Bad choice of words."

"He *was* an older man. He enjoyed a good, long life." And he was the last person Keeley cared to discuss with Dominic. "I didn't mean to get in the way here, Dominic. You go ahead—"

"No, please, sit with us. Or let us sit with you." He lifted a corner of his expressive mouth. "This table's as much yours as it is mine. Besides, you can't enjoy a Shanty cheeseburger unless you're with friends. Otherwise you've got time to examine it too closely. Come on. Can I buy you a beer?"

"No, I really—"

"Strawberry shake, huh? You always went crazy over strawberries."

Keeley read "back off" in the new flame's eyes, which was just enough challenge to make her forget the impropriety of horning in on Teri's date. She slid into the booth. "I can't stay long, but I—"

"Long enough for—" He motioned to the man behind the bar. "Hey, Jack, look who's here."

Jack Koski, owner of the Shanty, had put on weight and lost what little hair he'd had. He glanced up from the beer tap, pressed his glasses to the bridge of his nose and grinned. "The one that got away, huh, Dom? Howya doin', missy?"

"Good, Jack. How are you?"

"Gettin' old." He patted his round belly, as if it were a sign of age. "Enjoyin' every minute of it. You got your hands full there, Dom."

"So help me feed 'em."

"Cheeseburger, cheeseburger, cheeseburger?"

"Hold the grease, Jack. How're the strawberries?"

"It's June," he declared happily. "Which means they're great."

Dominic made an effort to include Teri in the conversation, but the years fell away, and Teri hadn't been with them then. Even though they spoke of the present, the increasingly familiar tone came from the past. Keeley knew little about his life, but still she knew him better than Teri did. And he knew Keeley better than she would have guessed. Over the years they had hoarded remembered intimacies, and now the carefully preserved memories played their role, prompting long looks and soft smiles.

The conversation skimmed lightly over the surface, covering up for the emotional undertow. Her husband's death was the most personal news either of them offered. She wondered about his marriage, but she wouldn't ask in Teri's presence. He was a carpenter now, had his own handmade furniture business, and he gave her his card. She didn't tell him she'd seen his listing in the phone book. She knew he lived in Bellefield now, and she didn't tell him how many times she'd thought of calling him, just to say hello. But she'd had better sense. Yes, she said, she had been back to the college a number of times over the years, but hadn't had time to revisit old haunts.

In truth, it was the heart she lacked, not the time.

When Teri reminded him that the movie would start at seven-thirty, he checked his watch. "Guess we'd better get a move on."

"I have to go, too," Keeley said quickly. The better part of the cheeseburger she'd craved lay cold on her plate. She had no idea how it had tasted.

"Listen. Maybe you'd like to see my shop if you get some free time while you're here. I'd like to show you what I do."

She studied his card. "I don't know how much—"

"If you get the time, stop by. I've got a piece I'm trying to finish up for a special order, so I'll be there tomorrow." He slid around the curve of the booth and stood next to Teri. "I'd like to see what an artist thinks of it."

"I'm an art dealer, not an artist." They were going out together. Keeley wondered at her sudden pang of jealousy. Of course they were. They had a date. He hadn't spent the past fifteen years in a monastery. But Teri was transparent. A bimbo. Hardly his type.

And they *were* going out together. Looking at them made her hurt. She fished around the booth for her purse.

"I *always* thought you were an artist," he said. "You were the only one who didn't believe it."

She looked up. Oh, those sweet, dark chocolate eyes. They eased the funny pinching she felt in her chest. "Not the only one." She smiled. "I'll try. I'll call first."

"Don't bother. Just come. Pound on the back door loud enough so I can hear you." He dipped his chin and smiled back. "I'll be seeing you."

Keeley skipped lightly up four flights of steps. Dominic, Dominic, Dominic. She felt like a teenager, thrilled simply because he'd *spoken* to her. And because he wasn't married. And because his smile was as beautiful as ever.

Wait a minute. Maybe he *was* married. She was certain she'd heard he was married. Maybe he was... No, not Dominic. If he was dating, then he'd gotten divorced.

So what? she asked herself as she headed up the hall. What difference did it make? He was just an old friend, and it was good to see him looking so—

Voices. The transom was open, the door ajar, and she heard familiar voices! She pushed the door open and stood there for a moment before Abby sprang from her chair and met her with unrestrained open arms. No one but Abby hugged this way, rocking back and forth like a buoy. It came unnaturally to Keeley, but she took the cue and bent down to accommodate Abby's stature. Bess followed with a less demonstrative greeting between fellow New Englanders.

Oh, they looked so good. Abby was short. There was no other word for it. Voluptuous and full of South Carolina sunshine, they had always teased her about being an exchange student, and she'd claimed to offer cultural enrichment and improved diction. Take it easy, say it slowly, you won't need to repeat anything.

And Bess was regal. Queen Bess. Tall, tailored and athletically trim. Bess seemed to sit back and watch over all proceedings. Once everyone else had overreacted, overstated and overcompensated, she would put things back into perspective with a simple gesture or a few words.

"When did you get in?" Keeley asked, glancing from one to the other. "I could have picked you up at the airport, Abby, if you'd only let me know. And you drove, didn't you, Bess?"

"Bess had a run-in with a cat, so that's why she was late, and I just—" Abby flopped back into her chair and offered a gamine smile "—got held up."

"A cat? You're kidding." She was rattling on, but she couldn't seem to stop herself. "Have you eaten? You know, I think they even have milk and crackers out in the kitchen. I've eaten, but I'll certainly join you. Or maybe we could sneak something back up."

They both declined, and the three of them set about unpacking, putting a sparse array of clothes and toiletries where once there had been a clothing jam, a shoe riot, a collection of bottles, tubes and sprays the size of Revlon's monthly shipment to Grenier Drugs, across the commons from the college gate. Keeley needed to keep the conversation going. Soon, she was sure, she would feel more at ease. She congratulated Bess on her promotion at work, and Bess asked about the gallery. An art gallery must have seemed almost like a frivolity to Bess, who was a senior vice president of one of the most important banks in Boston.

They spoke of Abby's job, her family, and surprisingly, she was able to make light of the demise of her marriage. Keeley caught Bess's glance and remembered their mutual assessment of Abby's husband: el jerko.

Uncouth. Uncaring. Totally unworthy of Abby. And now, finally, Abby agreed. It was a relief to share a laugh and finally break the ice.

The bed squeaked as Keeley slipped under the covers. She welcomed the cool night air from the open window above her head. "Do you think these are the same beds?"

"If they haven't repainted, why would they put in new beds?" Bess said.

"Oh, I think they must have painted the room, Bess," Abby put in. "They just didn't change the color."

Abby's ingenuousness always aroused affectionate laughter. Keeley had once thought Abby said such things to play the sugar-and-spice role, but she'd long since decided that the innocence was genuine. She was glad Abby hadn't lost it, even through a crummy marriage and a bitter divorce. Abby was close to her family, and Keeley remembered when Abby had called her the day after her mother's death and needed to talk. Keeley had felt favored. She, too, had lost a mother, but it had been so long ago, there was hardly any comparison. Nor had she been as close to her mother as Abby was to hers. But she hadn't said any of that. She'd grabbed for the opportunity to be the chosen friend. She'd told Abby she understood, and she'd caught the next flight out to be there for the funeral. So much like her mother, the relatives had said of Abby. And the relatives, so unlike Keeley's own situation, had been myriad. For Keeley it had been an uneasy time, but she had been there because Abby had chosen to call her that night.

Memories came easily in the dark, like friendly dreams. They traded them back and forth. Hairstyles had changed, and faces bore care lines. Clothing styles were different. Bess had even taken to wearing perfume, if Keeley's nose for scents hadn't failed her. But in the dark, the voices were still the same. They remembered things she'd forgotten. She reminded them of things they would rather have forgotten.

Weary. Weary. Recollections came harder as the past and the present began to drift.

"Do you remember Dominic Vitalli, either of you?"

"Of course," Abby said, and when no answer came from Bess, Abby yawned and drawled, "I think she's fallen asleep. What about Dominic?"

"I saw him this evening."

"Where?"

"I went to the Strawberry Shanty. He was there."

"What was it like, seeing him again?"

"Scary." Did that sound foolish? Probably. "He was with another woman."

"His wife?"

"No. She said she was the 'new flame.'" Keeley giggled softly. "He introduced me as his old flame. It felt very strange."

She imagined a candle flame, and then another. The new one was no brighter than the old one. No bigger. No hotter. No candles graced the tables at the Shanty, but even so his dark eyes had reflected a bright gleam when he'd smiled at her.

Come to think of it, it had felt warm, seeing him again. Old flame warm.

"I'm glad you're here, Abby. I'm glad we're all here."

"Me too."

Sunday

Coffee always did it for Keeley. It was the only thing about mornings that she truly liked, and for it she would rise, if not shine. Abby did all the shining after she'd managed to con the dorm kitchen out of a whole carafe of dark, delicious eye-opening coffee.

Thank God Abby hadn't changed. Back in the old days, you could count on Abby for a happy face in the morning even after she'd pulled an all-nighter studying for finals. She had kept her promise to the troubled masses by becoming a social worker, which Keeley had thought a grim ambition. But worrying about other people's problems professionally hadn't taken the cheery lilt out of Abby's southern drawl.

"Good morning, Keeley. It's a beautiful day outside."

"I know. Your grandmother used to say that."

"Even when it was raining cats and dogs," Bess put in as she held a cup while Abby poured.

"But it's stopped raining," Abby said. "You've got cats on the brain, Bess."

"Cats?" Keeley tossed the covers aside and swung her legs over the side of the bed. "That's right, you got held up by a cat yesterday."

"And a cat doctor." Abby handed Keeley a cup of steaming black coffee.

"I hope the cat doctor was able to pull a few more lives out of his little black bag, that's all." Bess had already put her makeup on and was working on her hair. Keeley wondered when all that had been accomplished.

"Well, I've done my job," Abby said. "I've fixed Keeley so she can't go back to sleep. Now that I'm here, I don't want to miss anything, and the first seminar starts in forty minutes."

The morning seminar on women's health issues held no appeal for Keeley as she listened with half an ear to the history of the birth control pill and its role in the Women's Movement. She'd long since forgotten about the effects of being "on the pill." Dominic's business card was secreted inside her purse like hot property, and like Bess with the cat, Keeley had handcrafted furniture on the brain. She toyed with the clasp on her purse, resisting the urge to take the card out and study it again. She knew every word printed on it. "D. Vitalli, furniture maker." There were no fancy claims like "fine furniture," or "custom woodworking." Simply *furniture maker.* Keeley decided the best thing she could do for her own sanity was to visit the shop and see what kind of furniture he made. Rather than explain her plan to anyone, she slipped away from the college before noon.

The Bellefield shop was tucked between a self-serve gas station and Pinocchio's Pizza on a side street. As instructed she headed for the back entrance. The aroma of hot cheese, tomato sauce and Italian sausage floated down the alley. Keeley rapped, knocked, then pounded on the door, before Dominic finally appeared, looking surprised. Keeley had a sinking feeling he'd forgotten all about his invitation. But then he smiled.

"Hey, terrific! Another anchovy lover."

"Anchovy?"

"I just put in the order. When I heard all the knocking, I thought, hey, that was quick." He stepped back and cocked his head toward the interior. "Come on in."

"I didn't mean to barge in on lunch."

He closed the door behind her while she took in the scent of pine, the racks of lumber and the assortment of benches and power tools beneath the fluorescent lights in the large open room.

"So how come you're here at lunchtime?" The arched eyebrow challenged her, followed by a smile that permitted her to relax. "Because you're hungry for pizza, right?"

"Do you still eat pizza every day of your life?"

"Nah, I had to cut back when I started puttin' on the weight." He patted his flat belly, stuck his thumbs in his waistband and grinned. He knew darn well he wasn't overweight. "Twice a week, though, at least, or my blood won't coagulate properly. How are your meetings going?"

"Fine. Fascinating."

"I'll bet." He put his hand on her shoulder, as though confiding in a buddy, and gestured expansively. "Welcome to Dominic's, where lunch is served among the pines." She took a deep breath, then sneezed. "Dusty pines," he added, and offered her a tissue from a box sitting close at hand. "And we've got oaks. Cherries. Some cedar. What we haven't got is old ladies spouting off about how many books you women have stuck away in your library up there, and why you don't want to go coed and let men mess up the shelves."

"That issue was settled long ago. We're a women's college. It's tradition as much as anything else. An old and venerable tradition." She blotted her nose and pocketed the tissue. "And I'm soon to be one of the old ladies."

He shook his head, eyes twinkling. "Yeah. You're gettin' old, Keeley. What, thirty-five now?"

"Thirty-six. Almost."

"June twenty-first. See? I remembered." He gave her an appreciative once-over. "You never looked better."

Well, then, she would say her line. "I never felt better. And, of course, you..." He had guided her past a series of workbenches to a low table, where a high-backed oak chair was in the final stages of being finished. Its sleek lines and dramatic height arrested Keeley's attention and forestalled another empty conversational claim. Instead she exclaimed, "Dominic, this is beautiful! This is..." She reached, then turned for permission to touch. He nodded. The wood felt like satin. "This is truly exquisite."

"You like it?"

"Oh, yes, it's a piece of... art."

"No kidding? I guess you'd know. Try it out." He moved it to the floor. "Go ahead. It's functional art, made to sit in."

She sat. "It's much more comfortable than it looks. In fact, it's really, *really* comfortable." The look he gave her said she was overdoing it, and she laughed. "You know how wonderful it is."

"And I can put up with being patronized by you only because I know it's bred into you, and you don't know any better."

"I'm not patronizing you any more than your comment about my youthful looks patronizes me. I didn't offer to buy it, did I?"

"It's not for sale. I designed it for a very rich, very grouchy old lady who has back problems."

She eased her spine against the chair's unique back and assessed its support. "This should certainly improve her disposition."

"Yeah, it has. This is the fourth one she's ordered. I don't usually make the same thing over and over again, but for good ol' Beatrice, I agreed to do four alike."

She stood up to admire the chair once more. "You mean, you wouldn't make a dining room set? This would be wonderful as part of a—"

"I used to, but now I like to do one of a kind pieces." He stepped around the chair and pointed out another piece. "Like this one. It was like the tree grew out of the ground and kept right on growing into this shape."

Keeley followed him to a low, sprawling cherrywood table with supports that looked like something that might actually grow in a forest. She touched the hand-rubbed surface. "Through your hands."

"Yeah. Through my hands. So if you wanted a dining room set, you might not get matching chairs. Or you might. People who know my work are willing to show me the space they have and leave the design up to me." With pride he added, "Nothing in this shop is for sale."

"I'm impressed." Even envious, she thought.

"I've waited a long time to hear you say that."

The plans on a drawing table caught her eye. "May I have a look?"

"Help yourself."

It was a scale drawing of a small side chair from several angles. A small preliminary sketch was clipped to the paper. Bold, sure strokes—nothing sketchy about it. "You used to talk about building houses."

He sat on the corner of the table, dangling one booted foot over the edge. "You used to talk about *building* sculptures out in front of my houses, shiny modern stuff for birds to perch on and kids to crawl under. Is that what you're doing nowadays?''

"No, I changed my mind. I'm selling art, instead. I have a gallery in New York." She glanced up from the sketch and offered a thin smile. "So, as it turns out, you're the artist." And well did he deserve the claim. He had spoken of none of these talents when he'd confided his dreams years ago. A contractor, he'd assured her, could rake in a ton of money. "Do you have people working for you?"

"Sure. The designs are mine, and basically I craft each piece. So when you order a Vitalli, you get a Vitalli. But I have two younger guys working for me, plus my Uncle Jake. I learned the business from him, but he's semiretired, works for me a couple of days a week for something to do."

"Did you buy your uncle's business?"

"No, I started my own. I used to work for Uncle Jake when I was a kid."

"I thought you worked in the paper mill."

He laughed. "That was for money, back when I was going to school. I worked for Uncle Jake for experience. After I got out of school, I, uh...I knocked around in construction for a while." He ran a finger over the edge of the table.

Times of trouble? she wondered. Time wasted?

He looked up again. "Then I apprenticed with the prince of furniture makers. Levi Tollman. Ever heard of him?"

"I don't think so."

"If you're into art, you should know about Levi. Here." He pulled a magazine off the shelf under the drawing table and flipped through the pages before holding it out for her inspection. "Here's some of his work. He died a couple years back, and people are already paying... Here, look at this one."

It was a slick trade magazine, one she would have had no reason to see before. Tollman's furniture was like sculpture. "Very nice. Yes, I see the mark of his influence in your work."

"Sure. Some. But I've got my own style. I've even developed a joint that I use mostly for tables...." He fanned through the pages until the magazine fell open to another page. "There, that's mine. I won an award for that bench."

He was like a kid showing off his grades, and she was the admiring friend. Nothing was forced. "Oh, that *is* beautiful. The way it curves...so graceful."

"There, that sounds more like you."

"More than what?"

"More than, 'I see the mark of his influence in your work,' for Pete's sake. You know a good thing when you see it, right?"

"That's how I make my living."

He wouldn't split hairs with her about her choice of words. He knew she'd never *had* to work a day in her life to earn a living. The choice between love and money probably hadn't been a difficult one in the end, although he hadn't been privy to any of the final deliberations. She'd chosen what she'd always had. He understood that now. She'd made the safer move, and probably the wiser.

But, damn, they'd been good together once. He smiled, remembering how sweet she'd looked the previous night, sitting in their booth, just like old times. "I couldn't believe my eyes when I walked into the Shanty, and there you were." He shook his head. "After all this time."

Her eyes were still on the magazine. "I didn't mean to intrude on your date."

"It was great to see you."

"Teri didn't think so."

Ah, she was angling for the scoop on Teri and him. He chuckled. "It's always interesting to see how a woman responds to meeting an old girlfriend. Remember how you told me once that your psych professor said you should always see how a guy acts when he's drunk before you make any commitments to him? The same principle applies."

"Did Teri pass the precommitment test?"

"Not a test, really. Just brings out another side. Her claim to *flame* was premature."

She closed the magazine and looked at him. "I'd heard you were married."

"Split the sheets five years ago." He took the book from her hands and set it aside. "Listen, I'm sorry for that crack I made about your husband being an old man."

"It's just an expression, isn't it?"

"Yeah, but I meant it literally." He raked his fingers through his hair and came up with sweat at his temple. It was getting hot in there. "I was thinking back to your wedding picture. He looked old enough to be your father."

"Murray actually had a son my age, and a daughter a couple of years younger. But we had a lot in common—friends, interests. We got along well." He flipped a switch, and an exhaust fan whirred. She had to raise her voice. "Where did you see my wedding picture?"

"My brother Brian's girlfriend found it in a magazine at the dentist's office."

"I think I can guess which magazine." Her father had sent them the announcement. "The kind you'd only look at if you were waiting to have a tooth filled."

"In those days, I wouldn't have looked at it at all, but now that I'm dealing with those country club people, I can flip through and say, 'Hey, ol' Charlie Oilwell's daughter, Tipsy, is tying the knot with Marvin Moneybags IV. Must be why Charlie's in such a hurry for his curio cabinet.' Of course, a piece of Vitalli is never rushed. Not for anybody." They looked at each other when the knock sounded at the back door. "Can you smell what's on the other side of that door?"

"Anchovies, pepperoni, Italian sausage—" she watched him hotfoot it across the concrete floor as though he hadn't eaten in weeks, and she pursued him with the litany of his favorites "—peppers, black olives, double cheese. A *whole* Vitalli is rushed when there's pizza at the door."

"Damn right. Every man has his price."

Dominic paid the delivery man, and Keeley thought better of offering to pay for her share. He carried the box as though he bore a precious gift, and he searched from unfinished project to cluttered tabletop to lumber-laden workbench, looking for a place to set it down. "This is going to be tricky, eating out of the box."

"We've done it before."

"Yeah, but you were never wearing an ice-cream suit." He offered a slow, lascivious grin. "In fact, I remembered one time when you weren't wearing much of anything, and I was a little concerned about dripping hot cheese on your—"

"It's been a long time since I've dined in a bikini." She laughed, then pointed to a tall drafting table. "How about over there? We'll eat standing up." She hung her white silk jacket over the back of a chair and followed the pizza to the table. With the flick of a latch he lowered the top to create a flat surface.

"Napkin?" He offered several of the countertop box variety. "I dare you to keep up with me and stay—" he eyed her suggestively "—as immaculate as you are now."

"Just watch me." Returning his challenging look, she rolled up the soft sleeves of her pale blue blouse.

Happy, he watched her ease a slice away from the pie, lift it on elegantly polished nail tips, then catch the dripping cheese and curl it around her tongue, nibbling her way up the stringy stuff until the point of the slice disappeared into her mouth. With his own first bite he imagined licking the spicy sauce off her lips. Like hell she'd keep up with him. If she wanted to try, she could forget all about staying *immaculate*.

He looked, she thought, as though he were waiting for her to drop something other than a sliver of anchovy, as though every savory bite of his favorite food were laced with anticipation. If any part of her came loose, he would devour it. He had before, with no more than a look, a smile, a silent invitation to dance.

They had met at a mixer in the fall of her junior year. On principle, she'd avoided mixers, but that Friday night she'd been between romances and bored with her social life. She'd talked Abby into taking a break from her books, and they'd gone together. The dance had already been underway close by in Howe Hall when they walked in. "I'm not staying long," Abby had warned, and to this day Keeley had no idea how long her friend had stayed.

The big blue-and-white banner proclaiming Welcome to the Virgin Island was enough to make Keeley want to turn around and walk out. It was a time when one woman felt as uncomfortable about her virginity as another woman felt about her lack of it, but Keeley couldn't see what the big deal was. Dating was like chess, and she was good at both games. She enjoyed the maneuvering, and her defenses were unbeatable. She enjoyed the social whirl too much to date one man forever. Would she do it for love? Skip Carver had once asked in desperation. Keeley had been in and out of love too many times to count, so the answer was no. She would do it in her own good time.

Then came Dominic, with his unnerving smile, his dark, deep-set, wellspring eyes, and his complete self-possession. He had told her his name as he'd taken her in his arms, held her closer than most boys dared to even after the prerequisite exchange of polite conversation, and made her move with him in a sensual hip-sway that required rolling joints and a liquid sense of rhythm. They shared both. The song was "Black Magic Woman," Santana's most hypnotic. The music and the motion were both memorable, and so was the moment when she realized that this was a man, not a boy.

"Where do you go to school, Dominic?"

"Will you have me thrown out if I tell you the truth?"

"You're not a student."

"Sure I am. Riverdale Tech. We don't have a rugby team, but we'll pitch pennies against your Ivy League boys anytime."

She laughed and introduced herself. "And, as far as I know, this is an open mixer, although I doubt we sent Riverdale Tech an invitation."

"Ordinarily, we'd have to turn you down, anyway, but it's an off weekend. No demolition derby tonight, so we thought we'd go slumming." He glanced at the banner. "Virgin Island, huh?"

"Ivy League humor."

"Funny as hell." Santana faded into Bob Dylan's entreaty, "Lay, Lady, Lay," and Dominic laid his cheek against her hair. "Interesting choice of music for a Virgin Island party. You feel like living dangerously tonight?"

"How... dangerously?"

"Venture off the island for a while." His voice was considerably more intoxicating than Dylan's. "'Cause if you don't, pretty soon I'll be mixin' it up with the preps waiting to cut in on me. That's not what they mean by 'mixer,' is it?"

"Hardly."

"So let's go grab a beer somewhere." She started to shake her head, but his was in the way. "Too dangerous? How about a shake?"

It had been a pizza and shake winter, and at first only Abby and Bess knew she was seeing him. She didn't want to explain him to anyone else. Where he came from, who his parents were, where he went to school—all were measures of acceptability where Dominic fell short and Keeley's brain had been marinated in the broth of her family's status to expect perfection. She took refuge in the college's rules, her father's rules, and delighted in the excitement of sneaking around. Dominic humored her, and a strawberry and sparkling wine summer followed. Rendezvous at the Cape Cod summer house when her father wasn't there, weekends in his neck of the woods—East Ridley, Riverdale, Bellefield, where she was ostensibly staying with a girlfriend. She dated other men for show, and they argued about it. He took other women out. Just to get back at her, she said. Just to refresh his memory, he said. She met his family, and after more than a year, she decided it was time he met her father.

Never, she thought, had two men with more in common despised one another so readily. In the end she had to ask herself, what *did* they have in common? And the answer: stubbornness. Each one was sure he knew what was best for her. Dominic had said she had a choice. Her father had insisted that choices were not as important as plans. *His* plans.

And now, with the choices all behind them, they were back to pizza.

"So how was your graduation present?" Dominic asked, as though he knew where her thoughts had taken her. "The last time I saw you was the day you got on that plane bound for Paris. I believe it was billed as a...summer art institute, right?"

"Yes." However it had been billed, she didn't want to talk about it.

"Always wondered whether you met some brooding French painter and had a quick fling." Her eyes flashed with shock. "Hey, it's been fifteen years. We can look back on it with a smile now, can't we? We were both pretty wild and restless."

"'Impetuous' was my father's favorite description."

"Yeah, well, he sure had a way of hitting the nail on the head, didn't he?"

She closed the lid on the pizza box. "There was no brooding French painter."

"No? Too bad. That was the best of the scenarios I conjured up. You didn't meet your husband over there, did you?"

"No. My father introduced us...much later." She glanced away from him. "I have wondered, from time to time, why you never wrote."

"I was never much of a letter writer. And I didn't want you to go, but you went anyway. You sent a few cheery postcards, a couple of letters." He crumpled a napkin and tossed it on the box, heaving a sigh. "Pride, I guess. That's why I didn't write. Long about September, I got loaded one night and called your dad. You still weren't back. I asked him for a phone number. He said you couldn't be reached."

"September?"

"Yeah, about then." He stuck his thumbs in his back pockets. "So, hey, you landed yourself a nice husband, made a nice life for yourself, and, uh...so did I." He nodded. "It's really good to see you again, Keeley. You've changed, maybe gotten more sophisticated, but there's something about you that's still the same." Leaning across the table, he confided, "Which is kind of hard to take, because I was hoping you'd turned into a miserable old biddy."

"I was hoping you'd gotten bald and fat." Oh, but he hadn't. She smiled. "Then again, I think of the way we were back then, and I wonder."

"I wonder, too. We must be feeling our age."

"Maybe so. This is kind of a sentimental journey for me, this time around." She brightened further. "Abby and Bess came this year! Oh, Dom, you'll have to stop by and see them. Neither one of them has changed a bit."

"Don't kid yourself. We've all changed." He lifted his index finger to make the point. "And that's good. That's the way it's supposed to be."

"Still, there's something about us that's still the same. Something that made us friends once and has nothing to do with our careers, our responsibilities and who we've become."

"You're still the woman among women, Keeley. Whenever I hear 'Black Magic Woman,' I have to look around and see if you're there." He folded his arms over his chest. "You ever listen to the oldies on the radio?"

"It's funny to think of our music as 'oldies,' isn't it? Glenn Miller is 'oldies.'" He groaned, and she echoed him. "Do you have children who tell you your music is old-fashioned?"

"I have a son. He's not into music." He raised his eyebrows. "You?"

"No. None of my own."

"Only your stepchildren?"

"And they were grown by the time we were married." Neither spoke for a moment, in deference to the children they'd once planned. Finally Keeley looked around for her purse. "I'd better get back to the college and let you get back to work. If you have some time this week, we're staying in the same dorm, the same room on the fourth floor. Lawrence Hall. You remember."

"I remember the fire escape quite well."

"Abby and Bess would love to—"

"How do you know? You probably haven't seen *them* much in fifteen years, either." She was fidgeting with her purse. He laid a hand on her arm. "Do you want to see me, Keeley?"

"You invited me to your shop, and here I am." She knew she was being perverse, but then, he knew why she'd come. "And I adore your work."

"Is that right?" He stepped back. "I'll check the schedule, see what I can work out, maybe give you a call. How's that?"

"That's fine. I enjoyed lunch."

"I'm glad."

Elizabeth Cady Stanton might not have approved the use to which the Bartlett alumni were putting the room named for her. On the top floor of Lockwood Hall, the room overlooked the chapel gardens and was a comfortable place for a quiet cocktail party. Shelves lined with books, overstuffed chairs and heavy maple antiques gave the room its character, but Keeley had seen another kind of furniture earlier in the day, and she could think of little else as she mingled, smiling practiced smiles and generally agreeing with whatever was said.

Bess homed in on her, picking up on the loneliness she hadn't been able to shake. "You're not with us, Keeley," she said.

Keeley's chin snapped up. "Yep, I am, but I'm a little tired. I enjoy these things, but after a while..." She raised her glass of zinfandel. "I'd be happy with milk and crackers and just the three of us back at the dorm."

"But Abby might not." Bess indicated their friend with a nod. "Remember Mr. Lucas?" She nodded in the opposite direction. Keeley looked from one to the other while Bess continued. "Catch them in the act of exchanging glances and you'll notice they've got a little electricity going."

"Is that Joshua Lucas, the psych prof?"

"Indeed. Abby's favorite."

"Mmm-hmm, I believe I see the charge zapping to and fro there." Keeley smiled at Bess. Bess smiled at Keeley. "Should we do a little bolstering?"

"I think so."

They moved shoulder to shoulder. Sometimes three heads maneuvered better than one.

Monday

The clay wanted to be a cat. Keeley's fingers merely pushed it along as it stretched its forelegs along the table, stuck its sleek behind up in the air and arched its tail, making a lazy Z of itself. Large ears, small face, splayed front paws—ooh, nice stretch, kitty. Bess had been worrying about a stray cat, and there in the sculpture studio, Keeley's haven, the feline figure was taking shape, sharing her break from the morning program. She would go back to the seminar soon, she told herself, and sink her teeth into those *issues* once again. Yes, of course, she cared about them. She had spent fifteen years molding herself, much as she did the cat, into an issue-oriented woman.

She had been a fair student, but Bartlett students were expected to be much better than *fair*. An exclusive preparatory school had groomed her for admission, but she'd been no brain. She had done respectably well in art, her major, but she hadn't been invited to write an honors thesis. In the company of so many smart girls, she'd felt fortunate just to be awarded a degree. Her summer in Europe had been intended to round out her education, and it had, but not the way she'd intended. Not the way her father had promised.

But you can't always get what you want.

The refrain of a lifetime. She'd learned to compromise, but stubbornly and with almost instinctive regularity she returned to her alma mater, the place where all things had seemed possible once, before any compromises had been made. Her friends were usually "tied up" and couldn't make it, but she came anyway, because she, busy as she might be, was never tied up. Her ties, in fact, were few. So now that her friends had finally come, why was she sitting alone in the sculpture studio playing with clay?

Because she loved this place, especially when it was almost deserted, as it was now. She loved the bright light that filled the tall east windows, the smell of wax and clay, linseed oil and wood. The creaky floorboards and the high ceiling were part of the old college's character, but the art building held a special charm for Keeley. In the corner of this room, where someone else's unfinished metal sculpture now stood, she had spent long hours shaping her own *Woman Waiting,* which had ultimately been cast in bronze. She kept it tucked away in a closet at home. Next door she'd spent a semester taking watercolor and deciding that it was not her medium.

Down the hall was the studio where she'd taken a course in life drawing and learned the meaning of artistic objectivity. She remembered glancing furtively at the faces of fifteen other female artists, hoping that someone felt the same sympathy she did for the naked model who posed center stage. No one gave any sign of noticing anything different when, after weeks of drawing females, a male model was hired from a neighboring school. Keeley's sophistication had fallen away when she returned to the dorm and described to Abby and Bess just how miserably the poor boy's deodorant and his jock strap had failed him. Fits of giggles finally gave way to serious debate over questions of grossness, male sexiness and who had borrowed Bess's deodorant.

"Nice work."

Keeley nearly jumped out of her artist's smock. Laughing, Dominic sat on the edge of the table and watched her straighten her shoulders, taking a deep breath to regain her composure.

"This place is as quiet as a tomb. How could you not have heard me come in?"

"I was off somewhere, I suppose. But you must have deliberately sneaked up on me."

"I clomped in here like an elephant. You must have been totally absorbed in what you're doing there." He tilted his head to study the cat. "I like it."

"Oh, I was just playing with the—"

He stayed her hand from crushing her work. "I like it very much. It reminds me of the figure you made me for Christmas way back when."

"A horse, wasn't it?" She remembered it well.

"I keep it on my desk at the shop. I didn't show you my office, did I?"

"No," she said, and then, almost in anguish, "Oh, no. You've got that sitting on your desk?"

"It's my only O'Donnell original."

"There are very few in existence, and I'd hoped they were safely under wraps by now. The artist never progressed beyond her 'early' period."

"Then it's about time she got off her duff and got on with it." He nodded toward the cat. "Obviously."

"This? This is typical of my dime-store knickknack stuff. Too cute to be memorable. No, my job is to discover people with real talent and find buyers for their work." Pushing her chair away from the worktable, she silently promised to put the cat out of its misery later. "How did you know where to find me?"

"Went to the dorm. The front door's quicker than the fire escape, but not as much fun." With a look, they shared a memory of the night he'd sneaked in that way. "I walked right up front, and there was Abby, just dying to tell me where I could find you."

Keeley smiled, knowing just how it had been. "She hasn't changed, has she?"

"Oh, I don't know. I think she's gotten prettier."

Humph. Had he said that about *her?* It was not a comment she'd intended to take seriously, but it felt as though she had. "So you're here. I'm a little surprised."

"I had an errand to do in the neighborhood. Thought we might have lunch on you this time. Unless you're tied up here?"

Tied up? Interesting choice of words. "No, I've had my clay therapy for the day. There's a lovely little tearoom—" Had she actually said *lovely?*

"Tearoom? Come on, Keeley, you know me better than that."

"Do I?"

"You used to."

She wiped her fingers on the smock. "We could take a rowboat out on the lake."

"There you go. How about that little deli? Is it still open?"

She pulled the smock over her head as she stood. "Shall we walk over to the commons and see? How much time do you have?"

"How much do you want, sugar?" He gave her full-skirted white sundress an admiring once-over. "I'm my own boss now."

A typical college-town deli called Portia provided the picnic. Without any need to confer, they ordered a loaf of sourdough bread, half a pound of sliced roast beef and rounds of Gouda and Camembert cheeses. Among the close-quartered shelves Keeley found Dominic's favorite brand of Greek olives, while he selected two baseball-size peaches from a basket. She filled a sack with cinnamon bears, jawbreakers, chocolate gold coins, Pixie Stix and red licorice whips, none of which was "penny candy" anymore, despite what the sign said. The clerk packaged everything in a plastic net tote, and Dominic paid the bill, despite Keeley's objection. They stopped at the tavern down the street for a cold bottle of liebfraumilch, and Keeley decided that her alumni sisters would not hear her views on the issues discussed that afternoon.

On their way across campus they saw Abby with Joshua Lucas. Abby and Keeley waved, exchanging the smiles that still said *Look who's with me.*

"That guy looks a little old for her, doesn't he?" Admonished by Keeley's hard glance, Dominic backed down. "Sorry, I forgot."

"You did not." With another smile, she forgave him, since she felt too lighthearted to be offended by "older man" remarks. "He was one of her professors. A very *young* professor at the time." She lifted her shoulder. "Still young by my ever-changing standard of over-the-hill. Besides, there's a bit of a difference in *our* ages, if you'll remember."

"Four years. Big deal."

"It was a big deal then. You seemed quite worldly."

"I'd seen New England and Southeast Asia, if that made me worldly."

"You never talked about Vietnam."

"You were a college kid. Vets weren't popular with college kids back then."

"I thought it was because it was too painful for you to talk about."

"I couldn't imagine regaling somebody like you with war stories. Life in the Vitalli household was about as shocking as you could handle."

Wounded, she looked at him sharply as they strode along the shady path past the new science wing. "That's ridiculous. Your family is delightful."

"'One bathroom for eight people?'" he mocked. "'How in the world do you manage?'"

She heard more than teasing. There was a larger truth. "Did I really say that?"

"You sure as hell did." He pointed to the library tower, with its castlelike turret. "Remember when you found that 'secret door,' and we got Abby to climb up to the top with us?"

"I thought that never-ending spiral stairway was going to do her in, but she made it."

"She's a good sport."

Keeley felt another small sting. Compared to a woman who was distressed by a dearth of bathrooms, Abby *was* a good sport.

At a fork in the path, they bore right. To the left, beyond a parking lot and a hockey field, they could see the manicured shrubbery and split-rail fences that marked the hunt course. Keeley felt a cold chill, despite the sun's warmth on her back.

"Do you still get dressed up like National Velvet and jump horses over those fences?" Dominic asked. "You used to look great in that outfit, but watching you do that stuff always scared the hell out of me."

"Really? You never told me that."

"I couldn't have stopped you, and I didn't want you to think I was chickenhearted. But I thought you took too many chances."

"Funny you should say that. You were the only man I knew who actually knew a bookie. I thought *you* took too many chances."

"I was worldly, remember?"

"Do you still play the horses?"

"I've gone from worldly to wise," he said, grinning as he swung the tote bag at his side. "These days, I only bet on a sure thing."

They'd reached the edge of the college's idyllic lake, and they walked out on a small boat dock, where several rowboats bobbed at the ends of their lines. "I hope we can bet on these things," Keeley said taking the groceries from Dominic. "Do they look a little rickety to you?"

He anchored one hand on a piling and hopped into a boat. "Maybe not seaworthy, but she's certainly lakeworthy."

Keeley handed the tote bag down and started to board the same way Dominic had, but his hands were there, waiting to lift her down. He was an artist with the hands of a carpenter. She hesitated long enough to look into his eyes and enjoy the come-hither sparkle in them. This was more than a courteous gesture. She steadied herself on the piling, but gave him her other hand. When he slid his arm around her waist, she gripped him tighter, transferring her balance to his shoulder as she went to him. She welcomed the excuse to touch this way.

He held her for a moment. "Don't rock the boat," he warned, but his voice wasn't quite steady, his chuckle a little off.

She brushed at her skirt and looked up at him. "I guess I'm not dressed for this adventure."

He smiled, remembering a time when they'd gone skinny-dipping at her insistence.

Her face colored as she remembered it, too.

"You sit in the bow, and I'll be your oarsman. I've always wanted to take a lady in a pretty dress out in a rowboat."

"I should have a parasol and a pair of white gloves, like a woman in a Degas," she said as she made her way to her seat.

"And I should have a flat straw hat and white pants." Sitting across from her, he took up the oars as he assured her, "I've seen those paintings, too."

He rowed the boat beneath a series of willows that lined the bank. Neither of them spoke for a while. They listened to the warbler's bright *weet weet weet weet* and the sound of the oars dipping and pulling against the water. He rowed with powerful strokes, taking them quickly to the middle of the lake. She closed her eyes and let the haze-filtered sun bathe her face. When he'd known her before, she'd always been as sun-bronzed as he. Clearly her skin had known less sun since. He rowed them to the far tree-lined shore and watched sunbeams play hide-and-seek in her hair as dappling shadows stippled the drapery of her full white skirt. Pristine, he thought, but there were champagne bubbles in those pale green eyes, just as there had always been, and he wondered what it would take to get her to shed that acquired polish along with the white dress and beckon him into the water as she had one hot summer night.

Dominic pulled the oars in and let the boat drift while they sat, knees to knees, and shared their first course of beef, bread and cheese. When they'd had their fill,

Keeley tossed a pinch of bread ashore, and soon the ducks came begging.

"Now look what you've started," Dominic teased as he held the bottle of wine between his knees and worked at it with the little corkscrew in his pocketknife.

Keeley raised a clear plastic cup, and Dominic poured. The sunlight twinkled in the flow of white wine. "Here's to Degas," he offered, touching his glass to hers. "For painting us a nice idea."

After several sips he opened the olives and sliced more cheese. Greek olives. It pleased him that she remembered a little thing like that. He offered her a slice of soft cheese, and she took it off the blade of his pocketknife. A small intimacy. It felt right, sharing close quarters with her and passing food from hand to hand. The past filled the present with the things they left unsaid, but all of it was right. It was as though they'd taken a leap over a stack of calendars just to spend this afternoon together.

When he poured the wine again, he made it his chance to move over beside her. She dragged the paper sack of candy from the tote bag and peered inside. "How long has it been since you had an old-fashioned jawbreaker?"

"Oooh, probably since the last time I had a tooth crowned." His smile betrayed none of his dental work.

She offered him a cellophane-wrapped red ball, spiced with a saucy smile. "Just suck on it."

"I can still do that pretty well." He pocketed the candy and sipped his wine, his eyes twinkling above the rim of the glass.

"How about a licorice whip? Would that loosen your dentures?"

The red string looked pretty good sliding between her teeth. "How can you eat that junk and stay so slim? I'll have a peach."

"One peach, coming up." She used her skirt to rub some of the fuzz off, then handed him the huge peach. "I'll take the candy back to the dorm with me and see if it brings back any old memories for the girls."

He sank his teeth into the peach and slurped the juice. It was a moment before he could resume his end of the conversation. "How does it feel to be one of the 'girls' again? You really haven't seen them in a while, have you?"

"Oh, we've kept in touch with cards and a phone call here and there. It's good to see them."

"Do you think you could still be friends?"

"I think so, if we weren't so far away. Bess is still a little hard to get close to in some ways. I've always admired her because she's such a strong woman."

"And you're not?"

"Not the same way Bess is. She's always been very much her own person."

"Whose person have you been?" She seemed not to hear him as she sipped her wine. "There was a time when you did as you pleased. We used to do some crazy things." He chuckled. "You were completely spontaneous. I had a hard time keeping up with you."

"I kept you a secret." Pressing her lips together, she savored the lingering taste of the wine. She was being truthful with herself now. This, she knew, was no news to Dominic. "If I had been my own person, I wouldn't have done that."

"You always had your reasons," he said casually.

"And you never liked any of them."

"I kept coming back, though, didn't I?" He tossed down the contents of his glass, then set it aside. "I guess I had my reasons, too."

"Do you remember what they were?"

"Yeah. I remember." He considered the peach for a moment, then looked up. "You?"

"I keep telling myself that time adds romance to the past, that I actually made choices based on...what seemed right at the time."

"Yeah, well..." With a shrug he admitted, "It probably was. You shouldn't have given up your own art, though. You're really good."

"And you're very kind. Your work is beautiful."

"Thanks." He held the peach near her mouth. "Want a bite? It goes good with the wine."

She sank her teeth into the fruit, eating where he had eaten, and the juice dribbled down her chin. He stayed her hand from wiping it away, and the moment stood still in her eyes and in his. The boat rocked gently beneath them. Somewhere a duck chattered. Feminine laughter tinkled in the distance, and it all blended together as Dominic moved closer. Keeley swallowed and caught her breath, and there was nothing but the touch of Dominic's tongue on her chin, his lips at the corner of her mouth, his hands on her shoulders.

"Much better than candy," he whispered as he put his arms around her.

Her lips parted for him, and they shared a kiss that tasted of peaches and white wine as the boat slipped through the water in the soft willow shade.

Tuesday

"Match point," Bess called out. Keeley flexed her knees and waited for the serve. The sun was hot, and it felt good to put on a pair of shorts and sweat after several days of wearing panty hose and a slip. The ball popped off Bess's racket and sailed for Keeley's backhand. She returned it.

Bess was good at everything. So self-assured, so knowledgeable. Keeley imagined her taking charge in a roomful of businessmen. She kept her private life private. Always had. She managed it the way she had managed to work part-time while she attended school full-time. She was the modern Scarlett O'Hara. She would never be poor again, but she wasn't about to bat her eyelashes just to keep that promise.

Keeley stretched to return another smooth shot.

Bess had it all together. She had never married. Why should she? She was doing exactly what she wanted to do, living the way she wanted to live. If she'd wanted to sculpt, she would not have set her dream aside. She would have sculpted. Not as a hobby, either, but as a commitment to express her ideas and maybe touch people through her work, the way Dominic did.

Keeley missed a shot.

"Whew! That's it!"

"I think that was in," Keeley teased, "but I'll give it to you."

"Give, nothing!"

"Okay, so you won!" Arms akimbo, Keeley stalked up to the net, full of sass. "So come on, now. Jump the net so I can congratulate you."

Bess tossed her racket in the air. It spun end over end and dropped back into her hand. She smiled, and the sun glinted off her dark glasses. "Rematch, anyone?"

Bess and Abby had plans for the evening, so dinner with them was out. And Dominic was an enigma. They had shared an afternoon full of sweet kisses and wine, but when he'd said goodbye, she'd found herself tongue-tied. She couldn't bring herself to say "Call me," and he hadn't said he would. Before she knew it, he'd left without offering any plans or promises, and the only message left at the bell desk for her asked her to return a client's call. She shifted from woman waiting for a call to woman handling a business transaction and back again.

Woman Waiting was her own creation. If she chose to fashion herself into such a figure, she would undoubtedly regret it. Not that she couldn't live with regrets— she had done that for years—but she wasn't about to turn herself inside out in the process. Besides, *Woman Waiting* had been a melodramatic statement, which was why it had been relegated to the closet.

It was Tuesday. They'd always met at the Strawberry Shanty on Tuesday nights. She wondered if he remembered. This nostalgic interlude in her life would only last a few more days. It wouldn't hurt to stick her neck out a little further. It wouldn't hurt to stop waiting and simply stop in.

No, but it might hurt if she did and he didn't.

Or if he stopped in again with Teri. But then, that would settle all questions, wouldn't it?

The familiar black-and-white '57 Mercury coupe was parked two cars to the left of the Shanty's door. It looked like a new car. Showroom shiny. Keeley wondered whether there was such a thing as nostalgia-tinted contact lenses that renewed all things. If they existed, she had to be wearing some. Resisting the temptation to peer through the rear window and reassure herself that the back seat was still there, she ran her fingertips over the trunk as she walked by and smiled to herself. She had a feeling Teri would not be there tonight.

Ah, the aroma of griddle-fried beef and deep-fat fried potatoes. Ambrosia for the young; anathema to the thirty-plus body. What hadn't seemed tolerable in years was suddenly irresistible when she walked through the door. As was Dominic. Dressed in jeans and a black Santana T-shirt, he was hovering over a frothy mug of beer and visiting with Jack Koski at the bar. Jack saw her first and nodded her way. Dominic swiveled on the stool and his eyes brightened with his smile. He'd expected her.

"You lost, lady?" he greeted her as he sauntered over, mug in hand.

"I don't think so. It's Tuesday, isn't it? If it's Tuesday, this must be the Strawberry Shanty, and there must be a table here somewhere with my name on it."

"You don't look like the type to carve up the furniture." With a hand at her waist, he escorted her to their corner table. "You want a shake?" She nodded. "Jack, bring the lady her usual."

"I can't believe you still have that wonderful old car. It's the same one, isn't it?"

"We've been goin' steady since I was in high school, so I didn't have the heart to junk her. Now I get offers for her every time I take her out."

"I'm sure they don't make them like they used to."

"Damn right. Seven miles to the gallon with a good tailwind." She slid into the booth ahead of him, and he joined her, sliding in close. "I don't know whether you noticed, but I do have a new car."

"I noticed. A silver sports car. I'm not into cars, but I've always liked the Mercury." She unrolled the napkin-bundled utensils at her place and smoothed the stiff paper over her green slacks.

"She's a classic. I've put a lot of work into that old bomb, and she's won me some trophies in a few classic car shows. Ever been to one?"

"No."

"It's kind of a hobby. The ol' Merc's got quite a reputation," Dominic boasted, then sipped his beer.

"She was the ruin of mine." Keeley spoke softly, but she did smile.

"*She* wasn't. *I* was." It sounded like another boast. He laid his hand over hers to let her know it wasn't. Still, he teased, "But I've turned the place where the deed was done into a sort of a monument. Like bronzing baby's first shoes."

"Sort of a Taj Mahal to my virginity."

"Exactly." He squeezed her hand and pressed his shoulder against hers. "So, uh...wha'd'ya say we go for a ride later?"

A saucy look. "In the memorial bomb?"

He laughed. "We might be a little older, sugar, but we ain't dead yet."

The car's restoration had been a labor of love. The 351 six-barrel engine roared at the flick of the key as faithfully as it always had. It was music guaranteed to empower a boy and thrill any girl. Dominic kicked the accelerator, just to tickle the tiger. The posturing youth in him smiled at the vestige of impressionable ingenue in her. Then he played her his car's sweetly tuned idle, and they shared a laugh with the people they had once been.

"There's this straightaway down by the river, where there are two trees that are exactly—"

"A quarter mile apart. I remember. What happens if we get caught?"

"I pay a fine. Ready?"

Keeley rolled her window down and let the wind make a flag of her hair. It was still light, but River Road was deeply shadowed, enveloped by hulking trees. Dominic's birch marker stood ten feet from a mailbox labeled "Rockstad." He gave Keeley his watch, because she wasn't wearing one, and nosed the front bumper even with the birch. Positioning his hands on the big steering wheel, he glanced her way. "How about if we just clock the takeoff, huh? Zero to thirty."

"Sounds sensible," she said, tilting the watch face near the window for some light.

He dropped his hand over the gearshift on the column and checked the mirrors. "Aw, hell, let's just—" Inertia plastered them both in their seats as the tires squealed. "Go for it!"

Equal measures of excitement and terror came in a quick rush as Keeley braced herself against the dashboard. When Dominic raised his voice against the screaming engine, the time was the furthest thing from her mind. She laughed and shook her head as the torque wound down. "I missed it," she lamented.

"He didn't."

Dominic saw the lights flashing in his rearview mirror and pulled over, hoping the cop wouldn't add to his humiliation by blasting a siren. Then he waited, staring ahead and wishing the guy would turn off the flashing beacon.

Feet shuffled, and a face appeared. "Dom?"

"Hey, Eddie."

"What the hell do you think you're doing?" The policeman noticed Keeley. "Hi there."

"Do you remember Keeley? We used to, uh..."

"Sure. How's it going, Keeley?"

"Fast," she said flippantly. "Things are going very fast."

"She's here for her college reunion," Dominic explained.

"Yeah, time flies, doesn't it?" The policeman patted the window ledge, almost affectionately. "So does this bomb, though, buddy. How much have you had to drink?"

"One beer, Eddie. I swear. We were just...acting like kids, I guess. *I* was."

Eddie chuckled. "You were, huh? Listen, if you're planning on doing any parking..."

Dominic forced a tight grin. "This is harassment, Eddie."

"Well, I can't get you for speeding, but I could call it exhibition driving."

"Just give me the balloon, or the citation, or whatever."

"You sure fixed this baby up, didn't you? You keep it up on blocks in your garage, I bet. This must be a special occasion."

"You know damn well where I keep it. Are you going to cite me or what?"

"You gonna let me win a few hands next Thursday night?" Straightening and stretching his back, Eddie tucked his thumb in his belt and tapped his fingers.

"Yeah, I know how it is, touching base with old times. You owe me one, Dom. On your way. But don't do anything I wouldn't do."

"Yeah, right." Dominic slipped the car into gear and gave it just a little juice.

The face appeared again. Eddie offered a salute as the car rolled away. "Good seeing you again, Keeley."

"Good seeing you, too." Then she muttered, "I guess."

"I guess." Dominic slid her an irresistible look of chagrin. "Sorry about that."

She smiled, thought a moment, then turned forty-five degrees in her seat. "You know what I want to do after it gets good and dark? I want to sneak into the strawberry field at the Shanty and eat strawberries off the vine. They're so sweet that way."

He laughed. "It'd be real sweet if we spent the night together in jail."

"I don't think Jack would press charges. I added a little to your tip." He lifted a questioning brow, and she explained, "I'm not as spontaneous as I used to be."

"Maturity weighs heavy, doesn't it?" He sighed as he braked for a stop sign. Left, back to the Shanty. Right... "Sure you wouldn't rather go parking?"

"Oh, we're much too old for that." She folded her hands in her lap and smiled primly. "Let's steal some strawberries."

The years had fallen away like drooping rose petals beneath the timeless night sky. Dominic resisted the urge to forewarn Jack so he wouldn't call the cops if they tripped some new alarm. They followed a dirt road along the fence line, parked in a stand of trees and climbed the fence. He helped her down, not that she needed help—she'd worn sensible sneakers this time out—but he wasn't passing up any chances to hold her hand or her waist . . . or whatever.

There was a patch of grass under an elm tree at the edge of the field, and beyond that, several acres of strawberries. They squatted over a row of plants and picked the ripe fruit by silver moonlight.

Dominic sat back, crossed his legs Indian-style and made a basket at the bottom of his shirt. "How much of a tip did you leave?"

"Twenty dollars." With her chin resting on one knee, she felt among the leaves for fruit. Bingo, a fat one. She wiped it off with her fingers. She ate as she picked, while Dominic collected first.

"I may have to give you the old heave-ho over the fence after twenty dollars' worth."

"Mmm, June strawberries. Uh-oh. If they catch us, I just dripped the evidence on my shirt."

"Keeley O'Donnell with a spot on her shirt?"

She thrust out her chest. "See?"

It was over her left breast, and he had to swallow before he could laugh. "Why don't you let me balance it out for you, put one on the other side. You'll have pasties."

"Is that another disparaging remark about my bust size?"

"*Bust* is too big a word." She protested with a *tsk*, and he laughed. "But as I remember, they're kinda cute." She bonked him on the nose with a strawberry. "Uh-uh, you have to eat all you pick. That's the rule." He held her ammunition up in front of her. "Open wide."

"That's what my orthodontist used to say, and you know what I did to him."

"You bit him," he recalled. "I'm sure he loved every minute of it. I know I did." He clutched a handful of berries close to his chest and stood up, knees cracking. "I think I'm getting too old for this. Let's go stretch out on the grass. You're welcome to bite me, but if you keep throwing your strawberries at me, I'm liable to bite back."

She plucked a few more berries before joining him in the shelter of the tree, the warm, sweet juice filling her mouth. Biting down on a little grit brought an occasional shiver, but that was part of the adventure.

Dominic offered Keeley his last strawberry. "Did you ever notice how all the fun things we do as we get older seem to revolve around eating?"

Sated, she nibbled at the fruit. "When we were younger, everything revolved around sex."

"Yeah, sort of. Those hormones make you crazy for a while." He lay back with hands clasped behind his neck and noticed the patterns the black patches of leaves made against the sky. "Took you a while to come around."

She lay down beside him, and he slipped his arm beneath her head. It was a natural gesture, requiring no formal offer, and it was a warm place to be. "Did you love me then, Dominic?" she asked.

"Very much. Didn't you know that?"

"Did you love me more for having made love?"

In those days, maybe, he thought, but that was no answer to give her. "I don't know. I guess I was pretty far gone beforehand, but once we'd made love, it seemed more like you belonged to me. Outdated thinking, huh?"

Outdated or not, it raised goose bumps even in places where she was warm. But that was no confession to make to him. "Obviously it doesn't really work that way."

"When two people are together, sharing everything, nothing held back, I think they belong to each other then." He turned his head toward her. "How come no children, Keeley? We used to talk about children."

"My husband had his children with his first wife. They were grown when I married him. What we had was an arrangement, not really a marriage in the sense...the way you just described. He was a friend and a mentor to me. He was..."

"A father?"

"Maybe."

"God knows you already had one of those. He's still around, isn't he?" She nodded. "Why didn't you want a husband?"

"Oh, Dominic." She sighed, long and deeply. "I didn't know what I wanted then."

It sure as hell wasn't me. He sat up and draped his arms around his knees.

She moved, too, turning on one hip and planting a palm in the grass. "Will you tell me about your marriage? What...why did you...?"

"We just didn't make it, that's all. We stopped trying. She thought it would be more fun to live in Connecticut with some insurance agent."

"And your son?"

His tone lightened, and she saw his smile, even in the dark. "Ricky will be with me for the summer, as soon as school gets out. His school runs a little longer than most. We'll be heading up to Canada in July. Ricky is a terrific little fisherman."

"Does he look like you?"

"Yeah, pretty much." The beauty of her elevated chin in profile drew him to reach over and touch, tracing the patrician curve with his thumb. "Pretty much," he mused again. He would welcome a second child, maybe a girl this time, with a chin like hers. "How did you know I'd be at the Shanty tonight?"

"I took a chance," she admitted. "What made you think I'd come?"

"Just wishing you would. It was Tuesday." He lifted her hair with the back of his hand. "So many things you think you've forgotten about."

"I know." Like the way he sensitized her with careful touches such as these. She hoped he would kiss her soon. "It's a funny feeling, isn't it? After all this time."

"Funny nobody's laughing."

His mouth moved over hers like swirling water, teasing, then less teasing, and still less, until he hovered over her for a moment, teetering on the brink, then making his move. He sank his tongue into her mouth to stroke hers. Shifting his body, he gathered her close, and she put her arms around his neck and gave him the taste of strawberries.

He had talked about not holding anything back, but he did. He tempered his passion. He longed to slip his hands beneath her soft knit top and touch her, but he contented himself with kissing her and rubbing her back, letting only the heels of his hands stray over the sides of her breasts. After many kisses, many moments, he drew back.

"Would you like to come over to my place?"

"I..." She straightened, confused. Too soon? Too late? *It was the best of times; it was the worst of times.* "I have to give a presentation first thing in the morning."

"First thing?"

"Yes." She gave a tremulous sigh.

He touched the spot on her shirt and smiled wistfully. "On what?"

"Investing in art." She brushed at the spot, straightened her top and smiled back as she found her voice. "I think people should invest in fine furniture, too. Wonderful, handcrafted furniture. I'm sure the value of one of your pieces increases, and if I knew more about the market, I would include that in my usual—"

"I have a waiting list. At least a year for a large piece. I'm doing okay, Keeley."

"Your work is beautiful." She wrapped her arms around her thighs and rested her chin on her knees. "But then, you know that."

"It gives me a lot of satisfaction." As did touching her wind-tossed, man-touched hair, which he did. "So maybe I'll drop in on your presentation tomorrow and see what you have to say. Would you mind?"

"Of course not. If you're interested. If you have the time for—"

"Then what?" he demanded. "What else do you have on your agenda this week?"

"Bess and Abby. I engineered this reunion with them, so they're on my agenda."

"You came to see me, too. You went to the Shanty."

"It was a coincidence at first—" A series of clicks and liquid sputterings cut her off. "Somebody's coming," she whispered.

"Some*thing*." He grabbed her hand and dragged her to her feet. "We'd better get out of here before we get—" she yelped when the water hit her, and he laughed, even as he ducked behind his upraised arm ''—irrigated!''

They were both drenched by the time they scaled the fence.

Wednesday

Yes, she had gone to see him.

He had come to see her, too. Front and center, there he was in the lecture hall, grinning up at her every time her eye lingered on the front row. She had to work hard at not grinning back.

"Prints have been a popular investment because they're inexpensive. If you guess wrong, and the print doesn't go anywhere, you've paid a reasonable price for something to hang on your wall. But the right print by the right artist can increase its value dramatically in today's market. Let's look at some slides...."

Keeley clicked through the slide series, displaying the work of painters who were already in demand and those who were up-and-coming. She ventured to make some predictions. She went on to textiles and sculpture, explaining methods and media and what to look for besides the artist's name. The work of other people. She supported it, collected it, appraised and marketed it. She was good at what she did, and she had a part to play in the art world. It was something.

She admired Dominic for finding his medium. She could sense his energy emanating from him in response to the creative energy depicted on the screen, even though he sat ten feet away. She remembered the loving way he had introduced her to his work. Through his hands the wood had continued to grow, he'd explained. Through his meticulous, inventive hands. She glanced at the porcelain child on the screen.

She had meticulous hands. *She* had an inventive mind. What was she waiting for?

She had no answer for her own question, but she ticked off answers to those from the audience with the assurance of a car salesman once the house lights went up.

Dominic lifted a finger in preference to raising a hand. "What about furniture?"

Keeley met his challenge with a quizzical look. "Do you mean antiques?"

"No, I mean handcrafted furniture. One-of-a-kind tables and chairs. Would you invest in that?"

"When I choose something for myself, the most important consideration is my own feeling for the piece. Do I like it? Do I want to see it in my living room every day?"

Sliding down in his chair, he cocked half a smile. His eyes sparkled. "Sort of like choosing a husband."

"Perhaps. Certainly different from speculating on a piece that you hope will turn a profit. Women no longer marry for profit, at least not—" she glanced over the audience for effect "—Bartlett women." The point was received with applause. She caught Abby's thumbs-up and Bess's okay sign.

"Still, it's an investment, isn't it? And what you're saying is, choose what pleases you and not what everybody else says is in."

"That's what I'm saying. And I do think that woodwork can be sculpture in the hands of the true artisan—" another meaningful pause "—*Mr.* Vitalli." His name drew a scattering of applause. "I'm more familiar with the market in fine art, but the beautiful furniture you make is bound to appreciate in value."

She was surrounded as soon as she stepped away from the podium, and she had to crane her neck to catch a glimpse of Dominic as he headed past her up the aisle.

"Just a minute, Dominic, I'd like to—"

"I'll pick you up at seven."

"For what?"

"I want to talk to you about this investment thing." He grinned. "And take you to dinner."

The Grandview was a small, quiet restaurant at the top of Ridley Mountain. Dominic had left the Mercury in the garage this time, a move he regretted when, after dinner, Keeley suggested that they park at the overlook on the way down the mountain and discuss the merits of the view. He did his best to cuddle her, despite the inconvenience of bucket seats and four-on-the-floor.

The river ribboned its way through the valley, doubling back on itself in an oxbow curve just below them. Small-town lights twinkled, and crickets vied with night birds for the opportunity to serenade. The air was cool, and the mist would soon gather in the low spots.

"So your dad's still kickin', huh?" Dominic remarked. "Do you see him much?"

"No, not really. I'm just as busy as he is now, which is nice. He has to fit into my schedule, too." She lifted her head from his shoulder to look him in the eye. "How about your parents?"

"My dad died three years ago, and my mom seems kinda lost without him. My kid sister Donna's still at home. She's a college girl, too." She heard his pride in Donna's achievement.

"I like your mother."

"Remember that first time I took you home with me? Ma got all choked up and had to leave the room."

She smiled. "You all looked at each other, your dad and you, your brothers. I never understood what that was all about."

"I hadn't brought a girl home since my high-school prom. I went in the army, went to 'Nam, she worried. I came back, went to school, she worried. Where were the grandchildren?" He laughed and squeezed her shoulders, letting her know that it was just one of those mother things. "I brought you home, she thought, this is it. He'll settle down. Then she found out how wealthy you were, and she decided you were not the girl for her son."

"She decided... I wasn't good enough?"

"'Money spoils,' she said. But I told her I was willing to overlook the money because you were a terrific lover."

"Dominic!"

"Money can't buy love. Sex, yes, but not love."

"I've never tried to buy love. But I did think..." She drew away slowly and sat back in her own seat, pondering. So long ago. She'd gone away thinking she had the world on a string. "Why didn't you write to me that summer?"

"When you went to Europe? Who knew where you were? Say, you never did visit my great-uncle Leonardo in Florence did you?"

She stared at the lights. Her smile was distant now. "You mean da Vinci?"

"No, Vitalli. Remember, I told you about him."

"I didn't get to Italy at all that summer." She hadn't gotten very far from Paris. She remembered how the lights had looked from the window of her room.

"You stopped writing. You stayed away too long, and after a while, when the letters stopped coming..."

"You never answered," she reminded him gently.

"You were only going to be gone for a month." He turned to her. "Your month lasted forever. After a while, when there weren't any more letters, I called your house. And when your father finally condescended to speak to me, he told me that you couldn't be reached."

"He told you that?"

"Ordinary people can always be reached, Keeley. It takes a lot of money to keep someone completely out of reach." He punctuated with a repeated flick of his closed hand. "But that was the way it was with you. You were here for a while, and then, when you were finished with that part of your life, you were beyond my reach." The hand opened, as though he were releasing some creature and setting it free.

"So you put me out of your mind."

"Hell, no, I couldn't get you out of my mind. I..." With a scowl he faced her. "Where were you? Huh? Where—"

"I've always wanted to be reachable, but..." No, the accusation wasn't fair. She tried. "I write. I call. People don't seem to try very hard to keep in touch. I guess no one has the time."

"Maybe they're afraid. After you graduated, you left here like Moses, vanishing up on the mountain. How are the rest of us supposed to—"

"I cook my own meals, pay my own rent, run my own business, just like everyone else."

"Okay, you've come down off the mountain." More gently he added, "I always knew you were real flesh and blood, Keeley."

Oh, yes. He touched her hand, as if to prove that she was. Within her flesh, her blood stirred.

Moments later, seemingly out of the blue, he wondered aloud, "Does your business ever make charitable donations?"

Donations? "We . . . try to do our part."

"I mean like, donate a piece for a worthy cause. A favorite charity of mine."

Requests for money always made her edgy. Not that she begrudged it, but she was cautious. And now, here was Dominic, always a proud man, suggesting . . . what? "You might send the information to the gallery. If it's a charity auction, we'll consider the merits of its cause."

"Just like everyone else's." He sounded disgusted.

"Well, yes. You know how these things go. There are a hundred worthy causes."

"It's something special, see. Something I'm kind of interested in." He seemed to stare through her. "But you're not, are you?"

"How important would my contribution be?" Oh, God, he seemed angry. Why would he be angry? "What would I be buying, Dominic?"

"I'm sorry I brought it up." He started the car, then turned to her again. "You ready to go back?"

She nodded, feeling as though he'd dropped a brick on her stomach.

When they'd been in school, the girls would have handled the troublesome midweek night differently. The minute she'd walked into the room and dropped into a chair, which would probably have been covered with all the clothes she'd worn during the first part of the week, Keeley would have complained to Abby about boy troubles. Abby would have offered sympathy and maybe hung a few things up for her. Bess might have had a word of advice. Maybe two, but it would have been succinct. Boy troubles were easily hashed over. Man troubles, once a woman had reached the age at which she should have known better, were not.

Dominic wanted something from her. Maybe it was perfectly innocent—a friend soliciting for his cause— but she hadn't expected that what he wanted from her might be money. Not Dominic. After some spring-loaded silence, she told Abby about it.

"Do you really think he wanted it for himself?" Abby asked rhetorically. "Dominic?"

"I don't know. I don't really know who he is after all these years." Keeley sighed. She'd thought no; she'd thought maybe. *Never.* But...maybe. "He used to gamble sometimes. After a while, that can be a problem for some people."

"He used to love the princess who lived in the big castle. After a while, *that* can be a problem for some people, too."

She turned away, exasperated, and found herself looking into a mirror. What princess? She whirled to face her friend. "That never had anything to do with...with anything, Abby. You and I were still friends, and Bess. My father's money didn't make me— I believe Dominic used the word 'unreachable.'"

Abby sat on the end of her bed and squeezed her hands between her knees. "You went off on a junket abroad, and the next thing we knew, you were engaged to marry Daddy Warbucks."

"It wasn't the next thing you knew. I wrote to all of you. I sent cards." Weary of it all, she sat, too. That damned trip. Nothing had ever been the same after that. "I had a difficult time with that trip...and afterward. I wasn't able to do things the way...the way I might have done them if I'd had the choice."

"You let your father choose. Is that why you treated Dom the way you did? Like he was something to be ashamed of?"

They were hashing that point over when Bess arrived. She was obviously troubled, too, and somehow the conversation dwindled into nothing while they fell quietly into their bedtime routines. Keeley knew that Abby had a point. When other girls had boasted of dating Dartmouth or Amherst, she'd never mentioned her boyfriend at Riverdale Tech. Instead she made mysterious mention of "a man I'm seeing."

"Everyone knew you'd never marry him, Keeley," Abby said matter-of-factly.

It rankled to think that something everyone had assumed about her had come true. Had she been that transparent, that shallow, then?

"I loved Dominic. I loved you and Bess, too. I kept in touch—" she raised her hand in a gesture of frustration "—much better than either of you did. More regularly."

"Your notes seemed to come from a place where no real people lived," Abby said. "No ordinary broke-at-the-end-of-the-month working people. It was hard to know how to answer you."

"I'm real. Didn't you call me when you lost your mother? It meant a great deal to me to know that you wanted to talk to me then."

Abby smiled lovingly. "And it meant a lot to me when you came to her funeral. You know that."

Keeley hadn't thought about it that way. Her friend had called her, and that was all she'd known. Now came an evening of revelation, of friends offering reflections, setting up the mirror for one another. And Keeley listened. Abby had always given, always helped. Did they think she never needed to be cared for or ministered to? she asked them. Bess, whom Keeley had set on a pedestal, said she was uncomfortable there. It was a lonely place. She had worked her way through school and had no time for the idyllic fun Keeley recalled so fondly.

And Keeley shared. "I remember when you defended me in that freshman art class we took together, Bess, and that wasn't a lark. Remember? We hardly knew each other then."

"Some real smarty ripped into something you said," Bess remembered.

Lying on her bed now, Keeley remembered exactly how humiliated she'd felt. "I described what I'd buy in a sculpture, and she made me feel stupid. You told her to put the shotgun away, that my opinion was as valid as hers, and that what a person liked should be the first consideration." She paused. "I said that during my talk today. I've never forgotten how good it made me feel."

"Anybody ever think about being thirty-five and childless?" Abby asked.

Thank God, Keeley thought. It bothers Abby, too. And that awful, raw, empty place inside her opened up. "I can't. I had a hysterectomy."

"Damn," Abby said softly. "Why?"

"I was...I had an accident. I guess I'm lucky I came away with just...that."

"*Just* that?" Abby echoed. "Oh, Keeley, why didn't you let us know?"

Bess knew. "Because it hurt too much."

"Yes," Keeley said. "I'll never be pregnant. I've tried to imagine what it would be like. I'd love to have a child."

"Me too," Abby said wistfully.

More perfunctorily, Bess added, "So would I."

But there was more to it than that. They all had dreams, disappointments, worries—and they shared them. Three friends. Three biological clocks, taking their lickings as they kept on ticking.

Thursday

Keeley was glad she didn't have to play field hockey against Bess. In tennis they might trade game for game on a good day, but when it came to field hockey, Bess was out for blood. Fortunately the reunion committee had been able to revive the old rivalry with a reunion team—aging less gracefully than the Bartlett women, to be sure—from Smithfield College, so Keeley didn't have to worry about being drafted to play. She and Abby stood on the sidelines and cheered their roommate on, just as they had in the past. But they soon realized they weren't the only ones with eyes for Bess.

"Get in there, Bess!"

The man straddling the forty-yard line and repeatedly slamming his fist into his hand was tall and rugged-looking, with curly gray hair. One of the umpires waved him back. He looked down, realized he'd overstepped his bounds and stepped back, searching the field until he found Bess again.

A cowboy, Keeley thought. How does this cowboy know Bess?

"Get in there and give 'er a good whack. Whoa, not the halfback! I meant the *ball*. 'Atta girl!"

Abby grabbed Keeley's arm and pulled her down for a secret. "Keeley, I think that's him."

She took another look. "You mean the cat doctor?"

"Bess's veterinarian." Unabashedly, they gave him the full measure of their assessment. "Does he look like Bess's type to you?"

"I don't know." Keeley had to think about that for a moment. "What's Bess's type?"

"I think . . . masterful."

Keeley slanted her friend an all-knowing smile. "Like Joshua Lucas, maybe?"

"Like Dominic Vitalli, maybe?"

"Look at us, Abby." But first they looked at the man, who'd bellowed something about high-sticking. Keeley laughed and shook her head. "We're Bartlett women. Do we really need men to make us happy?"

"Of course not. But if a decent one happens along . . ."

"And he's pretty good-looking and unattached . . ." They grinned at each other and nodded. "Oh, Abby, I haven't gotten giddy over a man in years. Have you?"

"Not since the last blind date you fixed up for me. And he was awful, Keeley. Rich or not, a yahoo is a yahoo."

"I know. He really was. Exactly what I should have expected Skip Carver to come up with."

The name made Abby grimace.

"I agree. Skip was . . . pret-ty skip-py." Keeley wriggled her eyebrows, and they remembered the way they used to joke about nicknames, Southern versus New England preppy. Another cheer directed her attention back to the field.

More seriously, Keeley wondered, "It's not possible to rekindle a relationship in a week's time, is it, Abby?"

"Aren't we doing that?" Abby put her arm around Keeley's waist, and they stood side by side, knowing that this interlude would serve to put them back in touch, at least for a while. The white ball sailed past them. Abby looked up. "I think you should call Dominic."

"Why?"

"Because you really want to see him as much as you can, and tomorrow night would be a good time to get him to come here."

"The banquet?" She thought about it for a moment, then shrugged. "Why not?"

It was noon before she could get to a phone.

"Dominic, I've been considering your charity proposal, and . . . well, we do it sometimes, but there are certain considerations."

The voice on the other end of the line was indifferent. "Forget it. It was a bad idea."

"No, it's just that I . . ." She turned toward the door of the phone booth. Abby stood several feet away, out of earshot. She gave a sign of encouragement, then went on her way. Abby would do this differently, Keeley thought, but Abby was Abby. "The gallery is a business, Dominic. If you need money, I wouldn't mind—"

"Wait a minute. You're thinking . . . *I'm* thinking we need to have a talk, lady."

"All right. Where shall I meet you?"

"I'm working right now. I *do* have to work, Keeley, but I also pay my own bills. I'll pick you up. Can we make it six?"

"That would be fine."

"Can we go to my place and talk? Can you handle that?"

"Yes, of course."

He picked her up in his Porsche. She'd called it a "sports car," and he wasn't sure whether that meant she wasn't one to notice the make of a car, or whether Porsches were commonplace to her. It didn't matter, he told himself. He wasn't hurting for status. But he wanted to *show* her, because over the years he'd convinced himself that what he was lacking was money. If he'd had that, or some promise of acquiring it, she would not have left him.

His professionally decorated apartment overlooked the river, and it had two bathrooms. "And most of the time there's just one person here," he pointed out as he gave her the tour, "so I can take my choice. I don't have to fight my brothers for my turn. There's a whirlpool in the master bathroom, and Ricky's got his own room when he's here. The complex has a pool and tennis courts. I've got several closets full of fancy junk around here, and more in storage. And I've been to Italy *myself* to visit Uncle Leonardo, just last year."

He folded his arms across his chest and eyed her coldly. "So I wasn't looking for a loan from you, Keeley. Certainly not a handout, and *certainly* not a stud fee."

The accusation felt like a slam in the chest, but she squared her shoulders and met it gracefully. "I'm sorry. I knew better, really." She shook her head, puzzling. "But the conversation was so strange. First wealth made me untouchable, and then you thought I might want to part with some of it in favor of your favorite charity." She spoke gently. "I thought you might be in trouble."

"Oh yeah?" He chuckled and took a seat on a brown leather sofa. "What kind of trouble?"

She shrugged, feeling like the child who had been called up to the teacher's desk to explain some horrible thing she'd said. "You used to gamble."

"I used to go to the track once in a while, and I still do. But I don't bet borrowed money. I don't bet to win big, so I don't lose big. I'm not a gambler. And I won't bite you—" He offered a slow, forgiving smile. "Very hard. Sit with me."

She sat beside him. He hooked his arm over the back of the sofa and massaged her shoulder. "And I didn't say *untouchable*. I said *unreachable*."

"I didn't mean to be. And I didn't mean—"

"We won't argue the point now, because we're long on attraction for each other and short on time. Right?" He lifted her hair away from her neck. The backs of his fingers grazed her nape, up and down, up and down. "Do you want to argue about money?"

"No."

"Good. I spent enough time arguing about money when I was married. Money and anything else that came up." With a sigh, he slid his hand away. "I may very well be in trouble. Again."

"Yeah?" she mocked, seeing her chance. "What kind of trouble?"

"The kind only you can cause me." Absently he patted his shirt pocket, then caught himself and braced his hands on his knees. "I thought we'd eat in. How would that be?"

"Fine. When did you quit smoking?"

"Before my son was born. You don't want to smoke around your kids, you know?" He wagged his head, pressing his lips together. "Sometimes I really get the urge."

"Like now? Are you nervous?"

"Me? Nah." He laughed. "Maybe a little."

"Quite a confession for Dominic Vitalli." She smiled, then surveyed the room. Neutral tones of leather and wood, but none of his work graced his home. Unless he'd made the oak bookshelves or the entertainment center. Her eyes were drawn back to him. He was watching her. "I'm a little nervous, too. Can you tell?"

Behind her back, he touched her hair again. "Why should we be nervous? We've known each other..."

"But there are so many new things." She turned toward him, and she felt his hand on her knee. She didn't look down. Just that touch made her thighs tingle. "And things...that we probably never bothered to know before," she added quietly.

"How long can you stay?"

"Long enough to discuss the question of—" she lifted her chin and smiled provocatively "—where charity begins."

"I've got a few thoughts on that subject. Would you like to see my whirlpool?"

No one was interested in the whirlpool, but Dominic's bedroom was a cool, blue, quiet place full of his things. That was interesting. Exciting. He was neater than she was. She noticed a pair of his sneakers sitting on the floor, a couple of newspapers and a plastic shopping bag with Toys First emblazoned on it in red. Otherwise, everything seemed to be in its place. She touched the back of his desk chair, then turned to him, and he took her in his arms.

"Not exactly a romantic bower, is it?" he asked.

"It's masculine, which is romantic from my perspective. And it's your bed, not some hotel's."

"I thought I'd never have you in my bed, Keeley. If you're wondering, I don't bring women here because—" He touched her cheek with his roughened knuckles. "I don't want any echoes or lingering scents, but you..." His open lips touched hers, and his tongue feathered across the corner of her mouth. "You leave yours, okay? Whisper nice things into my pillows, and I'll hear them when you're gone."

They closed their eyes and let their mouths seek each other out by touch, by taste. She massaged the back of his neck, and he kneaded the small of her back, her hips, her bottom. He unzipped her skirt and let it fall to the floor. Hips pressed against hips, they inflamed each other in deep, sensitive places.

"And what shall I take with me?" she whispered against his mouth.

"Anything you want." He unbuttoned her blouse, starting from the bottom. "Just tell me, sugar. I'll give you anything that pleases you."

He released the clasp between her breasts and replaced the cups of her bra with his hands. Touching her nipples with tough-skinned thumbs made a good start toward pleasing her. When his tongue replaced them, she caught her breath and swayed against him. He swept her into his arms and put her on the bed, where he lay beside her. Their kisses became urgent as they divested each other of clothing and tossed the bedspread out of their way. He touched her everywhere, made her moist for him, made her ready, and then he reached for a drawer in the nightstand. Heat-dazed, she looked up at him.

"There's nothing I want more than to make you pregnant, but not now," he explained, his voice gravelly. "Not yet."

"There's no need to worry. I'm...safe."

He looked down at her for a moment, questioning, nearly accusing, but she pulled his head down for a kiss. Then he slid over her and whispered into the hollow of her neck, "Are you sure?"

She cradled him between her thighs. "Oh, Dominic, I've missed you. Please make me feel whole again."

It was, in every sense, a reunion. Her body told his that it had been a long, long time, and his responded, *Yes, but all this time I have remembered you.* They made the most of every stroke, every breath and every soaring sensation. Her climax, then his, brought them home.

Moments later he propped himself up to look at her in the curtain-filtered daylight. Her eyes glistened, and tears had tracked her makeup.

"What's this? Have I hurt you?" He touched the dampness on her cheek. "Honey, I'm sorry. I didn't mean to—"

"No, Dominic." She placed a beautifully manicured finger over his lips and closed her eyes. She hadn't even realized their loving had brought her to tears. "You've never hurt me. And now you've made me feel alive again. Do you know how wonderful that is? I've been dead inside for so long. So long." She put her hand over her belly. "There's something of you alive inside me. How long will it live?"

"What?" It dawned on him what she meant, and he chuckled. "If you're 'safe,' not long. You sure you're okay?"

She glanced away from him. Blue curtains. Beyond them, blue haze. Dominic had always favored blue. She remembered wishing he could have seen the Paris sky late one afternoon when they'd gotten her up to sit by the window. "Not even you can make me pregnant," she said. "Not now. Not ever."

He brushed her hair back and traced her cheekbone with his thumb. "What's wrong?"

"Hold me, okay?"

With his arms around her, he pressed her head against his chest and entwined one leg with hers, making them inseparable. "Tell me."

"When I was in Europe that summer after graduation, I had an accident. I was thrown from a horse." He held her quietly, but she felt him stiffen. She drew a deep, tremulous breath and released it slowly. "Jumping a wall on a downslide. Dangerous stunt, and I went flying. There were other riders. I guess I was in the way, and some of them couldn't veer away in time. Not that I remember much. But the upshot was that I lost some major parts." She paused. "Like my womb."

It took him a moment to ask, "That's...why I didn't hear from you?"

"I was in a hospital in Paris for a while."

He turned, tucked her under him so that they could see into each other's eyes. "I should have been with you."

"I *was* unreachable then. Untouchable. Sometimes I prayed you'd come. Other times I prayed you'd never find out. I felt a terrible loss, as though my whole identity as a woman was gone."

"You still feel like a woman to me."

She smiled wistfully, resting her hand on his side. "I feel like a woman to me, too, but your seed was, as they say, wasted on barren ground."

"Who says? Who would dare to tell Dominic Vitalli what to do with his..." He grinned. Leave it to her to choose a poetic word like "...*seed?*"

"You said you'd like to make me pregnant."

"Sure I'd like to. I'd like to turn back time, too." He kissed her forehead. Twice. "Just a dream. At my age, who needs another kid?"

"I wish we could have a baby, Dominic. I'd be a good mother. Not that I had an example. I hardly remember my mother. But I think I'd know how to raise a child." She ran a finger over his arm, imagining. "I'd draw and paint with her. We'd make clay cats."

"Her?"

"Or him. Either one would be fine." He lay back on the pillow, still jealously guarding her in his arm. "I wish I had stayed here that summer," she said.

"Why didn't I know something was wrong? When you stopped writing, I assumed all kinds of things. Your father had turned you against me. You'd met another man. You'd never intended to see me after you were done with school. I worried about *me,* not you. 'The hell with her,' I said, and I brooded over it, went around telling everybody else to go to hell, too. It was pride, Keeley. Wounded male pride."

"You had a right to be angry."

"God, I should have been there. I should have been with you when you needed me." He turned his head, sought her eyes. "Was the old guy with you? Your husband—did he take care of you?"

"The old guy's name was Murray," she said instructively.

"Sorry. I shouldn't be disrespectful. After all, he's—" *Not a problem anymore.*

"He *was* a friend of my father's. When my father was notified that my condition was critical, they flew over together, and Murray was more...well, more understanding than my father was. My father can't stand being around sick people.'' Her sigh echoed down a long corridor of time as she remembered her fatigue, her lack of will, her resignation. ''I guess they both talked me out of calling you when I was well enough.''

''How the hell . . . ? What did they say to you?''

She groaned. ''Oh, Dominic, what does it matter? Obviously I listened.''

''You were laid up in the hospital. Captive audience. I guess it's all water under the bridge now, but I would have found a way to get to you, Keeley. You knew that, didn't you?''

''I knew you wanted children. Lots of beautiful children, remember? Besides, I weighed about ninety pounds then. I looked awful.''

''You think I would have been put off by that?''

''No.'' She turned her lips to his chest and kissed him. ''You would have been kind to me. But later you might have regretted...'' She lifted her chin and tried to smile. ''You see, you have a son, Dominic. And I'm glad.''

''I am, too. But that isn't the point, is it?''

''Murray had his family. All he needed was a companion. Sometimes an ornament. And I needed to get back on my feet. He helped me establish the gallery. We had very little...''

''Sex?''

She tipped her head in assent. ''Among other things. But he was good to me, Dominic.''

''I would have been good to you, too.'' Her breast didn't quite fill his hand. Small. Firm. Sweet. He smiled. ''We would have had a lot of sex.''

''We should have eloped that night. Remember? After my graduation. We talked about it.''

''Not seriously. It was another one of those crazy dreams we used to tease ourselves with.''

She hated the idea that she'd teased him in any way. "Dominic, I was so thoughtless sometimes. I was just what you used to call me when you got angry—a spoiled rich girl. I did love you, but I was a hypocrite. So much of my life has been spent—"

"Shh." He kissed away the futile admission. "There's more to spend. Much more."

"Teach me to love you well, Dominic." Tilting her hips toward his, she kissed his chin, because it was all she could reach. "Tonight. I'm not as selfish as I once was. Teach me all I need to know."

"What you need to know is that I think you're beautiful." Sliding his hand between them, he touched her belly. "When you feel empty down here, what you're missing is me."

It was a statement typical of his gender, and she smiled as she moved her hand over him and touched him. He sucked his breath in sharply. "Yes, that part," he whispered.

"This is not a replacement part, Dominic."

"I know," he said, rising to the occasion of being sheathed in her hand. "It's just a piece of me. Something I can use to help you replace what you lost. Physical pleasure. Physical love." He found the soft curls between her thighs. "But I have other ways. I'm good with my hands. I'm good with..." Stroking, stroking, he couldn't remember being good with anything or anyone but her. "Oh, God, I love you, Keeley."

"I love you, too."

Friday

Dominic had agreed to attend the banquet. So had Bess's veterinarian and Abby's professor. Excitement ran high Friday morning, and the consensus, after Abby's wardrobe had been dissected unmercifully, was that she badly needed something to wear. She wanted something *special*. Having taken "special" clothes for granted all her life, Keeley found new pleasure in the process of choosing the right dress for Abby.

"I don't think I'd get much wear out of this one," Abby would say.

Back to the racks.

"But, Bess, it's got to *dazzle* him."

On to a different store.

"Tell me the get-down-and-dirty truth, Keeley. Is this something *you'd* wear?"

Keeley laughed. At long last Abby was willing to be eye-catching, which actually made it a done deal. But the right dress would make her a true believer. A faceless mannequin in the Petites section of a classy shop wore a silk dress that would fit the bill if it came in another color. Keeley consulted with the clerk, who brought out a rich green version. Yes! Keeley thought. She envisioned Abby's face fairly blossoming in this one, and she delivered it aloft as though she'd found the Holy Grail.

But Bess had found one, too. Same style. Same color. Same dress! There could, after all, be only one absolutely perfect dress.

"How do you feel in this one?" Keeley asked Abby, who glowed like the girl who'd finally found her prom dress.

"Like I'm fixin' to dazzle that man."

Keeley returned to the dorm to find a message waiting for her at the bell desk. *Call Dominic.* She clutched the paper discreetly to her breast and prayed he hadn't changed his mind about the banquet. Shopping for Abby's dress had honed the edges of anticipation. This was the big date, and the preparations had reached spring prom proportions. At this point she wouldn't let him off the hook without a struggle, so she made certain no one was around before she sidled into the phone booth on the fourth floor.

He had plans. "Can you get away for a few hours this afternoon?"

"Sure." Relieved, she pushed the folding door open and sat down on the little seat. "As long as I get back in time to get ready for the banquet you remember you promised to take me to."

She heard him laugh. "You've got that line down pretty good already. Promises made in the heat of passion—"

"Are *still* promises."

"Are still promises," he echoed. "I've already sent my best suit to the cleaners. They promised I could have it back by five, which is about the time I should get back after I drop you off at the dorm. Deal?"

She smiled at the numbered buttons on the phone. "It's a deal. Where are we going?"

"I want you to meet my son."

"Oh," she said, immediately skeptical.

"Don't worry. His mother won't be around."

Good cheer returned. "Oh."

"Ricky's school is up in the Berkshires."

"Ohhh." It would be a pretty drive.

"Can you be ready in twenty minutes?"

"I'm ready now."

The previous night's intimacy spilled over into the afternoon. They spoke little at first, just admired the New England countryside, with its lush June shades of green broken by glittering granite road cuts and sun-washed towns with white church steeples. She pointed to an apple orchard. That it was pretty went without saying. He smiled and touched her hand.

As they neared their destination, Dominic claimed her attention from the scenery.

"Before we get there, I want to explain a little about Ricky. He's eight years old. He's a bright, lively, loving child. And he's totally, irreversibly deaf."

He didn't have to take his eyes off the road to know that the serenity had left her face.

It was a numbing piece of news. "Oh, Dominic, I'm so...sorry."

"Don't be. That's why I'm telling you this now. Ricky was born without any sense of hearing." He glanced at her and offered a piece of a smile. "Never had it. Never will. It took us a while to figure it out. You know, he was just such a good baby—didn't cry much, slept through anything, and he seemed perfectly healthy. By the time he was nine months old, we had to admit there was something wrong.

"I say 'we.' Actually, it was my mom. She said he ought to be babbling more, and we ought to be able to get his attention easier. She made me mad at first, and

I told her she didn't know everything there was to know about babies.'' He sighed. ''But the tests were done, and we got the diagnosis. Ricky couldn't hear a damn thing. That's just the way it is. See, once the questions are all answered, and you know, and you accept him the way he is, then you stop thinking about him as a deaf child and start thinking of him as Ricky.''

The exit sign for St. Mary's School was Dominic's cue to switch lanes. ''This is it.''

''Your favorite charity.''

''Yeah. Listen, forget about that. I never suggested it. I just want you to meet Ricky.''

The prospect was as intimidating as it was exciting. ''Will I be able to communicate with him?''

''We'll see. He signs pretty well. He's learning to read lips and to use his voice, which is tough when you've never heard it or anyone else's. Have you seen *The Miracle Worker?*''

''Yes, the story about Helen Keller.''

''I've seen the play, the movie—half a dozen times each. These people are miracle workers, too. Of course, Ricky isn't blind.'' He turned and smiled brightly. ''We're really lucky there, aren't we?''

''Yes. Very lucky.''

Ricky was in class when Dominic reported in at the school's simply appointed reception area. A soft-spoken nun in traditional habit promised Dominic a surprise, disappeared into a room down the hall and emerged with a curly-haired, strapping young man. He and Dominic clasped shoulders and shared an uninhibited embrace that would have done Abby, the consummate hugger, proud.

Dominic beamed. ''Keeley, this is Jon Goldman, who used to be a student here until he got too big for his britches and transferred to a public high school. You just graduated, didn't you, Jon?''

During the introductions Keeley watched Dominic's hands. He seemed hardly aware that he was signing as he spoke, and Jon watched his face rather than his hands. Keeley was entranced by the graceful gestures.

"I got accepted at Dartmouth," Jon announced proudly. His modulation was unnatural, but he spoke distinctly and with little trace of an impediment.

"Dartmouth!" Dominic laughed and punched Jon's shoulder. "What do you want to go to a wimp school like that for, Jon? I told you, Riverdale Tech's the only way to fly."

"Sorry. Big Green's my team, Dom. They offered me a scholarship, and I'll get to play football."

Admonishing Dominic with a look, Keeley explained, "Dominic's never appreciated the Ivy League, I'm afraid."

Jon touched Keeley's arm. "I have to be able to see your lips, Miss Douglas."

She felt foolish, even though no one gave her reason to. "Oh, I'm sorry. I was just teasing. It wasn't important."

"That's better." He grinned affably. "When you can't hear it, you know it's got to be important. I'll bet you were telling him to lay off the Ivy League. He always gives me a bad time about setting my sights on Dartmouth."

She nodded. Only Dominic noticed that she spoke too loudly. "He always gave me a bad time, too. I went to Bartlett."

"So you *do* know what you're talking about on that score," Jon told Dominic, feigning surprise. "Dom says the classiest women in the valley are at Bartlett, but you don't have to be an Ivy Leaguer to get them to go out with you. So I say, 'Hey, what Bartlett girl would have gone out with a hell-raiser like the young Dominic Vitalli?'"

"So now you know," Keeley said with a smile.

"Now I know. But you wouldn't have turned your nose up at a football player from Dartmouth who's maybe a little hard of hearing, would you?"

She laughed. "Somehow I don't think you'll have any trouble, Jon."

"Are you still tutoring?" Dominic asked Jon.

"How else can I afford to go to Dartmouth?"

"I'll call you, and we'll set something up for the summer."

"Ricky's doing great, Dom. I just stopped in for a visit, and I looked in on his class." No bell rang, but doors suddenly opened, and the corridor was soon filled with children. "You guys enjoy your visit," Jon said. "Big day tomorrow."

"Right," Dom replied, but Jon was already headed back into the office. At the same moment he was accosted from another direction when two small arms fastened themselves around his legs. A dark-haired boy with eyes as big and round as plums tipped his head back and grinned at the man he'd tackled. Dominic knelt to kiss and hug his son.

Keeley was introduced to Ricky and to Sister Edwin, his teacher. Her heart pattered at the sight of the child that should have—*could* have—been hers. He looked so much like Dominic. That bright-eyed smile stole her heart immediately, the way his father's had so many years ago.

Sister Edwin spoke with both her hands and her voice. "Tell your father what you made, Ricky."

"Ah ma-aid claaay." His hands fluttered like wings, while his eyes sparkled with excitement.

Dominic repeated the gesture. "You made a bird?"

"Out of clay?" Keeley injected. That was one word her hands knew intimately, and she showed her version of the process, kneading and shaping an invisible hunk of clay.

Grinning, Ricky nodded and signed. "Ah made ah claay buhd."

"Show me," Keeley said anxiously and offered her hand. Ricky watched her lips. "Can you show me?"

Ricky took Keeley and Dominic to the art room, where he took his drawer from a storage cabinet and showed off his drawings and finger paintings. His clay bird was his prize, and Keeley handled it as though it lived and breathed. She asked Sister Edwin for more modeling clay, and for the next hour she used her hands to make friends with Ricky.

After their visit, Ricky stayed at school. They were preparing a program for the parents, and Ricky had work to do. He would go home with his father on Saturday.

Dominic and Keeley were quiet as he drove them to the turnpike. They had to think about what they had just seen in each other. A man who cared for his child. A woman who related well through her hands.

Finally, Keeley asked, "Why didn't you tell me about Ricky before? And about your favorite charity?"

"Didn't I tell you it was a school?"

She shook her head.

"I told you it meant a lot to me. You didn't seem too interested, so I decided to drop it."

She remembered. On the tail of a sigh she admitted, "I guess I wasn't listening with both ears. I was playing rich and foolish. The noblesse oblige, even with a friend. You were going to invite me to share something with you, but I headed you off because I'm used to donating, not sharing.'' She shook her head, as if to dispel that image. "I'm not rich. I don't know if I've ever been rich, except maybe when I was in college. Those were rich times.''

"When you were with me?''

"Yes.'' And Abby and Bess. And when she had her drawer in the art room full of her own little prizes.

He smiled. "We had some rich times, Keeley. But don't you remember the arguments? How you used to slam my car door and prance away in a huff sometimes?''

"Those were wonderful arguments, weren't they?'' Wistfulness became hard reality. "Murray wouldn't argue.''

"Maybe he was too smart to argue with you, sugar.'' Dominic chuckled and cast her a cocky smile. "Or too old.''

"Too sensible. Too bloodlessly sensible.''

"Constant arguing can get pretty bloodless, too. Sometimes I thought it was just as well Ricky couldn't hear when he was around his mother and me.'' He stared through the windshield, opening and closing his hand on the steering wheel, then resumed his story. "Shirley, my ex-wife, never really wanted kids, but she finally gave in. When we found out about Ricky's deafness, we couldn't pull it together. She said it was my fault for making her have the baby. I said it was her fault for not taking care of herself when she was pregnant. Of course, it was *nobody's* fault, but we didn't have much of a marriage by that time, and kids don't fix things up for you.''

Chilled by the mere thought of another woman in Dominic's life, Keeley responded with the obvious. "It's not fair to expect them to."

"Shirley's never been able to accept Ricky the way he is. She doesn't work at signing, dropped out of the parent training program, so she can't get close to Ricky. He spent last weekend with her, and it was the first time in months. She usually backs out at the last minute. She trumped up some excuse to miss his program tomorrow."

"What time is the program?" Keeley asked, half hoping he'd ask her to go.

"One o'clock." He paused. "What time are you leaving?"

"I haven't decided. It's a subject we've all been avoiding."

"Let's avoid it a while longer."

They were all running late, but it wouldn't have mattered if they'd allowed themselves hours of leisurely primping time. Their excitement was uncontrollable. Shoulder to shoulder, they lined up before the mirror.

"Hold still, Abby, or you're going to have eyeliner all over your face."

Abby had never had much time or patience for makeup, but for this night she asked Keeley, the expert, to give her "the works." Keeley was an artist with a makeup brush, and "the works" was subtle but striking.

She took a look at Bess, who was working on her hair, then Abby and herself in the mirror. "Actually, ladies, I think we all have a pretty nice bloom in our cheeks."

"Especially for an old spinster, a widow and a divor-cée," Bess allowed.

"Marital status be damned." Abby lifted her chin and turned slightly to examine her completed makeup. "We're gorgeous."

"Yes, I'd say there's a bit of *Je ne sais quoi* on the loose in this room that seems to have revitalized us," Keeley judged.

"Something else is on the loose in this room," Bess wailed as she leaned closer to the mirror. "I think its adolescence. Could this possibly be a pimple?"

"Don't bother it." It was Abby's standard warning. "You'll have a scar."

"You should know. Your skin is flawless."

Abby suddenly took notice of the cotton sundress Keeley was wearing. "Keeley, you're not going to wear *that* dress, are you? Ish! It's too plain."

"Is it? Then maybe I'd better change into—" Keeley scrambled across Bess's bed and reached into the closet "—this one."

The sapphire sheath drew the requisite ooohs and aaahs. Then Bess announced she was finished with her curling iron if anyone needed it. Staring at herself in the mirror again, Abby ignored the offer. She smiled at Keeley, standing behind her.

"Keeley, honey, don't you need a little eye shadow or something?"

The way she said "ah shadah" cracked Keeley up. Abby turned from the mirror, and Keeley handed her a makeup brush. "Ah shore do, huhnny. Have at it."

Abby's smile dazzled, the way it always did, with or without any tint. "Well, you can't wear this color. You've got to wear Keeley colors."

Bess offered a tube to the cause. "I think this lipstick's about the color of the spot you had on your shirt the other night."

"Lemme see that." Abby checked the end of the tube. "'Mamma Mia Red.' Look out, Mr. Vitalli."

They shared a table at the banquet, and no one seemed to notice the predictable dryness of the Bartlett Inn's chicken. After the introductions, the three women wallowed in satisfaction, as though they had facilitated a summit meeting. The men found that they had mutual interests in addition to their interests in the three friends, and the conversation was lively.

"A '57 Merc! Are you serious? What've you got under the hood?"

"I made myself a set of bookshelves for my office in the psych lab, and I was hooked. I love the smell of wood."

"Do you think a pet's a good idea for a kid who's away at school a lot? I don't want it to be something else he has to leave behind on Sundays."

"Kids seem to adjust."

"He likes cats. He likes to feel the vibration when they purr."

"They'd be good for each other, Dom. Bring your son out to the clinic. I've always got some little critter who needs a good home."

After dinner, they danced by the light of Japanese lanterns strung across the Inn's patio. The five-piece band turned a few rock-and-roll numbers into jitterbug, then switched to standard romantic mood music. Dominic managed proper decorum through "Harbor Lights," but when the saxophonist launched his version of "Lay Lady Lay," he slipped both arms around Keeley and pressed her close.

"They're pretty bad, aren't they?" she said.

"Not so bad on the slow ones, which is all I want to hear tonight. I like to watch you boogie, but for my money, slow dancing's more fun." He rolled his hips subtly against hers. "Remember this one?"

She closed her eyes and felt her lashes brush his cheek. "Mmm-hmm. And I remember this particular move of yours. Pretty smooth."

"Where's the Virgin Island sign?"

"I doubt they're using that theme these days."

"Aw, c'mon. Word's out at Tech that Bartlett girls are so frustrated that if a guy can just get past the front gate, he'll have women crawling all over him."

"Typical male fantasy."

He blew a wisp of hair away from her ear. "There's plenty more where that came from."

"I've got one about the back seat of the Mercury."

"Whenever you say, sugar. It's parked right under your fire escape."

She groaned deliciously. "Why do I let you call me 'sugar'?"

"Because you don't want me to call you 'baby,' remember?"

They slipped away and, hand in hand, followed the path to the dorm, where the shiny bomb was, indeed, parked beneath the fire escape. She scooted close to him, and he drove, as he once had, with her head on his shoulder. They parked in the alley behind his shop. It was dark and quiet, and they necked a little, teased a little and necked some more.

"How can I get a piece of Vitalli?" she asked.

He chuckled and nipped at her ear. "Which piece are you interested in?"

"Seriously. Can I give you an order?"

"Not till we get to my place." Her dress fit her like a glove, and when he touched her breast, he could feel her nipple tighten against his palm. "You want me to put on my uniform? I think I've still got fatigues with stripes on the sleeves."

"Mmm, fatigues. What will I wear?"

"How about a baseball cap with scrambled eggs on the bill? I've got one of those."

"That's all?"

He kissed her and drew back to admire the damp polish his kisses brought to her lips. "That's enough. Then you just give the order and—" He winked. "I'll jump to attention."

"Will you salute me?" She was being cute. It was fun to be cute sometimes.

"Oh, yeah." He stretched his back and tucked his shirt more evenly into the front of his pants. He'd already shed his coat and tie. "I've got something to show you."

"Right here?"

"Right inside. Come on."

He unlocked the door and flipped on the lights. They both stood there, blinking and savoring the scent of wood shavings. Back in his office, which was spare and impersonal except for the awards that hung on the wall, he unlocked a cabinet while Keeley looked around. On his desk stood a framed photograph of Ricky, along with Keeley's horse sculpture. The cabinet yielded a large chest he was making. Stylized strawberry blooms and berries were chiseled into the unfinished lid.

"How's this for a piece of Vitalli?" he said, gesturing with a flourish.

"It's beautiful." She touched it tentatively. "Somebody ordered strawberries?"

"It's the only thing I've worked on since last weekend. It's for you."

"Oh, Dominic." Smooth, sanded wood, pegged joints, the work of his hands. It took her breath away.

"You can't tell much yet. It's far from finished."

"Ohhh, but I can tell." She fingered the carving, felt the edges of the lid, the corners, lifted it and peeked inside.

"I'll fit it with drawers and trays, but I need to know what you might keep in it. That's why I wanted to show it to you." He sat on the edge of the desk. "No, that's not why. I wanted to see if you'd be pleased."

"How could you doubt it?" She peered into the box again. "Let's see. It might just hold all the makeup I'm going to need in a few years."

"It might be a tight squeeze." He laughed when she cut a sharp, sideways glance his way. "It won't hold all your money, either."

"Rumors of my wealth have been greatly exaggerated."

"Not by me." He laid a hand on the box. "I thought it might make a nice artist's chest. You know, sketchbooks, pencils, brushes, clay."

"It would. But I have so little time for those things anymore."

"Make time. Do the things *you* want to do, Keeley. You're good," he urged. "You *are*. And you'll have to come back and pick this up in, oh, I'd say a month or so."

"Things could get complicated, Dominic."

He put his hands on her shoulders and pulled her closer, until she stood between his knees. "Or they could get very simple. Maybe we weren't right for each other fifteen years ago. Maybe time and some hard lessons—"

"I was more right for you then than I am now. I was physically whole then, able to—"

"Do you think I'm looking for a baby maker? I've lived half my life, Keeley. Does that mean there's only half of me left?"

"I only meant...a week of the way things used to be. That's what I wanted. That's why I came."

His hands tightened on her shoulders, and she thought how foolish and cowardly she must sound. "It's better than it used to be," he claimed. "I know who I am, and you're on your own, free to make your own decisions." His hands slid away. "You think about it. I'm going to finish this, but I'm not shipping it out to you. You'll have to come and get it. And you can fill it with whatever you want." She stepped back, and he caught her by the arm. "But it's genuine Vitalli. Show it some respect."

They went to his apartment and made love to each other, and she knew he was right. Things were so much better than they used to be. They had once been too young and too self-absorbed to share as freely as they did now. He'd said he was giving her an empty chest and leaving it to her to fill it. But he was full to the brim, and so was she. Some changes had been for the better.

She had felt ashamed of that empty spot inside her for a long time. It was habit. A state of mind. She couldn't ask Dominic to fill it, any more than she could expect Abby or Bess to cure her loneliness. Changes, yes, but many of the old bonds were still intact. And bonds gave strength.

What a joy it was to open herself, expose scars and dark cavities, and find that these precious people did not turn away.

Saturday

Bess and Keeley were packing in a pall of silence. Everything seemed up in the air. Abby wasn't back yet. She was still, presumably, with Joshua Lucas, and delighted eyebrows had been raised over the fact that Abby had actually been out all night. Bess spoke little of her evening with Will, whom Keeley still thought of as "the cowboy." Out of the corner of her eye, she watched Bess pack several jars of homemade jelly, carefully cushioning them with rolls of socks and T-shirts. Keeley was tempted to ask where the jars had come from. Had it been Abby, she would not have hesitated. But Bess would choose what to share and what to keep to herself, and Keeley had learned not to pry.

"I almost forgot," Keeley said. "I borrowed a pair of panty hose from you as well as Abby, didn't I? Let's see . . . I'm pretty sure I did."

"You usually do."

"I know Abby always keeps a dozen extra pair for me, but yours fit me better."

It was a long-standing joke, although Keeley didn't think it was *that* funny. She and Bess wore the same exact size, and somehow Keeley was always short a pair.

She grabbed her purse. "I'm going to pay you for them."

Bess laughed mirthlessly. "No need to do that. I brought an extra pair, just in case."

"I don't have the right change anyway, I guess." Keeley's eyes sparked. She loved to bestow gifts, and she'd been planning this all along. She had something for Abby, too. "But I did bring something else, just in case." She took a box from her suitcase. "I thought of you when I bought it."

Bess gave her a look of mock exasperation as she opened the box. "You borrow things, and you replace them with some trinket that costs you three times as much as...oh." With a rustle of tissue paper Bess lifted a small, hand-painted Chinese ginger jar from the box. "Keeley, how beautiful."

"I was in China last month. I met the artist."

"Keeley, I *will* treasure this, but please answer me one question." Bess gestured helplessly. "Why don't you ever have enough panty hose?"

"Does any woman ever have enough panty hose?" She held up one hand. "You do, I know. You're always prepared for a run." Keeley opened her arms, half worrying that it was a risk. But Bess returned the embrace. "I'm so glad you came."

"I'm glad we're still friends." When Bess drew back, she held up the vase and smiled. "I have a spot for this in my collection of panty hose that became something else."

"Nice things?"

"Always. But sometimes I needed the panty hose more." She laughed, this time more convincingly. "Not now, though. Now I need this to remind me whenever I look at it to give you a call."

Just then Abby burst through the door, up in the air, her spirits high. Keeley could have sworn "Short Stuff" had suddenly gained several inches on the other two of them.

"So where have you been?" Bess challenged, exchanging a secret look with Keeley.

"Out," Abby sang. "With the most wonderful of men."

"Doesn't Mr. Wonderful know about curfew?" Keeley quizzed.

"I knew I was locked out. So I just—" she twirled dramatically, grinning from ear to ear "—threw caution to the wind."

"I think the girl's a goner," Bess decided.

"Well, aren't *you?*" Abby poked Bess with a finger, then turned it on Keeley. "And you? We're all goners, aren't we?"

They looked at one another. And they muddled it over. And they considered varying degrees of "goneness." When the packing was done and the luggage was lined up beside the door, they exchanged promises and good wishes, and Abby, the consummate hugger, led them in a three-way group squeeze.

A package had arrived for Keeley at the bell desk. She loaded up her car, took the package in hand and headed for Dominic's apartment. She had hoped he would call, but he hadn't. She suspected his theory was, if she missed him, she knew where he'd be.

He answered the door, then invited her in with a welcoming gesture.

She stayed where she was. "You could have called me, you know."

"You could have called me," he said, hiking an eyebrow.

"I knew you were going to be busy today, but I thought, after last night . . ."

"I've told you how I felt about you before last night."

She looked at him for a moment and remembered what he'd said and the way he'd said it. Whispered into her hair, beneath her neck, across the plane of her belly. *I love you.* She shivered and stepped over the threshold, reminding herself that he hadn't called. She was making most of the moves here, and she wasn't used to that.

"Well, I brought this." She offered the package. He looked at it, then at her, questioningly. "It's an Ardelle Taylor bronze from my own collection. I had it expressed here for the auction. Tell them not to take any less than eight thousand for it, and they should get more."

"You tell them."

The package hung between them. "All right," she said quietly. "Tell me who's running this show, and I'll give her a call."

"It's Sister Edwin, and you could talk with her this afternoon if you'd go to Ricky's program with me." He took her hand. "Don't just donate. Share this with me."

Her heart puffed up like a birthday balloon. "I thought you'd never ask."

"I've been trying not to push you, Keeley. I was afraid you'd skitter out of my reach again. I was also afraid you'd think I was trying to force Ricky on you. I mean, we're a package deal."

"Force him on me? I may be a little awkward around him now, but I don't have much experience. I'll learn. I'd like to donate my services to the school's auction. I can acquire donations, do the appraisals, publicize the event."

"Whoa, wait a minute. What do you mean, you'll learn?"

"I want to be part of your life, Dominic. Yours and Ricky's. I want to take part. Give part. Participate. I'll learn to sign, and he and I can make clay birds and cats and maybe...maybe some other things, because I think it's time to move out of my early period, and I know damn well I can be fruitful even if I can't multiply."

"That was quite a mouthful." He chuckled as he pushed the door closed behind her and took her in his arms. "'Course, I'm still a carpenter. And you're still a lady."

Her arms went around his neck even as she protested. "I don't have that much money, either. Murray's children inherited his estate. I have the gallery. That's mine."

"I was never in love with your money." He dipped his nose into her sweetly scented hair. "But I don't remember a time when I wasn't in love with you."

"I won't let you down this time, Dominic."

"And I'll be with you when you need me. Even when you don't need me, I'll be there." He rubbed her back, and she wondered when she would ever not need him. "So you want to deliver your gift in person?"

"I'd love to see Ricky's program."

"Then the three of us will have dinner, we'll bring Ricky home, and then we'll see if you're still feeling charitable enough to discuss a cause that's about fifteen years overdue."

"Is this a personal cause of yours, Mr. Vitalli?"

"Would you marry me anyway?" He grinned down at her.

"And I'll help you raise your son."

* * * * *

Kathleen Eagle

People warn you about changing horses in midstream, and I've never considered myself to be a risk taker. Recently, when I said that about myself, my husband, Clyde, had a good laugh. "You married me, didn't you?" he said. Well, yes, but one risk in twenty years doesn't seem to qualify me as a risk taker. It meant making some changes, but I wasn't in midstream.

Still, he was, after all, worth the risk.

That was worth bearing in mind as I took the risk of changing my career in recent years. *Revising,* really. I was a full-time teacher for seventeen years, but I can't remember a time when I didn't love to write. I did both for a while, but the time came when I had to make a choice. I just couldn't keep up with two careers and a young family any longer. Becoming a full-time writer is a risky business, though, and giving up the real joys of teaching is not easy.

Writing stories is at once exhilarating and exasperating. It's wonderful to see the work in print, but it takes a lot of blood, sweat and tears to get it there. But then, everyone's heard that. What few people know is how lonely it gets sometimes, and how welcome are those letters from readers who tell a writer that it was worth the risk. The story came to life. It worked.

Working on interconnected stories with two other writers was a new challenge, and it brought new risks. Marilyn Pappano and Patricia Gardner Evans are writers whose work I've long enjoyed. And they're friends of mine. We created three friends and three stories that stand alone, but also come together as one. The process was all the things writing is—fascinating, frustrating, enlightening and finally...eureka!

I hope you enjoy the results.

Kathleen Eagle

LOVING ABBY

Marilyn Pappano

Summer Vacations

When I was a child, summer was always our time for vacations. Mom and Dad would take time off from their jobs and load the three of us kids into the car for a few days away from our Oklahoma home. Our vacations were never fancy—visiting relatives in Kansas and Arkansas, or camping at one of our state's numerous parks—but those simple times have left me with some treasured memories.

There was the cave—cool, dark and mysterious—that we explored on our first visit to the beautiful Ozark Mountains. There was the morning when my father, who loved everything about the outdoors, woke me early to witness a buck with an impressive rack of antlers swimming across the lake where we had camped. There was the Fourth of July we spent with relatives camped in a park where no fireworks were allowed; rather than deny all of us kids, my uncle swam under cover of darkness to the lake's floating dock and set off fountains for all to enjoy. There were ghost stories around camp fires, countless hours splashing in the water, a visit to a Civil War battlefield, sleeping under the stars.

After my husband and I were married, he decided to go back into the Navy. Suddenly, the places we were living were places other people came to for vacations: Charleston, South Carolina, with its beautiful old plantations, well-preserved historical district and lovely beaches; Mobile, Alabama, home to some of the most beautiful gardens in the nation and the battleship museum *U.S.S. Alabama;* San Diego, California, with its world-famous zoo, beaches, mountains and desert all only a short drive away, Mexico a few minutes to the south and Disneyland and Hollywood a few hours to the north; and our current home, Augusta, Georgia, which offers a mix of historic sites, prestigious sporting events and easy access to the mountains of Tennessee and North Carolina, as well as the beaches of Georgia and South Carolina.

Our vacations now are generally connected with business—I find myself looking at each scene, each new experience, and wondering how I can use it in a book—but are no less enjoyable for that. We usually include something historical for me and something educational for our son, and my husband, bless his heart, follows where we lead him. Our trips have included visits to New Orleans's French Quarter and to the Florida Keys, to aquariums in New England and NASA in Houston, to witches' museums and science museums, to historic cities where one can experience the past, and to newer cities where one can feel the future.

But sometimes, simpler vacations, like the one we took last summer, can still be the best. We went back to Oklahoma. We didn't do anything exciting—just visited with family and friends, went to the lake to swim and fish, ate picnic lunches. But I believe that just as I remember my childhood vacations, our son will remember this one: being old enough to finally drive his uncles' boat, going bowling with his uncle and his cousin, seeing his youngest cousin for the first time ever, spending time with his grandmothers. Because, although we didn't do anything exciting, we did something important: we made memories. And that's what vacations are all about, aren't they?

Saturday

Late again.

Abby Granger adjusted the rearview mirror to inspect her appearance in the dim interior light of the rental car, fluffed her short blond hair and added a touch of lipstick, then opened the door. She swung her legs out, careful not to let her feet touch the ground while she groped on the floor for her heels. She'd brought half a dozen extra pairs of panty hose with her, remembering her roommate Keeley's penchant for borrowing, but she didn't have the time to dig one out now if she ruined the pair she was wearing.

She wiggled her feet into the open-toed shoes, then stood up and stretched for a moment, unkinking muscles tired from the day's flight. Columbia, South Carolina, was a long way from East Ridley, Massachusetts. If she had arrived yesterday, as she'd planned, she would be rested, at ease and in the auditorium, where the ceremonies opening this week's festivities were already under way. But, softie that she was, when she'd gotten a frantic call yesterday from one of her fellow social workers involving a child abuse case, she'd postponed her morning flight and spent the day working instead.

How many times had it happened? she wondered as she leaned down to get her purse. How many times had she dropped whatever she was doing, changed her plans or canceled them altogether, because someone needed help that only she could give? How many times had she been a sucker?

She combed her hair once more as she slammed the car door, then started across the Bartlett College campus to the auditorium. She had all the time in the world to consider her shortcomings and less than an hour to enjoy this afternoon's ceremonies.

The campus was quiet as she followed winding paths between massive stone buildings. As she walked, the tension drained from her shoulders and the lines across her forehead disappeared. Being here at Bartlett was like coming home—even better than that, she thought, because her four years here had been a time of peace. Of innocence. Of hope. Her studies had been tough, and money had been tight, but she'd been young and full of plans for a bright future, and she'd been with Keeley and Bess, her two best friends in the entire world.

Now, for one week, she was back again. For one week, she would be with them again.

She heard the low rumble of applause as she entered the building. A moment later she passed through a set of double doors and found herself inside the brightly lit auditorium. It was filled with Bartlett College alumnae of all ages, from young women not more than two years past graduation to silver-haired matrons old enough to be their grandmothers. The group was primarily female, since Bartlett *was* a women's school. The few men in the room, Abby decided as her gaze skimmed across them, were members of the staff or tag-along husbands, attending yet another boring college function.

She found a place to stand at the back of the room, just as an announcement from the speaker up front caught her attention. It was time for the annual presentation of a delicate filigree key to each of the college's

Keystone Donors. She wasn't so late after all, she realized with a wide smile. Keeley O'Donnell—make that Douglas—was sure to be one of the recipients. She supported the college in every way that she could, while Abby did well just to support herself. But she had never minded her friend's wealth—envied it, maybe, but never resented it.

Sure enough, Keeley O'Donnell Douglas was the last name called. There she was on the stage, accepting the key—tall, elegant and beautiful—as usual, Abby thought. In fifteen years *she* had just gotten older, while Keeley had gotten more everything: poised, graceful, elegant, self-assured and, darn it all, even more beautiful.

Dr. Benedict called for a round of applause for the donors, and Abby complied. A moment later the formal ceremony ended with an invitation to renew old friendships over refreshments in the room across the hall. Abby slipped into the crowd, making her way toward the last place she'd seen Keeley. She saw several faces she recognized—mostly instructors, along with a former classmate or two—but there was no sign of Bess, and Keeley wasn't yet in sight.

Wishing for the millionth time that she'd been blessed with longer legs, she rose onto the tips of her toes to see better and searched the room for a glimpse of her roommate's auburn hair or the rich lemon yellow of her dress. She didn't find her, but her gaze did settle on someone equally interesting.

Joshua Lucas, Abby thought dazedly as she settled her feet on the floor again. When she'd come to Bartlett, he'd been a graduate student who taught a few introductory psychology courses part-time. By her junior year he'd been hard at work on his doctorate and was teaching only upper-level·classes, and she had managed to take every one of them. Because they were required for her degree, of course, she'd told anyone who noticed. Because she had a great deal of respect for his teaching abilities, she'd insisted. Because she'd had the biggest crush of her young life, Keeley and Bess had known.

Joshua Lucas. She hadn't even thought of him in ages, and she had never expected to see him again. She had certainly never expected to feel that excited tingling he'd always stirred in her again.

Just as in Keeley's case, the past fifteen years had only improved an appearance that had been perfect to start with. His hair was neatly trimmed, as befitted an instructor at a traditional school like Bartlett, and its rich brown shade showed no gray from this distance. His eyes, she remembered, were blue, intense, alive with interest and warmth and excitement. In twelve years of school and six years of college, she'd seldom met anyone who had enjoyed teaching more than Joshua Lucas, and it had shown in his eyes, his voice, his gestures. He'd made psychology come alive for his students and had passed his enthusiasm on to them. As a result, she hadn't been the only one half in love with him.

And it had all been for naught, she thought with a sigh. While he'd been many things to the girls at Bartlett—handsome man, beloved instructor, fantasy figure—first and foremost he'd been married. To a beautiful woman. With three beautiful children.

She realized she'd been staring too long when she saw that she'd caught his attention. He returned her gaze briefly, then started toward her. For an instant she considered disappearing into the crowd—she was so short that she would be hard to spot—but the nervous urge was overshadowed by her desire to talk to Joshua Lucas one more time.

He stopped in front of her, his hands in his trouser pockets, pushing open the tweedy jacket he wore, and gave her a long, head-to-toes look. It was followed by a smile she'd seen hundreds of times in the past—slow, warm, welcoming. "Abby Jenkins—or have you, like most of the others, taken a new name?"

Her smile came in automatic response to his. "It's Granger, Mr. Lucas—no, sorry. I presume it's *Dr.* Lucas now."

"Yes, it is, but I don't think anyone would mind if you called me Joshua."

She tried the name silently, then gave a slight shake of her head. In long-ago dreams she had called him Joshua and other names even more intimate, and she had even referred to him by his first name in late-night talks with Keeley and Bess, but to his face? Adult to adult? Equal to equal? How could she, when she suddenly felt far more like that giddy, lovestruck girl than the equal of this psychologist and professor?

"I was surprised to see you," he remarked. "This is the first time you've come back for a reunion, isn't it?"

"Yes, it is." The first few years, getting her master's degree had taken all her money and her time; then she had gotten married and had put her husband through college and law school. That had taken every extra penny for the next seven years. Then there'd been the divorce and her mother's death and a thousand and one other reasons for not making the long trip north. But this year Keeley had asked her to come, had teased and coaxed and sweet-talked her into it. Abby had learned long ago that when Keeley Douglas wanted something, she usually got it. "I haven't had time to look around much, but everything seems the same."

He leaned closer and said in a soft voice, "Everything's been pretty much the same here for the last hundred and fifty years, including some of the professors."

She laughed at the old student joke. They had thought they were being clever when they'd insisted that some of the faculty had been at Bartlett since its mid-eighteen hundreds beginning. They had never considered the possibility that their private joke wasn't so private.

She was pretty, Joshua thought, his smile fading at the sudden realization that he'd even noticed. After twenty years of teaching at an all-women's school, he had taught himself to see his students as simply that—students. Not girls. Not young women. Not pretty or beautiful or sexy or desirable. Just students.

But Abby Jenkins Granger was pretty. Put her in a ruffly, off-the-shoulders, Scarlett O'Hara dress and she would fit every northern man's image of a southern belle—fragile, with a delicate peaches-and-cream complexion, a soft, honeyed drawl and a totally feminine, totally enchanting air about her.

And she was sexy, too. And desirable.

And most likely married, he sternly reminded himself. Even though there was no ring on her left hand— had he always noticed such things, he wondered, or was that a habit he'd picked up after the divorce?—there was most likely a Mr. Granger waiting back home in Georgia or the Carolinas or wherever she'd gotten that drawl.

"Are you staying for the entire week?"

She nodded, the action making her blond hair shimmer with the light from above.

"Left your family to fend for themselves?" He watched as the emotions visible in her eyes shifted, a faint sadness replacing the warmth.

"No family," she replied. "Just me. I'm divorced."

Good. He stopped himself from saying it aloud, but he thought it all the same. "It seems to be that way with most of us these days."

Her gaze dropped to his left hand, as bare as hers was, then climbed once more to his face. "Your wife...?"

"Ex-wife. She's married again and living in Boston."

"I'm sorry."

He shrugged carelessly. "It happened a long time ago."

"And your children?"

Don't be too pleased that she remembered, he cautioned himself. Anyone who'd spent more than a minute in his office couldn't help but notice the photographs of his daughter and two sons all over the place. "Cassie lives with her mother. She and David both go to Boston College. Jason's at Harvard. I see them when I can." He shrugged again and changed the subject. "How do you like social work?"

This time it was Abby who looked pleased.

By the time he'd started teaching only upper-level psychology courses, his classes had been small enough that he'd been able to learn something about each of his students, to see each one as an individual rather than a nameless face in a sea of nameless faces. He remembered that Abby Jenkins had been one of the smartest girls in her senior class, that she'd been well liked and the first one her friends turned to in times of trouble. "Dear Abby," they had called her teasingly, but with a great deal of affection, too.

He remembered, too, that she'd been a pleasure to teach—eager to learn, conscientious about her work, quick to grasp new concepts. She could have been a major success in any field, but she'd chosen social work, a job that was usually difficult, sometimes heartrending, often unappreciated and always underpaid.

"It's all right," Abby replied, offering a shrug of her own. "It's frustrating at times and makes me feel completely helpless at others, but I enjoy it."

"And you're good at it."

Her smile was tentative. "Yes," she agreed. "I am."

"Listen, Abby—" He didn't know exactly what he was going to suggest. *Let's go someplace quiet? Let's get together tomorrow?* And he didn't have the chance to find out after a plump redhead swept between them and enveloped Abby in a hug.

"I can't believe you're here, Abby!" the newcomer cried. "Every year I come to these things, and I usually see Keeley, but you and Bess are always no-shows. And now, here you are!"

"You look wonderful, Glory," Abby said when the other woman released her. "You remember Dr. Lucas."

Joshua stood still for the woman's measuring look; then she shook her head. "Not very well. I found intro psych so boring—no offense meant, Doctor, you weren't the teacher—that not even a professor who looked like you could have gotten me to take more."

"No offense taken," he said dryly.

Glory turned her attention back to Abby. "Come on, Abby, there are some people here you have to see. Oh, and I just left Keeley over by the refreshment tables. She'll be thrilled to see you.''

Abby looked up helplessly at him, and Joshua bit back the urge to ask her to stay and talk to him a while longer. It would put her in the kind of situation ''dear Abby'' had always hated, torn between two friends who wanted different things from her—or, in this case, torn between an old friend and an old acquaintance who wanted to become a new friend.

He smiled and extended his hand. When she took it, he wrapped his fingers lightly around hers. ''I'll see you again.'' It wasn't a question or the meaningless kind of thing people said, but a promise.

With a faint goodbye, she pulled her hand back and allowed the redhead to lead her away into the crowd. When she was out of sight, Joshua returned to his earlier position, out of the way against one wall.

He should get in there and work the room himself, he acknowledged—speak to the department heads, greet their husbands and wives, and chat with some of the older, wealthier alumnae whose endowments helped pay his salary. After all, socializing at school functions was one of his duties as much as lecturing in class or grading papers or overseeing exams, particularly since he'd accepted the position of assistant head of the psychology department.

Reluctantly he moved away from the wall and back into the crowd, stopping to speak to a recent graduate, meeting her mother who had graduated twenty-four years earlier and her grandmother, Class of '42. He listened to the head of the music department debate budgets with the head of his own department and stoically endured the not-so-subtle hints of the music professor's wife. He found himself trapped for fifteen minutes with a long-winded, hard-of-hearing Keystone Donor and spent another uncomfortable few minutes with Dr. Benedict and his wife, one of his ex-wife's closest friends.

And the whole time he was searching the crowd for a petite blonde with a soft southern drawl and a gentle smile.

But she was nowhere in sight. After circling the room once more, he knew Abby must have escaped, gone off with friends or back to the dorm to get settled in. And escape was precisely what *he* would do, he decided, suddenly anxious to get away from the crowd and the noise and back to his quiet house. He'd put in an appearance and done his duty, and now he would go home. Alone.

Abby walked back to her car, feeling somewhat let down. It had been nice seeing Glory and a half dozen other friends, but her search for Keeley had been fruitless. Finally someone had told her that Keeley had slipped out shortly after making the rounds. There was no sign of Bess, either, and by the time she'd started looking for Joshua Lucas again, he was gone, too.

It was part of the curse of being short, she thought whimsically. Even in these cursed three-inch heels, she still felt like a dwarf among giants. Bess or Keeley could have stood in one place and gazed out over everyone else, but if *she* tried that, all she would see was bosoms or backs.

Stopping at the rental car, she fished out the keys and opened the trunk. "Packing light" had always been a foreign concept to her, according to her roommates, and staring into the trunk, she considered the possibility that they were right. For this one-week trip she'd brought the largest suitcase she owned, plus a garment bag, a tote bag and a nylon gym bag. How was she going to carry it all up four flights of stairs in three-inch heels?

She hauled out the suitcase and the tote bag, then dug a pair of tennis shoes from the gym bag. The rest would have to wait until morning, she thought as she closed the trunk.

Keeley had arranged for them to have the same room they'd lived in for four years. It was a sweet, sentimental gesture, Abby reminded herself as she trudged up the last flight of stairs. At the top, she put her suitcase down and pushed it the rest of the way, not caring if the scraping sound disturbed any early arrivals in the rooms she passed.

She reached their old room, fumbled with the key in the lock, then finally swung the door open. After turning on the light, she simply stood there for a moment. Home. She had come home.

She dragged her suitcase inside, closed the door, dropped the tote bag and her purse, and went straight to the bed, dropping down on it, resting her feet on the spread. This was where she'd slept for four years. Where she had giggled with her roommates and shared secrets in the night. Where she had schemed and dreamed and planned, and occasionally even cried.

The sound of another key in the door drew her gaze. She felt...excited. Nervous. Apprehensive. Was it Bess or Keeley on the other side? Were they anticipating this meeting even half as much as she was? And a more important question: would they be disappointed in the woman she'd become? After all, Bess had what she'd always wanted—a successful career and everything that came with it: respect, influence, power and money. And

Keeley—well, she'd *always* had everything. Would they think that Abby, with her divorce, her unimpressive job with the South Carolina Department of Social Services and her paycheck-to-paycheck life-style, had failed to fulfill her potential in comparison to them?

Once more the door swung open, and a scant second later Bess Hilliard walked in. As Abby had done moments ago, she paused and looked around, then slowly closed the door. After their initial greetings, she set her bags down, cast a chastening look at Abby's own suitcase, then, as if it had been only fifteen minutes since they'd seen each other instead of fifteen years, said in her no-nonsense way, "For heaven's sake, Abby, that bag's almost bigger than you are."

Abby jumped up from the bed and gave her roommate a hug. It was something Bess had never been used to when they lived together and apparently had never grown used to since. Abby could feel it in the slightly stiff way she held herself back. Slowly she released her and took a step away. "Oh, Bess, I'm glad to see you. I wondered on the trip up if you would actually come, or if you would change your mind at the last minute."

Bess's smile seemed taut as she went to her bed. "Well, I'm here. Is Keeley?"

"I caught a glimpse of her over at the auditorium, but she left before I could find her in the crowd."

"You should have climbed up on one of the chairs so you could actually see."

Abby smiled at the dry remark. All through college Bess and Keeley had called her "shrimp," and she had retaliated with retorts regarding their smaller-than-average bra size. If only they could trade, they had commiserated: a few inches of their height for a few inches of her too-lush—in her opinion, at least—curves. "Did you have a nice trip?"

"Abby, I live in Boston, remember? Less than two hours away? You're the one on a 'trip.' How was your flight?"

"It was fine."

Abby shifted a bit nervously. She had been looking forward to this reunion for so long, but she had never once considered how it might actually go. She had naively expected it to be just like old times. She hadn't expected this tongue-tied awkwardness. She hadn't expected Bess to look as if she would give anything to be back in Boston instead of here with Abby, waiting for Keeley.

For a moment she stood motionless, not sure what to do or say next. Then her gaze fell on her suitcase, and she lifted it onto her bed. The first item she took out of it was an oval pewter frame. Under the glass was a photograph that she had treasured for fifteen years, a candid shot of the three of them taken at the outdoor amphitheater: she and Keeley standing arm in arm, with Abby's free hand outstretched toward Bess, a little ways off, beckoning her to join them. Together but separate. She didn't remember now who had taken the picture and given copies to each of them. She wondered if the other two still had theirs, if the prints had been packed away and forgotten or lost altogether. She wondered if they would think she was disgustingly sentimental for keeping hers on the nightstand at home, or for bringing it with her on this week-long journey.

Then she smiled as she set the photo on the bedside table. What did it matter? She *was* disgustingly sentimental, and probably no one knew that better than Keeley and Bess.

While she began to unpack, she and Bess talked, with Bess telling her about hitting a cat on the drive up. Abby had just picked up another armload of clothing from the bag and was turning toward the bureau when the now-familiar rattle of a key in the lock stopped her. Laying the clothes down, she glanced at Bess, who was slowly rising from the bed, then turned her gaze to the doorway.

When Keeley walked in, Abby greeted her with a more exuberant version of the hug Bess had gotten. Neither roommate had ever been as physically demonstrative as Abby was, but Keeley came closer. Instead of merely tolerating the embrace, she returned it, then exchanged a more sedate greeting with Bess.

They talked while they unpacked: about jobs—*careers,* Keeley called them—families and friends; fifteen years of changes. It was an awkward conversation, Abby thought. Rambling words meant to fill the silence rather than the uninhibited, all-trying-to-talk-at-once chats they'd shared so long ago.

Then her marriage came up—or, rather, her divorce. Darryl was no great loss, she said with an airy shrug. She deserved better. When Keeley and Bess exchanged glances over choked-back laughs, she knew she hadn't said anything that they hadn't always privately thought. "So I was a little slow to catch on," she admitted, her laughter freeing theirs.

Conversation came more easily after they went to bed. Because they were rediscovering that old camaraderie that made confidences easier to offer? she wondered. Because three best friends couldn't remain strangers long, even after fifteen years? Or because memories were closer and easier to share in the darkness?

Do you remember...?

What about the time...?

How could you forget...?

The soft questions and softer giggles slowly faded into a warm, familiar silence. Abby was sinking into it, drifting away on it, when Keeley's voice, so elegant and cultured, filtered through. "I'm glad you're here, Abby. I'm glad we're all here."

She smiled sleepily and snuggled deeper under the comforter. "Me too," she whispered. Me too.

Sunday

Bess had always been an early riser, Keeley had liked to sleep in, and Abby herself had fallen somewhere in between. In that way, at least, none of them had changed, Abby reflected as she returned from her trip downstairs in search of a pot of coffee. Bess was wide-awake and already dressed for the day's opening session, Keeley was sleeping soundly in the corner bed, and she herself was awake but still wearing her robe, delaying the task of getting dressed.

She set the pot and three cups she'd filched on the bureau and filled each cup. The first went to Bess, the second was her own, and the third she carried to Keeley's bed. She knelt, protecting the cup so none of it spilled, and with a wave of her hand sent the aroma of hot, rich, strong coffee wafting across to her roommate's nose. "Keeley, time to get up," she called in a teasing, singsong voice.

The sleeping woman made a soft, grumbling sound and burrowed deeper into the pillow; then Abby waved her hand over the cup again and, perfectly-shaped nose twitching, Keeley opened her eyes. "Coffee?" she whispered in a sleep-softened voice.

Abby set the cup on the nightstand and stood as Keeley sat up and brushed her hair back. "Nice of you to join us. The opening session starts in one hour." She returned to her own bed and sat down, drinking her coffee while she skimmed over the schedule of events she'd found slipped under the door this morning.

The morning session would last several hours and consist primarily of speeches and announcements. The keynote speaker had graduated five years ahead of them and was one of the few female cabinet members. She was sure to be interesting, Abby thought, but not as interesting as Keeley's seminar on the art world scheduled for Wednesday afternoon—or Dr. Joshua Lucas's panel Monday morning on the varied uses of psychology in the business world. Although she knew nothing about art and less about business, those were two workshops she would be sure to attend.

With a sigh, she finished her coffee, tossed the schedule aside and rose from the bed. Keeley was coming alive, chatting with Bess about mutual acquaintances in Boston. Although the two women's backgrounds were as vastly different from each other as her own was, Bess's career in investment banking had provided them with a common link: Keeley was rich, and Bess helped rich people get richer.

Getting dressed was a simple enough task for Abby. Thank heavens—and Grandmother Jenkins—that she'd been given healthy, manageable hair that forgave everything she did to it, including sleeping on it. A few moments in front of the mirror with a brush lifted the flat spots, smoothed the wild ones and made her perfectly presentable again. Her makeup didn't take much longer than that. She'd never had the skill with makeup that Keeley possessed—but then, she'd never had as much natural beauty to work with, either. Not even the most talented application of makeup would make her a raving beauty.

"Oh, Abby, I forgot to stop by the store yesterday," Keeley said. "Can I borrow a pair of panty hose? Please?"

There was a moment's silence; then all three women burst into laughter. "Just like the old days," Bess remarked. "How many pairs has she 'borrowed' from you, Abby?"

"Dozens."

"And how many has she returned?"

"None." Then Abby grinned. "But she gave me this atomizer." She sprayed the perfume, then held up the crystal-and-silver bottle. "And once she gave me a book of poetry and a jar of those bath crystals I used to love that were so expensive. And some cologne to go in the atomizer and countless hamburgers at the Strawberry Shanty and..."

"It would have been cheaper to buy your own panty hose," Bess said to Keeley when Abby ran out of steam.

"But I always forgot, and Abby never did, and we wore the same size and style and shade," Keeley explained with a guileless smile.

"And she loaned them to you even if they were her last pair and it left her with none for herself." Bess gave a tolerant shake of her head.

"It's okay," Abby said, bending to open the bottom bureau drawer. When she straightened, she was holding an armful of brightly colored packages of hosiery. "I came prepared."

Keeley plucked out one package and looked at it. "Perfect, Ab. We're still about the same size."

After tossing one for herself on the bed, Abby returned the rest to the drawer. After all these years, she was still surprised that she and tall, willowy Keeley could wear close to the same size in *anything*, even though she knew they weighed the same. It was just that Keeley's weight was evenly distributed over a five-foot-eight-inch frame, while on Abby the same pounds were compressed into five feet three inches. That meant Keeley was tall and slim. It also meant Abby wasn't.

"Hey, Abby, it says here that Dr. Joshua Lucas is on the panel for one of tomorrow's workshops."

She glanced up quickly and saw that Bess was studying the schedule she'd had earlier.

"It's a good thing yours isn't scheduled at the same time, Keeley," Bess continued with a teasing smile. "Abby wouldn't know what to do: be a normal, curious woman and go lust after the good doctor or be a good friend and go listen to you."

Abby concentrated on putting on her panty hose and staying out of the conversation—but listening intently.

"There's no contest," Keeley said. "The good doctor is divorced now. If she passed him up to listen to me speak about art, I'd strangle her myself."

Finally Abby offered a fierce frown to both women. "Do you have to talk about me as if I'm not even here?" Then the frown dissolved into her usual smile as she padded across the room to the closet.

After a moment's consideration, she removed a khaki skirt in cotton and a summer-knit, pale pink sweater. It was somewhat casual compared to Keeley's silk and Bess's linen, she noticed, then shrugged it off. Even if she could afford silk and linen for daily wear, the sultry Carolina weather would make them impractical.

After dressing, she slipped into her heels, then, in unspoken accord with Bess, sat down to wait for Keeley to get ready. She'd spent many mornings just this way in the past, waiting for Keeley, who refused to rush in spite of her habitual oversleeping. It felt familiar. Comfortable. Warm.

When Keeley was ready, they left the dorm and walked side by side across the campus to the auditorium. It seemed that everyone there, whether older or younger, knew Keeley, although there were plenty of Abby's and Bess's old friends there, too.

Some of the speeches were interesting, particularly the cabinet member's, and some, Abby thought, were typically boring. She was relieved when the session came to an end. "You guys want to get some lunch?" she asked as she wriggled her feet into her shoes.

There was a moment's hesitation on the other women's parts; then Keeley begged off for personal reasons. She was sorry, Bess said, but she had other plans, too. But they would get together for tonight's cocktail party for sure.

And so Abby found herself heading across campus to the Town Tavern, situated on the street that acted as boundary between the college and the town, and facing her first meal back at Bartlett all alone.

But not for long.

She'd just settled into a corner booth and begun to skim the menu when a low, intimately husky voice intruded. "Mind if I join you?"

It was Joshua Lucas. She looked up at him for a long moment, taking in the differences in his appearance. Last night he'd been dressed as a proper New England professor—dress slacks, tweedy coat, button-down shirt and tie. Today he wore a striped polo shirt tucked into faded jeans and the most disreputable tennis shoes she'd ever seen. Last night he'd looked distinguished. Authoritarian. Today he looked handsome. Approachable.

Then her gaze slid down over his jeans again, and a tightness closed her throat.

Today he looked sexy.

She responded to his question with a nod, not quite certain she could manage a verbal reply.

He slid onto the padded bench across from her and folded his hands together on the tabletop. His fingers were long and thin, she noticed, and his hands, like everything else she could see, were nicely tanned. Not even a hint of the wedding band he'd worn so many years remained on his left hand.

"What did you think of the opening session?"

Abby turned her gaze back to the menu she still held and took a deep breath, hoping it would steady her voice. "It was interesting enough."

Joshua reached out and pulled the stained folder from her hands. "The menu hasn't changed in the twenty years I've been coming here. They still serve greasy hamburgers and greasier fries, foot-long subs and watered-down sodas." He closed the menu and pushed it to the edge of the table, then asked, "Do I make you nervous, Abby?"

She wondered briefly whether a psychologist-cum-professor had any special skills at identifying lies. Of course, she was so inept at telling them that no special skills were needed to recognize them. "Yes," she admitted honestly. "I think you do."

"Because I was your teacher fifteen years ago?" His smile made it clear that he needed no answer. "You're no longer a student, Abby, and for a few months, at least, I'm not teaching. So why don't you relax and treat me like any other old friend?"

She would like to be his friend, she thought. She had always liked him as an instructor, had always respected and admired him. Now she would like to know the man behind the teacher—*really* know him, the way she knew Keeley and Bess.

"All right," she agreed with a slight smile. "Friends."

He grinned a masculinely triumphant grin. "And you can start by calling me Joshua."

"All right. Were you at this morning's session, Joshua?"

"The faculty is required to attend certain events this week. Today was one of them. I slipped out before Dr. Benedict took the stage, though. I've heard his welcome-back-to-Bartlett speech at least fifteen times." He paused as the waitress arrived to take their order. "I saw you there with your two tall friends."

"Bess Hilliard and Keeley Douglas. They were my roommates when we were here."

"And you've stayed close friends all these years."

Abby tapped one fingernail thoughtfully against her lower lip. "Not as close as I would have liked. We've been together at the important times—marriages and funerals—and a few times in between. But Bess lives in Boston, and Keeley's in New York, and I live in South Carolina. It's not easy keeping long-distance friendships going."

"You seemed inseparable in college. Some of the faculty called you the Three Musketeers."

"Or the Three Stooges, depending on the teacher," she said with a quick smile.

Joshua felt the effects of her smile, dazzling and vital, somewhere deep inside. It was so genuine, so sincere, and it transformed an already pretty face into a beautiful one. The fact that she was utterly unaware of it made the impact even greater.

What would it take to seduce her? he wondered, then immediately banished the thought. Abby Granger wasn't the kind of woman a man carelessly seduced, then said goodbye to. She was too gentle, too delicate, too everything. Any man who set out to seduce her would run the risk of getting caught in his own trap.

It would be a thoroughly enjoyable captivity.

He looked away from her, forcing his attention to the dining room that was rapidly filling, but the exercise did little to control the desire knotting low in his belly. Had he ever known a woman who could make him ache like this without trying, without even being aware of it? Not even Marla had affected him this strongly, and he'd been married to her for almost twenty years!

"Hi, Dr. Lucas," a girlish voice called from a few tables over, followed almost immediately by a seductive woman's. "Hello, Joshua."

He murmured a response, then turned back to Abby. "Let's get the sandwiches to go. I know a quiet place on campus where we won't be disturbed."

His words seemed to create a moment's hesitation in Abby; then she nodded. "Okay."

Her agreement brought an absurd happiness with it. He was overreacting, he warned himself as he signaled the waitress. It wasn't as if she'd agreed to anything important—just lunch away from the curious eyes filling the restaurant. It didn't mean that she shared his interest. It didn't mean that she would ever see him as anything other than a former instructor. It didn't mean that she felt even one-tenth of his desire.

But it was a start.

Abby half expected Joshua's "quiet place" to be the privacy of his office, but instead he led her to the lawn in front of the library, stopping in the shade of an ancient tree. She sat down and removed her heels, then tucked her feet beneath the folds of her skirt. "This is nice," she said as he unpacked the paper bag that held their lunch. "It's been too hot and humid at home to sit out like this since mid-April."

"Where in South Carolina is home?" He checked one sandwich, found turkey inside and handed it to her.

"Columbia."

"And what do you do in Columbia, South Carolina?"

"I work and spend time with my brothers and sisters and their families."

Joshua stretched out on his side, supporting himself on one elbow. "You must have more of a life than that," he chided.

But she didn't, she thought with a measure of dismay. She put in long hours at work, she baby-sat for nieces and nephews, and she offered a helping hand, an encouraging word or a shoulder to cry on to family and friends when one was needed. That, in a nutshell, summed up her life. There were no men, no special occasions, no excitement, no glamour, no great accomplishments.

"No," she said with a shrug, as if the admission didn't pain her. "That's the extent of it."

"What did you do after you left Bartlett?"

"I got my master's at the University of South Carolina."

"Then?"

"I went to work for the state."

"And?"

She laughed and shrugged again. "And I still work for them."

"Come on, Abby, this is like pulling teeth," he teased. "*No one* can cover fifteen years of her life in three short sentences. You told me last night you were divorced. How long were you married?"

"How long does it take to get a law degree and establish a practice?" she replied flippantly, then immediately felt the heat of a blush. She hadn't meant to say that, hadn't meant to even hint at what a sucker she'd been in her marriage. Everyone else had seen Darryl Granger for exactly what he was: a scheming, manipulative jerk looking for a free ride. Everyone except *her*. Her family and friends had tried to warn her, but she'd been too foolish to listen. She'd been in love and had seen only what Darryl had wanted her to see. After eight years, though, he'd shown her the truth. *Thanks for the career,* he'd told her once the divorce was final.

"What about you?" she asked, deliberately changing the subject. From the wry expression on his face, she suspected that he'd expected it.

"What about me?"

"Now that you have your doctorate, why aren't you out practicing psychology in the big city and making a fortune instead of teaching a bunch of giggly girls and skipping out on Dr. Benedict's welcome-back-to-Bartlett speech for the umpteenth time?"

He took a long time to answer her question, time that he spent gazing off into the distance instead of looking at her. After a few moments passed, then a few more, she cleared her throat uncomfortably. "Poor choice of question, huh?"

He refocused on her and smiled absently. "It's one that my ex-wife asked on a regular basis for about three years."

"I'm sorry. I didn't mean to bring up painful memories."

"You didn't. By the time we finally got the divorce, about the only thing I felt was sadness that the kids were going to Boston with her." A troubled frown creased his forehead, as if he didn't like what he'd just heard himself say, and, his tone reflective, he tried to explain it. "Marla and I had been married nineteen years. She helped me get through school—not just financially, but emotionally, mentally. She was behind me all the way, pushing. At the time I thought I was lucky to have such a supportive wife, but later I realized that it wasn't so much support for me, but for her own ambition. She knew exactly what kind of husband she wanted, and she was doing her best to make me into it. She was pleased with my bachelor's degree, thrilled with my master's and absolutely ecstatic over my Ph.D."

Then he'd found out that the doctorate he'd worked so hard for—that they both had sacrificed for—meant vastly different things to each of them. To him it was the culmination of a lifetime of study and hard work, the key to becoming a full professor and, eventually, the head of his department. To Marla it had been the ticket to a new life, to money and prestige in someplace, anyplace, but tiny East Ridley, Massachusetts.

He had never known she wanted that new life, had never guessed that being able to say "my husband, the psychologist" instead of "my husband, the professor" was so important to her. He had never suspected that she found college life so distasteful. She had asked him to move, and he had refused. She had resorted to arguing, cajoling, pleading, demanding. Finally she had threatened: leave the college or lose her and the kids.

The former Mrs. Lucas, Abby thought darkly when Joshua paused to finish his soda, seemed to have a few traits in common with her own ex-husband: they had both used their spouses to fulfill their own desires. With their ambition, greed and drive, if they ever teamed up, they could conquer the world.

"When she brought the kids into it," Joshua continued, "I seriously considered doing what she wanted. The youngest was thirteen, the oldest sixteen. I wasn't ready to quit being a full-time father. But I would have been doing it strictly for them—not for myself and definitely not for Marla. They would have grown up and away, and I would have been left in a life I didn't want with a wife I realized I no longer loved. So they left, and I stayed, and we're still close. I'm still their father. They visit every month and call every week—collect, of course. We're all happy."

"So it worked out for the best. I have to admit, I can't imagine you doing anything besides teaching. There are plenty of good psychologists, but a good teacher is hard to come by." She stuffed the remains of her lunch into the paper bag, then leaned forward to collect Joshua's just as he moved to hand it to her. His fingers grazed her hand, then stayed there, moving just a bit, then settling.

Funny, she thought in a daze, that so light a contact could pack so much power. Her skin seemed to tingle, and she could feel it growing warm underneath his fingertips. His touch sent a tiny shiver that she was barely able to contain dancing up her arm, and it generated a longing for more.

What would it feel like if he *really* touched her? she wondered. If he drew her down to the ground beside him and caressed her? How would his hands, big and gentle and long-fingered, feel on her skin, in her hair? How would they feel undressing her, slowly removing each piece of clothing, brushing against her with each movement? How would they feel on her breasts?

Heat flooded through her. Arousal? Desire? Or shame at her shameless need? She didn't know. She didn't care.

Except for their brief handshake last night, this was the first time he'd ever touched her, Joshua thought. It was so clichéd, this electric sensation from so casual a gesture. But there was nothing clichéd or casual about what he was feeling.

But it was impossible. Abby was in Massachusetts for only a week, seven days, and one of them was already gone. Seven days wasn't long enough to build a relationship. It wasn't long enough to gain her trust. And it damn sure wouldn't be long enough to satisfy his hunger.

It would be best, he acknowledged as he slowly moved his fingers across her hand, if he avoided any further contact with her. It would certainly be best, he continued as his hand slid down to cradle hers, if he didn't see her anymore, if he didn't allow this arousal to build into something he couldn't ignore, something he couldn't control. And it would most definitely be best...

That last thought was lost when he raised her hand, small and delicate and nestled in his bigger palm, to his mouth. For a moment he hesitated, his lips mere inches above her skin. He could smell her fragrance, sweet and floral, on her wrist, could see each fragile link in the gold chains that circled it, could feel the pulse that beat erratically underneath it.

Then he pressed a kiss to the back of her hand, a gentle brush of his mouth back and forth. The pulse throbbing against his fingertip increased crazily when he touched his tongue to her skin, and from somewhere far away he heard her soft, sudden breath.

When he ended the kiss, he looked up at her, studying her face for some clue to what she was thinking. Her eyes, soft and brown and wide, reminded him of a startled fawn, and the peaches-and-cream complexion was more cream than peaches.

She was bewildered. That was one emotion he recognized—even shared. What should have been a simple, casual, meaningless kiss hadn't been. She had felt it as surely as he had.

"It's what I do best," he said softly, responding to her last comment.

She stared at him uncomprehendingly.

"Teaching. You said a good teacher is hard to come by. It's what I always wanted to do. It's what I do best."

Her gaze dropped from his face to her hand, still cradled gently in his. "I'm not so sure about that," she murmured.

Joshua tried to hide his grin, knowing she hadn't intended to speak her thoughts aloud, but it was impossible. When she blushed deeply, he lifted her hand for one more kiss, this one quick and impersonal, then released it and finished the task she'd started, stuffing napkins and wrappers and cups into the paper bag. "Are you going to the cocktail party tonight?" he asked casually.

"Yes. It seems like the best chance to see everyone." Abby paused, then hesitantly asked, "Are you?"

"My invitation, if I had one, would read along the line of 'the pleasure of your company is *required*.'" He stood up and extended his hand to help her to her feet, acting as a brace for her while she put her shoes on. "Go with me."

For a long moment she considered it: a date with Joshua Lucas. Wouldn't that be a great memory to take back home with her? So many years had passed since she'd sat in his class daydreaming about just such an event, and now that daydream could come true. All she had to do was say yes.

"You plan to go anyway," he said encouragingly. "And I *have* to go. But I would certainly enjoy it more with you."

"I'm flattered," she admitted honestly.

"Don't be flattered, Abby. I'm no one to be flattered over." He grinned appealingly. "Try being enticed. Tempted. Beguiled."

She wanted to say yes, wanted it with a fierceness that surprised her. But Bess and Keeley expected her to attend the cocktail party with them—those had been Bess's parting words this morning. Of course, they would understand if she told them that Joshua had asked her to go with him instead. It had been an accepted—even expected—behavior fifteen years ago: plans with a roomie could be broken if a date came along.

But that was fifteen years ago. A lot of things that had been acceptable then weren't now. Besides, she had come over seven hundred miles to see Keeley and Bess— *not* to get involved with a man she would probably never see again once the week was over.

"I *am* flattered," she said, then, at his chiding look, she added, "And enticed, tempted and beguiled. But I'm going to the party tonight with my roommates. It wouldn't be fair to cancel on them because I got another offer."

"For the sake of my ego, at least call it a better offer."

She smiled warmly. "All right, a better offer. But thanks for asking me." Then, in a helplessly hopeful voice, she added, "Maybe I'll see you there."

"Oh, you will. Definitely."

He was doing a good impersonation of the absent-minded professor tonight, Joshua thought as he looked blankly at the tie he'd just knotted around his neck. It was left over from the time when Marla, not trusting his judgment on anything beyond jeans, had bought his clothes for him: stylish but not trendy, traditional but not stuffy. Stylish or not, though, its burgundy-and-black stripes clashed with his gray suit and pale blue shirt.

He yanked it off and tossed it on the dresser, then removed another tie from the rack in the closet. Although normally he could dress in the dark and be perfectly coordinated, he wasn't surprised by tonight's mistake. A few moments ago he'd searched for cuff links before realizing that his shirt, in deference to the summer heat, was short-sleeved, and before that he'd gone through the closet looking for the belt that was already buckled around his waist.

It was all Abby Granger's fault, he decided as he adjusted the tie, then fastened it with a gold clip. She made him feel like a foolish kid—and, at the same time, very much a man. He couldn't remember when he'd enjoyed anything more than this afternoon's simple lunch on the library lawn. He couldn't remember when he'd last felt so relaxed, so at ease and, conversely, so aroused. He couldn't remember ever being this eager to attend any college function.

He wished she had accepted his invitation to to-night's party, although it really didn't matter, since she would be there anyway. Still, it would have been nice to pick her up at her room and even nicer to walk her home in the moonlight, to hold her close in the shadows, to kiss her good-night....

Clenching his teeth on a frustrated groan, he slid into his suit jacket. If he continued along that line of thought, he would wind up missing most of the party while he waited for the evidence of his desire to fade. After one last check to make sure he'd gotten everything right this time, he switched off the light and left the bedroom.

The house was quiet as he came downstairs. Before the divorce it had always been filled with noise, televisions, stereos, and good-natured—or not so good-natured—fights. When Marla had taken the kids to Boston with her, the silence had haunted him. He'd fallen into the habit of spending every possible hour someplace else, anyplace but here.

Now he was used to the silence. Now he called it peace. But there was something lonely about it, something that made him realize how alone he really was. Something that made it easy to imagine another voice here—a soft, slow southern drawl.

He locked the door behind him, then started down the driveway, passing his car where it had sat unused for at least a week. Most days, even when it was cold and snow covered the ground, he walked to work—across the street and a wide playing field, up a small hill and into the building that housed his office and most of his classes. It took less time than driving and finding a parking space would, and it gave him time to mentally prepare for an upcoming class or put a particularly taxing one behind him.

The night air was cool and fragrant. If not for one slender delicate blonde, he would skip the cocktail party and take a long, leisurely evening walk instead. Maybe he could persuade her to cut out on the party and share that walk with him. Then he would work on persuading her to go home with him, to make love with him, to stay with him.

The serious direction of his thoughts made him drag his hand restlessly through his hair. He was acting like Jason or David with their first crushes, and he wasn't a kid. He was forty-six years old—too old to be thinking in terms of a serious romance with a woman he hardly knew. Too old to rush into anything without considering the outcome. Too old for love—or lust—at first sight.

But Abby Granger, sweet, delicate southern flower that she was, had somehow managed to knock his always-planted-firmly-on-the-ground feet right out from under him . . . and without even being aware of it. That was just one of the things about this whole situation that he found so unbelievable and so refreshing. Everything Marla had ever done had been carefully calculated: she'd known exactly which buttons to push to get the proper response from everyone around her. Most of the women he'd dated since the divorce had been similar, a few more manipulative than his ex-wife, most much less so.

But Abby was different. She wanted to give to others, not take from them, and he doubted she would have the first idea how to manipulate someone. She was softer, gentler, more innocent, than most of the women he knew. Unfortunately, that made her more vulnerable, because people took advantage of the soft, the gentle, the innocent. People like her ex-husband...

He came to a sudden stop at the Stanton Room. He'd been so lost in thought that he didn't remember entering the building and climbing the stairs to the top floor. It was all Abby's fault again, he thought with a grin.

The party was in full swing, attended by the majority of the Bartlett administration and faculty, along with all the conference and reunion attendees. All in all, there were several hundred people in the room, and he was looking for probably the smallest one there.

The task didn't daunt him. He half believed he would somehow know when she was near—and considering the intensity of the desire she could stir in him, he wouldn't be surprised if the indicating signal was a purely physical one.

He stopped at the bar for a drink, then made a slow circuit around the room. It was tedious going. He knew at least half the people there, and the ones he didn't know seemed to know him. Nearly an hour had slipped away before he saw a tall, auburn-haired woman whose face was faintly familiar. Keeley something or other, he remembered from last night's Keystone Donor presentation. Abby's roommate. One of the Three Musketeers—or the Three Stooges. Where one went on campus, the others were sure to be nearby.

Sure enough, standing between Keeley and another tall, slim woman was Abby. She wore a summery mint-green dress that snugly followed every perfect curve and revealed the kind of legs men the world over would whistle for, shapely and sexy even though not long. She was listening to the conversation between her second roommate and another woman—*really* listening, the way so few people did—but after a moment her attention and her gaze began wandering, and when they did, they came to him.

Abby had felt Joshua's eyes on her as surely as an actual caress, the sensation increasing until she could no longer concentrate on Bess's somewhat unusual questions about a local veterinarian. When she had finally given in to the need, she saw him standing less than twenty feet away. He started to take a step toward her, but was brought up short by a demand for his time from old Dr. Wilkins. But even while he talked to the English professor, he continued to watch her, his gaze heavy with promise.

By the time Dr. Wilkins finished, Abby realized that both Bess and Keeley had noticed her preoccupation. As Joshua started toward them, she looked from one woman to the other. "Not one word, okay?"

Their smiles couldn't have been more angelic.

He stopped a respectable distance away. "Abby," he said with a nod, then glanced at her roommates. "I don't believe I've met your friends."

"Jo—Dr. Lucas, Bess Hilliard and Keeley Douglas."

They exchanged polite greetings, then Keeley laid her hand lightly on Abby's arm. "I'm going to get a fresh glass of wine."

"I could use a drink myself," Bess said, leaving with her.

Abby felt a flush warming her face at their transparency, but Joshua was grinning. "Not too subtle, are they?" she asked.

"No...but perceptive. Have you seen all of your friends?"

"Most of them."

"Then maybe you wouldn't mind stepping outside on the balcony with me."

"For a breath of fresh air?" she asked with a wry smile.

"For the moonlight and the stars and the privacy." Then he added, "Unless, of course, you're afraid to be alone with me."

She glanced over her shoulder at the double French doors that led outside, then back at him. "I think I should be," she replied softly as she led the way.

As soon as Joshua closed the door behind him, the noise level dwindled to nothing, then was slowly replaced with night sounds: crickets, birdcalls, the rustle of a lazy wind. Abby walked to the carved stone railing and rested her hands on it, feeling the warmth left over from the afternoon sun seep into her fingers and palms.

He remained by the door for a moment, watching her, then slowly approached. She could hear the soft sounds of his footsteps on the stone, could sense his nearness in the prickles that raced down her spine. He stopped close enough to make her insides flutter and turned to lean back against the rail. The position allowed him to study her in the dim light coming through the windowpanes, but, more importantly, she thought with a shy look, it allowed *her* to see *him*.

Heavens, he was handsome. Not pretty-boy cute like so many movie stars, but grown-up handsome. She wished for one wistful moment that that was all that drew her to him—his strong good looks—because that would make what she was feeling no more than lust. Lust faded in time; it passed without leaving any scars, without causing any pain. She could enjoy lusting after him for the next week without doing anything about it, and she could go home with her heart intact. She could deal with lust.

But it wasn't lust, and she couldn't fool herself into thinking it was. She could care about this man.

Be honest, Abby, she silently counseled herself. She already cared about him. In the short amount of time she'd spent with him, she'd found out that the respect, admiration and fondness she'd felt for him from fifteen years ago were still intact. She'd found her feelings for him rapidly changing from those of a student for a favorite instructor to those of a woman for a man.

And it scared her senseless.

She'd never had a broken heart before—by the time Darryl had divorced her, she'd suffered more from wounded pride than heartache—but that was exactly what she was heading for if she maintained this course. If she already cared for Joshua after only one day, how was she going to feel after seven of them? Just how much of her heart was she going to leave behind with him? How much of her soul?

"You look serious."

She shifted to look out across the campus. "I was just thinking."

"About what?"

"Going home."

"Is someone special waiting there for you?"

"No."

"Good."

That brought her gaze sharply back to him. "Good?" she echoed.

"I'd hate to think I'm competing against someone who isn't here to defend his claim."

"And what would that claim be?"

"You."

She turned away again, trying to ignore the warm rush of pleasure spreading through her. "You're not too subtle, are you?"

"You're only here for a week, Abby. I don't have time for subtlety."

She walked a short distance away, stopping to smell the heavy fragrance of some shadowed flowers planted in a giant stone urn. Then she faced him, leaning against the urn, hands clasped nervously in front of her. "That's right. I'm only here for a week. Trying to make something of that would be foolish, don't you think?"

He joined her, bracing his hands on the rim of the urn on each side of her, trapping her without touching her. "Trying to ignore what's between us would be even more foolish."

The shadows that prevented her from seeing the blue of his eyes didn't block the intensity of his gaze as it rested on her face. That gaze made her shiver. It made her long to cup her hands to his face and kiss him. It made her want to pull him closer until nothing but thin clothing separated their bodies. It made her ache.

"I would never hurt you, Abby," he said quietly. "I just want to see you. I want to be with you. I want to make the most of the time we do have."

And when it was over? she wondered. Would he pick up his routine as if nothing had happened? Would his life go on, perhaps slightly enriched from his brief summer fling? That wasn't the way it would work out for her. She didn't have affairs. She didn't even have relationships. She didn't know how to be casual about such things. She could be a friend, or she could be a lover—with the emphasis on "love." But she couldn't be a summer fling.

The closest set of French doors was flung open, and a small group of women moved out onto the balcony. Joshua and Abby both glanced at them, then back at each other.

"So much for privacy," she said, her lightness feigned.

"My seminar is tomorrow morning at ten o'clock. It lasts until noon. Will you have lunch with me afterward?"

No. It was on the tip of her tongue, poised to come rushing out in tones of self-preservation. The less she saw of him, the less she would care, the less it would hurt when she was gone.

But the refusal her mind dictated wouldn't come out, perhaps because her heart so desperately wanted just the opposite. And, as usual for her, in a process that often caused her inconvenience or hardship and, on a few occasions, pain, she went with her heart instead of her mind. "Yes, Joshua," she said softly. "I'll have lunch with you."

A few hours later she lay curled on her side in bed. The room was dark, the silence broken only by the even sounds of Bess's breathing on one side, Keeley's on the other. Abby didn't know if they were asleep and didn't bother to find out. Keeley had been pensive all evening, and Bess had something—maybe that vet she'd been asking questions about?—on her mind, too. Neither of them had asked about her meeting with Joshua, although they'd both taken notice of her disappearance.

She was glad they'd given her this night of privacy. She knew from past experience that their questions would come, probably tomorrow. Maybe then she would be better equipped to answer them, but right now she didn't have a single answer, even for herself. All she had now were questions, doubts, fears . . . and the suspicion that Joshua may be right. Trying to ignore what was between them *would* be foolish.

Even if it led to heartache.

Monday

Abby sat in the back row of the classroom where Joshua's seminar had taken place and waited while he and the other members of the panel talked quietly with small groups from the audience, answering questions, listening to problems, offering suggestions. She had enjoyed the two-hour workshop—enjoyed the workshop itself, she wondered, or two hours of listening to and watching Joshua? His portion of the presentation had dealt with the benefits a staff psychologist could offer a corporation, ranging from matching the right applicant with the right job to dealing with stress to making the workplace a more pleasant—and, therefore, more efficient—environment.

But finally he was finished and coming up the aisle toward her. He shifted his briefcase to his left hand and loosened his tie with his right, then sat down across the aisle from her. "Hi."

She responded with a smile and a wiggle of her fingertips.

"I wasn't sure you would show up today."

"You thought kindhearted, sucker-for-a-sob-story, can't-say-no Abby would stand you up?" she asked teasingly.

"Well, put that way, no. You wouldn't stand up even the worst blind date."

"And I had some awful ones when I was in school," she said, thinking with a mental shudder of some of the guys Keeley had set her up with. "I enjoyed your talk."

"Thank you. Are you hungry?"

"You bet." She stood up and smoothed her skirt down. She knew that Joshua watched her do it with a decidedly warm look in his eyes.

"Did you bring any casual clothes with you?"

She glanced at her cotton skirt and print camp shirt with dismay. "This *is* casual."

He stood up, too, and they started out of the room together. "Don't you southern belles ever wear shorts or jeans?"

"From time to time," she said dryly. "But I read a study once that said women in the South wear skirts and dresses more often than women in any other part of the country."

"If they all have legs as gorgeous as yours, I'm sure the men in the South are quite grateful. But for a picnic, I think you might be more comfortable in shorts and flat shoes."

"All right," Abby agreed—as if she could possibly turn him down after a compliment like that. Then she gave him the once-over. "Are you going in a coat and tie?"

"I thought I'd go home and change, then meet you at the dorm."

They separated outside, Abby turning down the walk toward her dorm, Joshua heading in the opposite direction toward his house. She'd gone about twenty feet when he turned and called her name. "I'm glad you didn't change your mind."

She smiled as she watched him leave. So was she. Heaven help her, so was she.

It took her less than ten minutes to change and find a seat on the broad rim of the fountain in front of the dorm. She didn't know where Joshua lived and hadn't thought to ask how long it would take him to get back, but she didn't mind waiting, not when it was such a pretty day. She leaned back on her elbows, stretched her legs out and tilted her face, eyes closed, up to the warm sun.

"Well, well, what have we here?" a deep, thoroughly amused voice remarked. "She's too small to be a keeper. I ought to throw her back in and see if maybe she gets any bigger than a minnow."

Abby's eyes flew open, and she sat up, coming face-to-face with the tall, dark, incredibly handsome man crouched at her feet. "Dominic Vitalli!" she exclaimed, leaning forward to catch him in a hug. "Oh, it's good to see you! I figured you would have left East Ridley behind years ago! How have you been?"

"Getting by. I'd heard you finally came back—and Bess, too."

"How did you—" She bit off the question. Keeley. That would explain the personal business that had taken her away at lunch yesterday. It would also explain her introspection at last night's cocktail party. "Heavens, you are *still* the most gorgeous man I've ever seen."

"You don't look too bad yourself, kid. How's life been treating you?"

She shrugged and borrowed his own response. "I get by. What are you up to these days?"

"About six-two."

Abby groaned at the stale joke. "You haven't gotten any funnier in the past fifteen years, I see."

"And you haven't gotten any taller. Still doing good deeds?"

"I suppose you could call it that. What do you do?"

"As little as I can manage."

She didn't believe that. She had always expected him to be a real success someday, *if* he survived his relationship with Keeley. Impulsively she reached for his hand. "Are you married?"

"Not anymore. What about you?"

"Not anymore," she echoed.

They fell silent for a moment, Abby waiting for him to ask about Keeley. Surely that was the reason he was here. She couldn't imagine him hanging around the campus for anyone else. She was about to bring Keeley into the conversation herself when he suddenly looked at her and spoke again.

"Remember the night we got you to climb the library tower?"

Sixteen years later the memory could still make her shudder. "And you went behind me so I couldn't chicken out and go back down."

The stairway in the tower was steel and spiraled up for four stories before reaching the library roof, and Keeley and Dominic had goaded her into climbing it with them. It wasn't bad, they had insisted, just a simple winding staircase. She had accepted their challenge simply to prove once and for all that she wasn't *truly* afraid of heights. But the simple winding staircase had turned out to be ancient, shaky and steep, and the tower it had wound through was dark and musty. It had been like climbing through a well, and it had taken both Keeley and Dominic at their most persuasive to coax her down it again.

"If you weren't afraid of heights before that night, you certainly were after," he remarked. "It was kind of a mean thing to do, wasn't it?"

She smiled. Here in the bright sunlight, her feet only twenty-four inches above the ground, she could afford to be generous. "It wasn't so bad."

The silence came again, and his black gaze shifted away, focusing on the water in the fountain for a moment, then back to her. "Is she in the room by chance?"

How many times in the past had they talked about Keeley without ever mentioning her name? Abby wondered. She'd just always known that the only "she" who ever mattered to Dominic Vitalli was Keeley. "No, she's not."

"I just came from the tavern and the deli, and I checked the dining hall. She's not at any of them. Any suggestions?"

They had each had their favorite places. Bess's had been the tennis courts, Abby's the amphitheater, and Keeley's... "Have you tried the sculpture studio?"

The suggestion seemed to make sense to him. He stood up, stretching tall above her. "I will. Thanks, Abby. I'll see you around."

"Take care, Dom." She started to watch him, but got distracted by another arrival: Joshua.

"A friend of yours?" he asked, gesturing with one hand toward Dominic. "Or maybe an old flame?"

Abby tilted her head to one side to look up at him. "A friend. And the old flame of another friend. Is that lunch?"

He set the wicker basket beside her. "'A loaf of bread, a jug of wine...'"

She lifted the lid and looked inside. "Fried chicken, potato salad and brownies. It smells heavenly. Where do you want to go?"

He gazed down at her for a long moment. Where he *really* wanted to go had absolutely nothing to do with lunch... but then, neither did what he was really hungry for. She had changed as he'd suggested, trading her skirt for a pair of neatly tailored shorts that bared a fair expanse of thigh. He could feel his temperature rising—along with other things—and none of it could be blamed on the sun high overhead.

"Why not the same place as yesterday?" he suggested in a slightly hoarse voice. He'd planned to take her to the lake on the northeast boundary of the campus, but the very things that had made it appeal to him in the first place—the quiet, the solitude, the isolation—now made him change his mind. He wasn't sure he could trust himself so completely alone with her, not right now.

Abby made no objection to the library lawn. When they reached the tree, he settled on the grass, leaning back against the trunk, while she unpacked the meal. Her movements were fluid and graceful, no fuss, no wasted motion. Was she like that in bed, too? he wondered.

He fully intended to find out.

The assertion—even though it was only to himself— made him uncomfortable, as if he had somehow lured her here under false pretenses. She had agreed to make time for him. She *hadn't* agreed to make love with him. He suspected that, at the moment, even the suggestion would frighten her away.

So he wouldn't suggest it... yet. He would wait until she was more comfortable with him, more trusting. Until she realized that making love would be the most natural thing in the world for them.

And if she didn't reach that realization before Saturday?

He had some free time—the rest of the summer. And he'd always wanted to visit the South.

"What do you normally do in the summer when there isn't a conference going on?" Abby asked, handing him a china plate filled with food—china, she thought, when at home picnics meant paper plates and cans of soda.

"I get ready for the next school year, catch up on my reading, do some writing. Occasionally I go back to school myself."

"Sometimes I'd like to have a regular break from my job. If I could work three months, then take a month off, that would be ideal."

It wasn't often, Joshua suspected, that she deliberately turned the conversation to herself. With a quietly sympathetic question, he urged her to go on. "Social work can be tough at times, can't it?"

"I'm on the local child protection team, so my caseload is primarily abused children. It's grim."

Was that why she hadn't had any children of her own? he wondered. She would be a natural for motherhood. She was a caretaker by nature; she'd mothered her entire dorm through four years of college, and he would bet it hadn't stopped there. She probably filled the same role for her friends, her co-workers and the children she worked with. So why none of her own?

He didn't realized that he'd asked the question out loud until he felt her sudden look. "Sorry," he murmured. "I was just thinking...."

"Then do so quietly, please." But her smile took the sting out of the tart request.

He waited, but knew she wasn't going to answer him. Just as she had avoided talking about her marriage yesterday, she was going to avoid this, too. But that was all right. Someday she would tell him everything.

"There are a lot of different aspects to social work," he said, returning to the subject. "You could do something besides abuse."

"I suppose so. But the kids need somebody."

"And for right now, you're it."

She nodded. "Don't get me wrong. I love my job. But it can be pretty bleak. Sometimes I think I'm not helping any. Things aren't getting better—they're not even staying the same, only getting worse, it seems. In spite of all our work, people are still doing horrible things to their kids, and it's still very difficult to get the courts to remove a child permanently from an abusive home, and too often the intervention comes when it's too late for the child."

"What do your roommates do?"

The seemingly unconnected question made her frown. "Keeley owns a very prestigious art gallery in New York, and Bess is a banking whiz in Boston."

Joshua twisted the cap off the thermos and filled their glasses with tea, then offered one to her. "Not that your points aren't valid, but I wonder if your disillusionment with your job right now doesn't have something to do with being here, being with them."

Abby tasted the tea and grimaced. "I lived here for four years and never got used to this stuff. Sometime I'll show you the proper way to make it." Then she responded to his suggestion. "I thought your passion was teaching, Doctor. *Not* analysis."

"It's an occupational hazard." He defended himself with a charming grin. "I can't help it any more than you can help worrying about the problems in your job when you're halfway across the country on vacation."

She drew a drumstick from the container and bit into it. After washing it down with the weak tea, she admitted, "You're right, though. As soon as I got on the plane to come up here, I began comparing my job to Bess's and Keeley's careers, and it didn't quite measure up. They both make a fortune, and they get to travel, and they meet important people. Working for the state, my salary falls well below the 'fortune' level, and the extent of my travel is to the local hospitals and the courthouse."

"But you meet important people, too," he pointed out. "Every one of those kids you work with. They're the most important people of all."

Abby stared at him for a moment before turning her attention to her meal. In that last sentence, he'd summed up all the reasons why she'd chosen social work as a career. A lot of people had never understood it, including her family and Darryl—especially Darryl. Only a fool went to college for six years to work in a field that paid little better than slave wages, he'd told her. After a few years in practice, he would be making five times what she was, he'd insisted. And he probably had been. She didn't know, because by then, of course, they'd been divorced.

But Joshua understood.

"It takes a very special person to do what you do, Abby," he continued quietly. "You can't compare your job to your friends'. You can't measure your success against theirs. I don't think money was ever that important to you, or you would have chosen a different field in the first place. I don't think travel or meeting people matters much to you, either. But helping people does. Knowing that you've done your best to protect one child, to make one child's world safer and happier—that's what counts. That's success, Abby. And you've done that."

His words and solemn voice gave her a warm feeling inside. She'd told herself the same things many times in the past fifteen years, but they sounded different coming from someone else—especially from someone she respected. They made her own occasional doubts and suspected inadequacies fade away, forgotten in the glow of praise.

The conversation turned to topics of little importance, subjects that required little concentration from Abby. She was grateful for that, since the only thing her mind seemed to want to think about was Joshua. What had drawn him to her? she wondered. What did he see when he looked at her? And, most importantly, what did he want from her?

There was no doubt of what she wanted from him: anything he could give. Everything. And she wanted to give him everything of herself in return. She wanted to be his friend, his lover, but she didn't want to suffer because of it. And, in spite of his promise last night that he wouldn't hurt her, there was nothing he could do to prevent it from happening anyway. What did she expect from falling for a man who lived more than seven hundred miles and another world away?

The tower clock chimed one o'clock while they talked, then one-thirty. Finally Abby reluctantly packed away the remains of their lunch, wiped her hands one last time on her linen napkin, then got to her feet. "I've got to go," she said reluctantly. "There's a workshop at two o'clock that I'd like to catch, and I need to change clothes first."

Joshua picked up the basket, and they started back toward her dorm. When they got there, Abby stopped on the third step to say goodbye. It put her on eye level with him. "Thank you."

"For what?"

"For lunch. For understanding about my job. For..." She sighed. "Everything."

He reached out with his free hand and captured hers. "You want to show your gratitude? Meet me right here at six-thirty."

She thought of the reasons why she should say no: she had come to see Keeley and Bess, yet she had spent little time with them so far; she was only going to be here five more days; she was already in over her head. Then she smiled just a bit sadly and nodded. "I'll be here."

Joshua took her to his house, a neat two-story structure that must have been a bit small with three kids but seemed big and empty for one man alone. Abby liked it from the moment she stood on the stoop and waited for him to unlock the door. She liked the contrast of the black shutters with the white siding, the symmetry of the three evenly spaced dormers upstairs, and the sprawling yard with its rosebushes and shade trees and wide open expanses just right for kids to play.

The inside was even nicer: welcoming, comfortably decorated rooms; gleaming wood floors; rough stone fireplaces; family photos everywhere, and a combination kitchen-dining-family room that stretched across the entire back of the house. After a quick tour of the downstairs, including Joshua's homey, cluttered office, they ended up in the kitchen, where she sat on a tall stool at the tile-topped cooking island while he started dinner. They didn't go upstairs, but the only thing up there, she reflected, twisting a small clay duck in circles, would be bedrooms. The mere thought of seeing

Joshua's bedroom, the place where he slept, the place where he loved, made her mouth go dry.

Did he want to make love with her? He'd done nothing overt to lead her to think so—that tiny little kiss on the hand didn't count—but she believed he did. She believed—hoped?—he wanted her as much as she wanted him.

And, heaven help her, she did want him. She'd been alone a long time, and it had never really bothered her. Oh, there had been times when she'd longed for a man's touch, for a nerve-tingling caress, for the sweet fulfillment only lovemaking could bring, but the man at those times had been anonymous, some faceless fantasy with no basis in reality, no identity. But Joshua was most definitely real. He was no fantasy, but a flesh-and-blood man standing less than four feet away, and she longed for *his* touch, *his* caress, *his* lovemaking.

But if he offered any of those things—or all of them—could she accept? Would she find the courage? Or would she run and hide, telling herself that it was better this way, that she wouldn't be hurt, that when she got back to Carolina she would forget the desire, the hunger, the need . . . and the man?

"How do you feel about being back at Bartlett?" Joshua asked as he set aside the pork medallions he'd been working with and began slicing the vegetables piled in a nearby bowl.

"It's been nice. I always liked it here."

"But not better than your big city."

"Columbia isn't so big," she protested.

"East Ridley has fewer than nine thousand residents. Columbia is your state capitol. It's got to be significantly bigger."

"Only about ten times or so. But it's nice. There are a lot of advantages to living in a city."

He sliced a thin piece of celery and ate it, then offered her the next one. "There are more advantages to a small town," he offered. "We have almost everything a city has except the crowds, the traffic and the crime. And we're less than two hours from Boston, if you really can't live without those things. We have virtually every business you'd find in a city, a hospital and some good doctors and dentists, and through the college we get plays and concerts and athletic events and—"

"You don't have to convince me," she interrupted with a laugh. "I liked East Ridley when I lived here before."

But had she liked it well enough to live here again? he wondered. Maybe he was rushing things—one thing he knew he absolutely could not do with her—but if he was going to romance this woman, he had to look to the future. And the simple fact was that if she gave him—gave *them*—a chance, that future looked pretty permanent. Not a frequent-visits-between-Massachusetts-and-South Carolina affair, but married-and-living-together permanence.

Of course, that didn't mean she had to be the one to move. He'd already known from their earlier conversation that the University of South Carolina was located in Columbia, and further checking had revealed several small private colleges there, too. Relocating would mean a setback in achieving the final goal he'd set for himself—head of his own department—but he could deal with that.

But, honestly, he had to admit that he would be happier staying right here. Dr. Saxon was scheduled to retire in two years, and Joshua was virtually guaranteed to be his replacement. He would still be within two hours of his kids, and finding a job would pose no problem for Abby. With a master's in social work, she could have her choice of positions, ranging from working for the state to something at the local hospital, from the county health department to the college.

He poured the vegetables into a large pan that smoked with hot oil, seasoned them and gave them a stir, then began hulling a bowl of chilled strawberries. "Tell me what you like most about South Carolina," he requested.

Abby filched a berry and bit into it, savoring its sweetness. "It's home. My family has lived there since the early 1700s. My ancestors fought at Cowpens, Kings Mountain and Fort Sumter." She finished the berry and licked a splash of juice from one fingertip, completely oblivious to the effect the gesture had on him. "More importantly, my family *still* lives there—my brothers and sisters and nieces and nephews and aunts and uncles and cousins. There are well over a hundred of us in Richland County alone."

"And you're close to your family?"

"I practically raised my brothers and sisters. My father was killed when the youngest was barely five, and my mother was never a strong person. Holding on to her job was all she could manage, so running the household and taking care of the kids fell to me, since I was the oldest. Mom died four years ago, so I'm more or less the head of the family now."

"And you help them out, loan them money, give them advice and take care of their children."

"Yeah, I guess so." She reached for another berry, and he playfully slapped her fingers away, then fed it to her himself.

"You do that with your friends, too, don't you? And the people you work with, and the rest of your family, and probably with complete strangers you meet on the street. If anyone needs advice, help, a favor or a sympathetic shoulder, they go straight to dear Abby, don't they?" He gave a shake of his head. "And what do you get in return?"

"Not a lot." She covered her frankness with a sweet smile. "What can I say? I'm a chump."

Joshua held out his hands, waiting until she hesitantly placed hers in them, then curled his fingers tightly around hers. "I'll make you a promise, and I want you to keep it in mind the next few days, okay?" At her nod, he solemnly continued. "I'll never ask for anything from you that I'm not one hundred percent willing to give of myself in return. Don't ever forget that, Abby."

He considered leaning over, pulling her closer and sealing the promise with a kiss, but the faintly acrid smell of near-burning vegetables forced him to put the idea out of his mind. Reluctantly he released her and turned back to the pans on the stove.

That was a close call, Abby thought, sliding off the stool and wandering away from the island. For a moment there, she'd thought he was going to kiss her—*really* kiss her—and if he had, she would have been lost. She would have told him that she didn't need promises, that he could have whatever part of her he wanted, that she would be happy with whatever part of himself he chose to give.

But she *did* need promises. She needed to be sure, needed to know that she wasn't on the verge of making another major mistake. She wanted to trust him, wanted to believe in him, but she had trusted and believed in Darryl, and look how that had ended. She had lost her pride and suffered a blow to her ego and self-esteem that she'd thought might never heal.

Joshua, if he chose, if he were that sort of man, could be even more devastating than her ex-husband had been. His training as a psychologist had taught him to hear what she didn't say as clearly as what she did, to read her emotions, to analyze her actions. Getting over Darryl would seem like a day at the beach compared to the misery Joshua could put her through.

She stopped in front of the framed photographs hanging on one wall. Jason, David and Cassie. Jason was twenty-three and looked a great deal like his father had when she'd first met him. He was handsome, with the same intense blue eyes that were watching her now from across the room. He was serious in most of the photos, but the last showed the same wicked grin that his father often used to his advantage.

David Lucas also resembled Joshua, but with a lighter air, more carefree, less responsible. He was probably a terrible tease, she suspected, and made his family's lives unbearable from time to time.

Cassie was the odd one out. If a stranger saw the three of them together, he would know immediately that Jason and David were brothers, but never guess Cassie was their sister. She had the kind of beauty that made people stop in their tracks and give her a second look. Her face was delicately shaped, her complexion pure porcelain, her hair black and her eyes... Abby stretched onto her toes and leaned closer to the largest picture to be sure.

"Violet," Joshua said from directly behind her.

She let her feet sink to the floor again and felt his chest against her back. "She's beautiful."

"Yes, she is," he agreed. "Marla—her mother—used to say that she couldn't quite believe we had created such a gorgeous child. Of course, every parent believes that his sons are handsome and his daughters are pretty, but Cassie..." He gave a bemused shake of his head, then glanced down at Abby. "You're shorter tonight."

She extended one foot. "Sensible shoes." She'd unpacked the only pair of jeans she'd brought and traded her heels for the comfort of tennis shoes.

He laid his hands on her shoulders, and she stiffened. It had taken most of her willpower not to move away reflexively when she'd found him standing so close behind her. Now she concentrated on not jerking free and taking refuge on the other side of the big room.

Slowly he turned her around and held her a short distance away. His eyes were as bright as she'd remembered in the classroom, but tonight his passion wasn't for teaching, but for her. Only her. No man had ever looked at her quite that way, she thought. No man had ever made her feel quite this way.

So *why,* she wondered woefully, was she so afraid to accept what he was so ready to give?

Joshua seemed to change his mind about whatever he'd been about to say—or do. Instead, he smiled absently, lifted his hands from her shoulders and said, "Dinner's ready."

She was relieved—and disappointed. She wanted to call him back as he walked to the table he'd set earlier, wanted to ask him to touch her again. She wanted to say that she wasn't hungry, that they could skip dinner and just make love instead. She wanted to tell him that she needed him close, beside her, against her, inside her.

And she wanted to tell him that she was sorry, but she simply couldn't risk this. She couldn't put her heart on the line. She couldn't trust him, couldn't even trust herself. Then she wanted to run away, all the way back to Carolina, where she would be safe.

But she did none of those things. She straightened her shoulders, found a smile and went quietly to the table.

It was nearly midnight when Joshua walked back to the dorm with Abby. They were quiet as they walked across the campus—because in the past five and a half hours they'd done nothing but talk? she wondered. Or because they might regret the things they would say on a seductively beautiful night like this?

Joshua drew her off the sidewalk and stopped beneath a tree twenty yards from the dorm. The low-hanging branches overhead sheltered them from the harsh glow of a nearby street lamp and offered them privacy.

"I have to go to Springfield tomorrow," he said softly as he leaned back against the tree. "I won't be back until about five. Will you have dinner with me again?"

"Yes."

"There's a concert in the amphitheater in the evening. Would you like to go?"

"Yes."

His smile was barely visible in the shadows, but Abby heard it in his voice. "You're being awfully agreeable," he teased as he reached out and, catching her hand, pulled her toward him. "Makes me wish I was asking different questions."

When he'd drawn her as close as he could, he lowered his head for one kiss, one simple, uncomplicated, good-night kiss. Her mouth was soft, her flavor sweet. He sampled it once, then again, then started to raise his head. He was surprised when Abby, until now submissive, suddenly raised her hands to his face, her fingers satiny warm on his jaw, and pulled him down again. She kissed him with a hunger that quickly fired his own, her tongue darting into his mouth, her kiss flavored with urgency, with heat and pure aching need.

He braced himself against the tree trunk and slid his arms around her, enfolding her slender body, pressing it against his own. Desire, swift, strong and relentless, swept through him, beginning and ending in the sweet, liquid heat of their kiss. While he wanted more, so much more, he could be satisfied, he thought in a daze, with this kind of passion, this kind of fire.

If she'd ever been foolish enough to have any doubts about what Joshua wanted from her or what she wanted from him, Abby knew they were settled now. Her entire body throbbed. Her breasts were swollen and achy, and the heated, shocky sensations that were swirling low in her belly made her tremble. She couldn't remember ever wanting—no, *needing*—anything as badly as she needed Joshua right this instant, and the heated, rigid length of his arousal pressing against her thigh assured her he was equally affected. If he'd kissed her like this at his house, she had no doubt she would have asked him—pleaded with him—to make love to her. If this didn't stop, she might ask anyway.

As if reading her mind, he forced an end to the kiss an instant later. Before she could do anything more than drag in a heavy breath, he threaded his fingers through her hair, pressed her face against his chest and held her tightly. His knit shirt was soft beneath her cheek. She could hear the thud of his heart, as rapid and uneven as hers.

Finally he released her as if he hated to let her go. "The concert starts at eight," he murmured, his voice unsteady. "I'll pick you up at six, all right?"

She nodded.

He touched her hair, smoothing his palm over it, then abruptly withdrew his hand. "Go inside now."

She left the shadows, passed the fountain with its softly splashing water and hurried inside the dorm. There she paused and looked back. She couldn't see him under the tree, but she knew he was there.

She could feel him.

Tuesday

Tuesday afternoon found Abby at the tennis courts, stretched out in the sun and watching Bess and Keeley play. Tennis on a lazy summer afternoon seemed such a waste of energy...unless you had excess energy to burn, which both women seemed to. She suspected that Keeley was involved with Dominic Vitalli again; in the past, their relationship had often led her to blow off more than a little steam. She thought Bess was seeing someone, too, although she couldn't imagine who. Dates had been few and far between for Bess when they were in college. Her part-time jobs and long hours of study hadn't left much time for something as frivolous as men. Whoever the man was, Abby hoped he appreciated what he had in Bess.

Shading her eyes against the sun, she checked her watch. Only four hours until she saw Joshua again. Funny how quickly things could change. A few days ago she'd been plodding along in her dull, routine, boring life, satisfied that this was as good as it would get. Now she felt like a giddy, full-of-hope, ready-for-her-first-romance schoolgirl. She felt younger and more care-free. She felt, for the first time in years, that life *could* get better.

And that when the reunion was over and she was back home in Carolina, it could go back to dull, routine and boring.

She pushed that thought firmly out of her mind. Like another southern belle, Scarlett O'Hara, she would think about that tomorrow—or a few tomorrows from now. For the present, though, she would enjoy what she had: Joshua, and lazy afternoons with Keeley and Bess.

It was just like old times. She couldn't begin to count the number of times she'd sat here on the grass, sunning herself while watching Bess and Keeley play a wickedly competitive game of tennis. She could, however, count the number of times she'd actually tried to play with them: three. Endowed with natural athletic ability—Bess—and natural grace—Keeley—her roommates had insisted on trying to teach her the game. Having neither athletic ability nor grace, she'd been utterly hopeless. Keeley had insisted such bad play had to be deliberate; no one with even a smattering of coordination could be as truly awful as Abby was. Bess had defended her and persevered with the lessons, until one of Abby's unfortunate backswings knocked her practically senseless. Then they'd decided she was better off on the sidelines, after all, or rather that *they* were better off with her on the sidelines.

The questions she'd been expecting from them about Joshua had finally come. What was he like? Did they have much in common? Did she enjoy his company? What did they talk about? What did they do? What had happened to his marriage? Was the man as good as the fantasy she'd cherished so many years ago?

And she had good-naturedly answered their questions, never considering that she would be perfectly within her rights to tell them it was none of their business. She hadn't even minded the questions that were a bit personal. They'd always gotten personal with each other—within limits, of course. After all, friends were entitled, weren't they?

Bess had ended the interrogation on a soft note. "Although there are dozens of women here who are green with envy," she'd said with a hesitant pat, "we can't think of anyone else we'd rather see win the good doctor's affection, Abby."

She had appreciated her roommates' sentiments, but darn it, she thought now, affection just wasn't enough. She wanted passion, respect, liking and lust.

When had she become so greedy? She'd spent most of her life mothering others, giving to others, and had been satisfied—more or less—with whatever they gave in return. Now that wasn't enough. She wanted Joshua.

She wanted love.

She wanted it all.

The grandfather clock in the hallway chimed five o'clock when Joshua let himself into the house. He went upstairs to the bedroom and began undressing. If he hurried, he would have time for a shower and a shave before he had to pick up Abby for dinner. He'd had a hard time—accurately phrased, he thought with a grin—getting to sleep last night, and when he had drifted off, she had been in his dreams with her lovely smile, her sweet southern drawl and her surprisingly passionate kisses. She'd been on his mind all day today. Now, in less than an hour, he would see her.

Noticing the blinking light on the answering machine beside his bed, he sat down, punched the playback button, then began unlacing his shoes.

"Hi, Daddy, it's Cassie. Heads up—Mom's on the warpath, and I'm sure she'll be calling you. I love you."

He rolled his eyes. That was a typical daughter-in-distress message. She always gave him warnings when Marla was angry, but she rarely offered any details he might use in her defense.

After a beep came her mother's call. "Joshua, this is Marla. If you're screening your calls, will you please pick up the phone? We have to talk about your daughter."

At least now he could judge the severity of Cassie's offense. When she was brilliant, well behaved or only slightly mischievous, she was Marla's daughter. When she'd done something her mother found totally unacceptable, she was Joshua's.

When the answering machine shut off, he dialed Marla's number. As usual, a stuffy, formal servant answered; then his ex-wife came on the line. "Where have you been all day?" she demanded. "I tried to call you."

"You left *one* message, Marla. Look, I just got in, and I've got to leave again soon, so make this short. What's the problem?"

Her voice changed from sharp to curious. "Why do you have to leave again?"

"I have a date."

"With anyone I know?"

"No." Thank heavens, he added silently. Abby had experienced enough difficult people without adding Marla to the list. "What has Cassie done now?"

"She's quit school."

"And?"

"She says she's going to be a model."

He shifted the phone and pulled his shirt over his head, then kicked off his tennis shoes and peeled off his socks. "Well, she's certainly got the face for it."

"Joshua, you're a college professor, for God's sake. You *know* how important education is."

The strident disapproval in her voice made him wince. He could remember a time—vaguely—when she hadn't spoken like that to him, when she'd always been sweet and encouraging and loving. Then she'd found out that he wasn't going to make her a prominent doctor's wife in Boston society, and all the softness had disappeared. "I wouldn't *be* a college professor, Marla, if you'd gotten your way," he reminded her. "Of course education is important for Cassie, but so is doing what she wants. If she really wants to be a model—"

"Don't be ridiculous. I don't want *my* daughter throwing away her future on something as ludicrous as modeling."

He lay back on the bed, his feet still on the floor, and closed his eyes. "Top models make top money, Marla. They're stars, known the world over. They have everything you used to find so important—money, prestige, celebrity. I'll talk to Cassie and see how serious she is about this, but if she really wants to be a model, I'm not going to discourage her. I'll give her all the support she needs—so you won't have to worry about it. I've got to go now. Goodbye."

He depressed the button on the handset to cut off the call, then simply lay there, still holding the phone. That brief, long-distance contact with Marla had dampened the high spirits Abby had kept him in all day. But just the thought of Abby smoothed the rough edges, drained the frustration, eased the tension. He would see her soon, would sit across from her at dinner, beside her at the concert, and he would kiss her again. Maybe that was all, just a kiss. Maybe it was still too soon to expect anything more from her…but it would be enough. Until she trusted him as much as she wanted him, her kisses would be enough.

Wednesday

Abby sat at the end of the sofa in the family room, her back against the padded arm, her bare feet tucked between two cushions, and watched Joshua while he talked on the kitchen phone. It felt natural, being in his house, making herself comfortable, watching him. As if she belonged here. As if she belonged with him.

This was her fifth evening in East Ridley, and she'd spent some portion of each one with him—Saturday and Sunday at the conference, Monday night at dinner here, last night at dinner and the concert, and here she was again tonight. It was getting to be a habit, one she could gladly live with.

She knew he was talking to his daughter, that incredibly beautiful creature whose photographs smiled at her from the wall. He'd told her last night about Cassie's dilemma—school or a modeling career—and her mother's response to it. She knew without asking that Joshua would encourage Cassie to do what was right for her. She knew, too, that what was right for Cassie didn't even enter into Marla's thoughts.

He was a good father. He loved his kids dearly and wasn't ashamed to show it. He was exactly the kind of father she had hoped Darryl would be, but, of course, he hadn't been. Children hadn't been in Darryl's plans. Nothing that would have diverted her time, attention or the money she made from him had been in his plans.

She stretched out her legs and slid a little lower on the sofa. Tonight had been one of the most pleasant evenings in recent memory. Recent? she silently scoffed. One of the most pleasant evenings *ever*. And the funny thing was, they hadn't done anything special. Joshua had met her at the dorm with a fragrant pale yellow rose plucked from one of his bushes. They had walked over to the Town Tavern for dinner, then had come here to his house. They had talked comfortably, companionably, like old friends—almost like old lovers—all evening until Cassie's phone call. A simple, unexciting evening, and she had enjoyed it tremendously.

"You have my word, sweetheart," she heard him say into the phone. "You finish the summer session, and I'll support you in whatever you decide to do afterward." After a pause for her response, he continued, "You know you can call me anytime. I love you, Cass."

When he hung up, he came to join Abby on the couch. "The longer the distance and the higher the phone rates, the more that girl talks," he teased.

"She's lucky to have you to turn to."

"I don't want to influence her too much on this. I'd like to see her get her degree, but I want her to be happy. And God knows she's getting enough pressure from her mother. She doesn't need it from me."

"You're a good father, Joshua."

He looked at her for a long moment, the way he'd been looking at her all evening. She was so pretty, so delicate, so *precious*, that just looking at her filled him with the ache to love her. She didn't have to speak, didn't have to do a thing, to start the longing. She only had to exist.

Slowly he shook his head in response to her remark. "I don't want you to see me as a father, Abby, or an instructor or a psychologist or anything except a man. I want you to see me as a man who wants very much to kiss you. A man who wants to make love to you.'' His voice became huskier. ''A man who wants to be a part of you. God, Abby...''

For an instant her expression was startled, and he feared he'd made a terrible mistake. Maybe she wasn't ready to hear this. Maybe she needed more time.

But *he* needed *her.*

Then she extended her hand to him and, when he took it, drew him closer. He moved to his knees beside the sofa, still clasping her hand tightly in his, using the other to brace himself as he leaned down to meet her kiss. There was nothing practiced about the kiss. It was, like Abby herself, sweet, innocent and incredibly sexy.

Once she'd begun it, she seemed more than willing to let him take control, and he did, pressing his mouth to hers, biting gently at her lower lip, savoring its softness with his tongue. When he probed, she opened to him, and he slid his tongue between her teeth, into the moist warmth that awaited it. Eyes closed, lost in the kiss, he was enveloped by hazy sensations of heat, scorching and consuming; of need that clawed in his belly, twisting and cutting; of desire so powerful that it made him weak; and, curiously, of despair that, if he loved and lost her, he would lose himself.

When she twisted her fingers, he released them and swallowed a groan the instant her hand flattened against his chest. She must be able to feel the pounding of his heart beneath her palm. It was so frantic that he could feel it in other parts of his body and could hear it echoing in his ears, along with the labored sound of his— her? their?—breathing.

Then she raised her other hand to his body, sliding them both down over the nubby texture of his shirt, pulling it free of his jeans so she could touch his skin. The branding made him groan with pure tormented pleasure, and he slid his fingers into her hair, holding her steady while he deepened the kiss.

So many sensations were coursing through her that her system was on overload. She was hot, as if a fever burned through her, and unable to think or reason—only feel. And what she felt was exquisite. Every nerve in her body was alive and tuned to Joshua, every one greedily crying for more.

She was dimly aware of pushing his shirt up, exposing more of his warm, velvet-soft skin to her hands. He left her mouth only long enough to pull the shirt off and toss it aside, then returned to kiss her again. She explored his chest and back with her fingers, taking pleasure in his pleasure, delighting in his shudder when her nails grazed his nipples. In spite of the kiss and his tongue in her mouth, she laughed softly deep in her throat, relishing his response, evoking another with her wickedly innocent caresses.

Then he offered his own caress, his long fingers gliding down to her breast, capturing her nipple, and her amusement faded in a rush of hunger so intense that it was painful. Teasingly, he removed his hand then, but she captured it and brought it back, then fumbled with the buttons that closed her shirt. Finally Joshua had to undo them for her. He tugged the fabric from the waistband of her slacks, lifted her and removed the shirt, then sent her bra following it to the floor.

For a moment after he lowered her to the sofa again, he simply looked at her, and she watched him. What did he see? she wondered. But she knew: pale skin, breasts too large for her small frame, and an average waist.

She was even more beautiful unclothed, Joshua thought, his emotions bordering on awe. Her skin was creamy and smooth, her breasts full and lush and crested with delicate rose-shaded nipples, and her waist was impossibly small. She was every fantasy he'd ever had. She was perfect.

Made uneasy by his stare, she raised her hands to cover her breasts, but he caught her wrists in a gentle grip and returned them to her sides. "No," he whispered. "Don't hide from me, sweetheart. Don't ever hide from . . ."

The last word was lost as his lips closed around her nipple, tugging at it, creating a sweet torture that made her cry out. She clung to him, one hand on his shoulder, the other buried in his thick, dark hair, while he suckled and teased and aroused her.

Gently he lifted her from the couch, laying her on the floor beside him, covering her body with his, then resuming his sensuously punishing kisses. His weight bore her into the thick carpet, his heat warmed her bare skin, and his hardness seared her thigh. He was thoroughly aroused, she realized. Ready to make love. Ready to take this relationship through its natural progression, from friend to lover. Ready to take it one step closer to blissful completion. One step closer to heartache.

That single word spread a chill through her, chasing away Joshua's warmth, denying her own arousal. *Heartache.* What else could come of this? What else could follow what was sure to be an exquisite sharing, not only of bodies, but of hearts and souls—or, at least, *her* heart, *her* soul? In three more days she would be home in Carolina. She would be alone. Without

Joshua. Without much chance of seeing him again until next year's conference/reunion. Without any indication that he would want to see her even then.

"No," she whispered, the small word heavy with fear and regret, with anguish and dismay. With pain. "No, Joshua, don't. Stop, please."

He was sure his clouded mind hadn't heard her correctly until he realized that her caresses had turned to a struggle to escape his greater weight. Puzzled, he moved aside, and she scrambled up, moving a safe distance away, turning her back to him and staring into the cold, empty fireplace. He lay on his side, braced on one elbow, and tried to figure out what had gone wrong. It wasn't easy when his body was protesting its loss, when his need was still so great that he gritted his teeth with it, when his disappointment was so strong his heart ached with it.

"Abby?" He spoke uncertainly as he reached out and touched the rigid line of her spine, bare to the waist, in a tentative caress. The muscles beneath his fingers grew taut, but he refused to withdraw his hand. If she suddenly found his touch unbearable, she would have to say so, because he couldn't simply switch off his desire for contact.

She gave a great shuddering sigh, then bowed her head. "I'm sorry, Joshua," she whispered miserably. "I'm so sorry. I thought... I didn't think..." She shook her head, her down-soft hair shimmering in the soft light. "I'm sorry."

"Is my timing off? Am I pushing you too hard? Are you afraid? Are you not ready for this?" Then he paused, and a shadow of hurt joined the bewilderment in his voice. "Is it *me,* Abby? You don't want *me?*"

She laughed, but it sounded more like a prelude to tears. "I never knew I could want so badly."

He sat up, too, adjusting his jeans over his swollen sex before settling behind her. "Then what's wrong, Abby? Tell me, please. Maybe I can help."

Nothing could help, she thought sadly, short of a vow of undying love or a promise of forever. Those were things Joshua certainly wasn't prepared to give, not for a few nights' sex. "I just need time," she whispered.

Cautiously he let his hand slide around to her shoulder. When she didn't protest, he moved closer behind her, his legs open wide to cradle her hips, his arms wrapped tightly around her, one above her breasts, the other below. "It's all right," he said, nuzzling his cheek against her hair. "Take all the time you need. I'll be here when you decide."

Would he? she wondered. Or would he go back to his other women once she was gone? Surely there *were* other women. He was too handsome, too virile, too darned sexy, for her to believe otherwise. Would he choose one of them to relieve the arousal she wasn't capable of satisfying right now?

She was afraid to consider the answer.

They sat there for a while in silence. Finally Abby stirred, moving out of his arms, reaching for the clothing he'd thrown carelessly to the floor. Keeping her back to him, she laid his shirt beside him, then quickly put on her own clothes. When she finally faced him, she couldn't quite meet his eyes. "I think I'd better go back to the dorm now."

But Joshua wasn't going to let her off so easily. He rose to his knees and caught her chin in a gentle grip, forcing her head up. "Look at me, Abby," he commanded.

Her gaze stalled when it reached his mouth, and he gave her a little shake. "Look at me."

Finally she did. Her eyes were troubled; his were concerned.

"What happened here isn't going to change things between us. You're not going to pull away or avoid me to keep me at arm's length. Things were moving a bit too fast for you, that's all. It's no big deal. I can wait. I can wait as long as it takes. Do you understand that?"

She nodded mutely.

"Understand this, too." He kissed her, swiftly fitting his mouth to hers, renewing the desire, rekindling the heat. Just as quickly, he ended it. "This is special, and it's not going to change. We don't have to rush into anything before we lose it, because we're not going to lose it. It'll be the same a week, a month, or even ten years from now. Understand?"

Once again she nodded.

He pulled his shirt over his head and tugged it down, then handed her shoes to her. "I'll walk you home now."

Abby sat in the middle of her bed, her knees drawn to her chest, her fingers laced tightly together. After the mess she'd made of this evening's date with Joshua, she hadn't wanted anything more than the peaceful anonymity of darkness and the snug cocoon of her bed. She hadn't wanted a serious discussion of flaws and shortcomings, of hopes and dreams and losses. But it had started, first with a discussion about Keeley's treatment of Dominic fifteen years ago, leading into her aloofness.

It hurt Keeley to hear that Abby and Bess had considered her remote. Abby heard it in her voice when she protested, when she reminded them that when Abby's mother died, *she* was the one Abby had turned to for comfort. It had meant a lot to her to be asked, especially since, she went on to add, it was the first time Abby had ever asked for anything from her.

"You were always so damn selfless, Abby," Bess put in from her corner of the dark room. "You never needed anything from anyone. You were always giving, never taking."

This time, Abby knew the hurt was in her own voice. "Do you think I enjoyed that? Don't you know there were dozens of times when I just wanted to say, 'No, I can't help you. Leave me alone'?"

"Then why didn't you?" Keeley challenged. "If you didn't like playing the selfless martyr, why didn't you just say no?"

"I couldn't do that."

"Why not?" Bess asked. "I did. Keeley did. Everyone did—except you. You let us all take advantage of you. You let us use you. Why didn't you tell Keeley to buy her own panty hose? Why didn't you tell me to find someone else to tutor me in French? Why didn't you tell everyone in the whole dorm to grow up and look out for themselves and quit relying on dear Abby to mother them?"

"You were my friends," she protested. "It's natural to do favors for your friends."

"Yes, it is," Keeley agreed. "It's your nature to be generous, Abby. But you carry it too far sometimes. You give to others at your own expense. Do you know how often we wished you would display even the tiniest bit of selfishness like the rest of us? Do you know how tiresome it was to live with someone who was *always* giving and never accepting anything from us in return?''

''You gave me something.'' Her voice was soft with pain, her southern drawl pronounced.

''What? Gifts? Trinkets?''

''Friendship. That was all I ever wanted from either of you, and you gave me that.''

''But not because you did things for us. We *liked* you, Abby,'' Bess said. ''We liked you for who you were, not for what you did.''

''It's okay to tell your friends no once in a while,'' Keeley added. ''If they're real friends, they'll love you anyway.''

She thought about the few times she'd tried to stand up to her ex-husband, the very few times she hadn't given when he'd asked. ''Darryl didn't.''

''Darryl was a jerk,'' the other two women said in unison.

After a moment's laughter, Bess continued, an awkward note creeping into her voice. ''You could have told us no, Abby.''

Abby leaned back against the headboard, letting their continuing conversation weave through the darkness around her. They would have liked her anyway—no, would have *loved* her anyway. Even if she hadn't given them so much of her time and attention. Even if she hadn't sacrificed her own needs and desires for theirs. Even if she had occasionally been selfish. They were real friends.

No matter how her romance with Joshua turned out, Abby thought with a bittersweet smile, she would return to South Carolina with a precious gift: the knowledge that Keeley and Bess were real best friends.

Thursday

Abby sighed softly and settled her gaze on the playing field in front of her. It was another warm day, and she fanned herself lazily with the wrinkled conference schedule she'd found in her purse. One of Bartlett's traditional rivals, holding its own reunion this week, had challenged the school to a field hockey game, and, since Bess was playing, Abby and Keeley had opted to come and watch.

They'd chatted for a while, mostly about the man on the sidelines whom they'd pegged as Bess's veterinarian. Abby had first noticed him when she'd seen that Bess's attention was often directed his way, and later his cheers—not for the team, but for Bess herself—had confirmed his identity. Then the conversation had moved naturally from Bess's man to their own. Ask Dominic to tomorrow night's banquet, she'd urged Keeley, without admitting that she hadn't yet found the courage to invite Joshua as her own date.

Her roommate had fallen silent, considering the idea, and Abby had turned back to watching the game. That seemed to be the story of her life, she thought morosely: always watching from the sidelines, never out there in the thick of things herself.

Oh, but that wasn't true. She'd been in the thick of it last night, and what had happened? She'd faltered. Dropped the ball, missed the serve, struck out. Maybe she wasn't meant for *any* type of physical activity, not just athletics.

Joshua had been so sweet about it. When any other man would have been furious and made insulting remarks about her character, Joshua had reassured her instead. He had held her and comforted and soothed her. He hadn't made any demands, hadn't used her guilt against her, hadn't tried to make her feel even worse.

So, of course, she did.

Maybe she should talk to Joshua, tell him what was on her mind. Tell him that she was afraid of getting hurt. Tell him that she was afraid to trust him. Tell him that she was just plain afraid.

Sure, she thought sarcastically. Finding the nerve to say all that was about as likely as her telling him that she wanted a future with him. That she wanted permanence. That she wanted to spend the rest of her life in East Ridley with him.

Wouldn't it be nice, she thought wistfully, if Bess stayed with her vet, if Keeley settled down with Dominic, and if *she* wound up with Joshua? To face the future arm in arm and side by side with the man and the two friends she loved the most? But would Bess give up her high-powered banking career for love? Or Keeley her renowned art gallery? There was no doubt what her own decision would be. She could find a job anywhere; a man she could love was harder to come by.

For a long moment she sat numbly. That was twice she'd put Joshua and love into the same sentence. Was her subconscious trying to tell her something? While she'd been worrying about caring too much for him, had she gone and fallen in love with him?

She was startled out of her reverie when Keeley dropped a brown paper bag in her lap. "For the hose," she said casually.

Abby opened the flat bag with little interest, expecting to find that, for the first time in their lives, Keeley had repaid panty hose with panty hose. But inside was a book, a bound volume with a title, stamped across the cover in gold, three lines long. It was the author's name underneath, though, that caught her eye. Joshua Lucas, Ph.D.

"The bookstore across the common has a section of books written by the college faculty. I found it there. I don't know if the subject interests you, but I knew the author would."

Abby drew her finger over the gold letters of his name, then turned and caught Keeley in a rib-crushing embrace. "Thanks, Keeley," she whispered. She would have been really disappointed, she realized as she opened the book and thumbed through it, if the package had contained a pair of panty hose. Although everything else seemed to be changing, she desperately needed some things in her life to stay the same.

She would have to get Joshua to sign the book for her before she went home. It wasn't a typical vacation souvenir, but it was a part of him she could take with her. For that reason, and because it was a gift from Keeley, she would treasure it.

Joshua sat at the desk in his home office, the results from his latest research project waiting to be entered into the computer in front of him, but his hands were idle and his mind was on other matters.

Two more nights and Abby would be leaving. He wasn't sure he could let her go... but he didn't know how to stop her. She was still so skittish, so uncertain. He knew she cared for him, but so did countless others—family, friends, colleagues, students. He wanted more than that from Abby. He wanted her to miss him when he wasn't with her, to be happy when he was. He wanted her to share his meals, not just for a few summer nights, but for the rest of their lives. He wanted her in his bed, living in his house, brightening up his life. He wanted to know when he walked in the door that she was waiting, that she would sleep in his arms each night, that she would be snuggled beside him when he awoke each morning.

He wanted to do things for her: to protect her from those who took shameless advantage of her; to make her life easier; to keep her smile bright and gentle; to give her the security of knowing that she was always deeply, tenderly, endlessly loved.

God, he loved her, but he didn't know if she was ready to hear that. Last night he had pushed her, and he had almost succeeded in scaring her away. Talk of love, commitment and forever might do just that.

He had to be patient at a time when his patience was woefully short. He had to move slowly, one step at a time. Sometimes, because of her insecurities and doubts, that would probably mean taking two steps back for each one forward. He'd already gained her affection and desire; next he had to earn her trust. He had to gently, tenderly prove to her that he deserved it, that he would never betray it, that he would never betray *her*.

Sighing heavily, he rubbed his face with both hands. How much of that could be accomplished in two days?

Not enough.

With another sigh, he switched off the computer and filed his research results away. The paper he was supposed to write would have to wait until next week. Maybe then he would know whether he had a future ahead of him to make the effort worthwhile.

But right now he was going to head over to the campus. According to the week's schedule, there was a field hockey game today, and since, again according to the schedule, Bess Hilliard had been one of Bartlett's star players, he was pretty sure he would find Abby there, cheering on her roommate.

But he'd made it no further than the office door when the phone rang. The possibility that it might be his ex-wife made him consider walking on out. The probability that it was someone else made him walk back to the desk and answer.

"Hi, Daddy, it's Cassie."

He sat down in the chair and cast a wistful glance out the window toward the campus. So much for his plans for finding Abby. By the time his daughter ran out of breath, the field hockey game would be long over and Abby would be gone. At least he would see her tonight.

Swiveling the chair around, he turned his attention one hundred percent to his daughter. "What's up, sweetheart?"

The restaurant Joshua had chosen for dinner was small, intimate and served the best Italian food in western Massachusetts, he said. Abby knew that Dominic had occasionally brought Keeley here years ago, so, if it was good enough for a Vitalli, she believed the claim.

After ordering dinner, she picked up the bag she'd brought along and withdrew the book inside, laying it on the table in front of him. He glanced at it, sipped a little wine, then set the glass down and picked up the book. "You didn't actually buy this, did you?"

"It was a gift from a friend. I want you to sign it for me."

The idea, she saw, both pleased and embarrassed him. "Why?"

"Because you wrote it. Because I asked you to. When I read it—"

"Read it?" he interrupted, flipping through the pages. "You don't really intend to read it, do you?"

"Of course I do. Otherwise, how can I tell you what a brilliant job you did?"

He laid the book aside and reached for her hand instead. "Brilliant in psychology can often be boring, Abby. I don't even ask my students to read that—and they *have* to read what I tell them to."

"Don't belittle it, Joshua. You should be proud of everything you've accomplished, including the book. Especially the book. Obviously a great deal of research and time went into it. So will you please sign it for me?"

"All right. I'll give it to you Saturday morning."

"Why not tonight?"

"Hey, we college professors don't get too many requests for autographs. Give me time to think of something appropriate, will you?" he teased.

"All right." His mention of Saturday morning brought a gloomy tone to the cheer she'd been practicing all afternoon. That was the closest he'd come to mentioning their future. Maybe he didn't mention it, she thought philosophically, because he didn't believe they had one. Maybe, as she'd feared earlier in the week, all he'd been looking for was a summer fling, and she'd been the lucky one. "I'll have to leave around nine-thirty to get to the airport on time, but I'll come by your house first.''

He released her hand at that and looked away, and after a moment so did she. That had been a perfect opportunity for him to say, ''I don't want you to go, Abby. I'll miss you. Will I see you again?'' But for a long time he didn't say anything, and when he did speak, it was only to ask if she would like more wine. Since she hadn't touched what he'd already poured, she simply shook her head.

The waiter brought their salads and a basket of hot bread sticks. The change in mood hadn't affected her appetite, Abby realized, or maybe it was just that the vegetables were too fresh, the dressing too tangy, the bread too rich and yeasty, to ignore because she suddenly felt melancholy.

''Have you enjoyed the time with your friends?'' Joshua asked.

It sounded like the kind of question people asked simply to fill the silence, but Abby grasped at it. ''It's been really nice. It's funny, you know... I've known them more than half my life, but I'm still learning things about them. We had a long talk last night that was really interesting.''

''And what did you learn?''

''That there's a limit to how much selflessness anyone can endure,'' she said with a rueful smile. ''That they wouldn't have minded if I'd occasionally told them no. That I didn't need to buy their friendship by always being so quick to do things for them. That they would have liked me anyway.''

For the first time since she'd mentioned leaving, Joshua brought his gaze back to her. ''You didn't know that?''

The disbelief in his voice made her smile falter. "I was never sure. You see, Joshua, I was eleven years old when my father died. My mother supported us, and I took care of things at home. She was always busy, always tired. What little spare time she had, she gave to the younger kids. She thought they needed her attention more than I did. I learned pretty quickly that the more I did, the more she appreciated me. The smoother the household ran, the better behaved the kids were, and the happier she was."

"So you earned her approval by doing things for her."

His attention was locked on her now. The intense light in his blue eyes made her wonder if she was talking to Joshua, her date and friend, or Dr. Lucas, the psychologist. But could she really distinguish between the two? Could anyone keep their private and professional personas totally separated?

She shrugged carelessly. "I guess I was insecure. The other kids didn't have to do anything to get her attention or approval, but I did. I felt inadequate. I began to believe that if my mother felt that way, other people must, too, so I did things for *them*. By the time I came to Bartlett, it wasn't a conscious action anymore. It had become the way I *was*. As long as I did things for my friends, they liked me." She broke off and smiled angelically. "I have to admit, it worked. I had more friends in college than practically anyone else I knew. I have more friends now than I ever wanted."

"But you're not sure if they're real friends—if they like *you* or the fact that you'll do anything for them."

"I'm sure about Bess and Keeley now."

"But not about the others. And not about me."

She didn't say anything but simply dropped her gaze from his. It hurt, Joshua realized. He had acknowledged just today that he had to earn her trust before their relationship could move forward, but it still hurt to be told so bluntly, even if without words, that she *didn't* trust him.

And it made him angry. He rarely lost his temper. He'd found anger to be counterproductive and a waste of precious time—and all his time with Abby was precious. But his hold on his temper now was tenuous at best. "Why aren't you sure of me, Abby?" His voice was taut, sharp-edged, barely controlled. "Have I asked for any favors? Have I taken advantage of you in any way? Have I done a single thing to suggest that I'm more interested in what you could do for me than in you yourself? What could you possibly give me that would be worth spending an entire week courting you?"

She was stunned by his outburst. "Joshua, I didn't mean to imply..." Her voice trailed off, then she tried again. "I didn't mean to insult you, Joshua."

"Of course not," he replied, sarcastically sweet. "*Dear* Abby would never insult anyone." Then, in a harsher tone, "Answer my question. What could you possibly give me that would make this past week worthwhile?"

She held his gaze and replied with quiet dignity, "An affair. A fling. Sex."

Could two people truly see the same relationship in such different lights? he wondered despairingly. *He* had thought he was leading her patiently, gently, to the point where he could propose marriage, while *she* thought he was looking for an affair to liven up his summer break. "If all I'd wanted was sex, sweetheart, I know at least a dozen easier places to get it,'' he said, each word deliberately cool and cutting.

He'd said it to hurt, but he couldn't look at her, couldn't bear to see the pain—pain that *he* had caused—in her soft eyes. He turned his head away from her, pretending great interest in the other diners. That was the way they finished their meal, and that was the way they made the drive back to campus.

He hadn't intended to bring her home so early. He had hoped—God, had wished and prayed!—that she would stay with him tonight, that she would let him make love to her, would let him *love* her. But she didn't trust him enough for that. Maybe it was time to face the fact that she might never trust him enough.

He parked in the closest lot, then walked her to the dorm. Before they reached it, though, Abby turned off into a small, elaborate, walled garden. After a moment, he followed her.

There was a sundial in the center, old and weathered and mounted on a stone pedestal. She traced her finger over the markings on it, then glanced over her shoulder, making certain Joshua was there. What she was going to say was difficult, and she would have hated to get it all out only to learn that he hadn't been there to hear her. With a sigh, she looked away again.

''I told you I was married once. My ex-husband's name was Darryl. Your story about your ex-wife and how she pushed you reminded me of him, only Darryl's ambition was all for himself. He was starting at USC just as I finished my graduate studies there. He was going to be the best lawyer in the state of South Carolina. But he didn't have any money to speak of, so he could only go to school part-time while he worked full-time. At that rate, he would have been an old man before he took the bar exam.

"It didn't take him long to learn what everyone else already knew—that I was a grade-A sucker. Need help? See Abby. Got a problem? Abby will take care of it. In trouble? Abby will fix it for you. We began dating, and after a few months he asked me to marry him. I'd fallen in love with him pretty quickly—he was handsome and charming, and he *needed* me. My family and friends tried to warn me about him, but I thought they were wrong. I believed he loved me. I *had* to believe that."

She broke off, wishing she had the courage to look at Joshua, to find out his reaction to her story. Would he think she was an even bigger fool than he'd already believed? Would he wonder how she could have been so stupid? Would he lose whatever feelings still remained for her?

She didn't know. She didn't have the courage to find out.

"So Darryl and I got married. He had our lives all planned out. I would work, and he would go to school. I would do the cooking and the cleaning, and he would study. Everything was all right until I asked for something that wasn't outlined in his plan. He was in his first year of law school by then. He had no responsibilities except attending class and studying. I did everything else for him: paid his expenses, fixed his meals, washed his laundry. He was better off than most of the other students in his classes.

"But I wanted to have a baby. I'd always wanted children. I was twenty-eight then, and the time just seemed right. I knew he would argue, so I had everything worked out in advance. My insurance would pay most of the medical expenses, and I could save my vacation time so I wouldn't have to take a leave of absence from work. My sister, who had two kids of her own by then, would take care of the baby when I returned to work.

"Darryl was furious at first, but when he realized how determined I was, he changed. Sure, you can have a baby, he said... in a few more months. And when those months passed, he asked for a few more, and a few more. I turned twenty-nine, thirty.... Then he graduated from law school. Of course you can have a baby, he said... just as soon as I get set up in practice."

Joshua knew what was coming next. When he'd asked her a few days ago how long she'd been married, she had carelessly replied, "How long does it take to get a law degree and establish a practice?" He had thought her answer odd at the time, but now he understood, and he ached for her.

"He had already filed for divorce before he told me. I'd fallen out of love with him by then, so I was surprised rather than hurt. I didn't contest it, and we didn't have much property to divide, so it was settled pretty quickly. Then he told me that marrying me had been the most expedient way to get his degree. Where else could he have found someone who would meet all his needs and ask for nothing in return?"

She laughed, but it was forlorn. "What made it worse was that everyone else either knew or suspected that was all he wanted from me. He couldn't touch my heart, but he almost destroyed everything else—my pride, my dignity, my self-respect, my self-esteem."

Joshua closed the distance that separated them and wrapped his arms around her, pulling her back against him. She raised her hands to rest on his forearms and laid her head on his shoulder, and the tension that held her body rigid drained out almost immediately. She was soft and relaxed ... and vulnerable, he silently warned himself. Too vulnerable, in spite of his own ever-present desire, for anything more than this embrace.

He regretted his angry words at the restaurant more than ever now that he knew more about her past. He'd been wary after his own divorce, and he'd never had a doubt that in the beginning Marla *had* loved him. How much worse it had been for Abby, who'd never had that comfort, who had never even known that she deserved to be loved.

A fine psychologist he was. He was supposed to have insight into other people's problems, but he'd been too involved in his own insecurities to look very closely at Abby's. He'd been too impatient, too anxious—too aroused, he admitted bluntly—and he had risked destroying something very special and very precious.

Last night he had promised her time, and that was what he would give her. Whether it took a few weeks, a few months or a few years, he would give her every moment she needed, free of demands, free of pressure. Free of everything except his love.

"Abby, I'm sorry," he murmured, his breath stirring her hair. "For what I said and the way I acted at the—"

"No. Don't be, Joshua."

"I told you I would never hurt you, then I did it deliberately. I'm sorry."

She twisted in the circle of his arms. "Oh, so the truth comes out now, does it?" she teased gently. "The great Dr. Joshua Lucas is human, after all. He thinks and he reacts and he feels pain—"

"And he inflicts it, too."

She stroked her fingers down his cheek. "And he heals it." Her fingertips reached his mouth, and she slid them slowly back and forth. His lips were full, soft, warm. She remembered the feel of his mouth on hers with a longing that was only intensified by the memory of it on her breast. She wanted to feel it there again, wanted to lie naked underneath him. She wanted to make love with him, wanted him to know her the way no other man ever had, wanted to discover him in ways no other woman ever had. She wanted to trust him with her body and her heart, with her very soul.

But she wanted to do all that without fears, without insecurities, without regrets.

Slowly she withdrew her hand and gently pulled away. His arms tightened briefly; then he let her go. She followed the path to the garden gate, where she waited for him to join her; then, her hand tucked into his, they completed their journey to the dorm.

"Tomorrow night—" They spoke at the same time, then laughed. Abby continued. "Tomorrow night is the banquet. I assume it's one of the events you're required to attend."

Joshua nodded.

"There will be dinner and dancing and stimulating company," she said softly, shyly teasing.

"And Dr. Benedict's umpteenth 'we are glad to have you and come back next year' speech."

"Well, yes, but maybe we can skip out on that." She glanced away, watching the fountain for a moment, then met Joshua's even gaze again. "Would you . . . If you don't have other plans. . . I would be honored if you would go with me, Joshua."

His grin, quick and powerful and purely masculine, made the difficult invitation worthwhile. "I'd love to."

Abby gave a relieved sigh. "Good. We'll make it a real date. I'll pick you up—"

He laid two fingers over her mouth to silence her. "Let's stick with our routine. I'll meet you here, as usual." He kissed her gently. "Good night, Abby. Sweet dreams."

She watched until he was out of sight, then went inside to her room. It was quiet and dark. Keeley was with Dominic, she thought, and Bess with her vet. She hoped their evenings ended better than hers.

After changing into a robe, she showered in the communal bathroom down the hall, then got ready for bed. It was too early to sleep, of course, so she wandered across the dark room to the window. The fire escape was a dark, spindly shadow. For some of the girls in the dorm, it had been a warm-evening meeting place, but not her. Rules had required a twice-a-year fire drill, but she had always managed to be elsewhere when it took place. Thank God there had never been a fire, since it had been a toss-up which would have scared her more: the flames or the rickety, steep descent down the steel stairs.

She'd been afraid of so many things in her life, she thought with a sad sigh. This week she'd added one more fear to her list: Joshua. Not the man himself, but everything he represented. Love, happiness, completion and fulfillment, and danger, risk, sorrow and loss. He was everything she'd ever wanted and everything she was afraid to take.

And she loved him.

It wasn't caring or affection or desire, or fondness or respect or admiration. It was love, pure and simple and incredibly complex. Love that would grow and mature but never fade. Love that would see her through whatever the years ahead had to offer. Love that would enrich her life and make it complete... if she let it. If she trusted in it. If she trusted in Joshua.

Love.

She used the word too often—signed all her letters, "love, Abby," told her nieces and nephews "I love you" every time she saw them, signed off phone calls with Keeley and Bess and most of her family with "love you." She had even, too many times to count, told Darryl that she'd loved him. But not once, in all the times she'd said it, had it meant the same thing it meant now. Because all those people, no matter how special, weren't Joshua.

So what was she going to do about it?

She sprawled across her bed, burying her face in the pillow. Was she going to tell him? Was she going to take a chance? Was she going to risk losing her love as quickly as she'd found it?

The simple fact was that Joshua had said nothing about love, much less about forever. He'd talked about desire, about time, about waiting, but those didn't add up to love.

But he'd talked, too, about courting her—a sweetly old-fashioned word that evoked all the right images. And at the restaurant he'd been hurt, even insulted, by her belief that all he wanted from her was an affair. *If all I'd wanted was sex*... Meaning he'd wanted more. But how much more? And how much was she willing to risk to find out?

Everything.

Joshua Lucas was an intelligent man who had never asked for a thing from her but a chance to develop the feelings between them. Not a chance for an affair. Not a chance to break her heart. Not a chance to use, then discard her, the way Darryl had. He thought he saw something worthwhile in her, and God help her, she *knew* she'd found something worthwhile in him.

And she wasn't going to give it up.

Tomorrow evening they would go to the banquet. They would have dinner with Keeley and Dominic, with Bess and Will Shedd. They would dance and even listen to Dr. Benedict's speech. Then Joshua would invite her back to his house, and if he didn't, she would invite herself. He would kiss her, and she wouldn't stop him. Instead she would encourage him. And she would tell him that she loved him.

Simple.

She swallowed hard. Simple. Yeah. So why was she already trembling inside?

Friday

"Make me beautiful tonight."

Abby remembered the request she'd uttered hours ago and winced. Those four words were all it had taken to set Bess and Keeley in motion and leave *her* feeling ragged. Bess had gone through her closet, ruthlessly rejecting every single piece of clothing she'd brought, while Keeley had sorted through first Abby's cosmetics, then her own, selecting and rejecting foundations, lipsticks, shadows and powders.

Then they had dragged her into town, into and out of every single shop that sold women's clothing in East Ridley and Springfield. They had selected lipstick in a brighter color than she normally wore, polish for her always-bare fingernails, and heels that were little more than narrow straps of leather, with a small, flat handbag to match. They had even dragged her through the lingerie departments, disdaining her simple half slips and perfectly acceptable beige bras, and badgering her into a sinfully gorgeous camisole and sexy lace-edged tap pants in silk as delicately shaded as champagne. The camisole's deep V meant she would have to go braless, she protested, but her objection had fallen on deaf ears. She'd wanted to be made beautiful, and they were going to do it, from the skin out.

She had tried on, at last count, twenty-one dresses, all of them gorgeous and not one of them her choice, but Bess and Keeley had found fault with every one of them. When she'd dared to point out a few dresses that she liked, the kind of simple, pale garments that she normally favored, they had shaken their heads in unison. "All those pastels, Abby," Bess had said in dismay. "They remind me of cotton candy. When's the last time you ever thought cotton candy was sexy?"

Keeley had found a dress in rich burgundy that Abby had loved, but as soon as she put it on, her roommate had shaken her head and ordered her to remove it. "The neckline's too high—doesn't show enough cleavage."

Bess had replaced it with one in royal-blue satin that draped lovingly over every curve...and plunged in a skin-baring V to her waist. Bess and Keeley had exchanged looks, and this time all three of them had shaken their heads. Too much cleavage.

Now Abby was tucked into an out-of-the-way chair in yet another store while her roommates scoured the racks for dresses they deemed suitable. She slipped her shoes off and rubbed one aching foot. Was all this worthwhile? she wondered, studying her reflection in a nearby mirror. The best Keeley and Bess could hope for was to improve what nature had given her, and it wasn't as if nature had been particularly generous in the first place.

But Bess had been right about one thing: with her pale blond hair, frizzing now from having so many dresses pulled over it, and her pastel print blouse and pale pink skirt, she *did* resemble cotton candy. Sweet. Definitely not sexy. She'd always gone for simple, for plain and basic, in both styles and colors. For anything, Keeley had said, that didn't draw attention to her. And for tonight she wanted exactly the opposite.

At least, she *thought* she did. At any rate, whether she wanted it or not, Keeley and Bess were going to see that she got it. "I hope you're impressed, Joshua," she murmured aloud as she caught sight of her roommates approaching from different directions.

They stopped a few feet in front of her, each holding up a dress: the same dress. Slowly Abby got to her feet. The fabric was silk, and the color was the richest, most vibrant, most intense shade of emerald green she'd ever seen. The style was simple and fitted all over, from shoulder to wrist, from tapered waist to slim skirt.

Neither Bess nor Keeley was surprised to find they'd chosen the same dress, she saw, because it was the *right* dress. It was beautiful. It was gorgeous. She couldn't help but look wonderful in it. Joshua couldn't help but be impressed by it.

She took one into the dressing room while they returned the other to the rack. After stripping off her own clothes, she took a deep breath, removed the silk from its padded hanger and slipped it on.

The bodice draped across to fasten with a single hook and eye at the waist on the right side, and the skirt, where the two sides overlapped, parted with each step she took. The sleeves were long, the shoulders slightly padded, the fit perfect. Absolutely perfect.

She combed her hair with her fingers, taming it the best she could, then left the dressing room. There were no effusive compliments from her friends. Instead they solemnly studied her front and back, then delivered judgment in unison. "Perfect."

Back at the dorm, they insisted that she start getting ready, even though it was only midafternoon. They wanted time to do her hair, her nails, her makeup, and needed time to get themselves ready, too. She stopped protesting and gratefully accepted their help.

Wearing nothing but a robe, her just-shampooed hair wrapped in a towel, she sat on her bed, hands resting on an empty shoe box, while Bess painted her nails. Feeling comfortable, relaxed and unexpectedly happy, she laid her head against the pillows propped behind her and rolled it to the side. There was the pewter frame and its long-ago picture: Bess, twenty-three, Abby, twenty-two, and Keeley approaching that milestone. She thought of the camera tucked in her bottom bureau drawer. She wanted another picture before they all left tomorrow, and she would send them copies. For herself, she would buy a double frame and display the two photos together, mentally labeled Before and After. Young and Older—But Definitely Better. Best Friends and Still Best Friends.

It was like old times—controlled chaos—as they got ready for their dates. Yet it was different, too. This time, for the first time, it was Abby asking and Keeley and Bess giving. Keeping her away from the mirror, Keeley did her makeup, Bess her hair, and they helped her with her clothes, ignoring her feeble protest about having to leave her bra in the drawer.

Finally they were finished—almost. When Abby reached for her cologne, Bess offered a bottle of her own. "Try this," she suggested.

Abby sniffed it and closed her eyes. It was heavenly.

Then Keeley brought out the crowning touch: a slim gold chain that she fastened around Abby's neck. Dangling from it was a diamond solitaire, sparkling, heavy, cool.

"Keeley, I can't—"

The other woman waved away her gasped protest. "Anything heavier would detract from the lines of the dress, don't you think?"

Finally they led her to the full-length mirror mounted on the door for the final unveiling. For a long moment Abby simply stared at herself. They hadn't made her into a great beauty, but this was even better. She was still Abby, still the woman she'd always been, but prettier. More polished. And, yes, she thought with a tentative smile, sexier, too.

Blinking at the moisture that filled her eyes, she hugged them both. "Thanks, you guys," she whispered.

Then there was a tap at the door. "You three have gentleman callers waiting downstairs, ladies," called an unfamiliar voice.

This was it, Abby thought nervously. Time to face Joshua. Time to face the future.

The look in his eyes was worth every moment of preparation and then some. He gave her a long, appraising study, then murmured, "You are beautiful."

It was the dress, she started to tell him, and Bess's hairstyle and Keeley's makeup job. But she caught the words before they escaped and simply smiled and said, "Thank you."

Joshua felt a bit as he did whenever he saw Cassie: in awe that this beautiful woman was a part of him. But she was—a part of his heart, a part of his life, an undeniable part of his soul. He had to struggle against the urge to tell her right now that he loved her, to beg her to stay with him, to plead with her to love him in return. But this wasn't the time or the place, he thought regretfully.

They left the dorm accompanied by her roommates and their dates. He was casually acquainted with Will Shedd, and he'd heard of Dominic Vitalli. Maybe, if everything worked out the way he wanted with Abby, he would have a chance to get to know them better in the future.

It was a short walk across campus to the patio where the banquet would be held. Linen-covered tables for six were set up across the flagstones—nice that they happened to be for six—and an area had been left clear for dancing. Dinner, dancing and stimulating company, Abby had said when she'd invited him. Considering the state he was already in, he could probably survive dinner, but dancing, he was afraid, might be *too* stimulating.

He took part in the conversation around the table but remembered little of it. All his awareness was focused on the woman beside him. Without looking he could see her; without touching he could feel her. The need that she created so effortlessly was starting to twist inside him, savage and relentless, blocking out everything else.

He ate his dinner without tasting it. He listened to Dr. Benedict's speech without hearing it. When the others left the table to dance, he wasn't aware of it until Abby gently touched his arm.

"I guess, since I asked you out, it's my role to ask if you'd like to dance."

"Just let me warn you. If we get that close—" He gestured to the couples on the floor. "I won't be responsible for what happens."

She smiled as she slid her chair back. "Being responsible all the time can get kind of old, can't it?"

Joshua took her hand and led her onto the dance floor. In her three-inch heels she was a perfect match for him. He folded his arms around her, brought her close and brushed his cheek against her hair. "Abby?"

"Hmm."

"Have I told you how glad I am you came to this reunion?"

"No."

"I am."

She looked up at him and smiled dreamily, then rested her cheek against his jacket again. His suit tonight was charcoal gray, impeccably styled and incredibly soft, but all she could think of was how long it would take to get him out of it. She wanted to make love with him, wanted it with a fierceness that both surprised and further aroused her. She'd never been aggressive before, had never gone after something she'd wanted with single-minded passion, but she was going to seduce Joshua or go up in flames generated by her own desire.

One dance slid into another, then another. When she could rouse herself to look, she found Keeley and Dominic in their own quiet corner of the dance floor, unaware of the couples around them. Bess and Will were lost in each other, too.

"Abby?"

"Hmm."

"Can we go now?"

His mouth was right above her ear, and the whispered words made her smile with their tickle. "Why?"

His voice took on a strained quality. "I'd like to take you someplace quiet."

It was quiet here, she thought, and achingly romantic with the soft music and the flickering light of the Japanese lanterns. But she knew what kind of quiet he wanted. The longer they danced, the closer he held her and the stronger his arousal grew. She stopped dancing and smiled up at him. "Lucky for you it's dimly lit here."

"Do you need to say good-night to your friends?"

She glanced at them once more and decided that they didn't need her intrusion. They would know where she'd gone...if they even noticed that she *had* gone. "No."

They stopped at the table to pick up her handbag, then followed the winding paths that led to the north edge of the campus. From there it was a short walk across one of the playing fields and along one street.

Joshua unlocked the door, then stepped back so Abby could enter. When he came in, he started to reach for the light switch, but she stopped him. He'd left a light burning in the family room, and it spilled into the hallway where they stood. She laced her fingers together and took a deep breath. She hadn't lost her desire or her determination, but sometime in the past few minutes, her confidence had started slipping. What if he rejected her? What if he could never love her? But what if he didn't reject her? What if he *could* love her?

"There's something I want to say to you, Abby."

She shook her head. "Later, Joshua."

"It will take just a minute, and I think—"

She leaned forward and kissed him, cutting off his words. He was surprised by the kiss but quickly warmed to it, laying his hands on her shoulders and drawing her nearer, hungrily kissing her back, greedily taking all that she offered. When the kiss ended a moment later, he said hoarsely, "I think it'll wait."

Resting her hand on the banister beside her, she gazed hesitantly upstairs. "Do you want me to stay, Joshua?"

He could have replied in a dozen flowery ways, but the reply he gave, simple and honest, was the absolute best. "Yes," he said. "I do."

Joshua stepped back, allowing Abby to climb the stairs before him. His hand rested lightly in the small of her back, offering support in case her heels or shaky knees gave way, guiding her into the bedroom on the right.

There she let him turn on the lights, a lamp on the nightstand and another on a corner table. The room was big, the furniture gleaming, the decor masculine. There were no woman's touches, no leftovers from his ex-wife, no left-behinds from his previous lovers. It was a man's room. Joshua's room. For this one night, and forever in her memories, part of it would be *her* room.

She was trembling, but with anticipation, she realized. Not fear. The fear was gone. Even if their relationship ended tomorrow when she returned to South Carolina, she would have the satisfaction of knowing that she had loved him, and loved well.

She braced herself with one hand on the bureau and removed her left shoe, dangling it by a thin strap before dropping it to the floor. The right one followed. But when she raised her hands to the closure on her dress, Joshua, watching her from across the room, spoke roughly.

"No. Let me undress you." He shrugged out of his coat and laid it on the chair next to the corner table. He removed his gold cuff links and dropped them into a crystal dish on the chest as he passed it; then he came to a stop in front of her. "I think of you in soft colors— pink and tan, lavender and blue and pale green."

"Cotton candy colors," she supplied in a thick voice.

"Those colors play up your sweet nature, your willingness to give, your capacity for love. This..." He fingered the fabric of her sleeve without actually touching her. "This plays up your passion, your sensuality, your fire. When I first saw you at the dorm to-night...'' There were no words to adequately explain what he had thought, what he had felt, so he gave up trying and concentrated instead on making *her* feel.

His fingers trailed up the sleeve to her shoulder and rested there, warming the cool fabric, sending his heat into her skin. His other hand made the same trip, coming to rest on her other shoulder, then slowly slid down. The caress confirmed what he'd suspected but had thought too dangerous to speculate on at the dance: she wore no bra underneath the dress. The awareness made his mouth go dry, and the weight of her breast in his palm made his throat tighten.

Her nipple was hard; he could feel it through the rich fabric with no more than that touch. He remembered the brief taste he'd had of her breast two nights ago, and his seemingly permanent state of arousal increased. Soon he would kiss her breast again. Soon...

Her heart was racing out of control, Abby thought, and he'd done nothing more than look at her and touch her breast for just a moment. When they were naked, when he kissed her, when he was finally inside her, the sensations would probably be more than she could possibly bear.

He took a step, and she instinctively backed away. He took another, and she felt the wall against her spine. He took the final step that trapped her against his body, lean and hard—exactly where she'd wanted to be—and threaded his fingers into her hair and kissed her with fierce longing and even fiercer control. His lips were pressed to hers, and his tongue was in her mouth, stroking, tormenting, feeding both her hunger and his own.

Just as suddenly as he'd started the kiss, he ended it, but he didn't move back, didn't release her. "Touch me, Abby," he said in a voice that was half command, half desperate plea.

"Where?" she whispered, stretching to press a kiss to the strong line of his jaw.

"Anywhere. Just touch me."

She pushed him back just enough to gain access to his body, then slowly, leisurely, undid his tie, leaving it hanging around his neck. Next she unbuttoned his shirt, taking her time, sliding her fingers between the buttons, kissing each bit of bare skin as it was revealed. When she tugged his nipple between her teeth, he groaned and tangled his hands in her hair again. To pull her away? she wondered, but instead he used the leverage to draw her closer.

Her delicate bites and kisses were refined torture. Combined with the continued exploration of her hands across his belly, unbuckling his belt, unfastening the button on his trousers, they were devastating. Joshua took a step back, forcing distance between them. His breathing was ragged, his hunger raw. "Do you know how badly I want you?"

The distance wasn't enough. Her fingers slid across his stomach and made a thoroughly intimate foray beneath the soft fabric of his trousers, and she smiled sweetly at what she found. "Yes, I do."

He pulled her hand free. "You look like an angel," he whispered thickly, "but you're as wicked as a devil."

Her smile grew even sweeter as she approached him once more, but he caught her hands and forced them to her sides. This time the torture was hers. He began with kisses, hot and wet, that followed the dipping neckline of her dress, nudging aside Keeley's diamond pendant, trailing down to the soft curves, barely visible, of her breasts. There he freed her hands and brought his own into play, sliding them inside the bodice of her dress, finding her breasts, still draped in champagne silk, and teasing them until they ached.

"Do you like that, sweetheart?" he asked, his grin as wicked as he'd accused her of being.

The sound she made was helplessly unintelligible and undeniably a plea for more. He obliged her, dropping one hand to the slit in her skirt that had tantalized him all evening. When he reached the silk heated by her need, he heard a gasp mixed with a groan. One was hers, the other his, but he didn't know which was which.

Swallowing hard, he found the fastener on the dress. A simple tug and it fell open. With another tug he pulled it down her arms and dropped it. It floated to the floor, a swirl of rich emerald against the beige carpet. His shirt was brilliant white against it, the effect softened an instant later by the pale gold of her camisole.

Still half-dressed, he lowered her onto the bed and drew her nipple into his mouth. She arched against him and cried out with the pure pleasure of it. While he continued the hungry kiss, he searched blindly for her hand, clasped it in his, then brought it to his body, pressing it flat against his stomach.

Abby understood his silent request and complied with gentle caresses. She shifted into a better position and used both hands, gliding them over his chest and down the long line of his back, sliding them around to open the zipper of his trousers, then inside the fabric to cradle the rigid length of his arousal in her hands. Her tender touch was like a brand, sending ripples of pleasure and pain through him, making him shudder. His control vanished, and need became everything, driving, throbbing, searing. With movements made clumsy by urgency, he removed the last of her clothing, then the last of his, and settled between her thighs.

For one agonizing moment he simply looked at her. Her hair was tousled, her delicate skin flushed, her muscles quivering. She was beautiful. She was the woman he loved.

Then she reached for him, and his restraint snapped. He entered her slowly, seeking her warmth, feeling her welcome, pressing gently deeper until he filled her. When his hips were snug against hers, he became motionless, giving her body time to adjust to the intrusion of his.

But she didn't need time; she needed *him*. She shifted restlessly beneath him, her hands on his hips urging movement, her mouth on his wordlessly pleading. They sank into a rhythm as easy as breathing and as natural as loving, each meeting the other, each enticing and capturing and claiming the other, until completion, long and wild and trembling, claimed them both.

Abby woke several hours later to find herself alone in the big bed, the covers pulled over her, the lights off and Joshua nowhere around. Closing her eyes again, she buried her face in his pillow, savoring his now-so-familiar scent.

Making love with him had been everything she'd expected and more. He'd made her feel things she'd never felt before. Beautiful. Desired. Loved. Of course, Joshua probably made every woman he took to bed feel those things. He was that kind of man—generous, tender and highly skilled.

How many times could they make love in one night? she wondered with a greedy smile. How many memories could she store up to take back to Columbia with her? How much of this lifetime's worth of desire could they satisfy in the next ten hours?

How thoroughly could she love him?

She heard a scraping sound downstairs and wondered where he was, what he was doing, what had drawn him from the bed in the middle of the night. Sliding out from beneath the covers, she found her gorgeous silk dress still on the floor and shrugged into it, fastening the hook, smoothing the skirt over her hips.

A light shone from downstairs, growing brighter as she approached it. She found Joshua sitting on a tall stool in the kitchen, wearing nothing but his gray trousers and balancing the phone between his shoulder and ear. He smiled when he saw her and beckoned her to come closer. When she did, he drew her between his thighs and, listening absently to his caller, bent to trace his tongue around her ear. "My daughter," he whispered, then nipped her earlobe. "There's wine in the refrigerator if you want some. I'll get off..."

His hushed murmur was interrupted by an exasperated, "*Dad*-dy, are you listening?" that even Abby clearly heard. Smiling, she moved away, letting him return his attention to Cassie and her problems. She took two wineglasses from the cabinet, found the bottle in the refrigerator and carried them to the sofa at the other end of the room. After filling the glasses, she carried one to Joshua, then sat down facing him, one leg stretched out along the cushions, the other bent. The slit skirt parted and fell to either side, revealing every inch of her thigh, but she made no effort to fix it when she saw Joshua's gaze grow warmer. Maybe it would encourage him to end his call more quickly—not that she begrudged Cassie his attention, of course. It was just that Cassie would have him as a father for the rest of her life, while Abby might very well have him as a lover only for tonight.

She sipped the wine, then tilted her head back, resting it on the sofa arm. *Only for tonight.* It seemed impossible that something so incredibly wonderful could end after only one night, but it was a possibility. He hadn't asked for anything more, hadn't hinted that he wanted anything more. She might have to be satisfied with this.

Was she wearing anything under that dress? Joshua wondered, the very thought making him gulp half the wine in his glass. It would be a pleasure finding out when he removed it as soon as he got off the phone. He loved his daughter dearly, but sometimes she had the worst timing. And he couldn't very well tell her that he had to go because he was dying to make love to Abby again. Cassie's first reaction would most likely be shock that her father even had a love life, followed by annoyance that he dared believe *his* turmoil even began to compare to her own.

But at last, thankfully, she was saying goodbye. He hung up, rolled his head to ease his neck muscles, then joined Abby on the couch, sitting at the opposite end. "I thought having a teenage daughter must be punishment for all my youthful sins," he said with a laugh. "I used to count the days until she started college and began really growing up, thinking that then most of our problems would be over. Was I ever wrong. Cassie's had more problems, disasters and crises in the last six months than in the previous twenty years combined."

Abby smiled gently. "But you're lucky to have her."

"Yeah, I am." He lifted her foot onto his lap and began massaging it. "Why don't you have any children, Abby?"

"I told you about Darryl—"

"But you've been divorced five years," he interrupted. "Why didn't you have one on your own? Finding a father would have been simple, and God knows you have enough love to make up to any child for having only one parent."

"I'd never met a man I liked and respected enough to consider as a candidate for fatherhood. I guess I'm a little too old-fashioned. I wanted a baby, but I wanted all the things that traditionally go with it—love, marriage, family."

"You haven't given up on getting it all, have you?" He pretended it was a casual question, not one that would affect the rest of his life if she gave the wrong answer.

"I'm thirty-seven years old. I don't have too many childbearing years left. Most men old enough to interest me have been married before and already have families." She shrugged, and the emerald silk shimmered. "How many men with grown children want to start again with diapers and bottles and midnight feedings?"

"I do." He hadn't meant to say it so bluntly, but the words were already out, spoken from his heart, not his mind. He loved children—his own and most others he came in contact with. He didn't know how good he would be with diapers, bottles and midnight feedings, since studying and teaching had commanded his life so thoroughly when his kids were infants that he'd missed most of that, but he was adaptable. He could learn. For Abby, he could learn anything.

She pulled her foot away and sat straighter. "You want another family?" she asked, not bothering to disguise her surprise.

"If it works out," he said cautiously. After all, it was always possible that, at thirty-seven, Abby could have trouble getting pregnant or carrying a baby to term. She was so selfless, so giving, that either of those things could take her away from him if she thought he had his heart set on starting a second family. If she had a baby, he would cherish it. If she couldn't have one, he wouldn't let her believe she'd cheated him of experiencing the joys of fatherhood again.

He finished his wine and twisted to set the glass on the end table. "There was something I wanted to tell you when we got home, Abby, but..." His smile was not the least bit rueful. "I got distracted. First, though, I want you to understand that there are no strings attached to this. No demands. No obligations. I'm not asking you for anything."

Now he'd made her sufficiently wary, she thought. What was he getting at? Maybe she should have listened to him earlier, should have delayed their lovemaking until she knew exactly what he'd wanted to say. No strings, no demands, no obligations. It sounded grim. It sounded like "affair." Not marriage. Not forever.

It sounded like heartache.

He glanced away, then studied his hands for a moment, gathering courage, she suspected, before he looked at her. When he finally did, she could read nothing on his face but nervousness. Because he'd promised he would never hurt her and was about to do it?

"Abby, I love you." He paused, then rushed on. "That doesn't mean you have to say you love me, too, and it doesn't mean that I'll make any demands of you or try to tie you down or force you to make changes you don't want in your life. It just means that...I love you."

I love you. She stared at him, the declaration echoing in her head. Had she really heard the words she'd wanted so desperately to hear? Then why didn't she feel happier, more joyful, more ecstatic? Why wasn't she telling him that she loved him, too?

No strings, no demands, no obligations. That was what he was offering. *That* was why she wasn't happier. She needed strings, demands and obligations. She needed the ties that bound two people together. She needed permanence. Commitment. Marriage.

"Abby?"

She focused her gaze on him. He looked unsure and a bit bewildered. She wasn't giving him the reaction he'd expected, and he was puzzled by it. She opened her mouth to explain, but the words failed her. With a helpless gesture she shut it again.

"Well..." He cleared his throat uneasily. "I have to admit that I envisioned this going over a little differently. Don't you have anything to say? Not even an 'oh, Joshua'?"

"I'm sorry, Joshua. It means a lot to me, really. It's just that I want..."

"What? What do you want, Abby? Tell me, and I'll give it to you if I can."

If he could. And if he couldn't? she wondered, feeling an edge of panic creep into her thoughts. What happened then?

He waited several moments, then leaned forward to clasp her hand. "Abby, talk to me, please. This is too important to ignore. Tell me what you want."

"Strings." The word came out shakily and freed those that followed. "Demands. Obligations. Without those things, all we have is an affair. It's not a relationship. It's not a commitment. It's not sharing our lives and raising a family and building a future." She broke off, then quietly finished. "It's not enough, Joshua."

The worry and fear faded from his eyes. "You want marriage?"

"Yes," she replied almost defiantly. "I love you, and I want to marry you. I want to have your baby. I want to spend the rest of my life with you."

Nodding thoughtfully, he released her hand and leaned back. She waited anxiously for some response. When it came, it was the last one she'd ever expected: he laughed. He tilted his head back and laughed. The hurt swept through her, all the way down to her toes, and it pushed her to her feet. Escape was the only thing on her mind—how to run far enough and fast enough to avoid this pain—but she was too muddled to think clearly. She needed shoes—upstairs beside Joshua's bed—and her purse, also upstairs. The sexy, silk lingerie could stay there for all she cared; she would never want or need to wear it again. That went for this stupid dress, too. As soon as she got back to the dorm—

Joshua caught her wrist as she passed and pulled her down, sprawled half across him and the sofa. "Can I take that as a proposal?"

"You can take it as the biggest mistake I've ever made," she said angrily, hating the tears that stung her eyes, praying they wouldn't fall until she was safely away from him.

He trapped her legs beneath his and wrapped one arm firmly around her waist. With his other hand, he lifted her face to his and said in a gentle voice, "Because if it is, my answer is yes. Yes, I'll marry you. Yes, I'll have a family with you. Yes, I'll spend the rest of my life with you, loving you . . . always loving you."

She stared at him, wanting to believe him, wanting to understand, but afraid. One scalding tear fell onto his hand. "But . . . why did you laugh?" she asked in a fragile, pain-filled voice.

He smoothed his hand over her hair, gently brushing it back from her face, tenderly stroking her cheek. "All this week I've been afraid of rushing you, afraid that if I pushed too hard, I would lose you. I thought you needed time—time to learn to trust me. Time to learn to love me. I was going to ask you to extend your vacation and stay here a little longer, or to let me visit you at home. I was going to ask for the time to convince you that you needed and loved me as much as I need and love you." Smiling, he shook his head. "And here you'd already reached that decision on your own. All this week I've worried for nothing."

His smile faded, and his expression became intensely solemn. "Will you marry me, Abby? Will you be my wife, my partner and the mother of my children? Will you live with me and share my life? Will you love me, the way I love you, for as long as we live?"

He was offering her everything she'd ever wanted, everything she had ever needed. All she had to do was speak, and it would be hers. *He* would be hers. Her throat felt tight, and her voice, when it finally came out, was mushy with impending tears—tears of happiness this time. Of joy.

"Yes, Joshua. Yes."

Saturday

Abby felt like a guilty teenager trying to slip into the dorm Saturday morning in the same clothes she'd worn to last night's banquet. The lovely silk dress that had been so perfect for dinner and dancing stood out at nine in the morning, glaring testimony to the fact that she hadn't spent the night in her own bed. Fortunately she met only a few people and none she felt compelled to stop and chat with.

Joshua had offered to come with her, to help with her bags, but she had gently refused. She had to say good-bye to Keeley and Bess, and she wanted to do it alone. He had kissed her long and hard, implored her to hurry back, then had rolled over onto the pillow where she'd slept. He'd been asleep again, she would bet, before she'd reached the front door.

What a week she'd had. Her family would be stunned when she flew home tomorrow afternoon—she'd canceled this morning's flight as soon as she'd gotten up— with a fiancé in tow. But as soon as they met Joshua, they would be happy for her. They couldn't help but see his goodness, his gentleness and the love that was as obvious when he looked at her as her own was when *she* looked at *him*.

She slipped her heels off inside the dorm and climbed the stairs barefoot. The closer she got to the top, though, the slower she went. Had this week been as favorable for Keeley and Bess as it had for her? Had Kee-

ley resolved her old relationship with Dominic? Had
Bess been able to build a new one with Will?

She desperately wanted them to be happy. They were
her best friends, and they were responsible for her own
happiness with Joshua. After all, if Keeley hadn't asked
her to come to the reunion, and if Abby hadn't wanted
to see Keeley and Bess so badly, she wouldn't have
come, she wouldn't have run into Joshua, and she
wouldn't be planning her upcoming wedding.

Besides, she admitted honestly, she would feel guilty
in her own bliss if they weren't happy themselves.

Even without Joshua, she thought, the week had been
a success. She'd learned a lot—about trust, about
friendship, about love. She had learned that she was
worthy of friendship and love based on nothing more
than the person she was inside. She had learned that
true friendship, the kind she shared with Keeley and
Bess, couldn't be bought and couldn't be bartered for.
She'd learned that it could survive petty annoyances and
major misunderstandings and fifteen years of near-
neglect and still be strong. After the last week it was
stronger than ever.

Bess and Keeley were already in the room when she
let herself in. They greeted her with smiles. Bess's was
somewhat troubled, but Abby stifled the urge to ask
what was wrong. Dear Abby was retired now. Bess
knew that if she wanted to talk, Abby would listen. That
was all that was needed.

As soon as she changed into a cotton skirt and
sweater—pastels, yuck, she thought with a wrinkled
nose—she hefted her big suitcase onto the bed. She
packed slowly, taking part in the idle chatter, but her
heart wasn't in it. As anxious as she was to get back to
Joshua, she dreaded the moment of saying goodbye to

her friends. How long would it be before she saw them again? Years, like before? Or would they make an effort to keep in closer touch—not just cards and letters, phone calls and Bess's "airport visits," but person-to-person visits, face-to-face sit-downs?

Just as it had been the first item unpacked, the photograph on the nightstand was the last thing into the suitcase. They'd had another taken at the banquet last night by the school photographer, and he'd promised Abby three copies. But for now, all she had was this, and she held it for a moment, tracing one fingertip over the frame. They'd been so young then, ready to take on the world, their entire lives unfolding ahead of them. They had grown up. *She* had grown up, and thanks to them and Joshua, she was still growing.

"Well?"

Unembarrassed to be caught sentimentally cradling the photograph, she tucked it into her suitcase and zipped it up, then turned to find both women watching her. She removed the diamond pendant from around her neck and returned it to Keeley with a quiet thanks, then took a deep breath. "Joshua and I are getting married," she said simply.

They promised to come for the wedding, whenever and wherever it was held. It would be a relatively small but traditional affair, she was certain, and she wanted them both to be her maids of honor. She was closer to them than to her sisters, who'd had their turn at her wedding to Darryl, and she wanted them at her side when she started her new life with Joshua.

Then, all packed and unable to delay any longer—and unable to resist Joshua's lure any longer—she hugged Keeley. Then she stepped into Bess's embrace. They would keep in touch, they all promised.

They would always be friends.

Now she was driving her rental car through the streets of East Ridley to a homey white house with black shutters and narrow dormers. To her new home. To Joshua. She let herself in with the keys she'd taken from his pants pocket and quietly made her way up the stairs. He was still in bed, his head bent at an awkward angle, his arms wrapped around her pillow.

Heavens, he was handsome. And sexy. And sweet. And she loved him so much.

She carefully sat down beside him and straightened his head on the pillow, then brushed her lips across his forehead. The morning sun shone through the windows, touching his face with its soft glow, warming his skin, lighting his hair. "You have some gray hairs," she whispered in surprise, unaware that he was awakening.

"Get used to them, sweetheart," he said, his voice groggy with sleep. "*You* put them there this past week."

He shifted positions, silently inviting her into his arms, and she snuggled down against him. He was naked beneath the covers, and his skin was warm and velvety smooth. "I forget sometimes that you're forty-six."

He opened one eye and looked at her. "But I've still got what it takes."

She thought of last night's loving, wildly passionate, fiercely tender, powerfully satisfying, and smiled in agreement. "You certainly do."

"Did you get Bess and Keeley packed up? Make sure they didn't forget their toothbrushes and their slippers? Check the drawers and the closets and under the beds so that nothing would be left behind?"

Abby teasingly punched him in the ribs. "Stop making fun of me."

"I'm not making fun of you, sweetheart. You're going to make a perfect mother someday. You've been training for it all your life." He yawned, then murmured, "I left something for you on the nightstand."

When she glanced around, she saw his book, the one Keeley had given her, sitting there. The one he had promised to sign for her and return before she left for Carolina. Wriggling out of his arms, she sat up and lifted it, opening it to the title page.

His handwriting was neat and well formed, rather like the man himself, she thought with an impish glance at him. The inscription was dated—Thursday, she realized. He had written this after their none-too-successful dinner date.

> To Abby, who has taught me much and given me more. Because you are selfless, I will always admire you. Because you are wise, I will always respect you. Because you are gentle, I will always protect you. And because you are you, I will always love you.

"Oh, Joshua," she whispered, touched beyond words; then she found them. "I love you."

"I know." Eyes still closed but smiling smugly, he pulled her back to his side, pausing only long enough to let her replace the book on the nightstand; then he reached blindly but unerringly to cradle her breast.

Desire curled lazily in her belly, seeping into her from his fingers. She dislodged his hand and unfastened the top few buttons of her blouse to give him easier access, knowing now why she'd uncharacteristically neglected her bra when she'd dressed this morning. When he began the sleepy caresses again, with his mouth instead of his fingers, she gasped. "Make love to me, Joshua," she whispered.

He raised his head and brushed a kiss across her mouth while his hands easily and swiftly removed her clothes. His eyes softened—by sleep, passion or love? she wondered and knew the answer—he moved between her thighs. With no more encouragement, no more loving than that, he was ready. He sheathed himself inside her with a single long stroke, then gazed down at her.

"Even when we're not touching, Abby," he said huskily, "we're making love."

* * * * *

Marilyn Pappano

According to my mother, ever since I was a small child, I've always loved making up stories. Before I started school and learned to write, I told them; then writing became my medium, and the tales became quite private, shared only occasionally and only with others who shared the need to create. But it was always a hobby to me. I never seriously considered the possibility of actually trying to sell anything I'd written until I was nearly thirty years old. My best friend was going to write a book, and in encouraging her, I convinced myself to give it a try, too. Although my first book was rejected, the second one sold. I considered myself one of the luckiest people in the world: I'd landed a job that I loved.

Selling that book and the ones that followed meant some changes in our lives. We went from an old-fashioned, traditional family with a breadwinning father and a stay-at-home mother to a two-career family with a mother who now had an excuse to let the house get dirty, let the laundry stay dirty and to forget about cooking dinner. People who had formerly known me as "just a housewife" showed new interest, and people who had never known me at all were now interested in meeting me. I was forced to overcome the intense shyness that had plagued me all my life. I gained a new confidence that allowed me to carry on quite intelligent conversations with strangers without secretly yearning to run away and hide. I also gained a new respect. Quirks, such as my refusal to fly unless absolutely necessary, that were once considered strange or odd now became eccentricities and were quite accepted. After all, everyone knows creative people tend to be eccentric.

But selling those books meant other changes, too. I wasn't free to run errands, do favors or spend a few hours socializing with other stay-at-home moms. I couldn't take our son to the park as often as he would have liked, couldn't volunteer hours each week to school, Scouts or soccer, couldn't do anything when facing a deadline but write. In short, I had traded one set of responsibilities for another.

But what a trade! I can mold my hours to my family's. While I may not be a school volunteer every week, I get to be there for the important events in my son's life. I don't need to search for a creative outlet to ease the stresses of my job, as so many people today do, because my job *is* my creative outlet. I can sit gazing into space for hours and, when asked what I'm doing, answer, "I'm working." I can create people who are important to me, people who are *real* to me, and give them problems and sorrows, just as we have in our lives. Better still, I can solve those problems for them; I can give them happiness to ease their sorrow. And best of all, I can bring a few hours escape and, hopefully, a few hours pleasure to those who read these books.

I can't think of anything else I'd rather do.

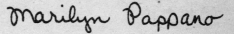

OVER THE RAINBOW

Patricia Gardner Evans

In remembrance of Bess Huntinghouse—
Auntie Bee—for being independent
in a time when women weren't, and
Harriet Huntinghouse Jackson—Ma—
for passing on her love of reading and the
old skills, and for Sally, for reminding me
of the priceless value of old friends . . .
and, of course, for Kathy and Marilyn

My Most Memorable
Summer Vacation

The back of an old vacation photograph of me reads "Happiness is being ugly and dirty and not caring." Judging by my appearance, I was ecstatic. This was also the vacation, if I remember right, that I lost the bottom of my bikini as I climbed back into a ski boat. No one had a camera then, fortunately.

I always start a vacation with the intention of staying at least presentable looking. I even began a week in the Nevada wilderness with five total strangers in a dress and heels, although accessorizing with a fishing-rod case, sleeping bag and overstuffed giant-economy-size duffel bag probably didn't create quite the impression I intended. Soon, though, the real vacation me appeared. I caught a glimpse of myself in a side mirror of the pickup truck we were abandoning for the horses that would take us on a twelve-mile ride through the rain and occasional sleet, and I knew I must be having a great time already.

And I *did* have a great time. My hair eventually dried, but it stayed straight because my butane curling iron was too cold to ignite in the mornings, and by the time the day warmed up, I'd found better things to do than mess with my hair. "Warm," it should be noted, is a relative term at ninety-five hundred feet in late September when one is standing under a solar shower that has "solarized" only a few degrees above freezing, but it really didn't matter. Much more important, my horse and I agreed that cantering was fine, but trotting wasn't, and I got the camp dog as a bed warmer since I was the only one who didn't have someone to sleep with. I made two wonderful human friends, as well, saw some of the most beautiful scenery imaginable and just generally had such a good time that even when I was attacked by the evil intestinal bug one of the others had brought along—learning, by the way, the laundering power of Coca-Cola when water is unavailable—I didn't care. Besides, it's those little unexpected happenings that make a vacation truly memorable.

I went home to continue another summer tradition. Every spring, the kitchen table is littered with as many garden catalogs as travel guides and road maps as I plan out the summer. About the time the seed orders start arriving, the peach and apricot trees bloom and the temperature drops back to freezing for at least one night. My neighbors no doubt wonder why I'm running around the backyard at three in the morning lighting fires around my fruit trees. They're not wondering any more than I am. The perennial battle with the bugs and weeds begins soon after, and I start noticing real-estate ads for yardless condominiums and town houses. Summer vacation is a reprieve from hoes and hoses, but I know I will return to find that the bean bugs and horsenettles—the cockroaches of the weed world—have staged a coup while I was gone. I start reading the condo ads more seriously.

Then comes the morning when I go out in the backyard to see two bushels of peaches that need putting up, a bucket of green beans that need canning, tomatoes to freeze and chile to roast, and I *really* look at the real-estate ads.

But even as I'm praying for an early frost, I know I'll do it all again next year. Just as a vacation is revitalizing, so, to me, is a garden. Every year begins with bare ground and brown branches; then, as if by magic, tiny green shoots and buds appear with the assurance of better to come, and finally, the promise comes to fruition. Life can be like that, too, sometimes—bare, brown and barren. A garden is a reminder that soon, a small bit of green will appear and the brown bareness will disappear as the green promise of better things to come grows and ripens into reality.

Pull a weed for me.

Saturday

"Is it dead?"

Bess Hilliard glanced up to see the three boys she'd driven past, seconds before the cat ran across the road, racing toward her. "No," she called and looked back down to the small body lying in the weeds.

It was a gray tiger-striped cat, the kind that had clones everywhere. A tremor passed through its limp body, and the shallow rise and fall of its side paused. She didn't realize she'd stopped breathing, too, until the motion began again, shallower and more erratic than before.

The boys squatted on the other side of the cat. They looked about nine or ten years old and wore the standard summer uniform of holey sneakers, cutoffs, faded T-shirts and assorted scabs.

"Do you think it'll die?"

Bess heard genuine sympathy as well as the normal ghoulish hope of children that something really gross and awful would happen. "I don't know. I don't know how badly it's hurt."

The boys were looking at her with the innocent confidence of children that an adult would take care of everything. So far she'd avoided giving the cat more than a cursory glance, because blood, even a few drops, turned her stomach. Swallowing the sourness already at the back of her throat, Bess forced herself to look down.

There was no blood. With a sigh of relief that was as much for herself as the cat, she began feeling gingerly through its short, soft fur.

"That other guy didn't even slow down." The bewilderment in the boy's voice made him sound even younger.

"Maybe he didn't know he'd hit anything," one of the others pointed out in fairness.

Oh, he knew. Bess made her silent, bitter contribution to the conversation. For a split second the brake lights of the car in front of her had flashed; then the driver had sped up. He'd known. She couldn't blame him for not being able to avoid the gray streak that had dashed across the road without warning, but that he hadn't even slowed down, much less stopped to see if he could help the poor animal . . . that was unforgivable.

"You don't know who it belongs to, do you?" She asked the question without any real expectation of a positive answer. If they knew, they would have mentioned it, and the uniform shake of their heads only confirmed that fact.

Easing the cat onto its other side, she noted that it was male. At least, she consoled herself, there wasn't a litter of helpless kittens waiting for mom to come—

The blood wiped all thought of the cat's sex out of her mind. It was bright and red and wet and had soaked the side of the cat's head from its ear to its shoulder. Dimly Bess heard a trio of gasps as her stomach heaved, and she swallowed frantically. Not giving herself time to think about what she might see next, she searched swiftly through the sodden fur for a wound.

After a minute she sat back on her heels, absently wiping her sticky fingers on her beige linen skirt. She'd found nothing to account for all that blood. A damp gust blew through her thin blouse, and she shivered. A thundershower had chilled the air, which seemed even colder after the July swelter in Boston she'd left a few hours ago. The wind gusted again; the cat appeared to shiver, too, and she thought of the sweater she'd tossed in the car as an afterthought. "Would one of you boys please get the sweater off the back seat of my car?"

All three of them scrambled up and were back in seconds, but even as Bess tucked the cardigan around the cat, she realized the futility of it. She had to do more than just keep the victim warm until the ambulance arrived. "I've got to get you to a vet," she muttered as she began to carefully gather up the injured animal, wincing as she felt small, fragile bones shift and praying that she wasn't doing it more harm.

"There's one down the road not very far," one of the boys volunteered.

"Yeah, right before you get to the creek," the smallest one added.

Bess looked at him sharply. "Which way?"

"That way." He pointed in the direction she'd been heading, toward East Ridley.

She suddenly recalled that it was Saturday afternoon. "He might not be open."

"He's always open," the tallest boy assured her. "He lives there, in a big white house. There's a barn, too. You can't miss it."

When "not very far" became several miles, Bess began to wonder if somehow she had missed it or the boys had gotten their directions mixed up. "Hang on, kitty," she murmured as she glanced down to tuck the sweater more closely around the cat lying on the other bucket seat. Looking back to the road, she noticed the time on the dashboard clock. In fifteen minutes Keeley would accept the gold filigree key that Bartlett College gave each year to an especially generous alumna, and she wasn't going to be there to applaud her old college roommate.

The ceremony was part of the annual Reunion Week activities. She hadn't planned on paying any more attention this year than she had to any of the other reunions since their graduation fifteen years ago, but the honor Keeley was to receive was important. Of course she would be there, she'd promised, before checking her work schedule, before she'd even thought about checking it. Keeley deserved the award, and she deserved to have people in the audience who were truly happy for her and proud of her.

If I hadn't stopped, Bess thought absently as she slowed for an oncoming curve, I could have been there.... She reached out to stroke the cat's head in silent apology for the small mean thought. Keeley would understand why she'd missed the presentation, and at least Abby, their other roommate, would be there. She'd stopped without thinking, of course, a natural impulse, just as her promise to attend the reunion had been. Both decisions had been made without the careful deliberation and weighing of consequences she usually employed because, too often, she'd learned, impulsive beginnings had unhappy endings.

As the curve straightened, she saw a large white house. It was a typical Massachusetts farmhouse, decades old, two stories, with a steep roof and a solid enduring grace. A barn sat behind it, and just beyond, the road crossed a short bridge—the "creek," she guessed.

A sign at the driveway entrance confirmed that she'd found the right place. Below Veterinary Clinic was the name Wm. Shedd followed by the appropriate initials.

Guided by an arrow, she bypassed the fork in the driveway that led to the front of the house and continued around to the back, stopping behind the large, older four-wheel drive vehicle blocking the end of it. Faded to a chalky orange, it was the only vehicle in sight, and there didn't seem to be a garage. The tailgate was down, and several paint cans sat on it, the slate-blue drips down the sides of them matching the freshly painted house trim. Behind the cans she saw what looked like drawers and small cabinets, as if the back of the vehicle were fitted out as a kind of tool chest. With a sinking feeling, Bess opened the car door. Despite the boys' assurance, it looked like the painter was the only one home.

A shady porch ran across the back of the house and, leaving the cat, Bess hurried toward it, almost tripping over a ladder lying on the ground, which she didn't see until the last second. She didn't see the man, either, until she stepped on the bottom step of the porch.

Halting abruptly, she stared up at the man staring down at her. His sudden appearance startled her, especially since she hadn't noticed him as she'd driven up; then she noticed the wet paintbrush in one hand, the can of paint in the other and the stepladder behind him, and realized why she hadn't seen him. He'd been painting back in the corner, hidden in the shade.

Her initial impression was size—a lot of it. He was wearing old jeans with the knees gone and a T-shirt that looked as if the sleeves had been lopped off with a hedge trimmer. The rag-bag clothes didn't make him look any smaller; rather, they emphasized the length of his legs and arms and the width of his shoulders. His face was shadowed by a baseball cap, but what she could see of it wore a day's growth of dark beard and an expression that made it clear he was not happy at having his work interrupted.

The amount of paint he was wearing said he was a general handyman rather than a professional painter. In other circumstances, his blue speckled appearance would have been funny, but in the current situation, nothing about his size and rough look or his silence was the least bit humorous. Without realizing that she did so, she edged back off the step.

He appeared to be giving her the once-over, his blatant stare lingering briefly at the level of her hips before dropping down her legs, and her unease was instantly overcome by an impatient exasperation. "Is the vet here?"

Her exasperation didn't lessen when he asked a question of his own instead of answering hers. "What's wrong?"

"I've got a cat that's been hit by a car. I can't see where it's hurt, but it's unconscious, and there's an awful lot of blood." To further her irritation, there was a tremor in her voice instead of the sharpness she'd intended.

He'd set down the brush and can and was starting down the steps even as she began to speak. With only a curt nod of acknowledgment, he headed toward her car without breaking his long stride, and Bess found herself having to run to catch up with him. He was opening the passenger door, intending, she feared, to take the cat out of the car, and she grabbed his arm to stop him. "Don't! There may be internal injuries. Only the vet should move—"

"I am the vet."

"Oh." Her response was something less than intelligent, but Bess doubted he heard her, anyway. He'd spoken with the same kind of absentminded impatience with which he'd shaken off her restraining hand. Crouching he swiftly unwrapped the cat while her fingers slowly curled over her palm. The brief contact with his arm had left her with far more than a brief impression. She knew exactly the warmth of his skin, the crisp silkiness of the hair covering his forearm, the strength of the muscles underneath that made any attempt of hers to restrain him ludicrous. Her fingers curled tighter, as if to be sure the knowledge they'd acquired wasn't lost.

He began to examine the cat, and unconsciously she leaned closer to watch. His hands were spattered with paint, several nails even coated with it, as if he were wearing one of the more bizarre shades of nail polish. It seemed impossible that such big, messy, rough-looking hands could be anything but clumsy and hurtful yet if she'd had any doubts that he was "Wm. Shedd, D.V.M.," they were settled now. His hands moved over the cat with a delicacy that made her earlier examination look brutal by comparison.

As he turned the cat's head, she looked away. Was he "William"? "Bill"? Neither name seemed to fit him exactly. She heard him getting to his feet and hastily stepped back as he turned to face her, the cat loosely wrapped in her sweater again and secure in his hands.

"I'll know more after I take X rays, but there's at least a concussion, and the right front leg is broken."

Nodding her understanding, she fell into step beside him as he started back to the house. Will watched her run up the steps ahead of him to open the screen door. He hadn't been pleased to see the car pulling into the yard and even less to see the woman getting out of it. He'd figured he had just enough light left to finish the painting and, after four straight days of it, he hadn't been in the mood for any interruptions that might make it five; then he'd seen the blood. She was well dressed, which made the dark stains on her skirt all the more startling, and he'd stared at the red smeared across her hips for a few moments, almost sick with fear that the blood was hers and enraged that someone had hurt her. He was looking at the grass and mud stains on her knees when she'd asked for the vet, and he'd felt a relief just as strong—and just as inexplicable—as his earlier fear. The woman was a stranger to him. Impersonal concern he could understand, but the reactions that had blindsided him were anything but impersonal.

Bess followed him through the waiting room and down a hallway into an examining room, where he set the cat down on a padded table. "I've got to clean up before I do anything else," he muttered and, moving with a speed that she hadn't gotten used to yet, he was already halfway out the door before she realized he was leaving her alone with the cat.

"No, wait! I—" The slamming of the screen door cut her off. "He'll be right back," she whispered encouragingly as much to herself as to the cat. The table appeared to be part of an X-ray unit; that and a stainless-steel, wheeled tray table were the only furniture in the room. The floor and walls were spotlessly white, as were the cupboards, drawers and countertop that took up one side of the room. An autoclave sat at one end of the counter, with a tray of surgical instruments beside it. Bess was trying to ignore the possible implications of those when the screen door slammed again, followed by the sound of running water and splashing.

He was drying his hands on a towel when he came back into the room. He still wore the same paint-smeared clothes, but his hands and arms had been scrubbed scrupulously clean, and as he walked around to the opposite side of the table she caught a whiff of turpentine and strong soap. He leaned over to look at the cat, holding his arms up and out to the side while he finished drying them. Bess followed the progress of the towel up one long arm. Small details, usually too insignificant to notice, suddenly took on new interest, as if her vision had somehow sharpened past normal—his biceps swelling powerfully as his arm bent tighter and the tendons stood out in strong relief, the contrast of the pristine white towel with his smooth sun-bronzed skin. The cloth ruffled the dense, dark hair on his forearm, then smoothed it on the downward swipe. A sequin of water glistened in the crease of his elbow, and with a peculiar feeling of suspense that seemed to center in the pit of her stomach, she watched the towel come closer and closer until, on the last pass, the thirsty cotton licked up the tiny drop.

She swallowed shallowly as he tossed the towel toward the end of the table. Turning, he took a stethoscope and ear scope from a drawer behind him. He looked briefly in the cat's ears with the otoscope, then began working the flat disk of the stethoscope down the cat's chest and abdomen, a slight frown of concentration on his face as he listened.

Her new avid interest in details didn't diminish. His face was square, the features strong, with a good jaw and definite brow ridge. His skin had a slightly rough, weathered look, not the pasty pale smoothness of men who spent their days in office buildings. His eyes were a clear golden brown and set deep under thick eyebrows. His nose showed signs of having been broken once, and his mouth was a little wide, the bottom lip fuller than the top. The decisive, mature set of it, more than the fine lines around his eyes or grooves around his mouth, told her that he was probably past forty but not by much. One eyetooth was chipped a little, and she wondered if it had happened at the same time his nose had been broken, or when he'd acquired the scar on his chin. Jagged and about an inch long, the scar showed whitely through the dark stubble of his beard. She glanced back up to the top of his head. His hair...

Bess sighed. His hair was gorgeous. From his beard and eyebrows she guessed that it had once been dark, but now it was silver, with just enough dark remaining to give it a contrasting tarnish that made the silver even richer. It grew lushly thick in a curly disorder that would defy any comb or brush to make it lie boringly neat and flat and, in marked contrast to the rest of him, it looked as if it would be soft to touch.

She slid her itchy, restless hands into her pockets. He reminded her of someone... It was something about the way he looked, the way he moved, although she couldn't think of who at the moment. He didn't, she added silently as he straightened up, look like anybody's idea of a veterinarian.

He glanced from the X-ray equipment positioned over the table to her. "I may need an extra pair of hands."

There was a question in his voice, but there was really no choice of answer. The cat had showed signs the past few minutes of returning consciousness, twitching and jerking as if it were chasing a dream mouse; he would need help holding it still, and she was the only help available. She'd dealt surprisingly well with the blood so far; she could certainly handle a few X rays or whatever, Bess assured herself, resolutely refusing to consider that "whatever" might involve that tray next to the sterilizer. "I'll help."

From a metal coat tree that she hadn't noticed behind the door, he picked off two garments that looked like the bulky, lead-lined apron she was given to wear whenever she had dental X rays taken. He started to hand one to her, then stopped before she could take it. "You aren't pregnant, are you?"

"No." She gave him a startled look at the bluntly personal question.

It was necessary, but not the kind she was probably used to from a total stranger, Will thought wryly. He handed her the apron, then put on his own. While she figured out the straps, he positioned the camera arm of the X-ray machine over the cat's body using it as cover to study her. The lines of her body were long and clean, although ten more pounds wouldn't do them any harm. She was tall, a few inches shy of six feet, with a trim waist and hips, rounded bottom and legs that all but reached her neck.

Her thin face didn't have a generic beauty or even prettiness—there was too much strength in it for either—but it was an arresting, interesting face that would only, he suspected, become more so as the years went by. Sliding a film holder into a slot in the side of the table, he wondered how long her hair was. She was wearing it up, in a tight, tucked braid. Neither blond nor brown, the closest thing to it in color he could think of was brown sugar. Hardly poetic, Will laughed to himself, but accurate. A loose wisp drifted against her neck, and her left hand reached up to tuck it back in place. It was a slim, graceful hand, practical nails, no rings—although that wasn't a guarantee these days. The soft material of her blouse pulled tight, detailing the firm, pointed thrust of her breast, and suddenly he was trying to remember if the sheets on his bed were clean.

The thought jolted him, almost as much as the urge that had prompted it. It was pure desire, stronger and faster than any he'd felt for a woman in years.

The exact second she finished fastening the apron, he turned to her. As if he'd been watching her out of the corner of his eye, Bess thought.

"I'll position the cat. All you have to do is make sure it doesn't move at the wrong time."

He arranged the cat on its side with its neck and legs extended. "I'm Will Shedd, by the way," he said, introducing himself without looking up.

"Bess Hilliard," she murmured in response. Will. That suited him.

"How do you do, Bess Hilliard. Hold the hind feet with your right hand, and put your left on the rump." Bess...a terse, no-nonsense name. Not unlike the woman herself, he had a hunch.

Bess did as directed, and he laid his hand over her left one to adjust the placement of her fingers. Her hand jerked uncontrollably. She sneaked a look to see if he'd noticed, but if he had, he gave no sign of it. It wasn't that his touch was unpleasant; it wasn't. His hand was warm and gentle, and his fingertips had an interesting roughness. It was just that his touch, his hand, felt so familiar—and it was a stranger's hand, a stranger's touch.

He withdrew his hand, and there was a click. "What's your cat's name?" Sliding out the used film, he inserted a new frame.

It took a second for the words to register. "I-it's not my cat. I saw the accident happen and stopped to help. Some boys told me where you lived."

He gave her a swift glance as he swung the X-ray arm over a few inches. "The driver didn't stop?"

"No." To her horror, tears suddenly burned in her eyes. Bending her head, Bess blinked furiously.

"Now the ribs. Leave your hands where they are."

Nothing in his voice indicated that he'd noticed the tears, either. There was another click, and he changed film holders again. "Last one. Put one hand on the shoulder and hold the head—gently, just enough to keep it in place." Bess repositioned her hands, giving silent thanks that this side of the cat's head wasn't the one with the blood. Again he laid his hand over hers.

She didn't flinch this time. Will adjusted the hand under his fractionally to make his action legitimate, then moved his finger to the remote button. "Ready?" He'd wondered if she didn't like to be touched. A moment later he slid out the exposed film and picked up the other two exposed frames. "It'll just take a few minutes to develop these."

When he came back into the room, she'd shed her apron, too, and was whispering to the cat, although she stopped the instant she realized she wasn't alone.

Ms., Miss or Mrs. Hilliard was as embarrassed to be caught talking to a cat, he realized, as she was to be caught crying over one. He slid an X ray under the clips at the top of the light box built into the cabinets over the sink and flipped the switch. "There's no sign of injury to the pelvis or back legs."

As he'd intended, she came to stand beside him. Her movements were quick and fluid, suggesting that the body hidden under the prim blouse and skirt was toned and supple. She would be soft, though, where all women were soft.

"What about the spine?" Her voice was soft, but it had an underlying firmness that suggested she was used to having her questions answered.

"Everything looks fine, and the response to stimulation was normal." He switched films. "Ribs look fine, too. I don't see any internal damage." She was close enough that he could smell her perfume. It wasn't the sophisticated scent he would have expected, but something light and sweet and flowery, almost old-fashioned, and very feminine.

He put up the last X ray. "Neck and shoulders are fine. The cat has a concussion, but there's no skull fracture. The right front leg is fractured, but it's a clean break and won't be any trouble to set." He pointed out the break in the X ray, and she leaned closer to look. He leaned closer, too, to get a better look at her eyes. He'd been trying to decide what color they were for the past ten minutes. Not really blue or green, they were a blend of the two, with a generous amount of gray mixed in that gave them an odd incandescence.

Bess stared at the X ray. She could see the hairline crack and the slight misalignment of the bone, but only because he had pointed them out to her; she never would have seen the break otherwise. And he had *felt* it. Bess looked at the large, strong hand silhouetted against the white light. It seemed impossible that those blunt, callused fingers could have such extraordinary sensitivity.

He reached for the switch on the light box, and it went dark.

"Okay, let's get to work."

He was obviously including her in that "let's." Bess watched him stock the tray table and, to her intense relief, he didn't include any of the sharp, shiny bits of stainless steel lying next to the sterilizer. After spreading a towel and lifting the cat onto it, he turned it over, exposing the blood-stiffened fur, and her stomach did a practice roll.

He set the broken leg first, manipulating the ends of the bone back together through the thick fur. The cat twitched once, but showed no other sign of feeling any pain. Bess glanced worriedly at the clock on the opposite wall. Surely, after all this time, it shouldn't still be so deeply unconscious; it felt like hours since the accident, but to her surprise, she saw that hardly more than thirty minutes had passed.

"Hand me a roll of gauze, will you? Do you live in East Ridley?"

Bess watched him rapidly wind the gauze around the broken leg. "No."

"Cut it here. Where're you from?"

She snipped the gauze with the scissors from the tray. "Boston."

"I need the splints now. Here on vacation?"

She found two metal Popsicle stick look-alikes. His voice was deep and a little rumbly. He didn't have the accent of a native New Englander; in fact, aside from a slight drawl, he didn't have any accent at all. "Not exactly. I'm here for a college reunion."

Finally. An answer of more than one syllable. He'd been wondering if he was going to need a crowbar to get information out of her. He aligned the splints on either side of the broken leg. He wasn't certain, but he thought he'd heard a trace of apprehension in her voice when she'd mentioned the reunion. "Tape. Bartlett College?" There was a community college in town, but her clothes, the luxury model import parked behind his old

Bronco and especially her manner said it was the exclusive women's school she'd graduated from.

"Yes." Fascinated, she watched him wrap the tape over the splints, his hand moving so fast it was almost a blur. The hand holding the tape paused, and she instinctively moved closer with the scissors again and snipped.

"The bottle and a square of gauze. Which reunion is it?"

Bess found a bottle identified as distilled water and a folded gauze pad. She snipped off the tip of the nozzle on the bottle and handed the items over. "The fifteenth. I haven't gone to any of the others," she added, not knowing why she did. He soaked the cat's fur, then scrubbed gently with the gauze pad, and a dirty red stain began spreading over the clean white. Bess hurriedly shifted her gaze upward to the vicinity of his chest.

Fifteenth reunion. That meant she was in her late thirties, although she didn't look it. "Another pad. Are you staying at a hotel?"

Bess put the pad in his hand without looking. Although he had the deep chest and fully developed shoulders of a mature man, he was really more rangy than brawny, and if there was an ounce of fat on him, she couldn't imagine where. His T-shirt was pulled tight across his broad chest, highlighting muscle and his small flat nipples. Where the fabric stretched tightest, there was a hole, as if the worn cotton simply couldn't give any more and had ripped. A tuft of dark hair had slipped through and formed a small curl, just about the right size to fit around her finger...

Abruptly she shifted her eyes again, to the blank wall. "No." She cleared the slight huskiness from her throat.

"One of my old roommates made reservations in our old dorm."

Will discarded the pad and water bottle. "Clippers. Have you seen your old roommates since graduation?"

Now that the blood was gone, she could watch him work again. As he clipped from the cat's ear down to its chin, the fur fell away, and a raw scrape began to show under the stubble. "A few times. I went to their weddings, but there was just time for cake and rice. And I went to Keeley's husband's funeral," she answered absently.

He made quick use of the opening she'd given him. "They didn't go to your wedding?"

"I've never caught the bouquet," she said with a small laugh.

She wasn't married, never had been. He glanced up swiftly to see if a smile accompanied the laugh. None did. She hadn't smiled yet, and he couldn't help wondering what effect it might have on her face, if a smile would warm up the cool aloofness in her eyes, soften the tight, almost prissy line of her mouth.

"Are you married?" It was a normal question, although Bess was surprised to hear herself ask it. A man's marital status usually didn't interest her.

"Not for the past six years."

Without taking time to figure out why his answer pleased her, she asked the natural follow-up question. "Do you have any children?"

"No." Just for a second his expression changed, but whatever the emotion was, it was gone before she could identify it. "Do you?"

The question would have been insulting a generation ago, but now, with the rising number of unmarried mothers, it was as legitimate as hers. "No."

The flat negative gave him no clue as to whether childlessness pleased or disappointed her. Just in time, he stopped himself from reaching for the swabs he needed next. "Some swabs, and we're about to be finished." She found the white packs of swabs on the tray and put one in his outstretched hand. "What do you do in Boston?"

Bess watched him pull out an oversize swab, the cotton tip at the end of the wooden stick already wet with a dark brown substance. "I'm senior vice president of a bank."

Pausing in the act of swabbing the scraped area, Will looked up at her. "That's quite an achievement for a woman."

There was no condescension in his words, no paternalistic praise equivalent to a pat on the head from Daddy, just acknowledgment of what she had accomplished and the sincere appreciation that it hadn't been easy.

"It was a goal I worked toward for a long time."

Again there was that same lack of emotion as when she'd said she had no children. Bess Hilliard had achieved success in a profession that was still overwhelmingly dominated by men, and to do it, she'd no doubt had to be pragmatic and unsentimental, more than a little cold-blooded and rigidly self-disciplined and focused—certainly not the kind of woman who would have grass stains on her knees, be worried about meeting a couple of old college roommates, or be blinking back tears over a stray cat.

The antiseptic on the swab stained the cat's fur and skin yellow-brown. "Surely all that blood didn't come from that?" Bess asked, frowning at the quarter-size raw spot.

"No. The eardrum ruptured on impact. It won't cause the cat any pain, and it'll heal up fine." He swabbed a spot on the cat's rump, then pulled a small glass vial from his back pocket and, before he could ask, she passed him a syringe. "This is a general purpose antibiotic," he told her, filling the syringe.

Bess averted her eyes as the needle began its downward arc. Needles ranked just above blood on her stomach's tolerance scale.

Watching her, Will groped with his free hand for the sweater she'd wrapped around the cat earlier, bunched it up and stuffed it in the empty film rack under the table.

She looked back as he dropped the empty syringe on the tray. "Well, kitty, I think you used up your nine lives and about a dozen others today," she told the cat softly, giving it a gentle pat before glancing up at him. "I know the injuries are serious, but it seems amazing that that's all there are."

She smiled, finally, and the smile did more than warm the cool aloofness in her eyes; it melted it, and softened the tight, tart line of her mouth into a sweet, lovely curve.

"Yes, it is amazing," he murmured.

The cat mewed suddenly, and her smile vanished.

"It's okay. It's just beginning to wake up," he reassured her. Picking up the cat, he started for the door. "It'll be more comfortable in a kennel. I'll be right back."

There wasn't, Bess realized abruptly, a reason to stay any longer, and she did, after all, have someplace else she was supposed to be. Remembering her sweater, she began to look around for it. Her glance skimmed over the towel with the blood-stained fur Will Shedd had clipped from the cat, and all the self-control she'd been congratulating herself on abruptly deserted her.

"The cat settled right in," Will began as he came back through the door. His next word was a vicious curse as the woman across the room crumpled toward the floor.

"Are you back among the living?"

His voice came from just above her, more gentle than she could ever have imagined—which only made her humiliation that much more complete. "Yes," Bess whispered.

She was lying on what felt like a sofa. There was a solid warmth against her hip, and she realized he must be sitting beside her.

"Are you planning to open your eyes anytime soon?" he inquired politely.

She wanted to say no, never, but that would only make the situation even more ridiculous.

His face was the first thing she saw, wearing an expression of mild exasperation. "Why didn't you tell me you can't stand the sight of blood?"

Bess wasn't surprised that he'd guessed the reason she'd made a fool of herself; it seemed natural, somehow, that he would know. "I wanted to help, and I thought I was doing all right."

Will watched his fingers brush a wisp of brown-sugar hair off her cheek. She'd scared the hell out of him, and with normal human irrationality, he wanted to give her hell back for doing it, but her face was still too white, her eyes too big. "You did fine, kid," he told her softly, then deliberately lightened his tone. "It's a good thing you didn't crack your head when you passed out and end up with a concussion, too. I don't have a kennel big enough for you."

Bess laughed in spite of her embarrassment, but her laughter faded as it occurred to her that she was still lying on the sofa snugged up against him, and she didn't feel much inclined to move. She sat up quickly.

She was in his living room, an unapologetically masculine room, with sturdy oak tables and tweed upholstered sofas and easy chairs chosen more for comfort than high style. It gave her an odd feeling to know that he'd carried her in here, held her, handled her body, and that she'd been unaware of it. It didn't make her uneasy; rather it made her... Disappointed? Bess shook her head once to clear it. Maybe she had cracked it after all, she thought dryly.

"Are you still dizzy?"

Bess looked up to see his frown of concern. As she'd sat up, he'd moved off the sofa to crouch beside it, putting their eyes on the same level. "No, I...just..."

Fortunately he didn't wait for her to come up with an answer that didn't involve the truth. "Here." He transferred a plate from the coffee table in front of the sofa to her lap. "You need something in your stomach to help settle it."

Bess gave the plate a doubtful look; she wasn't sure a piece of pizza was the prescription for an unsettled stomach, but she was, she noticed suddenly, hungry. Picking up the pizza, she took a big bite. "Oh, this must be from Mario's. They always made the worst pizza," she said before thinking. "But filling!" she added quickly.

His laugh, like his voice, was a deep rumble, and she grinned sheepishly around another bite.

"It was left over from the poker game last night." He handed her a paper napkin and a full glass of milk.

"Did you win?" She handed back the half-empty glass.

He was still crouched in front of her in what she'd always thought of as the "cowboy hunker," a low squat that looked like it would be torture on the thighs after the first thirty seconds, although he seemed completely comfortable.

"I broke even." His grin and shrug were so patently modest that she had to laugh. She was comfortable, too, she thought, completely comfortable.

Glancing over her head, he abruptly stood up in a smooth movement. "Excuse me a minute. Finish that," he added peremptorily, pointing to the plate on her lap, where only a fat roll of crust remained.

Bess made a face at his back as he left the room but took a bite of the crust, washing it down with milk. Curious to know what he'd seen that had caused him to leave, she turned around to look at the wall behind her. The significance of the clock didn't strike her until she heard him speaking to someone, too far away to hear distinct words. Of course. She should have known. Bess shoved the last bit of crust into her mouth and gulped down the remaining milk, then stood up in a rush. It was Saturday night, and he was a single man. He had a date, to whom he was no doubt explaining that he'd be a little late.

Will found her standing in the middle of the room, looking ready to leave. His relationship with the woman he'd called was casual, and he'd considered canceling their date entirely, but she didn't deserve such short notice.

"Thank you for everything," Bess said in a voice that said she wouldn't be persuaded to stay anyway. "I'll just go get my purse—"

"Don't worry about it. We'll settle up later." He saw her indecision. As he'd suspected, she intended to dump responsibility for the animal on him, with a generous check, of course. He'd already decided he wasn't going to let her get away with it.

She looked at him doubtfully. "I don't know when I can come tomorrow."

"I'll be here." Oh, yeah, he'd be here. Since she wasn't going to stay, he decided to hurry her on her way before she remembered her sweater. He walked to the front door. "If you don't get any answer at the house when you come, check the barn."

His brisk tone and the open door were an obvious dismissal. "Fine. Sometime tomorrow then," Bess said, a little annoyed. He didn't have to be so eager to see her leave. His date could darned well wait a few minutes.

He walked out with her, but only out of courtesy, Will told himself. "Nice car," he commented as she stopped beside the driver's door. It wasn't to his taste, but it was undeniably a fine automobile.

"It's very reliable and has good resale value."

Her testimonial was more resigned than enthusiastic. "But?" he prompted.

She shrugged diffidently. "It's frumpy."

Will swallowed a burst of surprised laughter. "What did you really want?"

"Oh—" she gave him a half-embarrassed glance "—I wanted one of those four-wheel drives you see in the television ads, always heading off into the boon-docks.'' She nodded in the direction of his Bronco. "Like yours, only smaller, but—" she shrugged again "—it wouldn't have been very practical."

He had to swallow another laugh. "No," he agreed solemnly. "There aren't too many boondocks in Boston."

"No, there aren't." Her expression was wistful, and he glimpsed a barely suppressed, restless excitement in her eyes. Then she blinked, and the excitement was gone; the wistfulness became a businesslike smile. "I'll see you tomorrow then, Dr. Shedd."

She offered her hand, and he took it, holding it a little longer and tighter than was precisely proper for "business," and just for a moment that restive excitement looking for escape stirred again in the blue-green depths of her eyes. "Tomorrow," he said.

Bess glanced at the white house growing smaller in the rearview mirror. She would be back, and not just because she needed to give Will Shedd a check, or because of the lingering tingle in her hand that she wanted to, but couldn't quite, ignore. She really did care what happened to that scruffy cat. With a helpless laugh, she pressed down on the gas pedal. She *had* cracked her head.

After another mile she saw the square bell tower of the Bartlett campus chapel rising among the sharp church steeples that pierced the skyline of East Ridley. Bess glanced at the dashboard clock. Abby and Keeley had no doubt given up on her by now.

Minutes later she closed the trunk of her car, then just stood still for a few moments to look around. The old buildings blended into the soft indigo light of early evening, their sharp silhouettes softening and blurring in the twilight the way memories did after a while, the details softening and blurring, too. The ivy was a little higher on the brick walls, the trees a little taller than she remembered, but otherwise nothing seemed to have changed.

She walked the block to Lawrence Hall, climbed the steps, opened the carved door and stepped back fifteen years. The oak floor gleamed as always with the patina of over a century of shoes and wax. The bell desk, where long-distance calls came in and "gentlemen callers" were announced, still stood off to the left. She hadn't received many of either, she thought wryly.

The desk was unattended, although a small sign advised reunion registrants to check there for their room assignments, so, deciding that someone would return eventually, she dropped her bags and went to see what else hadn't changed.

The dining room hadn't. At one table four women she didn't recognize were enjoying the traditional evening "milk and crackers." Each night, any dessert left over from dinner, crackers and peanut butter, and milk, of course, were put out at nine for anyone who wanted a snack. She and Abby and Keeley had eaten their share, she remembered with a smile.

The parlors were still furnished with the antiques and lovely carpets that bespoke graciousness and elegance. This had seemed like the grandest palace the first time she'd seen it, and it hadn't been until she was a senior that she had felt completely comfortable here.

By the time she returned to the desk, a young woman about the age she'd been the last time she'd manned it stood there. Bess signed in and got her room key, rec-

ognizing the number stamped in the brass immediately.
Keeley had gotten them their old room. With secret
amusement she turned down the girl's solicitous offer
to help her carry her luggage upstairs. She could remember a time when she, too, had thought that anyone over thirty-five must be ready for a wheelchair.

If the first floor was a palace, the residence floors
were boot camp. Nothing had changed here, either, not
even the paint. The concrete floor was the same dried-
mud brown and the bare walls the same yellowing
cream, just a little more yellowed. The small bathroom
that served the entire floor still had, she saw with perverse satisfaction, the same pukey green tile and
chipped radiators painted not quite to match.

Halfway down the hall, she stopped in front of a
scuffed door. She raised the key, then abruptly stopped,
staring down at the brass key poised by the lock. She'd
been looking forward to seeing Abby and Keeley for
weeks, yet now, standing outside their old room, she felt
an inexplicable reluctance, almost a fear, to enter it.
Drawing a deep breath, she put the key into the lock and
turned it.

"Bess!" The room's only occupant, a small blond
woman, turned with a welcoming smile.

"Hi, Abby. Had you given up on me?" Their hug
was awkward, since both of them had their hands full.

Bess dumped her luggage and purse on the bed near-
est the door out of habit, while Abby finished hanging
a dress in her closet. She explained briefly when Abby
admitted that she had been beginning to wonder,
quickly changing the subject when it seemed Abby was
about to ask for a few more details about the vet. She
did not, she discovered, want to talk about Will Shedd.
It was like when she was a little girl and had discovered

something wonderful—a beautiful butterfly just hatching out, a hummingbird's nest with tiny eggs. She wouldn't immediately run to tell someone, but would keep her discovery secret, just for a little while, to keep the wonderfulness of it precious and private. It was silly then, and even sillier now, but she still didn't want to talk about him.

"I guess Keeley's presentation went well," she said, glancing at the Gucci luggage at the foot of one bed. The two dormer windows formed small alcoves, each one just large enough for a single bed. In the old days, Keeley had had one of them and Abby the other, while Bess had taken the bed closest to the door so she wouldn't wake the others coming in late from work. "I'm sorry I missed it."

Abby, it turned out, had missed most of it, too. It was a familiar story. Someone—a co-worker, this time—had needed a favor at the last minute, and Abby, conditioned to always say yes and say it with a smile, had missed her plane. Something in her tone, though, made Bess wonder if the smile wasn't finally beginning to crack. Bess said softly, "Do you know where she is?"

"No, I don't." Bess detected Abby's mother-hennish unease at not knowing where every chick was. That was something else that hadn't changed.

Just as they finished their unpacking, the door opened and Keeley walked in. After the hugs and kisses, Bess and Abby sat in the old plush armchairs in one corner, but Keeley couldn't seem to settle. Flitting around the room like a hyperactive butterfly, she flitted from topic to topic, too, monopolizing the conversation. It was "hostess" chatter, bright, quick and meaningless. In response to Abby's question, she said that she'd just been wandering around town and decided to stop in for a minute at the Strawberry Shanty, an old hangout, but before Bess could ask her if she'd seen anyone they'd known, she'd flitted on to a new subject.

"I see there's still no elevator in this place. I'd forgotten how steep those steps are, especially with a full suitcase in each hand."

"But isn't it comforting to know some things never change?" Abby deadpanned.

Bess joined in the laughter automatically. She'd finally heard what was hiding under Keeley's bright chatter. Keeley's nervous, she realized. And so is Abby. It isn't just me. We're all nervous about how this week is going to work out, whether we'll get along as well as we used to, whether it might not have been a mistake to come.

The brief laughter died, and Keeley turned to her. "Congratulations on your newest promotion, Bess, although why we always find out about them from the change in your letterhead, I don't know."

Abby seconded the complaint. "Yes, Bess, why don't you ever tell us? You've done exactly what you said you would, and you should be proud of it. If it were me, I'd be taking ads out in the paper."

"Thank you," Bess murmured. She felt oddly discomfited, not by her friends' praise, but by the suspicion that maybe the reason she never told them directly was out of some kind of perverse vanity. Telling people that you'd done just what you said you would do seemed like the smuggest kind of boasting, but at least it was honest. She didn't use her letterhead to subtly announce another promotion; it was just easier to do her letter writing at the office—she'd thought. But maybe the real reason was that it gave her the opportunity to brag without seeming to.

The conversation moved on to family updates. "How's your sister, Abby?" Vaguely Bess remembered Abby mentioning on the card she'd sent last month that she was going to her sister's to help out with a new baby.

"Fine. By the end of the week, she was up chasing after her other two children and never missing—" Abby's laugh sounded strained "—an opportunity to tell me that I could be doing the same if I hadn't married the wrong man."

Privately Bess agreed. She and Keeley had decided that Darryl Granger was a sleazy jerk even before he'd dumped Abby after she'd put her own ambitions on hold to put him through law school. Abby, however, still made excuses for the creep and wouldn't listen to any criticism of him. "Well, he did seem like a good catch," Bess said carefully.

"He wasn't a catch, he was a fumble," Abby muttered sourly.

Keeley's eyes met hers. Abby had actually said something unkind—the truth, no less!—about her ex-husband. Both of them turned to stare at Abby, who looked as if she couldn't believe she'd said it, either, and then the three of them exploded in laughter.

An hour later Bess lay in the dark. The laughter had eased their awkwardness with each other, and after they'd gone to bed, the physical familiarity of the old lumpy mattresses had brought another kind of familiarity. They'd reverted to their old habits, talking, giggling, sharing the kinds of things that were easiest to share in the dark—dreams, hopes, plans, heartaches.

The sound of a passing car drifted in the open window. "That sounded like your old Singer, Abby," Bess murmured with a laugh. She'd christened Abby's old car with the nickname because it had sounded exactly like her sewing machine. It had also broken down with a monthly regularity that prompted numerous jokes only women could truly appreciate.

Abby's sleepy laughter echoed back. "The only car in history with PMS. What a clunker."

Their giggles faded away, and Bess felt herself drifting into sleep. She was happy she'd come, but she was sad, too, and frustrated with herself. It was fun to remember the funny little things that had happened when they were in school. The common memories connected them, made them close but she'd been hoping for more, she realized now, a different, deeper connection. She'd wanted to be closer then, but she'd felt so out of place. She'd been two years older, for one thing, a difference in age that was inconsequential now, but had seemed like decades then. Even with a partial scholarship, she hadn't been able to afford college right out of high school, so she'd spent the next two years working full-time, saving every cent for the education that would enable her to someday have more than thrift-store clothes, home-canned food and looks of pity. When she'd finally gotten to school, it still hadn't been easy. While Keeley and Abby were dressing up for dates, she'd been dressing up in a waitress uniform for the drudgery of the part-time jobs that kept her in school. Even after so many years and all her success, the memory still hurt.

A wet warmth soaked into the pillow beneath her cheek. Maybe the reason she hadn't had the closeness she wanted with Abby and Keeley was that she had been envious of them, even angry with them, because of the money and the clothes they had, and the fun she never had time for. And maybe they'd sensed that.

Well, she wasn't envious or angry anymore. She bought her clothes in boutiques, her food at gourmet delis and a look of pity hadn't come her way in years, she thought with a silent, watery laugh. She had the life she'd wanted—but she still wanted the closeness as much as—maybe more than—ever.

She closed her eyes and her thoughts skipped free, unguarded. How was that ratty cat doing? Was Will home yet? Asleep? Alone?

Sunday

"Are you sure you don't want the Siamese, Will? He's got papers."

"No, Jack. This is the one I want." Will swung open the door of a wire cage.

"It isn't a male."

"That won't be a problem." He hoped.

Outside, a few minutes later, he shook the older man's hand. "Thanks, Jack. I owe you."

The other man used the hand not covering his yawn to wave away his thanks. "With all the free care you give us, we owe you."

Will slid the cat carrier onto the front seat, then climbed in beside it and slammed the door. "Thanks again, Jack," he said through the open window.

"Anytime, Will." The man covered another yawn. "Though maybe next time you could make it a little later in the morning. Say about six?"

He got a grin and an upraised hand in response as the orange four-wheel drive began to pull away. "Hey! Will!" He yelled. "You forgot to tell me what you want it for."

"This is as bad as having an eight o'clock class."

"You never had an eight o'clock class, Keeley Douglas," Abby reminded her with a laugh. "You never took anything before ten."

"And I still couldn't sleep late, because of Bess, the human alarm clock," Keeley moaned plaintively. "Nothing's changed. She still gets up with the chickens."

"Poor baby," Bess said in mock sympathy. This morning could have been any morning years ago: Keeley grousing about having to get up early, Abby sneaking coffee up from the dining room to get her moving, the mass confusion as the three of them tried to get dressed at the same time. Keeley had even needed panty hose, and Abby had them all laughing again when she opened her suitcase to show that she'd come prepared with extra pairs. Keeley had always paid them back for things, although never with anything so practical as another pair of hose. She would drop a small package on the bed or leave it on the dresser as casually as she'd appropriated the panty hose in the first place, and inside would be something exquisite and utterly useless. It would be worth more than what a dozen pair of panty hose would cost, but at the time Bess would rather have had the hose. She couldn't wear a Waterford crystal candle snuffer, she thought wryly as she started to French braid her hair. She still had the snuffer, though, along with all the other lovely, impractical gifts. For a long time Keeley's useless presents had been the only beautiful things she possessed.

"Speaking of chickens, did you find yours, Keeley?" Abby asked.

Keeley looked at her blankly for a second, then winced. "I was talking in my sleep, wasn't I? What did I say?"

"'Where's the chicken? Where's the chicken?'" Abby's soft South Carolina drawl became Keeley's crisp

Beacon Hill tones. "I was about to wake you up and tell you we'd eaten the darned thing when you shut up."

Keeley's groaning laughter joined theirs. She and Abby had been entertained by Keeley's midnight monologues all through school; fortunately, they'd never been the blood-curdling scream variety, but about mundane things like chickens, which made them all the funnier. Psych major Abby had thought they were outlets for suppressed anxieties, but Bess had found that hard to believe. Keeley hadn't been born with the proverbial silver spoon in her mouth; she'd been born with an entire set, and Bess had never been able to figure out what a girl who never did the subtraction in her checkbook could possibly be that anxious about.

Looking in the mirror over Keeley's shoulder, Bess frowned and undid the braid. She needed something . . . looser.

"Bess, do you have a steamer?"

"In the outside pocket of my garment bag." She answered Abby absently as she experimented with a twist.

"Keeley, look! Bess still has Radar."

Bess shut her eyes briefly. She'd forgotten that she'd hidden Radar in the pocket, too. Turning, she saw Abby holding up the worn teddy bear. She'd never intended to bring him, but he was an old traveling companion, and she'd packed him out of habit. She'd stuck him into the pocket, thinking Keeley and Abby would never know. A gift from the two of them, she'd named the bear after a character on a television show who'd had one like it, and he'd sat on her bed for the next two years, then gone to Boston with her. The first night in the tiny furnished efficiency that was to be her new home, she'd looked around and nothing had been familiar—not the furniture, not the bedspread, not even the picture on the wall—and the enormous step she was taking had abruptly overwhelmed her. Then she'd spotted Radar, and suddenly her new job didn't seem so terrifying, the strange city so lonely . . . but trying to explain it would sound so foolish.

"He's the only male I know who doesn't hog the bed," she said flippantly as Abby sat him up against the pillow. It was no explanation at all and hardly true—she didn't know if the men she knew hogged the bed or not—but Abby and Keeley laughed.

The three of them were being a little silly this morning. A couple of times they'd stopped what they were doing just to smile at each other. For no more reason than they were simply happy to be together again, Bess suspected. The warmth and closeness that she'd wanted all those years ago were here now—but perhaps they had been there all along, and she just hadn't been smart enough or mature enough to know it.

Bess took a deep breath of the air blowing through the car window. The opening session of Reunion Week had ended just before noon, and when Keeley and Abby had gone off on errands of their own, she'd decided to skip lunch. Not that she was anxious to see him, but this would be a good time to go out to Will Shedd's. She wasn't really that hungry, and she had said she would stop by, and she did need to check on the cat, and there was still the bill to be paid, not to mention that she'd forgotten her sweater there, so, since she had the time, she might as well go.

Having explained things to her satisfaction, she concentrated on her driving. A passing car swirled a gust of air through the window. Spiced with fresh-cut hay, yesterday's rain and a sweetness that might be the yellow wildflowers blooming along the road, it was quite a difference, she thought as she breathed appreciatively, from car exhaust and Boston Harbor at low tide.

The road dipped over a creek, and on the other side was a familiar white house. The tumbling water threw up a mist that caught the sun to make a small perfect rainbow, which arched over the creek. The ephemeral ribbon of colors vanished when she drove onto the bridge, but she realized that it must be a common phenomenon when she read the sign on the railing: Rainbow Creek. She glanced in her rearview mirror after she crossed the bridge, and there it was again, as if the rainbow were magic and not a simple matter of water and light angles.

She saw the black sign for Will Shedd's clinic that she'd seen the day before, but today she noticed that it had been cleverly cut in the shape of a dog with a short jaunty tail and ears. When she realized who the dog-shaped sign reminded her of and what she'd just driven over, Bess laughed. She'd just crossed over the "Rainbow" and here was Toto. All she needed to see now was a little girl in a gingham dress and a scarecrow.

She saw Will Shedd coming out of the barn instead. He was wearing jeans again, shrink-to-fits that had, and another T-shirt, blue this time, with sleeves and without holes. Clean shaven today, he looked less rough . . . but not much.

She slowed to a stop and, although he hadn't seemed to be in any hurry, his hand was on her door handle before hers. Her stomach tightened as he swung the door open—a hunger pang, of course; she should have grabbed a hamburger. From the streak of sawdust across one thigh and the light dusting of it on the old running shoes he wore, he'd traded the paintbrush for a saw today. She'd been telling herself that he wasn't as good-looking as she remembered, and he wasn't. She sighed quietly. He was better.

Will noted the slight hesitation before she stepped out of the car, as if she were considering whether it was a good idea or not. She had on a "banker" dress today, dark blue, conservative, and her hair was still up, although the style was softer than yesterday's tight braid. It looked as though only a few pins were holding it in place. "Hi."

The wonderful smell of fresh-sawn lumber clung to him. "Hello, Dr. Shedd." His greeting had been relaxed and friendly, making hers sound stiff even to her own ears. "How's the cat?" she asked, striving for an ease to match his.

"The cat's doing fine." He shut the car door behind her. "Come on in and see."

They climbed the porch steps; then, swiping a hand down his jeans, he stamped his feet to get rid of the sawdust before reaching for the screen door and holding it open for her. The simple courtesy didn't surprise her; what surprised her was that she'd allowed him to do it. For fifteen years she'd been opening her own doors—making a deliberate point of it, in fact—doing everything she could to make people forget she was a woman, and she'd been so successful that at times even she forgot. Yet she hadn't reached for the door just now. She'd waited for him to do it, even moving slightly to one side and slowing a few steps to make the choreography perfect. It had all been automatic, following his subtle lead, which she'd been aware of on some instinctual level. Will Shedd made a woman remember that she was, very much, a woman.

"You've got a visitor, cat. Bess is here," Will called as they entered the kennel area. His use of her first name was deliberate. They weren't going to be "Dr. Shedd" and "Miss Hilliard," Will thought impatiently; they'd gotten past that nonsense yesterday when he'd held her in his arms and discovered a softness and pliancy he hadn't expected. Of course, she had been unconscious at the time, he reminded himself sardonically, but he could guess the reason she wasn't more casual. She would have learned quickly enough at the beginning of her career that she couldn't afford any kind of casualness, not even simple friendliness, or she would be "honey"—or worse—to some of the men. He only hoped she hadn't learned it too well.

The cat in one of the half-dozen chest-high wire kennels seemed to be the only boarder. It struggled to its feet, giving the bandage on its right front leg a perplexed glance. It meowed its disapproval of the bandage, the accommodations and, she suspected, life in general. "Poor kitty. You look like you're in jail. This isn't exactly your idea of fun, is it?" she crooned. The cat, sensing a sucker, mewed pathetically and stuck a paw between the wire bars, hooking it around her arm to pull her closer. Laughing, she looked up at the man standing close beside her. "I think it's trying to con me into letting it out." Slipping her fingers through the mesh, she scratched the cat's ear. "What's the matter, kitty? Are you trying to tell me that it's all a big mistake? That they've got the wrong cat? You're innocent?"

The cat loudly agreed, and she glanced up with a smile. "It seems to be doing amazingly well, Will, thanks to you." His first name came naturally this time.

Will shrugged off the compliment. He wasn't so successful with the sharp niggle of guilt. The cat rubbed its clipped, iodine-stained fur against her fingers. "What's the matter?" he asked, seeing her sudden frown.

Bess shook her head with a laugh. "It's hard to believe this is the same pitiful looking animal I brought in yesterday. It seems bigger and lighter in color. Probably, I guess, because its fur was so wet and matted."

"Probably." Will relaxed fractionally. He hadn't pulled a jackass stunt like this in years. The only good likely to come out of it, he thought disgustedly, was that the cat would get a home for life in exchange for a little inconvenience.

Bess concentrated on tickling the cat's chin. "I wasn't sure you'd be here yesterday." She hadn't been sure he would be home today, either, despite what he'd said, and she didn't like acknowledging even to herself how disappointed she would have been if he hadn't.

"Technically I'm not here. I'm on vacation for two weeks. But I'm here for emergencies," he added swiftly at her guilty look.

"But you might want to go somewhere." She felt even guiltier for hoping that he wouldn't.

He opened the kennel door and offered the cat a full food dish. "The only place I'm going is the lumberyard in town. I'm spending my vacation this year patching up the house and barn." And deciding to take his vacation at home was the best decision he'd made in years.

The food dish emptied as if it had a hole in the bottom. "It doesn't look like a broken leg affected its appetite," she said with a soft smile, watching the cat eat.

"No," he agreed, watching her. "It's really vacuuming up the food." He was still having trouble believing what a difference a smile could make.

"I wonder what its name is," she murmured.

"You'll have to give it one." Her scent teased him, as the memory of it had the night before while he'd lain in the dark, waiting for sleep to come. He'd waited, he remembered, a long time.

She frowned for a second or two; then the frown became a wide smile. "I know! Hoover."

Will looked at her blankly until he recalled his earlier comment about the cat's eating style.

The warm, rich sound of his laughter seemed to resonate inside her, where it generated a more tangible warmth. The cat apparently didn't appreciate it as she did, though; it interrupted its meal to give them both an annoyed look. "All right, Hoover," Bess said with a soft chuckle, "we'll leave you to eat in peace." As she turned away, a woof came from the direction of the dog runs, which she'd thought were empty, and when Will Shedd started in that direction, she tagged along, too.

The dog looked as though it had a cute floppiness normally, but it wasn't looking very cute today. One hind leg was immobilized in plaster, and lines of dark stitches showed where its white-and-tan fur had been shaved, giving it the look of an old moth-eaten stuffed toy that had been badly mended.

Opening the gate to the run, Will crouched and, without thinking, she knelt beside him. "What happened?"

"His encounter with a car didn't turn out as well as Hoover's."

Despite his injuries, the dog accelerated his limping progress toward them. "Hey, Scruffy. How're you doing, boy?'' He rumpled the dog's long ears gently, and the dog wriggled his way into Will's arms, his delight at being held by the big man obvious. She could understand that....

Despite the warmth of the room, a cool shiver curled down her spine. Abruptly she felt threatened, but the threat didn't come from the man beside her, as much as she wanted to convince herself that it did. She might, her subconscious reminded her with unnecessary glee, control her conscious thoughts, but she had absolutely no control over the subconscious ones. That was where this powerful attraction for a man she didn't even know came from, and it was a very real threat because she didn't, *couldn't,* trust something she had no control over.

Warmth seeped across the scant inches separating them, then seeped into her, and she had to fight an insidious desire to move closer to him. She smoothed the fur on the dog's shoulder, taking care not to touch the man's. ''Will he be all right?''

''He won't run as fast as he used to, but he'll be okay.'' The dog swiped his chin with a long pink tongue, then settled its head on his shoulder, cradled in his arms. Just like a baby, she thought, and she knew suddenly what he would look like with his child in his arms, how tenderly he would hold it, how capably, how lovingly.

When he closed the kennel door a few minutes later, a piece of paper Bess hadn't noticed before fell off the door, and she bent to pick it up. It was a sheet of tablet paper, the kind she remembered from elementary school. Drawn in crayon was a picture of a white-and-tan dog and the message, painstakingly printed in block letters: I MISS YOU SCRUFFY. PLEASE GET WELL. I LOVE YOU. MELISSA.

"That's Scruffy's get-well card," he said with a wry grin, taking the paper. "The little girl he belongs to brought it when she came to see how he was doing." He twisted the tape at the top of the paper through the wire mesh of the door to secure it. Bess knew he could have thrown the letter away, and the little girl would never have known, but he hadn't, understanding how important it was to her to have that contact, however tenuous, with her pet. A lot of men would have been embarrassed for anyone to know that they put up get-well cards to a dog, that they honored the foolish wishes of a child, that they had any sensitivity or kindness in them at all. Someone might think they were less than manly. Those were the men, she'd found, who were often uncertain of their masculinity. Will Shedd obviously wasn't uncertain, and neither was she. He was one of the most strongly masculine men she'd ever met.

She followed him out of the kennel area, feeling strangely deflated. The visit had been so...brief.

"I was about to take a break for lunch when you came. I imagine you haven't eaten, either, and I've got plenty for two."

He was holding open a door that she guessed led to his living quarters. "Oh, no," Bess said quickly. "I can't stay." The smell coming through the open door was wonderful. "I really should get back," she added, more slowly.

Will saw the discreet sniff and fanned the door a little to draw in more of the aroma from the pot simmering on the stove. "Do you have something planned for this afternoon?"

"Well, no..." Her nose twitched again. "But—"

"Good. Then there's no reason why you can't stay, unless—" he looked at her questioningly "—you don't like chili?"

Bess considered the offer. He wasn't making a big deal of it; it was just a casual invitation, and she *had* missed lunch. "I love chili," she told him with a happy smile.

The door opened directly into the kitchen, and as they entered, something that looked like a cross between a rusty steel wool pad and a Great Dane rose from the gray linoleum. Bess froze as it greeted them with a cavernous *woof* that showed an impressively lethal set of teeth.

"Sit, Hank."

The dog obeyed the command readily enough, but Bess remembered those teeth too well to make any sudden moves. "He's safe. You're in more danger of being licked to death than eaten." His large, warm hand on her arm reassured her, as much as his words did, and she allowed herself to be drawn forward slowly as he made the introductions. "Hank, this is Bess."

Gravely the dog offered a paw, and Bess, swallowing a laugh, shook it. "How do you do, Hank?" she said with equal gravity. She risked a pat on the dog's broad head and discovered his fur felt like a steel wool pad, too. When she took her hand away, he stretched his neck forward, trying to worm his head under her hand again, and she laughed. "Oh, you're just a big baby, Hank." She scratched the base of his bent ears and, with a blissful sigh, the dog closed his yellow eyes and leaned more of his considerable weight against her.

"The worst," Will confirmed dryly. "He'll make a real nuisance of himself if you let him." She was murmuring nonsense to the dog as she petted him, seemingly unconcerned that she was getting dog hair all over her dress. "Okay, Hank, that's enough lollygagging. Go lie down," he directed.

As Hank, with a last soulful look, went to lie down beside a chair at the kitchen table, Bess said wonderingly, "I don't think I've ever seen a dog quite like that."

"There's only one Hank," he agreed with a rueful grin.

He went to the sink to wash his hands, and Bess followed suit. In response to her offer of help, he pointed out the location of the dishes and silverware. "Where'd you get him?" she asked, taking down two stoneware bowls. He had, she saw, a complete set of dishes, not the usual bachelor odds and ends.

"One of the sheriff's deputies found him and brought him in." He opened the refrigerator; it was well stocked, a good deal fuller than hers, in fact. "He was a stray and had been staying alive by raiding garbage cans and chicken coops, which probably explains why somebody had taken a shot at him."

Bess's hands stilled on the spoons in the silverware drawer. "He was shot?"

"Yeah."

Bess heard the anger in his voice.

"And you decided to keep him," she said lightly.

He shrugged as he set a cantaloupe on the cutting board. "I didn't have a dog."

She hid a smile as she set a place at the chair at the head of the table, the one Hank lay beside, and one for herself next to it. "How long have you had him?"

"Almost three years. I got him not long after I moved here." He pulled open a drawer and took out a long knife, a ladle and an ice-cream scoop. His hands full, he bumped the drawer closed with a lean hip, reminding her again, if she needed it, that he moved with exceptional grace. He sliced the cantaloupe in half, then cleaned out the seeds with the ice-cream scoop with brisk efficiency. The sturdy pine table and chairs were antiques, but the rest of the kitchen had been completely modernized, and he clearly knew his way around it.

Will nodded toward the cupboard over the sink as he carried the cantaloupe to the table. "There's a box of crackers in that cupboard."

As she set the crackers on the table, her eyes strayed back to the most outstanding feature in the kitchen. He'd seen her startled double take when she'd first seen it, then watched her sneaking peeks at it when she thought he wasn't looking. "How do you like the wallpaper?" he asked blandly.

He must have seen her staring. "It's...unique," Bess said, settling on an opinion that was diplomatic as well as honest. "I don't believe I've ever seen that particular pattern before."

"I call it the 'Fighting Amish.'" He made a bet with himself as to how much longer she could keep a straight face.

Bess almost strangled on a laugh. "I can see why." The wallpaper depicted a Pennsylvania Dutch couple in several scenes of domestic bliss. In one the wife was clouting the husband over the head with a frying pan; in another he had her in an ear lock. To complete the "uniqueness" of it, the colors had a wonderful Halloween garishness.

"It's one of the reasons I bought the house," he said to nudge the odds in his favor. She glanced at him sideways as if to determine whether he were dangerous or just harmlessly insane. There was an odd choked sound, and he won the bet. Her laughter was as free and as infectious as a little girl's. She even looked like one, Will thought, with her cheeks pink and her eyes sparkling.

"I'm sorry," Bess gasped, "but that wallpaper is...is so..." Caught by a giggle, she gestured helplessly.

"Ugly?" he suggested. "Obnoxious?"

She nodded vigorously. "And the worst thing about it is, it sort of grows on you. After a while—" she laughed with a kind of despairing disbelief "—you might actually start to like it!"

"Not a chance. I've been here a year, and I still don't like it. I just haven't had time to do anything about it yet."

She giggled again, and the delightfully silly sound seemed to fill the kitchen, reminding him how quiet the big room usually was. The silence, he sensed, would have an emptiness from now on.

Abruptly he turned toward the refrigerator. "What would you like to drink? I've got milk, soda pop and beer."

"Milk's fine." She smiled her thanks as he filled her glass while she sat down. "How did you know I hadn't had lunch?"

"You look like a woman who skips meals on a regular basis."

Bess tried to decide if she should be insulted. He'd just told her, however subtly, that she bore a closer resemblance to a bean pole than a centerfold, but her mirror told her the same thing every morning, and being insulted by the truth now seemed a little hypocritical. She did miss meals, and too many of the ones she did eat came out of carryout cartons—corporate K rations, a stockbroker friend called them.

He took his seat and, without asking, picked up her bowl and ladled in chili until it was almost overflowing.

"That's all?" she complained as she accepted the bowl.

"You can have seconds," he promised solemnly. She didn't pick at it, but dug right in. "Somebody who didn't know better might think you're hungry," he murmured.

"I am," she admitted with a laugh. "But this is really good."

The amount of pleasure the compliment gave him was asinine, he knew.

He lifted his glass, and Bess monitored the disappearance of the milk by the smooth contractions of his strong throat, not the level in the glass. To distract herself, she asked, "You said you moved here three years ago. Where did you live before that?" Now that hunger was being satisfied, curiosity was next.

"The Boston area. Cambridge, to be exact."

"How did you choose East Ridley?"

He refilled his bowl. "After my divorce, I realized I'd be happier in a small town where I could have a small and large animal practice. It took me a couple of years to find exactly what I wanted."

"How long were you married?" Divorce was hardly uncommon, yet it surprised her that he was divorced. Intuitively she knew that if he committed himself to a woman, it would be for life, and she had to wonder what had broken the commitment.

"Seven years."

She abandoned any pretense of subtlety. "What happened?"

"We discovered we had different goals in life." He spoke in a matter-of-fact tone, although just for a second there was the same...something in his eyes that she'd seen yesterday when she'd asked about children, but again it disappeared before she could name it. "We'd planned to start a family as soon as her law practice was established, but she realized eventually that she didn't really want children." He picked up the carton of milk. "More milk?"

"Please." He poured the milk, and she picked up the glass and drank absently. There was no rancor or evidence of torch-carrying in his straightforward explanation. He and his wife had had a fundamental disagreement in which there was no compromise: he wanted children; she didn't. Bess had a mental picture of a woman who was completely focused on her career, a woman completely committed to her own success—a woman very like herself. Did his wife know what she'd given up?

Will picked up the ladle. "How about some more chili?"

"Just a little, please."

He reached for her bowl, wondering at the look of sadness he'd seen before her quick smile banished it. Deliberately he added another half ladleful to the bowl before handing it back with a look that dared her to object. He was teasing her, as much for himself as for her. He didn't, for several reasons, want to see a return of the bleak expression he'd seen a minute ago. He'd found himself wanting to hold her...just hold her, the need to comfort so sharp that it hurt. He just wasn't sure which of them he wanted to comfort most.

It seemed as if they had only just sat down to lunch and then he was walking her out to her car. As they passed his four-wheel drive, Bess glanced in the back window at what she'd thought yesterday was a handyman's traveling tool chest. "You've made your Bronco into a mobile veterinary clinic, haven't you?" she commented.

He nodded. "I probably treat as many patients out of it as I do here at the clinic." With a rueful laugh, he added, "The local kids call it the 'Broncosaurus.'"

Bess laughed with him. "I see the resemblance." With the heavy toothlike grill, bulky body, high clearance and deep-treaded tires, it didn't take much imagination to see the Bronco as some lumbering prehistoric beast. Stopping at her car, he stood facing her, relaxed, his hands in the back pockets of his old jeans, squinting a little against the late-afternoon sun. The sunlight touched his hair, turning it the color of molten silver. Her fingers played with the numbered push buttons below the door handle without pressing any of them. "Well," she said, looking up with a bright smile, "thanks again for lunch."

"You're welcome." When she'd announced that she had to leave, he hadn't tried to change her mind. He knew she needed a "legitimate" reason—checking on the cat, lunch—to be here, and today's quota had been used up. But there was always tomorrow.

"You're sure it will be convenient if I come tomorrow evening?" He'd already said it was; she was only postponing the inevitable.

"It'll be convenient."

As he spoke, there was a soft plop behind her. A look of annoyance crossed his face as he glanced beyond her, and she turned to see why. "Oh, you have a crab apple tree!" The tree stood in the side yard and bore a crop of reddish-gold apples, each one about the size of a fat cherry tomato. As she watched, another one dropped from the tree, joining the others on the grass below with another plop.

"Is that what it is? One of my projects this next week is to cut it down."

She turned to him, shocked. "Why? It's a lovely tree."

"It's also a major nuisance," he said flatly. "The apples are tiny, and so sour even the birds won't eat them. All they do is fall and rot on the lawn."

"They make wonderful jelly," she told him earnestly.

He gave her a dry look. "I don't make jelly, Bess."

She gave him a look of exaggerated patience. "Anybody can make jelly." She glanced back at the tree, and he heard her mutter under her breath, "It's really a sin to let them go to waste."

Will studied the tree thoughtfully. "It don't suppose you know how to make jelly?" The question was deliberately offhand.

She looked insulted. "I've been making it since I was eleven years old."

"I imagine it's pretty time-consuming."

"Not really. It takes two days, but that's only because the cooked apples have to hang in a bag for twenty-four hours so the juice can drip out. You actually spend just a couple of hours altogether making it."

He pretended to consider, then shook his head. "I think it'd be easier to get out the chain saw."

"Oh, Will, no! It's easy to make," she argued; then, to her utter astonishment, she heard herself say, "I'll show you."

His smile had the satisfied look of a cat who'd pounced and caught the mouse. "All right," he agreed softly. "We'll start tomorrow night."

"Bess, isn't planning to make jelly a little odd for a woman who's always claimed she despised it?"

Bess looked at her two roommates, Keeley's puzzled frown silently adding her opinion to Abby's. They were walking across campus to the cocktail party that was the real start of Reunion Week and talking about plans for the coming week, and she, without thinking, had mentioned that she would be making jelly.

She could understand their disbelief; she couldn't believe it, either. The endless hours she and her mother had spent putting up the surplus from their garden and small orchard had been a hated symbol of their poverty. She'd been overjoyed when her mother had married a well-to-do man, guaranteeing that she would never have to French another green bean or dill another pickle. That her mother persisted in doing it anyway bewildered and frustrated her, and yet, here she was, planning to do the very same herself. "Yes," she agreed thoughtfully.

A speculative look passed between the other two women. "You haven't told us much about this Will Shedd, Bess," Keeley remarked casually. "What's he like?"

She shrugged. "He's tall." She still felt a foolish reluctance to talk about him. "A few years older than I am."

Keeley was clearly going to press for more details when laughter ahead of them diverted her. Three summer school students were walking toward them, spotlighted by the late-afternoon sun filtering through the trees. It was like looking through a magic mirror back in time. The young women, light-haired and stair steps in height, could have been them years before, and from the soft expressions on Keeley's and Abby's faces, they were thinking the same.

The students caught sight of a workman working overtime on the library renovations. He was young, well built and good-looking, none of which was lost on them. Their voices became a little more animated, their laughter a little huskier, their walks a subtle sashay, while they studiously ignored him. He just as studiously ignored them back, but the three observers saw the quick flirting glances and small smiles passing among the four.

"Were we that silly?" Abby murmured.

Keeley laughed. "Bess wasn't. She was too sensible. She knew what she wanted, and she wasn't about to get sidetracked by a handsome face and tight jeans."

Hearing Abby's laughing agreement, Bess felt the same sense of exclusion she'd felt whenever Abby or Keeley had been lamenting their latest "sidetrack." She'd commiserated, but she'd felt like their eighty-year-old maiden aunt, closed out because she hadn't experienced their suffering. She'd had her share of secret crushes, but she'd understood that anything more, any kind of romantic involvement, was a temptation to be avoided at all costs and, irrational as it might have been, she'd envied Keeley and Abby their temporarily broken hearts.

The cocktail party was in full swing when they arrived, and Abby was soon claimed by her old psychology professor, Joshua Lucas. Bess and Keeley matched raised eyebrows over Abby's easy use of his first name, and suddenly Bess had a good idea how Abby had spent the afternoon.

"What do you bet he asked her to come with him tonight?" Keeley murmured as they watched Abby and her professor disappear into the crush, and Bess knew Keeley had come to the same conclusion she had.

Keeley decided to "work the crowd," as she put it; the opportunity to do a little fund-raising was too good to pass up. People stopped to talk, and Bess was surprised and flattered that so many remembered her, but she didn't join any of them when they moved on. For the moment she was content to hold up the wall and sip the wine she'd accepted from a passing waitress. After a few minutes she understood why.

Except for the handful of male faculty members and a few brave husbands, women made up the crowd, but it was the men she was interested in. None of them specifically, just in general—to compare to Will Shedd. Subconsciously she'd been picturing him here, wondering how he would fit in. He would, very well . . . and yet he wouldn't. He would stand out—and not because of his height and hair, Bess laughed to herself. The differences between him and the men in this room were physical, but more subtle, more basic, than hair and height. Most of the men were in shape, especially Joshua Lucas, but it was a fitness acquired in a gym or on a tennis court. Will's came from physical labor, and it gave his body a hardness the others lacked. He moved differently, too, with an ease and innate physical confidence that wasn't matched by any man here tonight. She stared sightlessly across the room, the mental vision of a tall, tarnish-haired man more vivid than any of the flesh and blood ones a few feet away.

"Bess? Bess Hilliard?"

From the puzzlement in the woman's voice, Bess realized that it wasn't the first time she'd spoken to her, and her attention snapped back to the short, plump woman standing practically under her nose. Not recognizing her, she glanced discreetly at the name tag on the woman's shoulder. "Eileen?" She tried to keep the disbelief out of her voice. "Eileen Beason?"

The other woman laughed ruefully. "It's Rhoden now, but yes, it's me, four babies and sixty pounds later."

"I don't have to ask what you've been doing the past fifteen years," Bess said with a wide grin. "Four children. What a nice family!"

Eileen gave her a wry look. "I'm not sure nice is the right word. What about you? Are you married? Any children?"

For the next few minutes they filled in the larger gaps in the past fifteen years. "Have you seen Abby and Keeley?" Bess asked.

"Yes. Abby was with Dr. Lucas, and I got the feeling I was interrupting something, so I didn't do much more than say hi, but I talked to Keeley for a while. I was sorry to hear about her husband." Eileen took a sip of the diet soda in her hand. "Actually I saw her earlier today, coming out of Dominic's shop, but I couldn't stop and talk then."

Bess almost choked on her wine. "Dominic Vitalli?"

"Yes. He's got a furniture-making business now, and I hear he's doing quite well."

Bess only half listened as Eileen described several pieces she'd seen in his shop. Now she knew why Keeley had been so vague about her afternoon activities, and maybe even why she'd been so keyed up the night before. The only real argument she, Abby and Keeley ever had had been over Dominic Vitalli. He'd been the town "bad boy," although she and Abby had never thought he deserved the label. Keeley had dated him, seemingly regarding the whole affair as some kind of romantic slumming. They'd pointed out that he seemed to be getting pretty serious and that she wasn't treating him fairly, and Keeley hadn't appreciated their opinions. Eventually she'd dumped him, and Bess knew Dominic had been hurt, but she'd always wondered if perhaps it hadn't been Keeley who'd been hurt worse. If she was seeing him again, she could well be setting herself up for more heartache.

Eileen changed the subject. "Keeley tells me you've got something going with East Ridley's most eligible bachelor," she said teasingly.

"Oh? Who's that?" Bess asked innocently.

"Will Shedd."

She shrugged. "I just took him a hurt cat I found." Feigning interest in the crowd, she took another sip of her wine. "Cuts quite a swath, does he?"

"He could," Eileen said honestly, "but he doesn't take advantage of it. He dates several of the single women in town, but he doesn't seem to be serious about any of them. Carlynn Sisk—" she nodded toward a woman a few yards away "—is one of them."

Bess studied the statuesque redhead over the rim of her glass. Carlynn Sisk used to have mousy brown hair and a flat chest. Was she the one he'd called yesterday to say that he would be a little late? "Do you know him well?" Now that she thought about it, she'd never particularly liked Carlynn.

"Pretty well, I guess. Bob, my husband, plays poker with him. He's got a good practice, does a lot of free work for the Humane Association, too. He takes in every stray that wanders by, but except for this one monster dog Bob's told me about, he always finds other homes for them.'' She laughed. ''Bob came home with a kitten one night.''

Bess laughed with her uneasily. Was that why Will Shedd had asked her to stay for lunch? Did he see her as another stray he felt sorry for?

Monday

"Joshua Lucas looks pretty good for his age, doesn't he?" Abby asked.

Bess exchanged an amused look with Keeley. Abby had just done a remarkably bad impression of nonchalance. She'd had a major crush on him in school, and from what they'd seen last night, maybe what would have been impossible fifteen years ago wasn't now. "Any age," Bess said dryly.

She went back to riffling through the meager selection in her closet, finally deciding on a slim white-and-blue polka-dot shirtdress.

"Did you make that dress, Bess?" Keeley asked.

"No, I don't sew anymore."

Abby looked at her in surprise. "Why not? You're so good at it. I've never known anyone who could sew like you."

"Because I don't have to wear homemade clothes anymore." Her answer was just a little short.

"Homemade?" Keeley laughed. "Your clothes didn't look homemade any more than mine did."

Bess looked at her two friends. She'd always thought they'd paid her compliments on her clothes because they felt sorry for her for being so poor that she had to make them. She'd brushed off their compliments, hating the pity she thought she saw in their eyes. But there was no pity today, only sincere praise. There never had been, she understood now. "Thank you," she said. For the compliment today and all the ones years ago.

She slipped the dress over her head, then stepped back to look in the mirror on the closet door, tripping over a shoe in the process. Picking it up, she stared around the room with a helpless laugh. "I can't believe it."

"What can't you believe?" Abby asked as she squinted one-eyed into the mirror to put on mascara.

"This room. We've hardly been here more than a day and it looks as bad as ever." Her sweeping gesture took in the shoes littering the floor, the clothes strewn over chairs and beds, and the mousse, hair spray, makeup, hairbrushes and other essentials taking up every other available surface.

"It does, doesn't it?" Keeley said, sounding impressed.

Abby surveyed the mess, too. "You know, I don't know why we asked for this room every year. The corner suites are bigger."

"Ah, but they didn't have a terrace," Bess reminded her, gesturing grandly toward the fire escape.

"Bess." Keeley's sharp voice cut into Abby's and Bess's laughter. Keeley stood beside the bookcase whose top had served all through school to hold curling irons, hot rollers and hair dryers. The assortment there now represented the newest generation, except for one. "Tell me these aren't the hot rollers you got with box tops when we were freshmen."

"What?" Abby said in disbelief. "She doesn't still have those, does she?" She went over to see for herself.

"Look at this, Abby," Keeley demanded, jabbing a finger at the inoffensive curlers. "The cover's gone, the base is cracked and one of the heat rods is bent."

Abby made an exasperated sound. "Really, Bess, I think you've gotten your money's worth out of these and then some. You can retire them now."

Bess stared at them, at a loss to understand why they were suddenly so annoyed with her, and over something as stupid as hot rollers, for heaven's sake! "They still work," she said mildly.

Shaking their heads at each other, her roommates favored her with another irked look. With a mental shrug, Bess finished buttoning her dress. Both of them were making workshop presentations today—maybe they were nervous; nerves could make anyone a little unreasonable.

She smoothed down her skirt. It wasn't just nerves, though. What had Abby said the first night? That it was comforting to know some things never changed? But things did change. *They'd* changed, and the changes hadn't all been good ones. Abby and Keeley had each suffered major losses that they all knew about, but there had been other griefs, too, she was sure, that hadn't been shared in the short scribbles on the Christmas and birthday cards they sent each other. She sensed that Keeley's silver spoons had tarnished, and that Abby was unhappy, too. She had her own dissatisfactions, as well, and she was beginning to wonder if all three of them hadn't come back to Bartlett hoping to recapture that simpler, happier time when all things had seemed possible, taking comfort in the illusion that the friends of that time wouldn't have changed. But of course they had, and now that the initial euphoria of being together again had worn off, the changes made them edgy with each other, because they had to face the reality that they couldn't go back in time. Mistakes couldn't be unmade, losses returned, wrong decisions righted.

* * *

"How many yards, ma'am?"

"Two, please." As soon as the seminars and workshops were over for the day, Bess had walked the few blocks to downtown East Ridley to find a fabric store. She hadn't been in one in years, and she wouldn't be in one now, she thought, if she didn't need some unbleached muslin to make jelly bags. Unlike Keeley and Abby, she'd never considered her sewing an admirable skill, only a necessity, and the day she started earning enough to buy her clothes, she'd put the cover on her sewing machine and packed it away.

While the clerk measured and cut, she glanced around the store. At one display table a woman fingered a bolt of a silky-looking tropical print that could make a gorgeous shirt. Nearby, a row of women and older girls pored over pattern books. Feeling an odd wistfulness, she watched them slowly turning the pages, as she had done once upon another time.

Back outside, she consulted her watch. Keeley and Abby had plans for the evening, so she'd decided to eat at the dorm, and they wouldn't be serving for another hour. She had time for a bit of window-shopping.

Coming to a corner, she glanced down the tree-lined side street and, seemingly on their own, her feet decided on a detour. The houses were older, but well cared for, with neat lawns and bright flowers, and almost every front porch had a swing and a pot or two of geraniums or marigolds. Children in swimsuits raced shrieking and laughing around one front yard, squirting each other with a garden hose. She'd forgotten, Bess thought with an unconscious smile, what a *nice* town East Ridley was.

Eventually she wandered back to the main street. Recognizing the building on the opposite side, she glanced up at the big old-fashioned clock mounted on the corner, then crossed the street. Knowing the front door would be locked already, she went around to the back and knocked on the heavy steel door. As she expected, the owner himself opened the door.

"Bess! I was wondering when you'd come by. Come in, come in!" Except that his hair had turned completely gray and there was quite a bit less of it, Lloyd Crosby was exactly as she'd remembered him. A little shorter than she, he had the prosperous, well-fed look of a small-town bank president, which was exactly what he was. He'd given her her first job in banking while she'd still been in college, and they'd kept in touch during the years since.

"I hope you don't mind my coming by without an appointment," she began as he ushered her toward the lobby.

"You know we don't worry about appointments here," he chided. Drawing her to a stop, he turned her around gently to face him. "Well, Bess, let's see what the big city's done to you." Obligingly she stood still for his inspection. "You look good," he said finally with a soft smile, then gestured around the lobby. "How do we look?"

Built around the turn of the century, the East Ridley National Bank looked the way Bess had always thought a bank should look, which was nothing like the glass and chrome pyramid she worked in. The outside was weathered New England granite, while inside were dark oak counters, brass tellers' cages and a silver-seamed marble floor. Everything had the appearance of integrity, stability and permanence, and appearances weren't deceiving. The bank was as solid as the three-ton polished brass door protecting the vault. "Everything looks wonderful, Mr. Crosby."

In his office, Bess heard what changes had taken place since she'd last sat across the beautiful antique rosewood desk from him. As she'd expected, the bank was as up-to-date as any Boston bank. Business was good; deposits were up. The only problem seemed to be who would follow him as bank president. The bank was family-owned, and a Crosby had always occupied the chair behind the rosewood desk. His wife was after him to retire, and he admitted that he was ready to, but, childless, he had no son or daughter to take over as president, and none of his nieces or nephews was a possibility. The stewardship of the bank was going to pass into a stranger's hands, and he was plainly concerned that the hands be strong and capable. He was looking for someone who would stay and become a permanent part of the town, not someone who would consider the presidency of a small bank just a stepping stone to a larger one. The salary and stock option he was offering were generous and, as he said, it was a good opportunity for someone looking for a wholesome, congenial, stable environment in which to settle down and raise a family.

"Well, enough about me." He leaned back in his swivel chair and clasped his hands over his comfortable belly. "You've come a long way from working nights here posting checks, Bess." He nodded his approval. "Senior vice president. You won't have any trouble now getting the presidency you've always wanted." He studied her for a moment. "You must be very happy."

"It's always been my ultimate goal," she said, and if he noticed that she hadn't directly answered his oblique question, Lloyd Crosby didn't mention it.

"It's not that I don't have faith in you, cat, but I've got to take advantage of every opportunity." Will raked a hand through his hair with a disgusted laugh. It was a sign of how far gone he was when he started explaining himself to a dumb animal. Shoving himself away from the counter, he began to prowl the kitchen.

He didn't believe in love at first sight, but he knew he was too old to be suffering from an attack of glands. He paused behind a chair to straighten the sweater hanging over the back of it. Whatever he was feeling for Bess Hilliard, the symptoms were just as severe, and he was almost certain she was suffering a few, too. His fingers kneaded the soft fabric under his hands. Part of what he was feeling was physical, he admitted, but there was a hell of a lot more to it than that, and he wanted the chance to find out just what and how much. If he didn't, he strongly suspected he would regret it for the rest of his life; yet, with only a week, he was desperately short of time. His head snapped up as he heard the sound he'd been unconsciously listening for all day. That was why, as he'd told the cat, he had to use any and every opportunity to keep her coming back.

She was just closing the door of her car as he came around the corner of the house. "Hi. I see you've got the ladder and buckets all ready."

"I'm ready," he agreed.

What was it Keeley had said? That she was too sensible to fall for a handsome face and tight jeans? Bess swallowed a half-despairing laugh. That just showed how much Keeley knew. "How's Hoover?"

"He's fine." Nothing like keeping your lies honest, he told himself caustically.

"Good." She clapped her hands together briskly. "Shall we get started, then?" It would be light for at least another hour, so they didn't have to hurry, but she wasted no time grabbing a bucket and starting to fill it. Will picked up the second one and headed for the ladder. She'd retreated back to her "business" mode.

He repositioned the ladder so he would have a clear view of her. She had her hair in a braid again, but there were braids and then there were braids, he decided. This one was so loosely plaited that it looked almost undone; it wouldn't take much to finish the job.

"How many of these things do we need?"

Bess looked up to see him standing halfway up the ladder. "If we fill both buckets, we'll have enough for a good-size batch."

"Damn!"

At first she thought he was grumbling about how many apples he would have to pick; then she saw that wasn't the problem. Directly behind his head was a dead branch spiked with small twigs, and somehow he'd gotten several of them snagged in his hair. He was trying to free himself but, not being able to see what he was doing, he was just making things worse.

"Will, wait! I'll help you." Pausing long enough to kick off her slick-soled pumps and hike up the skirt of her dress, she started up the back side of the sturdy aluminum stepladder.

"Damn it, Bess, be careful!" Cursing under his breath at her foolhardiness as much as the pain in his scalp, Will grabbed for her shoulders when it seemed she was slipping; then he saw that she was only hitching her dress up higher so she could climb up to the next brace. Never intended as steps, the braces on the back of the ladder were narrow and spaced widely apart, making climbing them precarious in pants and sneakers, much less in stocking-feet wearing a narrow skirt. But, in spite of himself, a part of him appreciated the length of sleek thigh she had to expose to do it.

"Bess, get down," he ordered impatiently. "You're going to tear your dress—if you don't fall and break your fool neck first." To his annoyance, she ignored him, and he dropped his hands to her waist to steady her.

"Nonsense," Bess said breathlessly, pulling herself up to the last brace. "My mother and I used to do this all the time when we picked fruit. Saved us from having to move the ladder so often." Bracing her thighs against the top of the ladder, she leaned cautiously around him. His hands tightened, and she moved even more carefully. Her balance was uncertain enough already.

"You've really got yourself stuck," she murmured as she began untangling his hair as gently as possible. Surreptitiously she rubbed a few strands between her fingers and discovered that they were as soft as she'd imagined. A few had pulled out, caught like silver silk threads on a broken twig. A bird would find them next spring, she thought with a soft smile, and make a special addition to its nest.

He winced as she had to pull harder to free one curl. "That chain saw is sounding better all the time," he growled, and Bess laughed sympathetically. She stretched up on her toes to reach the last tangle, and her laughter abruptly caught in her throat. She'd been able to deal with the feel of his long fingers around her waist and the shivery tickle of his breath past her ear, but now, with her on tiptoe, his breath was several inches lower. Another gust wafted through the thin material of her dress and the thinner lace of her bra, cool on her suddenly flushed skin. Her nipple shriveled yet paradoxically felt throbbingly full at the same time. As if in empathy, the other nipple drew up achingly taut, and a hot pang jabbed through her below her stomach. She knew she should move, but the swamping sensations felt too good.

He breathed again and watched the small pucker her nipple made in the soft fabric grow larger. He was so close, he could have touched his tongue to it, and he imagined the taste of her underneath, the color, the feel. Her scent he already knew. The sweet warmth of her seemed to surround him, and he breathed again. She pulled back, but slowly, as if moving in a dream, and when she looked down at him, her eyes had a heavy-lidded, almost sleepy look. Her mouth softened, and as he watched, her lips parted.

His eyes were clear and direct as he looked up at her. Bess felt his fingers spread and lock on her hips and ribs, his thumbs sliding up just under her breasts. Her hands went automatically to his shoulders as, with gentle, relentless force, he pulled her down off her toes toward him. Her eyes dropped to his mouth, and she saw it harden with intent as he drew her closer.

Her body seemed to go boneless in his hands, malleable and warm; then suddenly he was holding rigid stone. She ducked her head, turning her face away as her arms fell stiffly to her sides. "That's all of it. You're free now," she said in a tight voice.

His hands clenched involuntarily. That wasn't all, not by a long shot—but the top of a ladder wasn't the place to pursue it. Will forced himself to let her go, although his hands remained ready to grab her again if she slipped on the climb down. She didn't. She put on her shoes, straightened her dress and patted her hair, the cool composed all-business woman again, except for the feverish color in her cheeks. Then, without looking in his direction, she walked back to where she'd left her bucket.

Bess jerked a crab apple from the branch. She was a mature, experienced thirty-eight-year-old woman, not some sixteen-year-old who'd suddenly found herself in over her head in the back seat of a car. She'd known he intended to kiss her; she'd been anticipating it, *wanting* it, more than she'd wanted any kiss ever before in her life. And he'd known it. Then, suddenly, she'd turned into that sixteen-year-old—gauche, nervous... and scared. She yanked another apple off the tree and threw it into her bucket. And she knew why.

Since a romance that had ended several years before, her relationships with men had been either professional or very casual and superficial. Personal relationships simply weren't on her agenda, and frankly, she hadn't met anyone who'd made her think otherwise—until now. She was responding to Will Shedd on a deep, purely emotional level beyond her control, one that had nothing to do with logic or agendas. That was why she had acted like a frightened, immature child... because there was nothing casual or superficial about what she was feeling for him. But she could hardly tell him that, Bess told herself derisively. If he wasn't already wondering about her, he would be, thinking her even more of a child to take what had undoubtedly been just a simple pass and blow it so far out of proportion.

"So you and your mother used to pick a lot of fruit?"

After her hectic thoughts, the question was so prosaic that she almost laughed out loud, but it was exactly the conversational ordinariness that she needed to break the silence between them before it became too awkward. "Yes, bushels of it, every summer. Apricots, pears, peaches, plums, cherries, apples, everything. What we didn't put up, we sold." She clamped her mouth shut before she reached full-fledged babble.

"Your folks had a farm?"

She peeked over the branch she was picking from and saw that he'd moved the ladder closer while she hadn't been looking. "No, a backyard." She laughed briefly. "Some people collect stamps or coins. My dad collected fruit trees."

"Does he still collect them?"

"He passed away when I was eleven."

His pail full, Will glanced over and decided that hers was full enough, too. After climbing down, he folded up the ladder, and in response to his wordless cue, she picked up her bucket. "That must have been hard," he said quietly as they began walking together toward the house.

She glanced at him, then quickly away. "It was. Dad had started a small nursery business just before he became ill. Three months later he was gone. Mom couldn't run the business, so she sold it, but that just paid off the loan Dad had taken out. There were still thousands of dollars in hospital and doctor bills. There wasn't any life insurance or Social Security, but there was mortgage insurance on the house, so Mom paid it off, then turned around and remortgaged it, using the money to pay what she could right away and negotiating terms for the rest. She thought about selling the house to pay the rest of the bills but, as she said, we had to have a place to live.''

''It was just you and your mother, then?''

''Yes.''

''Your mother could have declared bankruptcy. It would have been justified in her situation,'' he said neutrally.

She looked at him again, meeting his eyes this time. ''Probably so,'' she said with a faint smile, ''but Hilliards pay their bills.''

That had a parental ring to it, and Will knew from whom she'd inherited that stiff-necked pride he'd already seen a time or two. He'd tried the most non-threatening conversational gambit he could think of to get her talking again, and it was working, with the side benefit that she was finally talking about herself. ''It couldn't have been easy,'' he said, careful to keep any hint of pity out of his voice.

She shrugged. ''It wasn't so bad. Mom had never worked, so all she could get at first was a minimum-wage job at a dime store, but she took night classes at the community college and eventually became a book-keeper. I learned to sew when I was twelve and made my clothes. We grew a big garden, and what we didn't put up we sold, along with the excess fruit, and that kept the house from falling apart, which—'' her laugh was wry ''—it tried to do at least once a year. And I was lucky enough to get a scholarship that paid for part of college.''

It was the most information she'd ever volunteered about herself, but what she'd left out told him more than what she'd said. Will thought of his own happy, financially secure childhood. His parents weren't wealthy by any means, but there had always been money for the things most kids took for granted—movies, vacations, hamburgers at a drive-in, clothes when he needed them. Just taking care of basic necessities would have taken every penny her mother made, and even then, he knew some of Bess's needs had gone unmet. Her comment about sewing her own clothes at an age when other girls were still playing with their Barbie dolls almost broke his heart. Her childhood had been cut short by her father's death, her life changed disastrously, yet there was no bitterness, no self-pity, in her voice as she spoke. She and her mother had pulled together and recovered from the low blow life had dealt them.

College couldn't have been easy for her to manage, even with a scholarship. There were government loans that would have made things easier, but after watching her mother owe her soul, he could understand why she hadn't applied for one. For the same reason, he could understand why she'd gone into banking. It was a natural for someone who'd learned early on the importance of money. He didn't feel sorry for the woman, because she wouldn't be what she was today otherwise, but he could feel sorry for the child, although he wouldn't tell her that. She wouldn't, he thought sardonically, appreciate his sympathy.

He leaned the ladder against the porch railing before they started up the steps. "What's your mom doing now?"

"Well, she went on a cruise a couple of years ago, and a wealthy widower followed her home." She grinned at his startled look as he opened the screen door. "It took him six months, but he finally talked her into marrying him, and now she's living very happily in New Hampshire."

He grinned back. "That's good." Six months. Stubbornness must be a family trait.

The door opened into a laundry room that Bess decided must also double as a mudroom, judging from the rubber boots and collection of slickers and jackets hanging above them. Besides a new-looking washer and dryer, there were two deep galvanized sinks, which had probably been the original equipment. The inside door was slightly ajar, and a four-legged reception committee met them as he reached past her to push it open to the kitchen.

"Scruffy? Hoover? How'd you two get out? Did Hank smuggle you in a saw?" Bess asked.

"I let them out for a little change of scenery." Will set his pail on the counter and reached for hers.

"Is that all right?" Bess asked uncertainly, adding quickly, lest he think she was questioning his veterinary skill, "I mean, Hank won't hurt him, will he?" One chomp of those teeth she remembered so well, and there would be one less cat in the kitchen.

She was calling the cat "he" now, Will noticed, which could be trouble, but all he could do was trust in the power of positive thinking. "I think it would be more the other way around," he said with dry humor. "Hank tried to be friendly and found himself up against claws and an attitude. He learned respect real quick."

Laughing, she crouched to pet the cat. "Are you *bad,* Hoover?"

The cat rubbed his chin against her fingers, and she laughed again when the nodding motions of his head seemed to confirm it. Hoover was enjoying the petting, but she was enjoying it even more.

"Did you have cats when you were little?" Will asked.

She shook her head. "No, no pets at all. My father was allergic to fur, and afterward—it wasn't possible."

Because she and her mother couldn't afford it, he supplied the reason silently; she'd been deprived even of that. Hoover deigned to allow the dogs their share of attention, and she hugged Scruffy gently as he nestled against her breast. It was irrational to envy an animal, he reminded himself. "Do you have any animals now?"

"They've never been allowed where I've lived."

It was the same emotionless tone in which she'd spoken of her career and childlessness, but this time her soft smile and stroking fingers revealed what her voice didn't. With obvious reluctance, she gave each animal a final pat, then stood up.

Watching Hank take his customary spot by the head of the table, Bess caught sight of the garment hanging over the back of a nearby chair. "My sweater," she said blankly. She'd completely forgotten about it, and she wasn't in the habit of forgetting her clothes or where she'd left them. She turned to the man leaning against the counter watching her. "I've been meaning to ask you about it." She would have, too—when she remembered.

"It was in the exam room." Which was true; she didn't need to know it had also been cleaned and spent two days in his closet. He'd debated keeping it longer, but with other inducements now to keep her coming around, he could afford to give it back—and returning it was a small sop to his conscience.

"Thanks for remembering it." Bess gave her sweater another bemused look. It was hanging on the chair she'd sat in yesterday at lunch. Merely a coincidence. After just that one time, he certainly couldn't think of it as "her" chair.

His slight nod acknowledged her thanks. "What do we do now?" he asked, indicating the two buckets of crab apples.

"Now we wash them, cut them up and cook them," she said briskly and, following her own instructions, went to the sink, set the stopper, poured in a bucket of crab apples and turned on the faucet. The water hit the apples and splashed. An apron should have been on her shopping list today, too, she thought as she jumped back.

"Here."

Bess turned to see him holding out a T-shirt that he must have gotten from the stack of clean clothes she'd seen on the dryer in the laundry room.

"You wouldn't want to ruin that pretty dress," he added softly.

His thoughtfulness, and the casual compliment, thrilled her ridiculously. "No...I wouldn't. Thank you." She took the shirt with a smile and quickly pulled it over her head.

Her smile was wide yet a little shy. She sent mixed signals, but he was learning to read them, and they only confirmed what he'd suspected even before the ladder. She wasn't a tease or coy; she'd wanted the kiss as much as he had. He'd seen desire and that restless, willful excitement in her eyes before the panicky confusion. That Bess Hilliard was self-confident and cool in an impersonal business situation he had no doubt; on a personal level, however, she wasn't so sure of herself. It was a chink in her armor of self-possession, and the unexpected vulnerability filled him with an odd tenderness toward her.

Bess smoothed the soft cotton shirt down over her dress. It was crazy, but she imagined that she could smell him on the fabric. All there was in reality was the faint lemoniness of laundry detergent; what she was smelling was a memory. On the ladder, she couldn't help but notice his scent, but she'd had enough to handle right then without thinking about how he smelled. It wasn't turpentine, antiseptic or sawdust today. It was nothing so strong as cologne or after-shave, either, but a mingling of subtle scents—hot sun on clean skin, cool woods, a fresh breeze. Pretty sexy, actually.

They sat at the table for the next step, Bess taking without thinking the chair she'd sat in the day before. Conversation between them as they worked was easy and comfortable, as if those few charged moments on the ladder had never happened. He asked after Keeley and Abby, surprising her that he remembered their names after only her one brief mention of them. She learned that he'd bought the house from a retired farmer who'd sold off his fields, migrated to Florida one winter and decided to stay, and before she wanted, the apples were cooking in his two biggest pans.

"How long do they have to cook?" he asked as she adjusted the burners from boil to simmer.

"About twenty minutes should do it."

He used the twenty minutes to show her something she'd been secretly dying to see—the rest of his house. The bathrooms had been renovated and modernized, but she was glad to see that the rest of the house hadn't been. The lovely old woodwork and hardwood floors gave it the same sense of permanence as the bank in town had. The house had sheltered families for several generations and would easily do so for several more.

And it could be a pretty big family, she thought as he opened another door upstairs. Although he'd taken half of the first floor for his clinic, there was still plenty of room downstairs, along with a partial basement and the entire second floor. It seemed almost a waste of space for just one person. Only two of the second-floor rooms were furnished, his bedroom and a spare, and she caught herself mentally furnishing the others, wondering if any of the previous owners had also thought that the corner one would make a perfect sewing room.

She liked the house. He could tell. Her compliments could have been simple good manners, but her eyes lingered, almost reluctant to leave one room to go on to the next. She'd seen the furnished spare bedroom and his own—where the sheets were clean, he reminded himself sardonically—but it was the empty rooms that seemed to interest her most, as if she saw something in them that he couldn't.

Back in the kitchen, she set him to mashing the cooked apples while she pulled needle, thread and fabric out of a shopping bag she'd brought with her and efficiently made up two pillowcase-size bags. The apples went into the bags, and she hung them on the hooks over the old laundry tubs. He hadn't even noticed the hooks until months after he'd moved in; the fact that she'd spotted them right away told him how interested she was in the house. "Do I need to do anything with these before tomorrow?" he asked, watching juice drip from the bags into the bowls she'd set in the sinks below.

"Not a thing. They'll be fine until I come back tomorrow night. After dinner," she added deliberately, just in case he thought she might be thinking about trying to cadge another free meal. The idea that he might think of her as some kind of stray still rankled.

As always he saw her to her car, although "always" was only three times, Bess had to remind herself.

"You've got plenty of sugar, and I'll bring the jelly glasses and paraffin tomorrow." The inexplicable sense of loss she felt each time she was about to get into her car and drive away was worse than ever. "That's all we need."

He nodded. "Almost." Then he moved.

Once when she was a little girl, some cousins and she had been caught outside in a storm. The thunder and lightning had been crashing around them as they ran across the pasture toward the house; then suddenly she'd felt a tingling over her entire body. Realizing what was about to happen, the oldest cousin had screamed at them to drop flat on the grass, and seconds later lightning struck a bush only yards away. She felt that same tingling now. Another lightning strike was imminent, she understood as his arms closed around her, and this time she wouldn't escape unscathed.

The kiss was hard, long, mind-stunning. His mouth didn't ask; it took. Not arrogantly, but utterly confident that she had no objections. She didn't. The paralyzing force that struck her took away any ability to speak, to move, certainly to think. All she could do was feel, and even that sense seemed impaired—or maybe just overwhelmed. Sudden heat surrounded her, and a tremendous strength completely sapped hers. Only her mouth seemed to be working, but not for speech. After the initial shock wore off, she began to respond with the mindlessness of pure instinct.

She was holding back, and he didn't want that, so he solved the problem with a nip on her soft bottom lip. Her small moan parted her lips. His tongue swept away the tiny pain, then found a taste sweeter than he could ever have imagined. His hand moved up to her hair, and his fingers destroyed the loose braid so the silky strands wound around them as he held her mouth where he wanted it. She moaned again, her hands clutching at his back, pulling him closer. Her tongue touched his, and she seemed to melt into him as her taste became darker, hotter.

When he finally released her, he had the satisfaction of watching her slide weakly down the side of the car until she collapsed through the open door onto the bucket seat. Lifting a hand that shook only moderately, he gave her a casual wave goodbye. "See you."

Tuesday

She hadn't been kissed like that in quite a while, and she'd enjoyed it. Bess emptied the quart glass measuring pitcher into the large pan on the stove while a small voice inside her laughed. Okay, she admitted, enthralled, transported, even enchanted, might be more accurate. *As long as you're being honest...* the voice taunted. All right! she growled silently. She'd *never* been kissed like that.

It hadn't been a simple pass, either.

"Do we squeeze the bags?"

"No!" She was thinking so hard about him that, paradoxically, his voice startled her. "The squeezings don't make the best jelly," she explained to soften the abrupt refusal. Actually the squeezings made fine jelly. The squeezed juice might not be quite as clear as the juice that dripped out, making the jelly a little cloudy, but it was foolish to waste it. Just as it had been foolish to buy the quilted jelly glasses with the pretty lids instead of the plain half-pint jars that were half as expensive. Cloudy jelly in sensible jars tasted just as good as clear jelly in fancy glass jars, it just wasn't perfect. And it had suddenly become very important to her that this jelly be perfect. Why, she wasn't sure. She'd just known that sensible wasn't good enough. Besides, if good sense was all that mattered, Bess thought wryly, she wouldn't be here.

"How much sugar do we need?"

"Six and three-fourths cups." He was wearing newer jeans tonight, with a madras sport shirt; she was the one wearing a T-shirt as an apron again.

Will measured the sugar, then she stirred it into the juice. Her hair was in a loose knot today, a few wisps curling around her face, and his fingers twitched with the memory of the silky softness of it. The mixture in the pan began to boil, and she stirred faster. He'd pushed her last night. He'd known it wasn't fair, and if he'd had more time, he wouldn't have—or so he'd told himself. But she seemed determined to deny that anything was happening between them; if she left at the end of the week still denying it, he would lose whatever chance he might have with her. A boiling bubble in the pan popped, splashing a few drops of the hot juice onto her wrist. She raised her hand, and the tip of her tongue darted out to lick them off; heat curled deep in his belly. Her response had outdone his best daydreams.

She raised the spoon, watching the juice drip off the side of it in two fat drops, gauging how close it was to being done, he guessed. "You and your mother must have put up a lot of jelly," he commented as she lowered the spoon back into the pan. Only someone with a lot of practice could work without a recipe book.

She laughed wryly. "My mother and I put up anything that couldn't run fast enough to get away from us. Our fingernails used to be black for a month from the acid in the fruit and tomatoes."

The words hadn't come out with the usual bitterness—because, Bess discovered, she didn't feel the usual bitterness. She didn't kid herself that he had any interest in making jelly; it had just been an excuse to keep her coming around, and she'd made the offer because she wanted to keep coming around. Yet a part of her truly had been sorry to see the apples going to waste. This evening and the last had been the most enjoyable she could remember in a long time, doing nothing more exciting than making jelly. Well, for a minute or two last night, there had been something a bit more exciting. Bess kept her head down to hide the sudden grin she couldn't help.

And the fun of working with Will made her remember the fun she and her mother had had working together. It hadn't all been drudgery; there had been a lot of silliness, too. They'd competed to see who could cut the longest peel when they were canning apples, then drape them over their ears to make long curls. There had been quiet talk, as well, and a shared sense of accomplishment in seeing the glass jars lined up in the kitchen cupboards. She began to understand now why her mother still put up food every summer, even when there was no longer any economic need to do so. It was a link with all those countless past generations of women who had provided for their families, perhaps one of the same reasons that men still participated in the annual ritual of a fall hunting trip when they had absolutely no need—or even desire—for the game. Preserving food was a ritual, too, in a way, one that maintained the long unbroken connection between the first women to gather seeds and berries and those who now used freezers and microwaves. The sense of connection with all those millenia of women and the fact that she was carrying on their traditions brought her an odd happiness, quite apart from the pure pleasure she felt at being with the man beside her.

She looked up at him suddenly and smiled, a quick smile that was so simply, dazzlingly happy that he felt as if he'd been kicked in the gut. Feeling a nudge on his hand, he glanced down and saw Hank looking up at him. The dogs and Hoover had enjoyed Bess's attention before she'd started on the jelly, and Hank, especially, had eaten it up. Heaving a wistful-sounding sigh, the dog went back to watching her, too. I know exactly how you feel, Will told the dog silently.

Out of the corner of her eye Bess saw Will's hand drop to pat Hank's broad head. Those long fingers had caressed her last night, tangled in her hair, showed her her own heretofore undiscovered capacity for passion. The discovery had frightened and confused her, almost as much as it had fascinated and delighted her, and whether it, too, made good sense or not, she wanted him to touch her again.

Deliberately, Bess forced her attention away from him and back to the boiling pot. "I've been trying to place your accent. Where're you from?" she asked with forced casualness.

She'd been watching him pet Hank, and where he'd grown up wasn't, he thought with a smile, what she'd been thinking about. "Everywhere. My dad was in the Air Force until he retired to help run the family cattle ranch. He took my mom and I back to Nevada when I was fourteen."

"You were a cowboy!" Bess laughed delightedly. She'd been driving herself crazy trying to think who he reminded her of, and now she knew. He had the drawl, the hunker, even the walk—that slick-hipped, long-legged mosey. It took no imagination at all to see him in boots, a ten-gallon hat and a shirt with pearl snaps. The fact that he wore T-shirts, a baseball cap and sneakers only made it better, because it proved that the walk and everything else were completely natural.

He grinned at her reaction. "Yeah, I was a cowboy."

The mixture in the pan began to sheet off the spoon, indicating that it had reached the jellying point, and Bess moved the pan off the burner. "I think every little boy I've ever known wanted to be a cowboy," she said reminiscently. And every big girl simply wanted one, the small voice sneaked in. She ignored it.

"The first time you turn a bull calf into a steer, the life of a cowboy loses a lot of its romance," he said dryly and laughed at the face she made.

"Do your folks still live there?" She reached for the ladle, and he began passing her the sterilized jelly glasses.

"Still. I go back every fall to help with the roundup."

"You didn't want to go into ranching, too?"

As he shook his head, one corner of his mouth turned down in a wry grimace. "The only part of ranching I really liked was rodeoing."

Pausing with the ladle over a half-filled glass, Bess stared at him. "You competed in rodeos?"

"Part-time. It paid my way through school."

"Wasn't it dangerous?" It was ridiculous, she knew, to be worried about something he'd done almost twenty years ago.

One broad shoulder lifted negligently as he took the ladle out of her hand and tilted the pan to get the last bit of jelly. "I got a few nicks."

She wondered if the scar on his chin, his chipped tooth and broken nose were some of those "nicks." Picking up the former dog food can that, along with a small saucepan had become an impromptu double boiler to melt the paraffin, she began to pour a skin of wax over the top of each glass to seal it. "How did you end up here instead of Nevada?'' That was something else she wondered about. He'd lived in Cambridge because of his wife's law schooling, but after his divorce, he could have been expected to go home.

''My father was stationed not far from here for a couple of years, and I always wanted to come back. It was the only place I ever lived that felt like home,'' he said simply.

Bess glanced around the kitchen with its antique oak, state-of-the-art appliances and goofy wallpaper. He'd gone home, after all, and found a wonderful one. For a moment she considered the concrete and plastic high rise she called home.

As she finished with the last glass, Will glanced at the time displayed on the microwave. Perfect timing. ''If we hustle, we can make the next show at the movie in town.''

Now, watching red taillights disappear around the corner, Bess raised her hand slowly to her lips.

They'd made the movie.

Finally she turned and opened the dormitory door. He'd followed her back to the dorm so she could drop off her car and ride with him. He would follow her anyhow, he said, because he didn't want her driving alone late at night, so she might as well go with him. It wasn't the first time he'd exhibited chauvinistic tendencies, but she didn't feel the annoyance sexist oinkings usually aroused. It wasn't machismo speaking, but concern. It was unnecessary—she'd been taking care of herself for years—yet his protectiveness, like the small courtesy of opening doors, made her feel feminine...and special. She drifted across the lobby toward the stairs. Very special.

After they'd finished the popcorn, he'd taken her hand. Holding hands at the movies sounded so adolescent, yet it hadn't seemed adolescent; it had seemed exactly right for her hand to be clasped in his big, warm, rough one, their shoulders brushing, their wrists entwined . . . just as it had seemed perfectly natural when he'd kissed her good-night. She'd been ready, waiting for it tonight. With an unconscious smile she touched her mouth again lightly. Lightning could, indeed, strike twice in the same place.

When she opened the door, the dorm room was dark, and she thought Abby and Keeley must already be asleep; then she heard Keeley's soft call, from the "terrace." Sometimes, back in school, Bess and Keeley had carried a mattress out to the fire escape on warm nights so they could sit out there and enjoy the stars. Abby, as always, stayed safely just within the doorway. Bess sat down on the mattress and leaned back against the railing.

"Nice night," Keeley commented.

"Gorgeous," she agreed softly.

They sat in companionable silence until Abby spoke. "I enjoyed your presentation today, Bess."

Bess smiled at Abby. Her talk had described the mentor program she participated in, where inner-city high-school students were matched up with professionals to give them the guidance and practical help they needed to stay in school and achieve their goals. "Thank you. I was impressed with your child abuse intervention program." Abby, as part of a panel discussing the problem, had described the program she'd designed and implemented. "The woman sitting next to me said your program has served as a model elsewhere. You must be very pleased."

Abby laughed shortly. "I can't match your one hundred percent rate."

It was too dark for her to see Abby's expression clearly, but Bess heard the sour frustration in her voice. "I've only worked with four girls, Abby, who were already headed in the right direction. All they needed was a little push. You've turned around the lives of dozens of children. My success rate is meaningless compared to yours."

"At least you two have successes to rate. I don't." Keeley laughed mirthlessly. "Unless you count mingling and good clothes—my two talents."

"And what's wrong with those, Keeley?" Bess asked her sharply. It was the kind of self put-down Abby and she were used to from Keeley, but not with such bitterness. "You know as well as Abby and I do that all the good intentions in the world can't produce success without some money to go with them. You know people with money, and you're extremely successful in getting them to part with it precisely because you do know how to mingle and dress well. Look at all the money you've raised for Bartlett's scholarship fund. And what about all the young artists who've gained recognition, not to mention the money to enable them to pursue their art without worrying about eating, because you brought them to the attention of the right people? Abby and I could never do that."

"Yes, Keeley, if that isn't success, I don't know what is," Abby seconded forcefully.

Lying awake in bed later, Bess replayed the scene again. Maybe because she was suddenly trying to cope with so many new and overwhelming emotions herself, she was more sensitive to others'. Underlying Keeley's words—and Abby's, too—she'd detected what had sounded disturbingly like a sense of failure, not in some minor aspect of life, but in life itself, and that saddened and worried her. Her two old friends were more important to her than she had ever realized. The three of them weren't professional friends, their relationship cemented by the mutual advantages of networking, or political friends, interested only in promoting common causes. They were and always had been friends simply because they wanted to be—the best kind, and she wanted so much for them to be happy.

Although she didn't agree with their feelings of failure, she could understand them, better than she wanted. The past few days she'd heard a great deal about children and husbands from the women she'd talked to; everyone, it seemed, had one or the other if not both, everyone except Abby, Keeley... and her. She'd never thought one had to have either to be happy, yet... what did the three of them have to show for the past fifteen years? No husbands, no children, no one. They were exactly as they had been fifteen years ago—alone.

Wednesday

"Are we finished already?"

Will looked at the scraggly-haired woman staring at the stripped wall in disbelief. "Some of us did more work than others," he reminded her, and she gave him a cheeky grin. She'd worked like a dog the past three hours, and because of her help, he'd finished the job in a day instead of the two he'd resigned himself to. He'd thought they would go see the other movie they'd debated seeing the night before; he'd never intended for them to spend the evening stripping wallpaper, but she'd come a little sooner than he'd expected—and a lot later than he'd wanted—and caught him still working. She was an old hand at working with wallpaper, she'd informed him as she set down her purse and picked up a scraper. Another skill she and her mother had acquired, he guessed, trying to keep their old house together.

She wiped the sweat off her forehead. "You know, I kind of miss the 'Fighting Amish,'" she said with a wistful-sounding laugh. "Maybe we should have saved a little section of it."

That "we" had a nice sound to it. "There's still a leftover roll down in the basement. We could frame one panel of it and hang it up as a memento."

With a quick laugh, she nodded her enthusiastic agreement.

She reached up to pick off a bit of paper still cling-ing to the wall, then tugged automatically on the legs of her shorts. Will smiled slightly; she didn't have to tug them down for his benefit. Covertly he appreciated the sleek length of her thighs and the firm muscles in her shapely calves shown off by the old gym shorts. They were his shorts, but with the difference in their anato-mies, they fit her perfectly, although she seemed to think they were too short. She gave the black nylon an-other firm pull. He'd given her the shorts and one of his T-shirts so she wouldn't ruin her dress, and she'd come down the stairs with a self-conscious shyness that gave him an intense satisfaction, because it meant she didn't wear a man's clothes often enough to be casual about it, which also meant that she wasn't often with a man in the kind of situation where she casually pulled on his clothes afterward, either.

They began to clean up the mess littering the floor. It was silly, Bess thought as she stuffed another handful of trash into the garbage bag, to keep looking at the line of jelly glasses on the counter and think they looked like sparkling, sunshine-colored jewels. It was even sillier to have used the excuse that the glasses needed another layer of paraffin, which they didn't, as an additional reason for coming tonight. Hoover was a good one, but another didn't hurt. And it was silliest of all to take such pleasure in seeing them. Her eyes slid inexorably to Will punching down the scraps in another bag so he could tie the top. Almost as much pleasure as she took in seeing him.

Realizing that she was staring, Bess grabbed the broom leaning against the counter and began sweeping energetically. "What are you going to do with the window over the sink?'' There was a cracked and yellowed roller shade there now.

He glanced at it and shrugged. ''I haven't really thought about it. I'll probably get some of those skinny blinds.''

''Curtains would be nice.'' She'd seen some yellow chintz in the fabric store that would be perfect. Café curtains, she decided, a double tier. She swept a small wad of paper and glue ahead of her, and Hoover, who again had the run of the kitchen and had been amusing himself with the bits of paper on the floor, swatted the paper puck. ''Nice slap shot, Hoover,'' she congratulated the cat with a laugh.

Will looked at her speculatively. ''Are you a hockey fan?''

She shook her head. ''I played it. Field hockey, in college.''

Will swallowed a laugh. At first glance five days ago he'd taken her for one of those tailored, aggressive, humorless, goal-driven women who frankly held little appeal for him, and almost immediately she'd surprised him. He looked at the slightly grubby woman across the kitchen, with her straggly hair, hand-me-down clothes and a streak of white dust on her cheek. She was still surprising him, and he had a hunch that, fifty years from now, she would *still* be able to surprise him. ''Were you any good?''

''Bartlett took the league championship my last two years in school. I was all-league for three years, too,'' she said with patent modesty.

''Sounds like you could have gone pro,'' he said solemnly.

"I considered it, but who needs all that money and adulation?" she said with equal seriousness, then giggled.

Will looked down at her, her dusty cheeks flushed, her hair a mess, her eyes glowing with the incandescence of happiness and laughter, her mouth curved in a sweet smile, and he felt his breath catch in his chest. "Yeah, who needs it?" he echoed absently. He needed. Her.

"Actually I'm playing tomorrow in the annual alumni game between Smithfield and Bartlett. We'll probably get creamed," she predicted cheerfully.

"What time?" he asked diffidently.

She groaned. "Eight-thirty in the morning."

He made a mental note to set his alarm half an hour ahead.

Hoover was still batting the wad of paper across the floor. It ricocheted off Hank's nose where the dog lay under the table, and the cat chased it between the chair legs. "Hoover sure is frisky for a cat with a broken leg."

There was puzzlement in her observation, but no suspicion. "He's not in any pain, and the exercise is good for him." Two truths, he congratulated himself sarcastically. He ought to tell her, but he couldn't risk it yet.

Accepting his explanation, she turned her attention back to her broom. More hair came loose from the knot on the top of her head to dangle in her eyes, and with an exasperated sigh she yanked out the pins, then gathered her hair and started to twist it up to repin it.

"No, leave it down," he said quickly.

She looked up at him for a second, then lowered her arms, and her hair tumbled loose in an endearing disorder of brown-sugar curls around her face and shoulders. "All right."

Bess tried to finger-comb her hair into some semblance of order, but finally gave it up as a lost cause and went back to sweeping. Her hair—*she*—was a mess, but, uncharacteristically, she didn't care. How, she wasn't sure, but Will Shedd had the ability to draw her out of her normal inhibitions, draw her out of herself. She glanced sideways as he paused for a moment to gently rub Scruffy's head. Maybe it was because he was like his home, a little weathered, showing a few signs of wear and tear, but still unassailably strong and attractive, with an air of security and comfort that she was finding harder and harder to resist.

Will set another full trash bag by the back door. The radio was on, playing in the background. It was "golden oldies" night, and she'd been humming and singing along under her breath all evening. It had been hard, fast rock 'n' roll earlier, but now he heard songs he remembered slow-dancing to in a small high-school gym more years ago than he really cared to remember. She was sweeping up the last of the litter, her hips swaying gently as she danced unconsciously with the broom, singing along softly with the slow, bluesy version of "Do You Wanna Dance?" The invitation was too hard to resist.

The broom was taken out of her hands; then a pair of long, strong arms closed around her. As if they'd danced together a hundred times before, Bess linked her arms around his neck without missing a step. She laid her cheek against his shoulder and shut her eyes. Hips…thighs…chests brushed in time to the lazy, sexy beat, while the words played through her subconscious. With a small sigh, she nestled against him. There was no moonlight as in the song, but she could pretend. He shifted her closer, one big hand moving down to the small of her back, urging her closer still. His head moved, his hair brushing softly over her cheeks; then his mouth found hers, and moonlight was unnecessary.

In contrast to the slow, dreamy music around them, the kiss was immediate and demanding. His hands slid down to her hips, his long powerful fingers digging into her soft flesh as he widened his stance. She stepped into his strength, feeling his thighs lock around her and the full brunt of his desire. For the first time she understood just how much he wanted her. It frightened her, but not enough to keep her from pressing still closer, her mouth as demanding as his. Then her own desire, which had been simmering just under her awareness for days, boiled over.

One hand left her hip to insinuate itself between their bodies, and they echoed each other's small groans of satisfaction when its journey ended. His hand cradled the weight of her breast, his thumb teasing the nipple under the thin cotton and thinner lace into an impertinent little nub. Will felt her shivers as his mouth roamed hungrily over her throat and shoulder, his hand impatiently dragging his shirt out of the way.

Bess flinched at the wet tickling assault of his lips and teeth in the hollow of her shoulder, then shuddered at the warm, soothing sweep of his tongue. The hand on her breast left, but before she could moan her disappointment, it had returned, slipping under the shirt. She resented the tissue-thin layer of fabric that kept skin from skin as his broad palm rubbed slowly, creating an ache that almost had her sobbing, but not from pain.

"Let's go upstairs," he murmured.

The skin under his lips went cold, and another shudder shook her body, but he knew it wasn't a shiver of desire. With a vicious curse that he barely kept under his breath, Will jerked his hands to her shoulders and snapped her away from him so he could see her face. "What the hell—?" He clenched his teeth together in an effort to get his frustration under control before he said something he would regret. The wild excitement he saw in her eyes, telling him that she wanted as much as he did to let things reach their natural conclusion, didn't help.

"I'm sorry," Bess whispered. With a hideous sense of déjà vu, she diagnosed another relapse of sixteen-itis. "You have every right to be angry."

The abject misery of indecision he saw in her face helped him find control. "What happened, Bess?" he asked quietly. She'd averted her face, and with a gently firm hand, he turned her chin so that she had to face him.

He knew it cost her, but she met his eyes directly. "I don't sleep around, Will, and I'm not a tease."

"I know that, Bess." As the more physically vulnerable, it was the woman's right to set the limits, Will reminded himself. But there were other kinds of vulnerability, too. He realized his hands were still clamped so tightly on her shoulders that he must be hurting her, although she'd never given any indication of it. Maybe she thought she deserved it, he thought, half-ashamed. Loosening his hold, he rubbed her shoulders gently as he consciously lightened his tone, too. "You're obviously attracted to me, and I'm having trouble remembering my name."

Bess managed a rueful laugh. "So am I. I'm just not—" Struggling for the words, she finally shrugged helplessly, feeling more gauche and juvenile than ever.

"Ready?" he suggested softly. "Sure?" She nodded miserably, and he felt a rush of tenderness toward her. "Okay." He pulled her in for a quick kiss, then set her briskly away from him. "I'll pick you up for dinner tomorrow night at seven."

Panic quickened her tongue. "Oh, no! I don't—"

"The evening will end when and where you want, Bess."

Searching his eyes, Bess saw nothing but the truth. She nodded soberly. "I'll be ready."

Bess turned over on the narrow bed for the fourth time in as many minutes. As Abby, Keeley and she had been getting ready for bed, she'd sensed that she wasn't the only one who'd had an unsettling evening. With each of them preoccupied with her own problems, there had been little conversation except for what politeness demanded, and after the lights had been turned off, even politeness had disappeared. Their lights-out conversation hadn't drifted into pleasant dreams tonight.

Perhaps what had happened was inevitable, she thought, turning over again. The tensions had been building since they'd arrived, old tensions from old resentments, and new ones, too. Occupied with other concerns tonight, their careful self-control had slipped, and some of those tensions had been relieved. Although it had been emotionally traumatic, she wasn't sorry. She'd learned a lot tonight, and not all of the lessons, especially those she'd learned about herself, had been pleasant, but she was very grateful for the knowledge.

Keeley, the one who had never shared personal problems, who had always maintained the front that her life was just as perfect as one would expect from someone who had the money to buy anything she wanted, didn't have a perfect life and never had. Her marriage had been a cold sham, her dream of children forever shattered. Abby and Bess had been hard on Keeley about her callous treatment of Dominic, especially when it seemed that history was once again repeating itself, only to learn that Keeley's heart had been broken then, too. From that point on, her life had gone wrong, and she didn't seem to know how to make it right again.

Abby, too, had her problems. After she'd revealed her unhappiness in her role as the everselfless giver, Keeley and Bess hadn't offered sympathy, Bess thought sadly; instead they had taken the opportunity to tell Abby how much her goody-two-shoes selflessness had annoyed them. Now her own selfishness and insensitivity made her ashamed. All of them had been self-centered when they were young, not aware of—or even wondering about—each other's needs. They hadn't valued each other, hadn't *cared* about each other, nearly as much as they should have, but she couldn't help feeling that she was guiltier of those sins than either Abby or Keeley. Consumed so by her own ambitions, she hadn't wanted to see anyone else's problems, much less help with them. As she'd gained a new understanding of her old friends, seen them clearly for the first time, she'd gained a new understanding of herself as well.

Gradually she became aware of the faint, familiar smell of something hot. With an annoyed sigh, she slipped out of bed and felt her way across the room to the octopus plug by the bookcase that held all their hair paraphernalia. She moved carefully, trying not to make any noise that would disturb Abby and Keeley, if they should be lucky enough to be asleep.

Noiselessly she pulled the plug that belonged to her hot rollers, which she'd somehow forgotten. It would be a memorable reunion, indeed, she thought sourly, if the curlers overheated, set the hay that was rumored to be the insulation in the hundred-year-old walls on fire and the dorm burned to the ground.

"Bess, what are you doing?"

That answered half her question; Keeley was wide-awake, too, and sounded no happier about it than Bess was. "Unplugging my hot rollers. I forgot and left them on."

"If you had one of the new sets with the automatic shut-off, you wouldn't have to worry about it." Abby, too, was awake, and just as annoyed about it.

"I'll look into a set when these wear out," Bess promised shortly, heading back to bed.

"The damned things wore out years ago," Keeley said acidly. "You don't need to prove anything to us. We know how poor you were and how far you've come. You don't need to rub our noses in it, Bess."

Stunned by Keeley's attack, she was even less pre-pared for Abby's. "You always seemed to think you were better than us, Bess, because you had to work so hard for your education, and we didn't. We knew how hard you worked, and we admired you for it. We wanted to help you, but every time we tried to do something to make things a little easier for you, you slammed the door in our faces. Well, you've suc-ceeded, just like you said you would, and without any-one's help, least of all ours. You can afford to throw those damned curlers out now and buy a new set!"

With a surge of righteous fury, Bess opened her mouth to deliver a blistering counterattack—but no words came. Why, she thought absently, had she thought she would escape without a few wounds to-night, too.

The silence lengthened into an acute uncomfortableness, and Keeley cleared her throat, as if she were going to try to ease it, but Bess spoke first. "You're right," she said quietly. She honestly had kept the curlers for no other reason than that they still worked, but everything else Abby and Keeley had accused her of was, sadly, true. "I did slam the door in your faces. I was so sure you pitied me because I was poor, that you felt sorry for me . . . because I felt sorry for myself. I imagined everyone saying 'Poor Bess' behind my back, when in reality I was the only one saying it. I was jealous because I had to work hard. I envied you your big family, Abby, and I envied you your beautiful clothes and your money, Keeley." Except for her voice, the room was absolutely still, the other women pale, motionless blurs as they sat up in their beds, listening. "I used to love to beat you at tennis, Keeley, because it proved that you didn't have everything. After the other day, I finally realized how meaningless those wins were. I even envied both of you your infatuations and broken hearts, because I was too afraid to risk one." She laughed hollowly. "But there is one thing I can't envy either of you for."

She paused before continuing in a flat voice. "You said you were sorry, Keeley, because you would never know the misery of morning sickness. It's not so bad, actually. At least, mine wasn't." She heard the two indrawn breaths. "It only lasted a month or so, and wasn't anything more than a few extra seconds in the bathroom every morning. The man—" She sighed softly. "The man doesn't matter. The affair was over before I knew I was pregnant. I planned to tell him he was a father after the fact, because he had a right to know, but I didn't want anything from him. Although it was a definite surprise—" she chuckled wryly "—I never had any other idea but to have the baby. I'd never wanted children, or thought I wanted them," she corrected herself, "but suddenly I wanted this baby very much. I didn't tell anyone at first, especially anyone at the bank, because I wasn't sure what effect my pregnancy would have on the bank management, but I didn't really worry about it much. I had savings, and after the baby came, I knew I could always find another job.

"Finally, though, I had to tell them." Her laugh was rueful. "It was the start of my fifth month, and none of my clothes fit anymore. The bank was very supportive. I knew that, realistically, I couldn't expect to advance as fast, but that didn't seem so important anymore. I went shopping that weekend for maternity clothes and began pricing cribs and layettes and thinking about buying a bigger condo or maybe even a house." She smiled to herself. "I looked at teddy bears, too. There was one that looked like Radar's big brother, and I almost bought it, but I decided to look a little more, to see if I could find one a little bigger. Sunday night I started hemorrhaging."

She was quiet for several seconds. "The doctor said it was a girl. I lost her the day before your mom passed away, Abby. I got out of the hospital on the day of the funeral," she said absently. "The next day I took back all the maternity clothes. Fortunately, I hadn't worn any of them. I remember thinking it was lucky, too, that I hadn't bought the teddy bear, so I didn't have to return it, as well.''

Only a quiet sob broke the long silence that followed. "I did do what I said I would, Abby," she said finally. "I got everything I wanted. I guess that proves you should always be absolutely certain of what you want." Her soft laugh was bleak. "You just may get it."

She didn't know whether it was Abby or Keeley who snapped on the light. The three of them looked at each other, their faces stark and colorless in the harsh light. She saw the tears glittering on the other women's cheeks, and something warm splashed onto her hand. She looked down at the wet spot, put her hand up slowly to her own cheek, and was vaguely surprised to find hers was wet, too.

"You should have told us, Bess," Keeley whispered. A choked, wordless sound from Abby eloquently seconded Keeley's gentle reproof.

"I know." And, as she read the empathy, compassion and understanding in her friends' faces, she *did* know. Foolish pride—the fear of showing vulnerability or admitting weakness or being seen as less than perfect—had kept all three of them from the support they had needed and that the others would have been only too happy to give. Those fragile bonds of friendship forged between them when they were young mattered more than she ever could have imagined then. Perhaps only now that she was older, and needed them even more, could she truly appreciate those delicate strands that still reached between their hearts. As her eyes met Abby's and Keeley's, Bess knew that they understood, too.

Who moved first, she didn't know, but suddenly the three of them were in the middle of the room, their arms wrapped around each other tightly. "We're a sorry-looking bunch," Bess said with a watery laugh as they broke apart and got a good look at each other's red noses and puffy eyes.

Keeley grabbed a packet of tissues and passed it around. "We certainly are," she agreed, blowing her nose.

The three of them grinned at each other, not caring in the least.

Thursday

Standing on the sidelines of the grass playing field, Will watched the twenty-two women battling in the middle of it. A tall, leggy blonde in a red Bartlett jersey and old gym shorts faked out the opposition's goalie with a feint, then slapped the white, baseball-size ball over the goal line, and his whistle drowned out most of the cheers around him. The Smithfield team put the ball back into play, the umpire whistled a foul, and Bess leaned on her stick, tugging automatically at her shorts in a gesture he already knew well. She was wearing his colors, he thought with a smile. She'd worn the clothes he'd loaned her back to the dorm last night, and she was wearing his shorts again this morning. His smile became a wince as play resumed and one of the Smithfield backs whacked her across the knee trying to steal the ball. She would be wearing some black-and-blue tomorrow, too.

The game ended twenty minutes later, and the spectators loudly clapped and yelled their appreciation. Will grinned at the two women who'd been eyeing him ever since Eileen Rhoden, who was standing with them, had nodded in his direction. A blonde and a redhead, one was a little taller and thinner than the other, and they'd spent as much time looking him over as watching the game. They smiled back tentatively, then started purposefully toward him.

"You're Will Shedd, aren't you?" The shorter one had a slow southern drawl, confirming her identity before she introduced herself. "I'm Abby Granger, a friend of Bess Hilliard."

He shook hands with Abby and the taller woman who was, as he'd thought, Keeley. "I'm happy to meet you, Will," she said. "Eileen Rhoden's been telling us what an interesting practice you have."

That innocuous comment had initiated a subtle and very thorough interrogation that would have impressed a veteran police detective, Will thought wryly a few minutes later. By the time the losers had congratulated the winners and were starting for the sidelines, Abby and Keeley had confirmed his marital status, childlessness, fiscal soundness, community standing and general trustworthiness. He answered their politely nosy questions seriously, appreciating the fact that they wanted to be sure he was right for their friend.

Apparently deciding that he had no major skeletons in any of his closets, they offered their congratulations on a well-played game to Bess when she arrived, then took themselves off. "You lost," he observed, wrapping a companionable arm around her shoulders.

"The ball didn't work." Slipping her arm around his waist, Bess grinned up at him as he laughed and hugged her tight against his side. She knew she looked as bad as she had the night before, only sweatier, but he didn't seem to care, so neither did she.

As they started toward the locker room, a big, red-haired woman with an even bigger dark-haired man in tow hailed them. Bess turned around in time to be enveloped in a hug that had Will wincing again, concerned for her ribs, this time.

"Will," she said a little breathlessly as she disengaged herself and turned to him, "this is Louise Detwiler and her husband, Charles. Louise and Charles, Will Shedd." The Detwilers shook his hand, smiling amiably, then Louise continued her enthusiastic congratulations.

"Great game, Bess! You're still the best dribbler I've ever seen. I wish my girls could see you play."

Bess thanked her gravely, then explained for his benefit, "Louise coaches field hockey and basketball at a women's college in Virginia. Charles coaches football at the nearby men's school." She smiled at the other woman. "I'm sure you can show your team all they need to know, Louise. You were always an excellent player," she said graciously.

Louise shook her head mournfully. "Not anymore. My knees gave out, you know," she confided. Taking his cue from Bess, Will nodded in solemn sympathy.

A few minutes later, they were walking toward the locker room again. Bess looked at Will questioningly when he leaned down to peer at her legs. "I'm just trying to see if your knees show any sign of giving out," he explained.

She favored him with an exasperated look that was already dissolving into a grin as she disappeared through the locker room door. While he waited, Bob Rhoden came by and mentioned the poker game he was organizing for Saturday night. Will didn't commit himself; he expected to have other plans, he thought as Bess came out, minus the borrowed shin guards and jersey and wearing his T-shirt as well as his shorts.

Before she reached him, another old classmate waylaid her. While they stood talking, the woman's small son ran around them, playing with a large ball. He would throw the ball, chase it down, then throw it again. He caught up with it again and flung it away once more, straight at Bess. Will didn't think she saw it, but just as the ball was about to hit her, she caught it and tossed it back gently to the little boy. Clearly pleased to have somebody to play with, he flung it back. The ball went back and forth, Bess keeping up with both it and the conversation. She matched her tosses to the boy's catching ability, and gradually he began to gain more control over the ball by imitating her. It was the first time Will had seen her with a child. Although she had none of her own, she seemed to have an instinctive rapport with them.

Eventually Bess and the other woman ended their conversation. Will put his arm casually around her waist when she was within reach.

"I was surprised to see you at the game," she said neutrally. While she'd been changing, it had occurred to her that he might have come to cancel their dinner date for tonight. After what had happened, she couldn't really blame him if he'd had second thoughts.

Will glanced down at her, wondering at her flat tone. "I've always been fascinated by women who dribble well," he said lightly.

Her sudden smile dazzled him. "Wait until you see me at dinner."

Will placed the phone receiver back on the holder mounted on the dashboard of his Bronco.

"A problem?" Bess asked him quietly.

He glanced across the cab of the Bronco. "A problem," he agreed with a grimace. "Maybelle is stuck again." Her bewildered look prompted him to explain. "Maybelle is Mildred Aldhizer's pet Guernsey cow.

Mildred forgets to lock the barn door every once in a while, and Maybelle heads straight for the bog on the other side of the pasture. That's where she is now, mired to her belly, and the vet covering for me is out on another call. The cow can wait, but Mildred is frantic.''

"Then we'd better go rescue Maybelle," Bess said reasonably.

He looked at her again. "Are you sure? We may lose our reservations. The cow can wait."

Despite his reassurance, he was worried about the cow and her owner. She smiled. "Yes, but Mildred may not be able to. Let's go."

They lost their reservations, and her dress, Bess knew, would never be the same, but they saved Mildred and Maybelle.

"Stay in the shower until you warm up," Will instructed as he laid clean towels and a bathrobe, that was going to swallow her, on the lid of the commode in the bathroom.

"I will." Bess tried to stifle a sneeze with only partial success. He frowned at her worriedly, and she tried to keep a straight face, again with only limited success.

"What's so damn funny?" he growled.

"Have you looked in a mirror?" she inquired politely.

Maybelle had gotten herself well and truly stuck, requiring Will to wade out into the bog to wrestle a sling around her, then use the winch on the front of his Bronco to pull her out. Despite the coveralls and boots he'd put on, he'd gotten covered with mud and muck from head to toe. Her nose wrinkled, but not from another incipient sneeze. He'd acquired another unique scent. His hair was plastered down and dripping, but it was probably the only part of him that was clean. As they'd been winching Maybelle out, it had rained on them, a cloudburst that Will had seemed to regard as a mixed blessing.

"Have *you?*" he retorted.

She shook her head. "No, but I can't look any worse than you."

Without speaking, he swung the bathroom door shut to reveal a full-length mirror, then drew her over to stand in front of it.

She was wrong. She could look worse. The coveralls and boots hadn't protected her any better than they had him. Her silk dress was limp and streaked with things she would probably be better off not trying to identify. That pungent smell, she realized, wasn't coming just from him. Her hair, too, was wet and dripping, but being longer, there was far more to drip, and the rain hadn't gotten hers as clean as his. "Oh, Lord," she said weakly.

For a reply, he leaned into the shower and twisted on the spray; then, with a significant look from her to the shower, he departed, closing the door behind him.

Her next look in the mirror half an hour later was a definite improvement over the last one, she decided objectively. She was clean, smelled better, and the robe, while it did overwhelm her, was a nice green, not a brown-streaked rose. Her hair, while stick-straight, was almost dry and back to its normal color.

Rolling up the sleeves on the robe, she went back downstairs to the kitchen. Will, barefoot and wearing clean jeans and a T-shirt, was rooting through his refrigerator, muttering under his breath. Scruffy and Hank lay on the floor under the table, while Hoover occupied a chair, all three animals watching him interestedly.

He straightened up from the refrigerator with a disgusted look. "Well, the best we can do for dinner without waiting for something to thaw out is peanut butter and jelly sandwiches and chicken noodle soup." He looked across the kitchen at the phone on the wall. "Or we can have a pizza delivered."

"Soup and sandwiches are fine," Bess said quickly, remembering the pizza.

They did have to defrost something after all, because the only loaf of bread he had was frozen. Since they decided they wanted the peanut butter and jelly on toast, he bypassed the microwave and just put the bread in the toaster, turning the knob to the darkest setting to compensate for its frozen state.

The first pieces of toast popped up accompanied by smoke. Muttering again, Will pulled out the blackened pieces of bread.

"Ah, Cajun style," she said approvingly.

Will chuckled reluctantly as he set the toaster to a lighter setting. She'd gotten filthy dirty, ruined her dress, probably caught double pneumonia, and now she had to settle for peanut butter and jelly instead of a gourmet meal. After all that, any woman had a right to lose her sense of humor, yet she hadn't. If anything, she seemed happier now than she had before tonight's fiasco.

Sitting down a few minutes later, he looked over the meager meal. "This wasn't exactly what I had planned for tonight."

"What *did* you have planned?" Bess asked, ladling soup into their bowls.

"*Poulet à la moutarde,* a good chardonnay, candle-light, soft music, maybe a little dancing."

His obvious perturbation at the ruination of his plans touched her. She understood how important she must be to him that he was feeling so annoyed. "Hmm." She looked at him thoughtfully. "Sounds like the classic seduction scene."

His grin widened slowly. "Yeah."

She hid her answering grin by sniffing the glass of milk in her hand, then took a mouthful and rolled it around on her tongue. "Mmm. The vintage is Tuesday, I think. Unassuming, with a hint of clover, and a slight aftertaste of alfalfa." She took a sip of soup. "While I must say I was looking forward to the *poulet* whatever, this is awfully good *poulet* noodle."

He understood what she was telling him. There was no need for the big seduction scene. Mud and muck and peanut butter and jelly with him was better than a big night on the town with any other man. If he hadn't already been in love with her, he would have fallen right then.

He picked up his glass and took a long swallow of milk to cover the sudden shiver that went through him. It was the first time he'd admitted it to himself. It still made no sense, seemed impossible, too fast, but he no longer doubted the truth of it. He'd fallen in love with a smart, funny, independent, tenderhearted, stubborn, prickly, vulnerable—in short, difficult—woman. He watched her sneak the last bit of her soup to Hoover. But he really hadn't had any choice, he thought ruefully. "What about the peanut butter?"

She gave him a patient look. "Peanut butter is peanut butter. However—" she popped the last bite of her sandwich into her mouth and grinned at him "—the crab apple jelly is outstanding.'' She raised her hand to lick a dab of jelly off her finger.

Catching her hand, he brought it to his mouth and touched his tongue to the sweetness. ''You missed some.'' He held her eyes, watching them turn dark and smoky, while he linked his fingers through hers, bringing their palms together slowly.

Dinner, Bess thought vaguely, was over. Her stomach clenched with a hunger that couldn't be satisfied by peanut butter and jelly and chicken soup. He tugged on her hand, and she stood up with him. Another tug and she was in his arms, closing her eyes as his mouth came down on hers.

''Mmm.'' She felt him smile. ''You're right about the jelly. Outstanding.'' His lips touched hers again lightly. ''What about the music, dancing and candlelight?'' he murmured.

''We danced last night,'' she murmured back. ''There was music then. There wasn't any candlelight, but—'' her mouth teased his as he'd teased her ''—I'm sure there was moonlight.''

It wasn't a flashfire—all flame and no heat and over in seconds—as she'd been afraid it would be.

The only light in his bedroom came from the old rose lamp on the dresser. The dark wood of his bed gleamed dully in the soft glow, while the cool, rain-sweetened breeze through the open window tinkled the slender prisms hanging from the glass shade, flashing slivers of rainbow around the room. Bess stood still as his hands slipped up to her shoulders.

''I'm going to make love with you, Bess,'' he said quietly.

She nodded soberly. All her life, without even realizing it, she'd been waiting to feel the emotions washing through her now, threatening to sweep her away. If she was swept away, though, it wasn't because of him. She was too mature—and too honest—to put that responsibility on him. She was responsible for herself. For so long she'd lived a life devoid of passion, emotionally dead, because it was safer. Then this man had shown her what was missing in her prescribed, proscribed life. He'd plumbed depths of passion in her that she'd never ever expected, and she didn't want safety anymore. She wasn't sure where this would lead, whether they had any future beyond tonight, but she knew that if she didn't have at least this night, she would be dead for the rest of her life.

Her eyes captured the dim light of the lamp, intensifying it and shining it brilliantly back to him. He undid the belt of his robe and slowly parted the edges. His eyes traveled down the length of her naked body, here shadowed, there highlighted, by the lamp glow. Her small, firm breasts were all in shadow except for the pale pink tips, which budded slowly under his long, feasting look.

He shrugged out of his T-shirt, and she had a glimpse of a dark wedge of hair narrowing down to a thin ribbon bisecting his hard, flat abdomen; then his arms closed around her again. His hands brushed off the robe as they slipped down her back, then back up, slowly bringing their bodies together. He took her mouth the same way, deepening the probing thrusts of his tongue at a leisurely rate. The crisp hair of his chest brushed deliciously across her aching breasts as he slowly rubbed her bare body back and forth over his in a rhythm that thrummed through her until it seemed as if her breathing and the blood pumping heat through her body beat at the same steady, drugging pace.

Bess panicked. She wasn't a practiced, artful lover. Already he had shown her a sensuality far beyond anything she'd ever experienced before, and they were just beginning. If he expected equal skill from her, he was going to be bitterly disappointed and she was going to be humiliated.

"Ah, Bess, you feel so right." She heard his rough whisper as he strung soft sipping kisses down the side of her neck and across her shoulder. He expected nothing, she finally understood, and in understanding that she was able to give him more than she could ever have hoped to.

She pressed slow, openmouthed kisses across his chest, her teeth teasing his nipples while her nails dragged softly down his belly. He shuddered once; then she was swung up dizzyingly. She felt a cool sheet against her back before she fully comprehended what was happening. He stripped off the rest of his clothes and followed her down. His hands roamed over her body, exploring, touching, lingering, while he took her nipple into his mouth and suckled strongly, as if to quench a soul-deep thirst.

Her scented warmth enveloped him, and he felt as if he were drowning. As he lifted himself over her, her thighs relaxed, creating a warm cradle for him. He felt her shock at the touch of his body in hers, and her thighs closed reflexively, taking him deeper into her heat. Sensing the subtle relaxation of her inner muscles, he began rocking slowly, building the tempo, taking her in long, easy strokes.

She knew only pure sensation. Dimly she sensed some impending cataclysmic pleasure, but what she felt right now was so good that she couldn't think about the future. The pleasure built, and small tremors rippled through her, faster and faster, as the rhythm of his body moving inside hers picked up speed.

He was being buried alive in her, but there was no sense of panic, just a desperate need to burrow even deeper. The shivery sensation along his backbone signaled that he was close, and Will gritted his teeth in the effort to hold back. Her fingers feathered at the base of his spine, and the last thin strand of his control snapped.

A tidal wave of terrifyingly glorious pleasure broke over her as she heard his hoarse cry. She drowned, surfaced briefly, then drowned again.

She couldn't stop trembling. Her heart still hammered; her breath still tore from her lungs, loud in the midnight quiet of the room. Aftershocks of shivery sensation still careered through her as she clung to the hard, warm body crushing hers so reassuringly.

"It's all right, Bess." His ragged-sounding whisper calmed her, along with his hand stroking gently over her body, soothing the spasmodic shivers still jerking through her. His mouth brushed soft kisses over her nose and cheeks and forehead. "It's all right, sweetheart. It's just the shock of coming back down from such a height." She felt his body jerk and shudder. "I feel it, too."

"It's never—" Her whisper caught. "It's never been like that before." The words might be trite, but she'd never said anything truer. She thought she'd known what sex was, but she hadn't known anything. The sensations she'd just experienced were all new, all wondrous . . . and a little frightening.

She murmured a protest as he eased his weight from her, levering himself up on one elbow to look down at her. He smoothed her tangled hair back and dropped a warm kiss on her shoulder. His finger circled the spot slowly. "It had been a while for you, hadn't it?"

"Yes," she whispered. The urge to hide her suddenly burning face under the pillow was almost overwhelming. Had she been that inept? Too humiliatingly eager? Too—

"I'm glad." A peculiarly sweet smile softened the rugged lines of his face. "For me, too."

So there, Carlynn! she thought with a wickedly smug satisfaction that was faintly shocking.

He rolled onto his side, taking her boneless body with his, and their arms and legs tangled satisfactorily. A huge yawn caught her unexpectedly as she snuggled her head deep into his shoulder, and he chuckled softly.

"Good night, sweetheart."

Her sleepy giggle and hug answered him, and she closed her eyes on a wholly satisfied sigh. His arms tightened around her. There was nowhere else on earth she would rather be, she thought dreamily as she fell asleep.

Friday

The pearly glow of first light illuminated the woman sleeping next to him. She lay on her stomach, the sheet twisted around her waist, one knee drawn up, one hand tucked under the pillow. A faint smile curved her soft mouth. Her hair was tangled, her face rosily sleep-flushed, and she looked nothing like the sophisticated, uptight, slightly hard woman he'd first seen. Leaning over her, he brushed several tendrils of brown-sugar hair off her cheek with his hand. Although he knew he hid it well, his size often made him feel like a clumsy hulk with women. But not this woman. This woman made him feel sure and powerful, tender and protective, and a dozen other things he ached to tell her. She fit him perfectly, in all ways.

He leaned farther, letting his mouth trail thistledown kisses along the beautiful slope of her bared shoulder. How long would he be able to keep her? He only needed forever. He'd considered the risk that if he couldn't have her forever, having her for only a few brief moments might heighten the pain of losing her. His smile was bittersweet as he rubbed his cheek over the top of her silky head. There was no ''might'' about it, but he'd known he would take the risk, even before he'd visited Lloyd Crosby yesterday to confirm that he was still looking for someone to take over the bank. He'd known before he kissed her the first time, before he'd held her in his arms after she'd fainted—hell, probably before he'd even gotten a good look at her legs, he'd decided with a silent, rueful chuckle.

It had surprised him that she wasn't a virgin, although he didn't really know why. It would have been ridiculous to expect that she was; certainly he had no right to expect it. He'd hardly been one when he married, and he hadn't been celibate since his divorce, yet some vestigial chauvinism made him regret that he hadn't been the first. Probably, he thought wryly, because he wanted so badly to be the last.

Something was tickling her shoulder. Bess raised one hand languidly to swat it away and found cool, empty air. Sighing sleepily, she nuzzled her body deeper into the mattress. The phantom tickler returned, and she opened one eye reluctantly.

"Hi," Will said softly.

She opened both eyes. "Hi," she returned, even more softly and with a shy smile.

"How are you feeling?" he asked in the same gentle tone that made her feel oddly like crying.

"A little awkward," she admitted in a whisper. She shifted her legs under the sheet. "And a little sore." She groaned silently at that unthinking revelation. Sixteen-itis wasn't a chronic condition, was it? She felt her smile widen into a grin. "And wonderful."

He grinned back; then his expression gradually sobered, and he seemed about to say something, but she guessed he changed his mind, because suddenly he threw off the sheet and stood up in one fluid ripple of muscle.

Picking up his robe from the floor, Will held it out to her. "If you want to take a shower, I'll go down and start breakfast." He wanted to suggest that they share the shower, but self-assurance in the boardroom didn't extend to the bedroom, he reminded himself. She was looking him over frankly, but there was a faint tinge of pink along her cheekbones, and the sheet remained clamped over her breasts as she stretched for the robe. She slipped it on with a studied casualness that made him want to laugh, and revealed a glimpse of one rosy breast that made him want to yank the robe out of her hand and show her a better way to start the day than with a shower. Seeing him watching her, she shrugged self-consciously and grinned at her own foolishness, and he almost told her what else he wanted, what he'd almost told her a few minutes ago. Keep it light, he had to caution himself again. He couldn't risk pushing her too far too fast, no matter how much he wanted.

"This reminds me of getting ready for 'gracious.'"

Bess smiled at Abby's comment as she carefully unwound another of the small round curlers Keeley had persuaded her to try. "Gracious" had been the noon meal on Sunday back in school when they'd been required to dress up and practice their best manners and dinner conversation. She set the last curler in the box and stared doubtfully at the giant pin curls dangling around her face.

Keeley paused as she pulled on a pair of Abby's panty hose. "Now you finger-comb it, then finish off with the pick," she said. Bess did as instructed and studied the result. Her stick-straight hair was a mass of unrestrained curls, a little wild looking, even. She loved it.

Keeley caught her eye and looked toward Abby meaningfully. Tonight was the final official function of reunion week, a semiformal dinner to which guests might be invited. It had come as no surprise to any of them when each had announced who she had invited—

especially after last night, Bess thought with a silent, rueful laugh. She'd been wondering how the others would take her absence from her bed last night, only to discover this morning when she'd returned to their room that none of their beds had been slept in.

Keeley took up a position on one side of Abby, and Bess took the one on the other. She and Keeley had decided that Abby was going to have a night she would remember if she lived to be two hundred. They'd selected her clothes, done her hair, and now, with the combined contents of their makeup bags in front of them on the dressing table, they were going to finish the make-over.

"I don't know...." Abby gave her image in the mirror a doubting look a few minutes later. "That lipstick is awfully bright." Bess and Keeley ignored her. "Well...I guess it's all right. It draws attention away from my nose."

"Your nose is fine," Bess told her patiently.

Abby looked down at herself and grimaced. "Too bad it's not bright enough to draw attention away from my hips."

"Your hips are fine, too," Keeley said. "Especially if you swing 'em just a little." She demonstrated.

Bess stepped back to get the full effect of their handiwork. "You're going to knock Joshua so dead, it'll take you a week to resuscitate him," she announced.

"You may have to do a little resuscitation yourself, Bess," Keeley told her dryly.

"I certainly hope so," Bess said gravely, then giggled along with Abby and Keeley.

"We like him, Bess," Abby said quietly. "He seems like a wonderful man."

"I think so." She gave her friends a lopsided grin. "But then, I'm not sure I'm very reliable where he's concerned."

She did like him, Bess thought again hours later. She liked the way he looked and talked, the feeling of security she had when she was with him, the fun, the feel of his strong, hard body against hers. She watched him loosen his tie and drape it over the back of a kitchen chair. In fact, there wasn't anything she could think of at the moment that she didn't like about him. That thought added to the odd melancholy she'd been feeling all evening. She reached out to touch the petals of one of the roses in the bouquet gracing the center of the old table. Yesterday morning, while he'd been in the shower, she'd picked them from the rambler that had gone wild at the corner of the back porch, then put them in an antique blue glass canning jar forgotten on a shelf in the basement. They were old-fashioned roses, with blush pink petals like ruffled crisp organza and a strong, sweet fragrance.

She glanced up as he shrugged out of his dark suit jacket. Why she felt melancholy, she didn't know. The dinner had gone well. The men, as might be expected in a small town, knew each other and obviously got along. The six of them had had a good time together; nothing had happened to make her feel so oddly forlorn.

Will met her glance with a smile. "Do you want some coffee?" With a strange solemnity, she shook her head. Her hair tonight was a froth of frivolous curls, and they bounced gently around her grave face. She had been quiet during dinner and become more withdrawn as they'd been driving back. He didn't know if she was sad at the prospect of saying goodbye tomorrow to her friends or if there was another reason—that she was sorry because she thought she had to say goodbye to him, too. There was a third possibility, one that he didn't want to consider at all: she might be regretting the night before.

"No, I don't want any coffee," she said, not as if she were reinforcing the shake of her head but as if she suddenly knew what she *did* want. Her eyes met his, and he saw an urgent, almost desperate hunger that matched his own. Silently he held out his hand, and with the same silence that communicated volumes, she rose and put her hand in his.

She thought she knew what to expect now, but she was wrong. Her body ran hot and cold with the avalanche of sensation from his pleasuring hands and mouth and body. She wanted to move, to pull him closer with her own ravening hands and mouth, until there weren't two separate bodies, only one, but she couldn't. It was all she could do to breathe. His tenderly rough hands tracked lower, blazing an icy-hot trail across her belly, while his teeth nipped at her earlobe, not hard enough to hurt, just enough to send another current of chills and fever through her.

Suddenly she had to move as his hand found her, and she arched helplessly. She couldn't be feeling such impossible pleasure, and abruptly she was afraid, afraid to let him continue, and even more afraid that he might stop. In a purely instinctive act of self-preservation, her suddenly fierce hands dragged his body up hers.

Will looked down into eyes as fathomless as fog, and he was hopelessly lost, his soul reaching deeper and deeper into the insubstantial mist. The mist burned away, and her eyes shimmered brightly as his body took possession of hers. An almost uncontrollable craving demanded that he take her fast, consume her totally, physically and emotionally. That craving warred with his desire to be tender and careful of her body and her fragile emotions.

"Ah, Bess...you feel so...good."

His raw rasp was full of exquisite agony. His face was taut, honed by the battle for control raging within him. She felt the strain of his conflict in the trembling of the muscles under her restless hands. Yet still his body caressed hers with a slow, easy beat. It wasn't nearly enough; the furious hunger gnawing through her wouldn't wait any longer to be satisfied.

With a low, feral growl, Bess arched upward and had the glorious satisfaction of feeling his control shatter. For a split second more she savored her victory; then she was caught up in a frenzy of sensation that swept her along like a bit of paper in a whirlwind. Bolts of sensual lightning whipped through her one after another, yet dimly she sensed the gathering of an even greater force. When it finally struck, she exploded in a fiery, soul-consuming pleasure.

For what seemed an eternity their exhausted, sweat-slicked bodies remained anchored together. Finally Will found the energy to move. Her eyes were still wide and stunned, and he knew his own mirrored the same shock. Tears trickled from the corners of hers, and he began soothing his hands over her shoulders and throat as he kissed the salty wetness away. A long shudder trembled through her into him, and he moved his lips over her face with soft kisses and wordless murmurs of wonder and appreciation. Finally she smiled up at him tremulously, a heartbreakingly beautiful smile. He eased aside, pulling the sheet over their cooling bodies.

He pulled her back into his arms and waited, but she didn't relax. He kissed the top of her tousled head, then asked quietly, "What's wrong, babe?"

She didn't pull away from him as he'd half expected, but turned in his arms to lay her head against his bare chest with a sad-sounding sigh. "I lost my baby five years ago today," she said softly.

Will couldn't help his startled jerk. Whatever he'd been expecting, it hadn't been this. "What happened?" he asked with equal softness.

The story was much easier to tell than she would have thought, if she *had* thought about it. A small part of her was amazed that she'd answered his question honestly, but a much larger part thought it only natural that she share what had been a secret sorrow for too long.

Will listened in silence, feeling himself growing angrier and angrier as she gave him the heart-wrenching details. He wasn't angry with her; he felt no censure, only a deep empathetic sorrow. He was angry with the man. He had no rational reason—or even right—to, but he was ready to get up and find the guy and beat him to a pulp.

Finished, she fell silent. He closed his arms tighter around her and felt the damp flutter of her lashes against his shoulder. "I lost a child, too," he said quietly.

Bess looked up at him. "What happened?" she asked, unconsciously echoing his earlier question.

"My wife became pregnant with our child and realized that a child was the last thing she wanted. She didn't tell me she was pregnant. She decided alone to end the pregnancy." With a tired sigh, he drew her closer. "I knew something was wrong, and finally she broke down and told me what she had done. I filed for divorce the next day."

She understood all that his stark telling had left out. His wife hadn't wanted a child who might interfere with her career, but she hadn't wanted to lose her husband, either, so she'd thought to solve the "problem" without telling him. In the end, he'd lost his child as surely as she had. Fiercely she wrapped her arms around him. "I'm so sorry, Will."

He felt the twin splashes of wet warmth on his chest as she hugged him. He tightened his arms around her, and for long minutes they lay together, giving each other silent, heart-healing comfort.

His quiet, deep voice finally broke the silence. "Don't go back to Boston tomorrow, Bess. Stay here with me for another week."

Slowly Bess raised her head to look at him. "I..."

He watched his hand brush a loose curl off her cheek; then his eyes suddenly shifted and caught hers, holding them in an implacable grip. "Just another week," he repeated.

"I don't know," she finally said, knowing even before she spoke what a sorry, nothing answer it was, but after a long moment of silence during which his eyes searched hers, he nodded, apparently satisfied with it. He tucked her head back against his shoulder, then pressed a sweet, loving kiss to her forehead. "Go to sleep, love. We can talk about it in the morning."

He went to sleep almost immediately. Bess lay in the dark, warm and secure in his arms, yet felt the panic rising inside her. A blind woman could see where Will was hoping the extra week would lead, and her vision was twenty-twenty. This wasn't a whim with him. He wasn't a man for whims. He'd spent three years looking for the right town and another two for the right house. She'd seen the work he'd done on the house, the sturdy stalls and corral he'd built for the horses he would bring from Nevada in the fall, all showing the same careful planning and thought. It seemed almost impossible that a man who planned so deliberately and patiently could be so certain after only a week that he wanted her, yet she didn't doubt it for a second. She didn't doubt, either, that he would be faithful, loyal and honorable, or that she would be loved, protected and the most important thing in the world to him. He seemed almost too good to be true. She knew he loved her, not from the endearment he'd whispered just before going to sleep, which could have meant nothing, but from the way his eyes softened each time he looked at her, the rather high-handed way he tried to take charge of her for her own good, the fun they had together doing nothing, the total absorption with which he made love to her—those were the things that meant everything. What she doubted was herself.

He was so sure of what he felt and wanted, and she was so uncertain. This wasn't a financial statement, with neat columns of assets and debits that could be added and subtracted to arrive at a decision concerning the soundness of a proposed venture. Feelings couldn't be reduced to assets and liabilities. Her week-long journey into the past and into herself had also been a journey into the future, she saw now, and the possible destination terrified her.

She slipped from the bed and began as quietly as possible to gather her clothes.

"It's tacky to leave without saying goodbye, Bess."

She jumped, as much from the sudden light that flooded the dark room when he switched on the bedside lamp as from his voice, and dropped the few items she'd managed to find. Slowly she turned to face him. He was raised on one elbow, watching her, and she was suddenly, excruciatingly aware of her nakedness. "I thought it was . . . for the best," she said lamely.

He sat up, seemingly unaware that the sheet had fallen away from his lap. "Why?"

She shrugged. "Because it would be a mistake to stay."

"Why?"

"Because." She gestured around the room taking in the rumpled bed and their scattered clothes, lying where they'd heedlessly tossed them in what seemed like another lifetime now. "This is just chemistry and libido. We were both on vacation, taking a little time away from reality. It would never work between us."

"I know it would."

She shook her head with a sad smile. "It wouldn't. This way we can remember each other . . ." She struggled for a word. ". . . fondly."

His mouth tightened at her choice of vocabulary. "That's not what I want."

"What if the reality doesn't live up to your expectations?" There was more than a trace of desperation in the question.

"I think it will surpass them, and even if it doesn't, it would still be more than worth it."

She tried another tack. "You're making the same mistake all over again, Will, choosing a woman just like your former wife."

He moved so fast that his fingers were locking around her upper arms before she'd fully comprehended that he had moved. "Don't you think I'm old enough and smart enough to know what I want, Bess?" he said with deceptive softness as he shook her slightly. "I can assure you it's not a clone of my former wife."

He resisted the urge to shake her again. He understood her panic attack, but his patience was strained to the limit from a mixture of frustration, disbelief and what he knew was just plain male outrage. How could she be so stupid as to be even thinking of turning him down? "Damn it, Bess, I'm in love with you."

"I know," she said in a small voice and took advantage of his momentary shock at her ready admission to twist out of his hold. She scurried around the room, frantically trying to collect her wits and her clothes. She knew she was handling this with absolutely no aplomb and even less intelligence or maturity. She threw her clothes on in no particular order, speed being the main criterion.

"Damn it, Bess! If you know that, why the hell are you leaving?"

An observer of the scene, she thought absently, would probably find the sight of the two of them—the big, buck-naked man standing with his hands on his hips and the nearly naked woman scuttling around the room like a demented crab, frantically throwing her clothes on—hilarious. "Because it's for the best," she repeated mechanically as she found her half-slip peeking out from under the sheet.

His opinion was succinct and obscene, and suddenly Bess had no more energy for specious arguments. Taking a deep breath, she faced him across the bed. "Because I lose a little of myself when I'm with you—and it terrifies me," she said quietly.

"I don't want to change you, Bess," he reassured her just as quietly. His mouth quirked up in a crooked grin. "I like you just fine the way you are." He sobered again. "I know what I want, Bess. I want a companion, not a sex doll. I want a woman who has a life of her own, friends, a career, who doesn't want me to be her whole world, but who has room for me in hers, and for our children." He reached his hand cautiously across the bed. "I want you," he finished softly.

Bess stared at him helplessly, tears running down her cheeks. After an agonizingly long minute of indecision, she was starting to reach out to him when Hoover jumped up on the bed and intercepted her hand.

Taking advantage of the last-second reprieve, Bess concentrated on petting the cat. Hoover flopped over to have his belly rubbed, and she obliged.

Suddenly she went very still, and Will cursed long and fluently under his breath. Now, of all times, he didn't want to deal with what was coming.

"This isn't the cat I brought you." As she'd been rubbing the cat's belly, she'd suddenly remembered something that the shock of its injuries had temporarily driven out of her mind. She looked up at him accusingly. "That cat was a male. This is a female. What happened to it?" Even as she asked, a look of sick realization settled on her tight features.

"It's fine, recuperating at home," Will told her readily. "The boys who directed you here were equally helpful to the cat's owners when they were searching for it later that evening. They showed up about ten minutes after you left. I got this one at the Humane Association the next morning." He tried a charmingly lopsided grin. "It was the best I could do on short notice."

She didn't smile back. "Why?"

"Because it was the only way I could keep you coming around," he said matter-of-factly.

The fact that she had wanted to keep coming around made her suddenly furious. "So—" her voice dripped scorn "—you shaved a poor animal's head and crippled it just to provide yourself with a little vacation fling?"

He counted slowly to ten in an effort to hold on to his temper. "The fur will grow back and the cast is just a sham, hardly anything that will permanently harm him. For a little inconvenience, he gets a home." She gave him a supremely derisive look. "And as long as we're talking about flings to liven up a vacation," he added in a deceptively mild tone, "wasn't that exactly what you were doing, Bess?"

She felt tears pricking her eyes again and blinked furiously. That wasn't what she'd been doing, and he damned well knew it. Without a word, she grabbed her remaining shoe and virtually ran out of the bedroom.

With a curse, Will started after her, realized his lack of attire, and stopped long enough to jam on a pair of pants, zipping them as he went down the stairs three at a time. She was standing in the middle of the kitchen, staring at the jars of jelly lined up on the counter.

"May I have a jar of jelly?" she asked formally.

He shrugged, indicating that she should help herself. She picked up one jar and tried to make a place for it in her purse. Impatiently he yanked open the cupboard under the sink and took out an empty grocery sack and handed it to her. Without looking at him, she transferred the jelly to the sack.

"Take a few more," he said gruffly.

She put three more in the sack, then folded the top over neatly. She fiddled with the folded top. "What about Hoover?" she asked diffidently.

"Hoover has a home for life here," he said neutrally. "Besides, I don't think he'd be very happy in Boston."

A look of regret passed over her wan face. "No, he wouldn't," she agreed very softly. She didn't move for several seconds, and Will simply waited, tense and biting his tongue. "Well," she said finally, "goodbye."

The shock of realizing that she was really leaving kept him frozen for the several seconds that it took her to cross the kitchen and open the door. "Bess, wait!" he said urgently, starting after her at last.

She paused as she stepped through the door, and for a second his heart stopped as he thought she was coming back. She gave him a brief, bleak smile. "I love you." With that exit line, she was gone.

Saturday

Bess parked her car in her designated space in the garage beneath her apartment building and turned off the key. The sound of the engine and the rhythmic squeak of the windshield wipers died abruptly. It had started raining almost as soon as she'd left East Ridley, and had continued nonstop all the way to Boston. She watched the last of the raindrops slide sullenly down the windshield. Finally, with a weary sigh, she unlocked her seat belt and pushed open the door.

Minutes later she set down her purse and the luggage she'd carried in. Pulling out a chair, she sat at the ultramodern chrome-and-glass table in the tiny kitchen. With the rain, the late-afternoon light coming through the narrow window did little to illuminate the room, but she made no move to turn on a light.

She pulled her suitcase toward her and took out the remaining two jars of jelly. She'd given one each to Keeley and Abby just as they were leaving. They'd all promised that they would keep each other apprised of how things were going. Their friendship had grown deeper, richer and more mature in the few days they'd had together, and she knew the promise would be kept.

The room gradually grew darker, but still she made no effort to turn on a light. She would be seeing them again soon, at whoever's wedding happened first, Keeley's or Abby's. They'd both seemed to have reached the conclusion this past week that while you couldn't go back and undo your life, it was possible to go back to where you'd made a wrong turn and try a new direction. There was no guarantee that the new road would be any less bumpy or potholed than the old one, but there was a good—a very good—chance that it *might* be, especially if there was someone with whom to share the bumps and jarring jolts.

And they each had someone. She was happy for Keeley and Dominic, and for Abby and her Joshua, but her happiness had just a tinge of bittersweet. The four of them had taken up their lives after long separations without, apparently, any of the uncertainty or cowardice that afflicted her.

She picked up one of the jars and stared at it without seeing it. All the way back to Boston, she had deliberately tried to avoid thinking about the past week. So much had happened, too much, and her emotions were too near the surface. But memories kept sneaking out insidiously.

She tried to hold them at bay by telling herself she'd been right; he had been too good to be true. Only a jerk would pull such a dumb stunt. He'd made a fool of her, she kept telling herself self-righteously, ignoring the possibility that she might have made a fool of herself. It had been a dumb stunt, but an inventive and flattering one, that small annoying voice put in.

As she had before, she ignored it, but a picture of Will holding Scruffy so tenderly in his arms snuck out while her attention strayed. She'd tried to tell herself that much of what she'd been feeling was simply her biological clock ticking down, the same reason the anniversary of the loss of the baby had become harder to ignore with each passing year. Perhaps she should pay attention to that ticking.

It wasn't the urgency of the clock running down, though, that had prompted her feelings. One of the few truths she'd told that last time was that she loved him. And it terrified her. She rolled the jar between her palms. Despite what the magazines had said a decade ago, a woman couldn't have it all. Compromises had to be made, career and family goals balanced, maybe even set aside. For years she'd adhered to a rigid agenda. To even consider changing it now was so frightening. Her life would change drastically if she accepted Will's unspoken offer. She couldn't ask him to move back to Boston; he would never be happy as a "city" vet. That meant some of her old goals would never be met, but there would be new ones, and possibly a purpose and meaning in her life that had been lacking. Sometimes people clung to a goal because they'd sacrificed so much to achieve it, and they were loath to admit that maybe, ultimately, it wouldn't be worth the sacrifice. Was that what she was doing?

She closed her eyes tiredly and rubbed at the dull, continuous pain that seemed to be centered near her heart. She'd gone over the rainbow a week ago, but not for the first time. The first time had been fifteen years ago, when she'd gone off to Boston—her personal Oz. She'd had wonderful, terrifying, exciting and unpleasant adventures, and she wouldn't have missed a one of them. She grimaced to herself. Well, maybe one or two. Was it time now to click the ruby slippers and go back . . . to Kansas? Was Will Shedd home?

Whatever they had together wasn't going to bring on world peace or cure the common cold. Life wasn't magically going to become ideal. There would always be that constant fine tension that came from the compromise between independence and oneness. Yet, twenty years from now, what was she going to regret? Not attaining the bank presidency that she knew now she would have—but maybe no longer needed to validate herself? The lack of children? Husband? Could she be content with a lesser goal... that might be so much more?

She opened her eyes and focused on the small jar of jelly in her hand. It was a bottle of sunshine for just such a cold, gray day, for her equally cold, gray apartment in a cold, gray city. She shook the jar of sunshine gently. It seemed now that her life was like the crab apples they'd picked—sour, small, but with the addition of sugar they made something sweet. Was Will Shedd her cup of sugar?

Yet what he wanted wouldn't be a temporary detour that she could make before getting back on the main road at some point in the future. She would have to do as Abby and Keeley were doing, take a fork in a one-way road, with no possibility of a return. Her destination would be irrevocably changed—and she just didn't think she had the courage for that.

She raised the jar in her hand in a mocking salute to the utilitarian, lifeless walls surrounding her and gave a bitter smile. "There's no place like home."

Epilogue

The sound of a car driving up gave him a depressing sense of déjà vu. He shouldn't have turned down the poker game, he thought. He'd thrown the robe she'd worn into the washer, along with the sheets from the bed, put the jelly in the darkest corner of the basement and succeeded in wiping every sign of her brief presence away. Yet still there was a sense of something missing, as if the house were no longer a home now that she was gone.

The knock on the kitchen door came a minute later, and he willed the person on the other side to go away. He'd let her go, telling himself that she wasn't gone for good. She couldn't be. She just needed some time, and then she would be back. A few hundred more repetitions and he might even believe it.

The knock became more insistent, and Hoover and Hank looked at him puzzledly, as if wondering why he wasn't getting up to answer it. With a muttered curse, he pushed himself out of the chair.

"I discovered I was out of peanut butter."

This time, instead of an injured cat, she had a jar of crab apple jelly in her hands.

"I think I can spare some," he said neutrally, trying to tamp down the elation surging through him.

He held the door open, and she came in, stopping a few feet inside the door. "What's that?" He nodded at the obviously heavy case she'd set on the floor.

"My sewing machine."

He nodded again. "A present?" he asked, not seriously.

"More in the way of a loan, actually. The kitchen window needs curtains." She was serious.

He moved farther into the room, and she followed. "What are the terms?"

"Zero down, zero interest, no monthly payments for the first fifty years. There might be a couple of balloon payments, though," she warned.

He leaned against the back of the chair he'd been occupying. "How much?" he asked, matching her businesslike tone.

"Children, at least two. Boys or girls, or one of each, I'm not choosy."

He considered for a moment. "Well, I don't know. There's a lot of competition among financial institutions to give out loans nowadays. Most offer an incentive. Maybe a toaster?" he suggested.

She didn't miss a beat. "No toaster. How about companionship? Love?"

"Sex?" he counteroffered.

"That, too."

He smiled slightly. "Just checking. What happens at the end of the first fifty years?"

"We negotiate a new deal."

Nodding decisively, he straightened away from the chair and moved toward her. "Sounds good to me. Where do I sign?"

She held out her left hand hesitantly, then pointed to the fourth finger. "Right here."

He reached for her hand as if he meant to shake it, then the next thing Bess knew he'd jerked her into his arms and she was being crushed against his hard, warm body.

"You had a week," he growled in her ear. "Then I was coming after you."

She pushed against his chest, and he let her move back just enough so she could look up at him. Her mouth was pursed with annoyance. "I should have waited. I could have gotten better terms."

"Not a chance," he murmured, kissing the annoyance away. Swinging her up into his arms, he started for the stairs.

Hours later, he raised his head to look down at her, his expression suddenly sober. "You're sure, Bess? You can leave Boston, the bank, be satisfied with a small town, maybe a small bank?"

She smiled at him slyly. "Definitely a small bank." Her smile softened as she traced the weathered planes of his beloved face. "I'm sure, Will. I love you." Home was in his eyes. "I finally realized Boston isn't Kansas."

At his puzzled frown, she laughed softly and pulled his mouth back down to hers. "I'll explain," she whispered, "on the first anniversary of the loan."

* * * * *

Patricia Gardner Evans

There weren't many other children around to play with when I was small, so I spent a lot of time playing with dolls and Tinkertoy people, telling them what to do and say. When I began first grade, I soon learned that the other children did not go along with my "I'll say and then *you* say..." style of play. For that, I had to go back to my dolls. They weren't much as friends, but they didn't keep messing up my brilliant stories with ad libs.

Writing any of them down was never even an idle daydream. My dolls and toys became childhood history; I completed two college degrees, married, had a child, taught school, kept house, did the usual things. My major vice was a tendency to read perhaps a bit more than I should, but there weren't really *that* many dinners that got scorched because I wanted to just "finish this chapter."

A bad back changed all that. Recuperating from surgery to fix it, I realized with horror that I'd read all the library books I'd stocked up on and couldn't drive yet. I was considering the literary potential of the wrapper on the toilet tissue when my daughter brought in several sweet romances she'd traded for at school. I'd never read a category romance before, and, as I finished the last page of the first one, I thought how quick and easy it must be to write one. True, I'd never had even a high school creative writing course, but, really, how hard could it be? I'd been contemplating a career change; why not become a romance writer? It seemed like a rational decision at the time.

A year later, I'd discovered that nothing about writing was quick or easy, certainly not success. I did, fortunately, have sense enough to realize it might help to read a few more as I started out so I would know what I was supposed to be doing. I read about five hundred that first year, wrote two and collected rejection letters. The phone call telling me that my third attempt had sold was a lifetime thrill second only to the birth of my daughter. When it was published, I went around to local bookstores and loitered in front of the book racks displaying *my* book. I'm embarassed to say I still do it each time another one is published.

I'm still not sure I know what I'm doing, but I'm having a wonderful time anyway. I've traveled, made very precious friends among other writers and an editor, gotten fan letters that let me think perhaps I do know—sometimes, at least—what I'm doing. My only regret is that I can't read as much as I'd like because I'm too busy writing—a small sacrifice.

I do worry about one thing, though. Sometimes, I suspect I'm still playing dolls, still telling them what to do and say, the only change being that now I play with a computer instead of Tinkertoys. Overhearing Kathy Eagle and me discussing long-distance our stories and characters for this book, my daughter commented, "It sounds like you're playing Barbies by phone." Maybe I've never grown up. If that's true, I hope to avoid it forever.

Patricia Gardner Evans

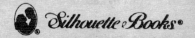

FOUR UNIQUE SERIES
FOR EVERY WOMAN YOU ARE...

Silhouette Romance®

Tender, delightful, provocative—stories that capture the laughter, the tears, the *joy* of falling in love. Pure romance...straight from the heart!

SILHOUETTE *Desire*®

Go wild with Desire! Passionate, emotional, sensuous stories of fiery romance. With heroines you'll like and heroes you'll *love*, Silhouette Desire never fails to deliver.

Silhouette Special Edition®

Stories of love and life, these powerful novels are tales that you can identify with—romances with "something special" added in! Silhouette Special Edition is entertainment for the heart.

SILHOUETTE·INTIMATE·MOMENTS*

Enter a world where passions run hot and excitement is the rule. Dramatic, larger-than-life and always compelling—Silhouette Intimate Moments will never let you down.

SGENERIC